W9-AFP-214

DREAMWALKER

Novels by
C. S. Friedman
available from DAW Books:

The Dreamwalker Chronicles
DREAMWALKER

The Magister Trilogy
FEAST OF SOULS
WINGS OF WRATH
LEGACY OF KINGS

The Coldfire Trilogy
BLACK SUN RISING
WHEN TRUE NIGHT FALLS
CROWN OF SHADOWS

THE MADNESS SEASON

THIS ALIEN SHORE

IN CONQUEST BORN
THE WILDING

C. S. FRIEDMAN

○———————○

DREAMWALKER

Book One of
The Dreamwalker Chronicles

DAW BOOKS, INC.

DONALD A. WOLLHEIM, FOUNDER
375 Hudson Street, New York, NY 10014
ELIZABETH R. WOLLHEIM
SHEILA E. GILBERT
PUBLISHERS
www.dawbooks.com

First Hardcover Printing, February 2014
1 2 3 4 5 6 7 8 9

DAW TRADEMARK REGISTERED
U.S. PAT. AND TM. OFF. AND FOREIGN COUNTRIES
—MARCA REGISTRADA
HECHO EN U.S.A.

PRINTED IN THE U.S.A.

For Kim and Larry,
Best Family Ever

Acknowledgments

This book could not have been written without the support of some very special people. First and foremost I'd like to thank Russ Galen and Betsy Wollheim, for their usual creative input and encouragement. Next, Larry Friedman, Kim Dobson, David Walddon, and Bradley Beaulieu, for providing key plot points that helped me deal with some rough spots in my story. And of course my loyal beta team, whose constructive criticism (and occasional hand-holding) made it possible for me to leave my literary comfort zone and tackle a whole new kind of project without going totally crazy: Zsusy Sanford, Carl Cipra, Jennifer Eastman, and (yes, it's a repeat) David Walddon.

Thanks to Captain David Short of the Sterling Volunteer Fire Company for helping me understand how a house fire progresses, which generated some good story ideas along the way. It was a fascinating lesson, and I hope I did it justice.

Thanks to Tara Flewelling for her hospitality and support, and to all the troubled teens who opened their hearts to me in Sacramento so that I could have insight into their world.

Thanks to my new copy editor, Marylou Capes-Platt, who provided some wonderful creative criticism. This is a much better book for her input.

Lastly, I would like to express my appreciation for two very special people, who, sadly, were taken from us this year. Judy Gerjuoy, a.k.a. Jaelle of Armida, was chair of the Darkover Council for 35 years and inspired writers, fans, and history buffs around the globe with her boundless enthusiasm for the genre. Chazz Mahan was a gamer of remarkable creativity and a man of generous spirit who was always ready to offer a helping hand to people in need.

They were good people. May they never be forgotten.

PROLOGUE

WITH A LAST FURTIVE GLANCE behind him, the grey man began to climb down the ladder. Its metal rungs were damp from recent rains, making them dangerously slick, and the jagged walls of the narrow passage scraped against his shoulders, but it was not the first time he'd come this way, and he moved quickly and confidently into the cool depths of the earth. Summer in this version of Virginia was hotter than in his own, and he was glad that his business today was underground. Was this a price the locals had to pay for all their fancy technology? Or was it just a quirk of nature, part of the natural variation of the universe? This close to the heart of creation one could never be sure.

The tunnel grew darker as he descended, the light of sun-drenched land slowly giving way to the underworld's all-consuming darkness. It didn't bother him. His great black eyes drank in what little light there was, and when he looked up they flashed green, like a cat's. Darkness was an ally to men of his Guild, and with his mottled grey skin and neutral-colored uniform he knew he was all but invisible in such lighting. Indeed, for as long as the sheen of summer sweat still lingered on his skin, he was a near-perfect match for the rain-slicked stone surrounding him, almost impossible for an observer to pick out.

A useful quality for someone in his line of work.

At the bottom of the ladder the tunnel opened out into a small natural cavern. A narrow strip of steel grating had been suspended several feet above the floor to serve as a walkway, with rusty handrails flanking it. The metal grate shuddered as he stepped onto it, and he could hear a thrumming vibration run down its length, like a bass note traveling down a guitar string: the music of the underworld.

He removed the glow lamp from his belt and activated it, casting beams of cool blue light about the cavern. Normally he avoided the use of artifacts from home while on duty, but here in the depths of the earth no one was likely to question him. The small globe of energy hovered steadily in its sealed compartment, the etched sigil of the Guild of Elementals glowing like a tiny thread of blue neon on the metal hood.

Recent rains had worked their way down into the earth and as a result the cave formations glistened, making it seem as if the entire chamber had been coated in glass. Tiny puddles of water had gathered in pockmarks along the limestone floor, and reflections from his lamp twitched across their still surfaces like fairy flames as he began to walk, jerking in time to his footfall. There was a time when such effects had fascinated him, but familiarity had dulled the edge of novelty. And today he had bigger things to worry about.

Maybe the Shadows already know what's happening here, he thought nervously.

Maybe I won't have to be the one who breaks the news to them.

The steel walkway led him to a sizeable chamber, a large circular cavern with rippling stone formations on every side. Tourists had crowded in here not so long ago, eyes wide as they listened to tales of how bootleggers had once partied in this chamber, far from the watchful eyes of Prohibition authorities. How exotic those ancient parties must have been, with the sounds of drunken revelry echoing from every stalactite! In such a setting it was easy for a man to envision the fabric of this world giving way to another, allowing the dead—and perhaps the living—to pass through.

These days there were no tour guides. The owners of the property had fallen on hard times in the late 90's and been forced to sell this land as part of a bankruptcy settlement. How their children had wept when it was time to say goodbye! Such a cavern was a perfect playground for the young, its walls riddled with secret nooks and crannies filled with ink-black shadows. Slip into a crevice, hold your breath for silence, and your own mother could stand five feet away and not know you were there. But finances had forced the family to surrender its holdings to a new owner—one who had no children and who didn't intend to let tourists visit the place—and now it was lost to children forever.

No one had ever questioned the source of the financial ruin which forced them to sell the caverns. Of course. The grey man's Guild was good at what it did.

A great stone archway dominated the far end of the chamber. Once it had been a simple enough structure, a sleek limestone arch inscribed with the usual patterns. But calcium-rich water dripping down from above, combined with tremors of temporal seepage from within, had resulted in an explosion of formation growth. Now every inch of the arch was covered with clusters of crystalline needles, some of them as tiny and delicate as flowers, others breathtakingly dramatic in size. Some of the longest needles had even sprouted secondary clusters, which glittered against the absolute blackness of the Gate like stars in a velvet night sky. Beautiful but treacherous. The grey man had snagged his clothing on them more than once, and last week a haughty apprentice had scratched her arm in crossing, necessitating a Healer's attention. Sooner or later he was going to have to take up a hammer and start clearing them all away.

But not yet. Not until he had to. Creations this beautiful—and this rare—should never be destroyed lightly.

Off to one side of the arch, the grey man's charges were waiting: a dozen sleeping bodies carefully arranged on wheeled tables, white sheets covering them from head to foot. The corners of the sheets had been neatly folded so that their points all hung precisely the same distance from the floor, he noted. One of his assistants was a bit on the compulsive side.

All was as it should be.

Ignoring the nervous flutter in his stomach, he set his glow lamp down on a limestone stump and waited.

There was little prelude to his visitor's arrival. Perhaps the air shimmered ever so slightly within the arch, for less than a second. Perhaps if one listened closely enough one could hear echoes of another world . . . or whispers of the dead. Perhaps someone whose Gift was strong enough would be able to sense a glowing pattern take shape within the archway, for only a moment.

A cold wind gusted into the cavern, raising goose bumps along his arms. Then a tall, thin man stepped through the arch. Or perhaps it was something else, that wore the shape of a man. His skin was translucent white, with cold blue veins that fanned out from his eyes. His long, dark hair curled in the air like wisps of smoke. And his eyes! They were as dark and as colorless as the abyss between the worlds, and it seemed to the grey man that as the visitor gazed around the room he sucked all the heat out of the air. There were spirits stirring in the depths of those eyes that no living man should ever have to learn the names of.

That was something the grey man never got used to.

"My Lord." He bowed his head respectfully, trying to look calm even though his heart was now pounding in his chest. "How may I serve you?"

The man wore the robes of a Master of the Guild of Shadows, but whether he was here in his leadership capacity or just running errands was anyone's guess. The hierarchy of the Shadows was based upon concepts no living man could grasp, and the grey man had long ago given up trying to make sense of them.

"I came to see that you are prepared for tonight's passage." The visitor looked around the chamber. It was impossible to tell whether he was pleased or displeased by what he saw.

"Yes, my Lord." Because the grey man took pride in his work he gestured toward one of the bodies and offered, "This youngest one is HIV positive. That seemed a good match for Master Roland's condition—"

The black eyes fixed on him—empty, unreadable—and the grey man flushed. Had he really expected a Shadow to care about the fine points of his Guild's work? As long as commerce flowed steadily from one world to another, the Shadows had little interest in how it was managed. Only when things went wrong did they start asking questions.

The grey man shivered inwardly, remembering the last time he'd had to answer such questions.

The Shadow said, "Passage is set for eight o'clock local time. Be ready."

The grey man bowed his head, acknowledging the order.

His visitor looked about the cavern, hollow eyes drinking in everything. Had the Shadowlord ever been here before? Or had he perhaps devoured the memories of someone who had been here before? No matter how often the grey man dealt with his kind, he never quite got used to that concept.

"A rather large expedition is also being planned for later this month," the Shadow said at last. "Several Guildmasters wish to bring their apprentices with them. Some kind of *training exercise*." His mouth curled in distaste. "Will you be able to accommodate them?"

"How many people are we talking about?"

"A dozen at least. The list is still growing. Probably two dozen, by the time all are accounted for."

"I'm surprised you're permitting so many to cross at once."

The Shadow's lips tightened but he said nothing. Clearly he was not about to discuss the business of his secretive Guild with outsiders.

Two dozen visitors. It wasn't beyond the capacity of the grey man's operation, but it would certainly strain his resources. "Will there be children in the group?"

"Given the nature of the party, I imagine so." The Shadow raised an eyebrow. "Will that be a problem?"

"Of course not," he said hurriedly. "But I'll need extra time to gather the necessary supplies."

"You will have two weeks. No more, no less."

The grey man nodded tightly. There were beads of cold sweat on his forehead, but he didn't want to do anything as obvious as reach up to wipe them off. In truth, he hated dealing with children. Infants weren't a problem—transporting them was his bread and butter—but once a child reached the age of puberty things became . . . well, complicated. They changed so fast it was hard to get everything right. He knew of one case where the improper handling of a teenager's passage had resulted in a three-week temporal displacement. Which wasn't a major issue as far as *his* Guild was concerned—it was well within the bounds of acceptable distortion—but the boy's parents had been livid. Something about a university examination he had missed, lifetime opportunities now compromised forever, etc., etc. Far be it for the grey man to point out that maybe if the exam had been so important the boy should have been home studying for it, rather than playing walkabout on strange worlds. But logic bore little weight in such a dispute.

It was rumored that the operator responsible for that incident had been reassigned to a mosquito-laden swamp in the middle of nowhere, which might or might not be true. No one had heard from him for a long time.

"I'll need their profiles as soon as possible," the grey man said.

The black eyes glittered coldly. "I'm familiar with what the process requires."

The grey man flushed. "Forgive me, my Lord. I just . . . I just want to make sure everything goes smoothly."

"It will go smoothly," the Shadow said coldly. "I'm certain of it." The unspoken message was clear: *nothing else is acceptable to us.*

The grey man bit his lip and said nothing. It had taken him years to accumulate enough seniority to be assigned to this prestigious post, but he knew that he could lose it all in a heartbeat. Rivalry within his Guild was fierce, and the displeasure of a Shadowlord could impact who was promoted . . . or demoted. If anything went wrong at this facility he might well find himself assigned to some dreadful backwater, where the locals hadn't worked out the basics of personal hygiene yet.

And in fact, something *had* gone wrong. Odds were that more than one head would roll for it in the end. Maybe even his own.

For one brief, mad moment he was tempted to keep his silence. Let someone else tell the Shadows the bad news. Let someone else explain why their usual strategies wouldn't fix things in this case. *It isn't my fault*, he told himself defiantly. *Surely they will see that!*

As if the Shadows were known for their sense of justice.

As the visitor turned to leave, the grey man thought he saw a wisp of darkness flit across his robe. A ghost, perhaps? Some said that the Shadowlords drew spirits of the dead to them like flies, in such quantities that even common men might see them. Others claimed that the dead were as wary of the Shadows as the living were, and that only a ghost who had lost all vestige of free will would ever come within ten feet of one.

The grey man was glad he did not belong to the Guild whose job it was to keep track of such things.

The Shadow paused before the archway, bracing himself for passage. A faint golden light seemed to flicker about him.

Tell him what's wrong, the grey man urged himself. *Right now. It will only get worse if you wait.*

"My Lord." The words came out in a hoarse whisper. The sweat on his forehead felt like ice.

Slowly the Shadow turned back. His eyes were mirrors that reflected the grey man's own fears back at him. Perhaps other men's fears as well. Who could say how many souls were hidden behind that gaze, each one passing judgment upon this moment? The thought of it made his skin crawl.

"They know," the grey man told him. "They developed a science we didn't foresee, discovered things they weren't meant to learn. They're talking to each other now, all across this world, asking questions as a group that no one would have thought to ask alone. And others are starting to listen."

The Shadowlord stared at him. There was no way to read that half-dead expression or to guess at what thoughts lay behind it. Anger? Condemnation? Uncertainty? The grey man held his breath, bracing himself for the worst.

Then, with a sharp nod of dismissal, the Shadow turned back to the arch. He paused for a moment in concentration, then quickly stepped through. Wisps of darkness that might have been ghosts followed him into the void, like pet dogs at the heel of their master.

And then there was silence.

After a long moment—when it was finally clear that no one else was going to come through the Gate—the grey man dared to breathe again.

I did my job. Now the Shadows know the truth. They'll decide how to handle this mess.

It wasn't a reassuring thought.

1

Manassas
Virginia

"OMMY?"

No answer.

I pushed the door open the rest of the way and stepped into the house. The interior was gloomy, not at all what you'd expect on a summer afternoon. It took me a few seconds to register that all the curtains had been drawn shut.

I called for my brother again. "Tommy?"

Still no answer.

On a normal day, that wouldn't have worried me. My little brother generally spent more time in imaginary worlds than in the real one, and I strongly suspected that his "chest cold" earlier that day had more to do with a World of Warcraft game taking place during school hours than anything rooted in biological causes. He was probably hooked up to his computer right now, ear buds blasting game feed straight into his brain, and wasn't even aware that I had come home.

But.

I locked the door behind me—careful to include the deadbolt— and as I pushed a strand of wet brown hair back from my face (*next time check the weather report before biking to school!*) all I could think about was the disturbing text message he'd sent me earlier in the day. Doubly disturbing since it had arrived while I was in the mid-dle of a trig test, and I hadn't been able to read it until nearly an hour later. Precious time to lose if he was in some kind of trouble.

133 WATCHD, he'd texted.

133 was our house number.

A cold feeling was growing in the pit of my stomach, and I won-dered if I should call for help before searching the house any further. I'd shown Tommy's message to two of my friends before leaving school, and they probably would come running if I called, but it would take them time to get here. There was always 911, of course. I fin-gered the cellphone in my pocket nervously, wondering if the police would take me seriously if I called them. *Truant brother—weird text message—yeah, right. Call us when you find a body.*

I was going to have to deal with this on my own.

Heart pounding, I crept through the house, trying to move like the cops did on TV, sliding my back along the wall as I approached corners and doorways. It was harder than it looked—walls have things on them—and I almost knocked over a vase as I slid past Mom's china cabinet.

Finally I reached the door of Tommy's room. There was no noise coming from inside, which could be a good thing or a bad thing. I wasted a few seconds debating between a stealthy entrance and a sud-den one, and decided that without some kind of backup I was best off going with the first option. Slowly I eased the door open, every nerve on high alert. Nothing seemed to be moving inside. I pushed it a little more, to where I could just see my brother's bed. It was in its usual state of chaos; only in cyberspace did Tommy value order. It took me a minute to parse the various lumps of blankets, discarded clothing, and video game controllers into meaningful patterns. When I finally did, I exhaled noisily in exasperation and stalked over to the bedside.

"Hey."

The lump that was my brother did not move.

"Hey!" I shoved the bed hard, and when he still didn't move, jerked the blanket off him. He was wearing his *Lord of the Rings* pajamas, and the face of Gollum had gotten twisted onto his butt. "Get up and talk to me, jerkwad!"

I knew why he was so tired, and it really pissed me off. If you're going to stay up all night playing games with people in Australia, so that when morning comes in America you're so tired you can't even keep your eyes open, and you have to moan and sneeze and pretend you're sick in order to stay home from school so you can catch up on sleep, that's your business. But if you then send your older sister a weird text message about how the house is being watched, and then don't follow it up with an immediate explanation of what on earth you're talking about, or even let her know that you're still alive . . . well, you'd *damn* well better be waiting at the door when she gets home!

At last the kid was stirring. He turned his head, and his eyes cracked open a bit. They were bloodshot. "Jesse? You're home?"

Understatement of the year. "Yeah, I'm home. What the hell was that text about? Who's watching the house?"

The eyes closed again. "She's gone now."

I couldn't tell from his manner if he was fully awake yet. Maybe he thought he was dreaming this conversation.

"All good," he said. "I checked."

I shoved the bed again with my knee. Hard. My heart was finally beginning to settle down to its accustomed rhythm, but I was still pretty pissed. "Who is 'she'? When was 'she' here? Talk to me!"

Finally he seemed to get the message. His eyes opened all the way. They were dark eyes, heavily lashed, just like Dad's. The resemblance was disconcerting sometimes. "I looked out the window this afternoon and saw some woman there. She was just standing in one place, not doing anything. Staring at our house. Then when I went to get a sandwich later I saw her out the front window again, and it was just . . . weird. I think she wanted to walk around the house, to get a better look at it, only she realized she couldn't. That's when I texted you." He shrugged stiffly. "Then she got into a black car and drove off. Never came back."

Walking around our house wasn't easy. There was a regional park right in back of us whose dense woodland merged into our backyard without visible border. Between that and the placement of neighboring houses, it was hard to find a clear path around the property. "Did you see what kind of car it was?" I pressed. "License plate?"

He shook his head. "She parked behind the bushes. I could see that it was a regular car, not an SUV or anything, but no more than that."

"What did she look like?"

He scrunched up his face, trying to remember. "Thin woman. Bony face. Black hair, kinda goth. Couldn't see much else." When I kept glaring at him he protested, "That's all I know, honest!"

I couldn't think of any reason why a strange goth chick would want to spy on our house. Maybe Tommy's marathon gaming session had warped his adolescent brain, leaving his imagination stuck in high gear. Which still wasn't going to get him off the hook as far as I was concerned.

"Don't *ever* scare me like that again!" I snapped. "Jeez, I nearly called 911 on you! How would Mom feel about that, if they called her at work to tell her you were in some kind of trouble? All because you couldn't spare the five minutes it would take to let me know what was going on?"

He flushed slightly. "I'm sorry." It sounded sincere, for whatever that was worth.

I sighed heavily, torn between feeling relieved and angry. With Tommy you never knew which way to go. He was so tied up in his online games that sometimes it carried over into his real life. I wasn't sure he always knew where World of Warcraft ended and the real world began. It worried me sometimes. It worried Mom, too. And he didn't have to describe everything that had gone on during the day for me to guess at the bigger picture. When he first caught sight of the strange woman, he'd probably been busy gaming, so of course he wasn't going to contact me right away. Later on when he took a break and saw her again, he texted me, then went right back to his gaming. Never stopped to think about how much I'd worry when I got that crazy message.

Maybe the woman wasn't even real. Maybe she was just some fan-

tasy inside his head that had managed to breach the wall between realities and slip into this world. Or maybe she was real enough, but her
visit had no significance. A strange woman had gotten out of her car
for perfectly mundane reasons, looked around to find some kind of
landmark or street sign to tell her where she was, then driven away.
Welcome to the DC suburbs.

But even if that was all there'd been to it, he'd scared the hell out
of me with that text message, and I wasn't going to let him forget that.

"Mom said I should order pizza for us when I came home." I
kicked the bed one last time as I pushed myself back from it. "I'm
going to go do that now. If you're out of bed when it gets here you can
have some; otherwise I'm eating all of it."

He turned over again and buried his head back in the pillow. Gollum stared up at me. I shook my head as I headed toward the door
and added maliciously, "You want anchovies on your half, right?"

The lump stirred. "No anchovies," a muffled voice protested.
"Pepperoni."

"Double anchovies, all over your half. Got it." I nodded as I took
hold of the doorknob. "And get dressed. You know it'll upset Mom if
you don't."

"No anchovies—!"

I shut the door before he could protest further.

IIIIIIIIIIIIII

By the time the pizza arrived I had the house looking somewhat normal again. The outer curtains in the living room were open now, but
I'd left the sheer inner layer closed. I did have a creepy feeling that
something was outside the house, but that wasn't enough to justify the
whole living-in-darkness thing. In our neck of the woods there were
always creatures wandering around the property; animals in the park
sometimes mistook our yard for their rutting grounds and our garbage cans for their food supply. I'd seen some things wandering by
after dark that I couldn't have named if you'd paid me.

Mom had left us twenty dollars for pizza. That was guilt money. If she'd planned for us to eat without her she would have made us something for dinner and left it the fridge. But she hadn't, which meant that her boss had called her in to work at the last minute. Again. He liked to do that to her. He knew that Mom couldn't afford to lose her lousy waitress job or be assigned to crappy shifts. So whenever someone couldn't make it to work, she was the first one he would call in as a replacement. He figured she couldn't afford to say no.

Which was, sad to say, accurate.

I once read a Dean Koontz novel in which there were monsters living among normal people, and they looked just like everyone else, but they were really creatures who fed on human misery. So they were constantly working to cause people pain, in a thousand little ways. I figured Mom's boss was one of them.

When Tommy finally emerged from his inner sanctum he was still barefoot, but he'd pulled on a pair of jeans and a T-shirt, all wrinkled but clean. Good enough. I'd never understood why Mom thought that someone who stayed home sick from school needed to get dressed at all, but she did, and I didn't want her to come home and start fighting with Tommy about it. Life was tough enough without people yelling at each other, and with Mom constantly stressed out from working two jobs—with a Dean Koontz monster for one of her bosses—it took a little extra work to keep the peace.

Yes, that was me: peacekeeper, pizza provider, and surrogate mother for a thirteen-year-old gaming junkie. Truth be told, the last one wasn't quite as bad as it sounded. On the Sibling Annoyance Scale, wherein a score of one would be *"Tommy who?"* and ten would be *"get him out of my face NOW!"*, Tommy ranked somewhere in the five or six range. Some of my friends had to live with sevens and eights, and Jenny Cedric's brother was a whopping eleven, so actually I was pretty lucky. Tommy rarely caused trouble for anyone. He'd be happy to just sit in front of the computer and play games all day, occasionally posting videos in which he talked about sitting in front of the computer and playing games all day, if Mom and I didn't force him out into the sunlight now and then.

The pizza was New York Style, made by a vendor from Brooklyn who supposedly knew what New York pizza really tasted like. It had thick orange oil on top, that trickled down your hand no matter how you tried to contain it. Some of it dribbled onto the countertop as I ate, and I found myself swirling it into fractal patterns with my index finger. First a circle to represent our house, then a larger circle surrounding it, to indicate the scrutiny of the strange woman. Then little curlicues leading off from that one, representing all the places she might have gone. I stared at the design for a few minutes, then added a little circle at the end of each curlicue. Other houses the woman might watch? Appointments later in the afternoon? The fate-portrait was interesting, and I wondered if there was some way to press a piece of paper toweling down onto it to preserve it. Maybe I would base my next art project on it. Title: *Invader.*

Tommy started telling me all about his Australian game, and I did my best to listen attentively because I knew how important it was to him, but as usual, 99.99 percent of it went flying straight over my head. Something about a raiding team with twenty-five people who had to confront a massive "trash mob" (annoying bad guys) on the way to confronting an "epic boss" (big scary bad guy), but the tanks didn't do their job right, so all the healers got killed, which meant that nobody could get resurrected, which meant that Tommy's buddy Josh (who was playing a bikini-clad elf with double-D breasts . . . now tell me *that* wasn't weird) was now going to have to hike back from wherever it was that people went when they died. Death having been reduced by the game to a temporary inconvenience, as opposed to . . . well, you know, *death.*

Mom's sudden arrival cut the recitation short. She looked really tired, and I could feel exhaustion radiating from her skin like heat from a sun-baked sidewalk. The pizza was cold by then, so I jumped up to put a slice in the toaster oven for her. Mom never ate at work, no matter how hungry she got. It was like the story of Persephone, an ancient Greek beauty who swallowed seeds in the Underworld and then had to stay there for six months out of every year. Or changelings who got whisked away to a fairy realm, then foolishly ate food there and couldn't ever come home. On some deep, visceral level, I suspected that was how Mom felt about eating food at work. Like if she took anything from the Koontz Monster's world into herself, he'd own her soul forever.

She came around the island to hug me hello, then went to hug Tommy. He wasn't really comfortable with such overt physical affection, and I could see him stiffen up a bit, though he didn't actually pull away from her. Mom could sense the resistance, but as usual she gave no overt sign that it bothered her. Doubtless she hoped that if she just kept acting like everything was okay, someday it really would be.

She had once told me that Tommy was a highly affectionate toddler, always trying to climb into her lap, begging to snuggle while she read him bedtime stories, even hanging onto her leg while she cooked. At moments like this you could see how much she wanted to have that closeness back again. But when Tommy was three Dad had walked out on us (or was thrown out, depending on which version of the story you believed), and that changed everything. Tommy never talked about that time—even to me—and a counselor last year had assured Mom that he probably didn't remember the details of Dad's departure. *People don't remember things clearly from when they were three years old,* she said. But she was wrong. A kid never forgets the day his father walked out on him. It changes the world in subtle ways that a three-year-old might not have words for, but the fact that he can't talk about his scars doesn't mean they're not there.

I suspected that's what all the gaming was really about. It gave Tommy a world that he could control, a universe with clearly defined rules that stayed the same no matter what he did. Turn the machine on when you want to play, log off when you want to stop. Simple. Always works. He could make himself look like anything he wanted to, spend hours with friends who didn't care about how insecure he really was, and create fantastic tales that ended the way he wanted them to. Hell, even death had been reduced to a minor story variant in that universe. It was the perfect escape for a little kid.

I had an escape world too, but it wasn't anything that Mom knew about. There were echoes of it in my artwork, but they were pretty well disguised, and thus far no one had caught on. Some of my paintings were on display at the school right now, and people could look at them on their way to the main office. Sometimes I saw visitors staring at my interlocking fractal patterns and metaphorical spiderweb designs, and once I overheard comments about how *unique* my paintings were, and how incredibly *innovative* I was. But none of those people had a clue about what those patterns really meant. Or the dreams they came from. Tommy was the only one I ever told about those. I knew he sometimes used ideas from my dreams in his gaming universe, but he'd promised me once, on a stack of D&D rulebooks, that if anyone ever asked about them he'd say he dreamed them himself, so no one would bother me about them. He also promised me that if he ever made a million dollars turning one of my dream stories into a game he'd split it with me fifty/fifty, which was a nice fantasy for both of us, so I said okay.

A short while after Mom came home, Tommy went off to bed. Of course he never said a word to her about the strange woman he'd seen that afternoon. Tommy wasn't forward about that kind of stuff with anyone but me. I found myself staring down at my pizza oil drawing as Mom asked about my school day, knowing in my gut that I really should tell her about the incident myself. But then what would happen? She'd just get all stressed out—like I had earlier in the day—but she couldn't actually *do* anything about it, could she? She couldn't call the police and tell them, *Hey, a strange woman was standing outside my house five hours ago, and no, she didn't do anything wrong, but my thirteen-year-old son just thought it was kinda weird, y'know? So could you maybe come by and take a look?* They'd just laugh in her face. Meanwhile you could see from the deep lines in her face and the exhausted glaze in her eyes how much working two long shifts had already drained her of energy today, and I couldn't bring myself to add an imaginary crisis to her load.

So I told her about my math test instead, and how bummed I was that I hadn't been invited to a party that some girls in my class were throwing, and about the piece of American History homework I'd stupidly lost in study hall that morning, which might or might not wind up screwing my grade for the whole quarter. It was our nightly ritual. She tried her best to pay attention, and she nodded and "hm-hmmed" in all the right places, but I knew that she just didn't have the kind of energy it took to connect with me on any meaningful level. I gave her credit for trying, though.

While I talked I tore pieces of paper toweling off the roll to wipe the orange oil up from the counter, reducing my composition to a fatty orange smear, obliterating its secrets forever.

"I'm going to bed," Mom said at last. She came around the island to kiss me on the forehead, her lips lingering there for a moment longer than usual, as if she was too tired to remove them. "Don't stay up too much longer, Jesse."

"I won't," I promised.

She gave me a hug, and I returned it, knowing as I did so that all my hugs counted double because of the issue with Tommy.

"And don't forget," she said as she exited the kitchen. "We have that appointment at the lab tomorrow. I'll pick you up right after school."

My heart skipped a beat. But Mom was looking the other way by then and did not see the expression of dismay on my face.

Jeez. I'd forgotten all about the lab appointment.

I could always pretend to be sick tomorrow. If I could convince Mom that I had some kind of bug—maybe the one that laid Tommy low today—she wouldn't want me to get within ten miles of a medical facility. There were way too many people with compromised immune systems in a place like that, she would say. Best for everyone's health that I stay home.

But Mom wasn't looking forward to our lab appointment any more than I was, especially as she'd had to give up a shift at work to make time for it. Making her go there alone, with no one to help distract her in the waiting room or offer her emotional support afterward, would be the height of selfishness.

It's going to be all right, I told myself. *Mom said nothing could possibly go wrong, didn't she? This is all just a formality.*

With a sigh I headed off to bed, knowing that I probably wouldn't sleep a wink all night. Goth spies at the windows. Crazy paranoid father ruining all our lives.

Welcome to a day in the Drake household.

2

MANASSAS
VIRGINIA

*D*OORS.

More doors.

Doors all around me, as far as the eye can see. They're scattered randomly about the landscape, identical in form, stark in aspect. Like tombstones with doorknobs. Each one is set in a wooden frame, but the frame connects to nothing. No walls surround these doors, no houses support them, and they seem to have no purpose. Beneath them is a smooth black floor that glistens like polished glass; around them there is only darkness.

What is this place?

Some of the doors stand alone in the darkness; others seem to be gathered in clusters, carefully arranged, as if the houses they'd once belonged to had been lifted up and carried away, leaving them behind. In their arrangement I can see the ghostly echoes of rooms and hallways. And yet even that isn't quite right. Because all the doors are facing me. The ones that are alone, the ones that are in groups—every single one of them facing me. Whatever purpose these doors were meant to serve, it centers around me.

A shiver runs up my spine.

Part of me knows this is a dream. And God knows, I'm used to strange dreams. Some of mine are so weird that Tommy can't even share them with his gaming buddies. That's the highest bar there is for weirdness.

But though this dream may be tame in appearance, something about its essence chills me to the bone. For a moment I'm frozen in place. I know these doors are significant, but I'm not sure I want to find out why.

But in the end curiosity wins out over caution, and I walk hesitantly toward the nearest one. The black floor is cold beneath my bare feet, as if I'm walking on ice. Though it's dark all around me I can see the doors clearly; they are exuding a strange mystical light that renders them visible, while leaving the surrounding landscape in darkness. Really creepy.

Then I'm standing in front of one of them. I draw in a deep breath, bracing myself to confront whatever might be behind it. This is only a dream, I remind myself. As if that ever helps.

I put my hand on the doorknob—smooth metal, ice-cold to the touch—and slowly turn it. I hear the latch snick open: a normal, mundane sound.

Heart pounding, I open the door.

On the other side I see . . . my living room. It's kind of hazy, like the whole thing is slightly out of focus, and some of the items in it aren't arranged the same way they're supposed to be. A lamp that my brother broke last week is back in its place by the side of the couch. The jacket I used to wear when nights were cooler is draped across the back of a kitchen chair, as if I'd just dropped it there.

My mother is in the room, and she looks afraid. Someone else is there too, and my gut knows who it is before my brain finds the courage to give him a name.

Dad.

He looks angry. Really angry. I can smell the alcohol on his breath from where I'm standing.

"Don't lie to me!" he screams at my mother. "I know the truth!"

The words make my stomach clench in a knot, so powerfully I

want to vomit. I know that I should grab the door and slam it shut before this scene goes any further. But my hand is frozen on the door-knob, and I can't make myself look away.

"He and I were friends," Mom protests. "Just friends." She's clearly struggling to sound composed, but it has a false edge to it, like a person who's trying to pretend she's calm in front of a rabid pit bull. "You knew about my past history with him when we got married."

"And you said that you would stop seeing him!"

"I did, I did. I couldn't help—"

"I SAW THE PICTURES!" He takes a step toward her, and I can see the fear in her eyes. Instinctively I begin to move forward to pro-tect her, but I find I can't pass through the doorway. It's not like there's anything physically blocking my path, or any supernatural force that I'm aware of. It's simply not possible for me to cross the threshold.

I'm forced to watch the scene unfold, and nothing more.

I can't.

I can't.

Somehow I manage to reach out and shut the door. The scene behind it is extinguished like a snuffed-out candle flame.

Thank God.

There are several other doors nearby. After a moment I start to walk toward one of them. I dread finding out what's behind it, but I need to discover what these doors are all about, and I can't do that without more information.

Breath held, I pull the door open.

"Sixteen years!" My father is screaming. "Sixteen years I've been paying to support a child who isn't even mine! Paycheck after pay-check, bleeding me dry . . . Don't try to tell me she's mine! I SAW THE PICTURES!"

I'm about to shut this door as well, when suddenly a flicker of movement from the far side of the room catches my eye. It's coming from the very place where I had once hidden myself, listening in hor-

ror as my own father disowned me. But this time I'm not the one who's eavesdropping.

It's Tommy.

"I'll tell you what," Mom is saying. A shadow of strength has come into her voice "We'll go and get tested. All right? You and me and Jessica, all together. And then the doctor can show you that the DNA matches up and she's really your daughter, and then you can go home and work on some new conspiracy to get all upset about, but I WILL NEVER SEE YOU IN MY HOUSE AGAIN!"

I slam the door shut.

Is this what's behind every one of them? A rerun of that terrible night? No, Tommy's presence implies there's something more to this. Despite my horror, I can't deny the sharp bite of curiosity. It's like when you drive by a gruesome car accident. You don't want to look at it, but you have to.

Trembling inside, I begin to open other doors. Each one seems to have the same scene going on behind it, but in a slightly different version. At first the changes are small: maybe the room is decorated differently, or my parents use different words to say the same things—inconsequential stuff. But the further I get from my starting point, the bigger the changes become. Until at last I open one of them and the room behind it is deathly still. There's blood splattered all over the place and a sickening smell in the air. My mother's body is lying motionless on the floor. One side of her head has been crushed. A broken lamp lies next to her. My father is nowhere to be seen.

I turn and run.

It's only a dream, I tell myself, tears streaming down my cheeks. Only a dream. I can wake up if I want to. But when I try and it doesn't work, I know I'm trapped in this terrible place.

Suddenly I am standing in front of another door. I reach out and open it, not because I want to, but because the dream has taken on a momentum all its own, and I am helpless to do anything else.

"I'm sorry," this version of my father is saying. Tears are running down his face. "I'm so sorry, Evelyn! I've been such a jerk to you and

*the kids. Can you ever forgive me? I mean, I know we can't just turn
back the clock, but if you'll give me a chance to make things right—
any chance at all—I'll see that you never regret it."*

*It's all too much. Too much! Sinking down beside the doorframe,
I start to cry. "Please," I whisper. Praying to whoever controls this
terrible place. "Let me go home now. Please."*

*And the blackness surrounding me gives way to a gentler dark-
ness, and then, mercifully, to dreamless sleep.*

The waiting room at the lab was decorated in a disturbing mix of
techno and Victoriana: artistic schizophrenia. The walls and ceiling
were stark white, the floor was polished to an antiseptic sheen, and
the chrome-and-glass furniture in the receptionist's space was aggressively ergonomic. God help the germ that wandered into this place.
But someone had apparently questioned how comfortable the setting
would be for actual patients, and so had stolen a dozen heavily uphol-
stered chairs from the set of *Masterpiece Theater* and set them up in
a corner of the waiting room. To my eye, the ornate wooden chairs
seemed to be screaming in aesthetic agony: *Get me out of here!* Never
before had I had such an overwhelming urge to ship furniture back to
England.

Mom and I sat in overstuffed chairs and riffled through an unin-
spiring pile of magazines. *Better Housekeeping, Sports Illustrated,
Highlights.* If you picked one not intended for your age and gender,
would they note that on your intake form? I picked up a *Highlights*
and briefly relived my childhood as I flipped through the pages, my
hands trembling ever so slightly.

"Hey." Mom reached out and put her hand over mine. "It's all
going to be all right. Really."

"I know," I muttered.

"This is to calm your dad down," she reminded me. "There's no
real question about the outcome."

I sighed and put the magazine down. "I know."

There were all sorts of questions I wanted to ask Mom, inspired by stuff I'd seen in my dream, but since I normally didn't tell her about my dreams at all—not the weird ones, anyway—I didn't know how to start. Finally I ventured, "About Dad. Was he really . . . well, you know . . . crazy?"

Mom sighed and looked down at her lap. "Your father had some problems," she said quietly. Picking her way through the words as if tiptoeing through a mine field. "He didn't know how to deal with his feelings, so sometimes he didn't handle it well."

My throat tightened. I remembered all the versions of my father that I'd seen last night. The smashed lamps. My mother's crushed skull.

It was just a dream, I told myself stubbornly. *Pull yourself together, girl.*

"Hey." Mom leaned over and put an arm around my shoulders, squeezing me gently. "It'll be okay. Really."

The words came out before I could stop them. "Why did he leave us?"

Mom sighed heavily. "Your dad was full of fear, Jesse. He was afraid that if he didn't control everyone and everything around him, he would lose it all. The trouble is that sometimes, when you hold onto a thing you love too tightly, you can crush the life out of it." She paused. "Or drive it away."

"Do you still love him?"

A shadow of pain crossed her face; she touched her lips gently to my forehead. "You can't raise two children with someone and not love him," she whispered. "That doesn't mean it's right for us to be together."

Someone coughed gently. We looked up to find an orderly standing at a respectful distance. She was wearing dress scrubs with a sprinkling of tiny planets and stars all over them, reminding me of Tommy's Star Wars pajamas.

"The doctor will see you now," she said.

She let us through a pair of glass doors at the end of the waiting room, down a squeaky-clean hallway flanked by claustrophobically small exam rooms, and into a consulting office. It was a spartan space, with only a desk and a few chairs in it. As we were in the process of sitting down, an Indian-looking man in a lab coat arrived.

"Ms. Drake. I'm Dr. Gupta. I'll be discussing your test results with you." He turned to me and offered a well-rehearsed smile. "And you must be Jessica."

We all shook hands. I tried to make my grip feel strong and confident, even though I felt anything but.

"Will Mr. Hayden be coming?" the doctor asked. "We do prefer to speak to the whole family together in situations like this." Maybe it was just that my nerves were on edge, but I thought he stressed the last three words slightly.

"He's away on business right now." Mom had actually gone out of her way to schedule this meeting at a time when Dad couldn't come, but the doctor had no way to know that. "I'm sure he'll get in touch with you when he comes home."

"Very well." Dr. Gupta sat behind the desk and cleared his throat as he opened a manila folder with my name on it. A shadow crossed his face as he read. He closed the folder, rested his elbows on the table, and steepled his hands in front of him. "Ms. Drake . . . Jessica. . . ."

My heart skipped a beat. Call me paranoid, but I've never seen a doctor do that when the news was good.

"I'm afraid the results of the paternity test were negative."

For a moment the words just hung there in the air between us. Like a ball had been thrown to us, that no one wanted to catch.

At last my mother spoke. "Are you saying that Mike isn't Jessica's father?"

The doctor nodded. "I'm afraid that's the case."

"But that's not possible."

"The test results are quite clear. I'm sorry, Ms. Drake."

"No. No." She shook her head emphatically. "You don't understand what I'm saying. It's not *physically* possible."

"I'm afraid the data—"

"Unless you're suggesting some kind of immaculate conception —"

He raised up a hand to still her protest. "Please, Ms. Drake. Please." He waited until she calmed herself and then said, very gently, "The issue isn't only with your husband's DNA."

Mom blinked. "What? What do you mean?"

"Jessica's genetic profile isn't a match to yours, either."

Say what?

Had he really just told us that I wasn't my mother's daughter? The thought was so crazy my brain could hardly process it. Maybe I'd misunderstood him.

Mom reached out for my hand and squeezed it so hard that I thought her nails would break skin. "That's not possible," she said firmly. "Jesse is my daughter."

So then he explained to us about how DNA testing worked, and why the results meant what they meant. I only half-listened. I mean, we've all watched *Law and Order*, right? So everybody knows about spectrum analysis, and the bands of marking that look like bar codes, which tell you what your genes are like, and how, if you put a child's bar codes next to her father's—or her mother's—some of them are supposed to match up.

Then he showed us the sheets of plastic our bar codes were on, mine and Mom's and Dad's, and no, they didn't match up at all.

Zero percent, he said. Those were the odds that Evelyn Rose Drake was my mother. Ditto for Michael Glenn Hayden being my dad. Not even one percent. Zero.

To say that I was confused would be an understatement. I felt as if someone had struck me square in the gut. My hand could no longer feel Mom's nails biting into it. My mind could no longer process a rational thought. I felt disconnected, like a boat whose anchor had suddenly been cut loose, and there I was in the middle of a stormy sea with nothing to keep me from being swept away and lost forever. I felt like throwing up.

"It just isn't possible," my mother protested. But with less conviction this time. She watched *Law and Order*, too.

He explained to us about mitochondrial DNA, and how that's passed down straight from mother to daughter, and so they had checked that too, just to be sure. He showed us the printouts. Still no match.

I hated him for the pity that was in his eyes, because it was so obviously rehearsed. How did it feel to deliver news like this to someone? To know that with a handful of words you could tear the soul of a family to pieces? I felt hot tears coming to my eyes, but I struggled to blink them back. I didn't want this man to see how badly he had upset me. No stranger should have that kind of power over me.

This can't be happening, I told myself. *It's all a bad dream. I'll wake up any minute now.*

"Hospitals do make mistakes sometimes," the doctor was saying. "It's unfortunate, but even in this country, with all its safeguards, babies do get mixed up."

"Labs make mistakes too," my mother challenged him. "Maybe your test was wrong. Maybe your samples got switched around. Isn't that a more likely scenario than someone handing me the wrong baby?"

"Our lab protocols are meticulous," he said coldly. "And we have safeguards in place to avoid just that kind of mistake."

But Mom wouldn't accept his reassurance. And In the end he agreed to do the test a second time. He even agreed that the lab would pay for it. Which was a good thing, because insurance didn't cover this kind of thing.

So I sat there numbly while they stuck a swab in my mouth— again—wondering what my life would become if this was really true. It was too scary to think about.

Mom and I were silent for most of the trip home. I pressed my face against the car window and watched the scenery of Route 28 pass us by without really seeing it. If I wasn't really the daughter of Evelyn and Michael Hayden, who was I?

As we crossed the I-66 junction I muttered, "Am I adopted?"

Mom glanced at me. She said nothing. A few hundred feet later there was a wide enough shoulder for her to pull off onto, and she did so, putting the car in park. Then she turned to me and took my face in both her hands.

"*You are my daughter*," she told me sternly. "I gave birth to you in Manassas Hospital, with your father present. They took you out of my body and cleaned you up and wrapped you in a towel and put you in my arms, and then your dad came and touched your hand, and your little fingers curled around his fingertip—"

I could see tears brimming in her eyes, which made tears come to mine.

"I have a birth certificate with your name on it. You can look at it if you want to. Jessica Anne Drake-Hayden. *My daughter*."

"Are we going to tell Dad about this?" I whispered.

I could see a flicker of fear in her eyes. It had been ten years since he'd left us, and she was still afraid of him.

She turned back to the road, turned her left signal on, and put the car in drive.

"When we have to," she said.

⸻

Mom didn't tell Tommy about the tests results, just that there had been a problem with the original procedure, and it had to be repeated. He was a smart kid, though, and he could probably tell from our expressions that something was seriously wrong. But Mom had decided to spare him the truth—at least until the test results were confirmed—and I went along with that. Later, when Tommy would normally have grilled me for more information privately, he surprised me by not asking questions. Maybe he sensed that if I tried to talk about what had happened at the lab I would break down in tears, or put my fist through a wall while I screamed curses at the heavens, or . . . something. Like I said, he was a smart kid.

Sample contamination. That's what Mom told him. The original samples had gotten contaminated, so we'd been asked to provide new ones. Now we had to wait for new results. Ten days.

Dad would be back by then.

||||||||||||

Midnight. I couldn't sleep.

No, that wasn't accurate. I wasn't *willing* to sleep. Because this was the kind of night when I usually had weird dreams, and right now I just wasn't up to dealing with them.

I read in bed for awhile, my body positioned between the lamp and the door so that Mom wouldn't realize I was still awake. Then, come midnight, when I figured everyone else had fallen asleep, I turned off the lamp, left my room, and sneaked quietly downstairs.

The "office" was actually a walk-in pantry, which Mom had outfitted with a computer desk and a few filing cabinets. The files themselves were pretty well organized, so it didn't take me long to find my birth certificate, along with all the other paperwork that had accompanied my entry into this world. I even found a form with a pair of tiny footprints on it, and for a moment I was tempted to ink up my fully grown feet and see if they matched. But what would that tell me? If two babies had been switched at the hospital, it could have happened before those prints were made.

I put everything back where I'd found it and started back to my room.

On the way I passed Tommy's door. And I stopped. After a moment, I opened it quietly and slipped inside. The room was dark, but the slatted blinds hadn't been shut completely, so thin bands of moonlight fell across the bed, illuminating a mound of blankets, toys, and Tommy.

As I stared down at him I felt a mixture of love and confusion so strong that I didn't know how to handle it.

You're not really my brother.

I formed the words in my mind, testing them, but they had no real substance. No reality.

For thirteen years this crazy kid had been part of my life. I'd hated him and loved him and resented him and needed him— sometimes all of those things at once. I'd tormented him when he was learning to walk and comforted him when he fell off his bike, and climbed into Mom's bed with him the night that Dad left us, so that the three of us could cry quietly in the darkness together. Which bonded us together in ways no words could ever capture. Since then I had been like a second mother to him, filling in for Mom while she struggled to make ends meet.

Now, after all that, five simple words threatened to come between us: *You're not really my brother.*

What did those words mean, really? That a couple of genes weren't arranged the way they should be? So what? That didn't change who I was, did it? Or dictate who I was allowed to love?

Maybe the lab really *had* screwed up the test, I thought. Maybe they would call us in a few days to tell us that, and then everything would go back to normal. But as much as I hoped that would happen, deep in my gut I didn't really believe it. Ever since childhood I'd felt as if something in my life was out of kilter. There was nothing concrete that I could ever point to and complain about, just an indefinable sense of *wrongness* that had always haunted me. Now, at last, that feeling had a name. Things with names didn't just go away.

I recalled a *Law and Order* episode I saw once, in which a nine-year-old boy learned that he'd been kidnapped from his birth-parents back when he was just an infant. Years later they found him and applied for legal custody. The judge ruled in their favor, and so they took that happy kid away from the family who had raised him, the only family he'd ever known. DNA trumps love. I still remembered the look on his face when that ruling was announced. Like his whole world had been destroyed.

At sixteen, I was past the age when such a thing was likely to happen to me. At worst, a couple of strangers calling themselves my "real mother and father" might visit, and we'd all try to be polite to one another as we joked bitterly about the lousy security in the hospital where Mom had given birth. And then they would go back to their house, and I would stay in mine, and we'd all try to put the pieces of our lives back together again, as if nothing had ever happened.

Yes, I thought stubbornly. *That's how it will be.*

Looking down at my brother, I felt a sudden wave of tenderness and fear come over me, so powerful it brought tears to my eyes. *I will always be your sister,* I promised him silently. *No one will ever be allowed to come between us. I swear it.*

Then I sneaked out of his room as quietly as I could, leaving him to dreams that were sure to be more peaceful than mine.

3

MANASSAS
VIRGINIA

Dear Ms. Drake,

In response to your question, it is the policy of our hospital to record the footprint of each newborn during the post-delivery examination. This takes place by the side of the mother and in her full view, immediately after childbirth. Babies and mothers are also tagged with matching bracelets at that time, which they wear until they leave the hospital.

These procedures have been in place since 1992.

Please let me know any further questions you may have.

Sincerely,
Janeen Dover
Director of Risk Management
Manassas Hospital

||||||||||||||

Two footprints. One tiny but clean, rendered with professional precision. The other somewhat messy, the kind of mark you'd expect if a teenager swabbed her foot with calligraphy ink and tried to then roll it onto a sheet of printer paper. It was hard to make out its loops and whorls even where the impression was good, and in most places it wasn't good. Only the ridges on the big toe could be examined with any certainty. But those appeared to match my own.

That should have been good enough, shouldn't it? Jessica Anne Drake-Hayden had been carried straight from her mother's womb to the ink pad, a journey witnessed by both of her parents and half a dozen delivery room staff. Her ridge patterns matched my own. I was indisputably that child.

So the DNA lab must have made a mistake. They'd switched samples somewhere along the line, or else confused the reports. The new test would sort that all out.

Right?

Only the lab we'd gone to wasn't one of those fly-by-night outfits in which quality control took a back seat to sales quotas. This facility was hardcore, as befit a business whose findings had the power to destroy marriages, resolve million-dollar lawsuits, or even send people to jail. The smallest weak link in its chain of protocols would have brought the whole thing crashing down long ago. So the likelihood of them mixing up our samples wasn't zero percent—nothing in the universe was zero percent—but it was low enough that you'd need scientific notation to write it down. So where did that leave me?

A chimera, I thought soberly. *Right on the outside and wrong on the inside. A creature that should not exist.*

Great stuff for a science fiction movie. Sucks for real life.

|||||||||||||

The sign outside the school library said, *SO YOU THINK YOU CAN PAINT?* Which had to be the lamest title for an art display ever. But the artwork itself wasn't bad. Our teacher Mrs. Fletcher encouraged us to embrace our craziest ideas and to mix media without inhibition, which sometimes produced interesting results. The school liked to put them on display, which I figured was kind of like a parent putting his kids' drawings on the refrigerator. Visitors to the school seemed to find it impressive, which I'd been told had significance in fundraising circles.

Three of my paintings were in the show. At first glance they appeared to be nothing more than geometric designs with a bit of a crazy edge to them (less crazy if you were familiar with fractal art) but in reality they were much more than that. Each line, dot, and fractal squiggle *meant* something. If you read my paintings right they revealed all sorts of things about human relationships, patterns of behavior, and sometimes my own hopes and fears. And they told you about my dreams, as well. Because every painting of mine was based on something I'd seen in a dream. If you stared at one of them long enough it was like getting inside my head.

No one outside of my family knew anything about that.

Now, looking up at my work, I felt grounded again. I'd been walking about in a daze for the last day or so, disconnected from the world around me. Like I was a stranger in Jessica Drake's body, and if anyone looked at me closely enough they might detect the masquerade. But whoever I really was—*whatever* I really was—these paintings were uniquely mine. They were reflections of Jessica Drake's true soul, and seeing them on canvas like that helped anchor me to that identity.

"Jessica?" The voice from behind broke into my reverie. "Oh, I'm so glad I ran into you!"

I turned around to see Mrs. Fletcher standing there: a short, plump woman with rosy cheeks, who looked like she should be off baking apple pies for a county fair somewhere. Her button-up smock was criss-crossed with streaks of paint and dye that would probably never wash out. They were marks of honor for her, much as facial scars were for a Prussian duelist.

"There's someone who wants to buy one of your paintings," she told me, her blue eyes crinkling from excitement. "She said they were as good as anything she's seen in a gallery, and she wants one to hang in her home! She asked if she could come by after school tomorrow and talk to you about it. Are you free then?"

I blinked. "Uh, yeah."

Something about my expression must have seemed odd to her; she cocked her head and asked, "That's good, isn't it?"

"Of course it's good." Truth be told I wasn't sure that it was, but clearly that was the response she expected.

"You don't have to sell something to her if you don't want to," she assured me. "It's perfectly reasonable for you to want to hold onto your work at this stage in your life."

"I know."

"But it's flattering, yes?"

I nodded. "Very flattering."

"Your mother should be there for this. Can she make it?"

I shook my head. "Working. Sorry."

"Ah, well. She really should approve any sale, but I guess you could at least get the details and talk to her later."

The bell rang suddenly, startling us both.

"Come by my office after school tomorrow," she said backing away quickly. "This is so exciting!" Then she turned and trotted toward her classroom.

Yes, by all human measure it should have been exciting. It was the kind of thing that high school artists dreamed about. The kind of thing I had dreamed about, once.

But now, as I looked up at my paintings, I wondered if I could bring myself to sell one of them to a stranger. If you poured your soul into a painting and then gave that painting away, would that part of your soul be lost forever?

Then the second bell rang, and I sprinted down the hallway, existential questions driven out of my brain by the looming abomination called Trigonometry.

⁞⁞⁞⁞⁞⁞⁞⁞⁞⁞⁞

I had the door dream again that night. Only this time all the doors were locked, and try as I might I couldn't open any of them. I knew there was a key that I was supposed to have, but I couldn't find it. Had

I owned it once, but lost it? Or never possessed it in the first place? The question seemed to matter, but I had no way to answer it.

I wandered the black plain for a long time before the dream finally faded.

‖‖‖‖‖‖‖‖‖‖‖‖

Noise. In the distance. Subtle sound, barely above the threshold of hearing. Enough to wake you up only if your nerves were already stretched to the breaking point.

I sat up in bed and focused all my senses on the noise. It seemed to be coming from downstairs. The subtle rustling of fabric in motion. The creak of a wary footstep on wooden floors. Someone was moving around as carefully as possible, not wanting to be heard.

Heart pounding, I eased myself out of bed. Part of me wanted to hide from the unseen threat, or perhaps call for help, while the other part of me wanted to investigate, so that I would know what was going on before I woke up the whole family. Because if it turned out there wasn't really anything wrong, I would look pretty stupid shouting an alarm.

The latter instinct won out by just a hair, and so I eased my bedroom door open and slipped into the hallway, my bare feet silent on the carpeted floor.

Now I could see that there was a light on downstairs, somewhere at the far end of the house. A burglar would use a flashlight, I told myself, not turn on the light like that. It was mildly reassuring.

I worked my way slowly down the stairs, trying to avoid the spots that I knew would creak the loudest. Once I got to the first floor I could see that the light was coming from the office. The door was half closed so I couldn't see who was inside, but I assumed it was someone who belonged here. Like I said: flashlight.

I walked to the door and pushed it open slightly. Just enough to see inside, not enough to draw attention.

It was Mom.

She was sitting at the desk with her back to the door, staring at a piece of paper. One of the file cabinet drawers was open, and I could see where a manila folder had been removed. A lump formed in my throat as I realized what folder it was.

I came up behind her, no longer trying to hide my presence. If she heard me, she gave no sign of it.

In her hand was the hospital document with my footprint on it. She was just staring at it. Not moving, hardly even breathing. Just staring. And I knew what she was thinking, as if I were inside her head. *I could compare Jesse's footprint to this one. We'd know the truth, then. But what if she thinks I'm doing that because I don't really believe she's my daughter? That could hurt her in ways no DNA test would ever fix.*

"Hey," I whispered.

"Hey," she whispered back.

I put my hand on her shoulder. "It's okay, Mom."

She nodded. "I know."

"No. Seriously. I mean, it's *okay*."

Leaning on her for balance, I lifted up my right foot so she would look at it. And okay, call me an idiot for grabbing the bottle of indelible ink last night, when I was reaching for the washable stuff. What can I say? It was dark, and I was upset, and the labels were really small. But maybe God does have a purpose in everything, because when she looked down at the blue stain on the sole of my foot I could feel some of the tension go out of her body, and that wouldn't have happened if I'd been able to clean all the ink off.

"I take it you're my real kid," she said.

"Yeah." No need to share all my paranoid fantasies at this point; it wasn't that kind of moment. "Looks like it."

The corner of her mouth twitched as she shook her head: almost a smile. "And here I thought I could get rid of you at last."

I shook my head. "Not gonna be that easy, Mom."

We laughed a little, in a strange way that was almost like crying, and then she hugged me and said I should go back to sleep, because I had school in the morning. So I headed back up the stairs as she closed up the office, and as I entered my room I could see the light downstairs go out, leaving the house in darkness.

I was halfway to my bed before I realized someone was sitting on it. I jumped backward, startled, and felt a scream well up in my throat. But the figure was too small to be a burglar, and after a second my brain shifted into the proper gear, and I realized who it was.

"So," Tommy said, "You gonna tell me what's going on? Or do I have to keep spying on you and figure it out for myself?"

4

Manassas
Virginia

I WOUND UP TELLING Tommy everything. Not just because I hungered to talk to someone who wouldn't think my fears were totally crazy—though there was that—but because I'd seen him go into spying mode before, and I didn't want to have to sweep my room for hidden cameras every night before I went to bed.

Try the internet, he suggested. As if every mystery in the universe could be reduced to a single web page, and all you had to do to gain spiritual enlightenment was plug the right search term into Google.

I tried the internet.

First thing I discovered was that a scary number of people out there thought they'd been raised by the wrong families. Whole networks of them, in fact, going on and on about how they didn't look like either of their parents, or didn't have the same interests as their siblings, or were smarter or dumber or taller or shorter or better at foreign languages than the rest of the family. Whatever. Most of their logic wouldn't survive five minutes in a high school genetics class, but some of it was disturbingly reasonable. Yes, there were only a handful of verified cases of "baby switching" in the US, but how many remained undiscovered?

Some of the posters were just plain crazy. One guy claimed that he was really a space alien, and that he had been planted on Earth to serve as a spy for "the grey men." Another insisted that faeries (she spelled the word with an "e") had stolen her mother's real baby and left her in its place. Yet others blamed Middle Eastern slave traders, or the Illuminati, or any one of a dozen global baby-snatching conspiracies. These people clearly had problems that went beyond the question of who their parents were.

Was I crazy, too? I was beginning to wonder.

Meanwhile, thank God for Tommy. I'm not sure why talking to him helped keep me grounded during all this, but it did. Not just because I needed someone to confide in, though that was certainly the case. I think it was because, for him, this mystery was all so . . . well, *normal.* I mean, the kid hung around with elves and trolls and went on dragon-hunting expeditions in his spare time. So what if his sister was a chimera, whose very existence defied the laws of science? It was just another puzzle for him to solve. Another game. Come up with the right answer and you get experience points.

I posted brief comments on some of the discussion boards, hoping to connect to someone else who was in a situation like mine. But if other chimeras existed they weren't talking.

llllllllllll

Mrs. Fletcher's office was at the far end of the art studio, so you had to walk past all the works-in-progress to get to it. This week she was teaching us how to sculpt human faces in clay, which meant that there were now disembodied heads lined up along both sides of the room. I was reminded of how an ancient tyrant might impale his enemies' heads over the castle gate, warning detractors to behave.

Her office was separated from the main room by a wall of glass, and maybe, at one time, you could have seen between the two rooms, but there was so much artwork hung on it now that only narrow peepholes were left. As I approached the open door I could feel my heart flutter in anticipation. Yes, I was flattered that someone wanted to buy my artwork, there was no way around that.

Two people stood up as I entered the room. I saw that some of my art had been spread out across a table; were these the pictures someone wanted to buy? I frowned. Some of them weren't my best work.

"And here is the artist herself!" Mrs. Fletcher announced. You could hear pride echo in her voice. "Jessica, this is Miriam Seyer, the woman I told you about."

The second figure held out her hand as I raised my eyes to look at her—and I froze.

The room froze.

Time and space froze.

"Jessica," Seyer said, holding her hand out casually, as though I hadn't just become incapable of human motion. She was smiling; I couldn't tell if the expression was genuine or not. "I'm so glad to meet you."

She was a small woman, probably early thirties, with pale skin and large, dark eyes that were outlined a bit too heavily in kohl. Her hair was jet black, the kind of color that rarely appears in nature, and it was cut in a shoulder length pageboy, with a thick valance of bangs hanging down to her eyes. The bones of her face were prominent, with high, arching cheekbones that accented the elongated eyes, reminding me of an ancient Egyptian queen.

Or a goth chick.

After a moment I managed to get a hold of myself, and I forced a smile to my face. "Hi." I didn't want to touch her but there was no polite way to avoid it, so I shook her hand. One brief up-and-down, a light squeeze, then I let go. I resisted the impulse to count my fingers afterward to make sure they were all still there.

This was Tommy's stalker. I knew it in my gut. And for the life of me I didn't know how I was supposed to respond to her.

Fortunately Mrs. Fletcher reached in between us, dispelling an awkward moment. She offered me a bottle of flavored water, bright cranberry in color. I took it gratefully, glad to have something to do with my hands.

Who was this woman? Why was she here? What had she been doing at my house?

"Mrs. Fletcher has been showing me your work," Seyer said. Her voice was as smooth as silk, too controlled to be trustworthy. I realized with a start that my most recent drawing was among those on the table. Did she have a clue what that one was really about?

It depicted two sun-shapes, one dark and one light, hanging side by side in a sullen sky. Their rays interlocked like the spokes of a gear, each one breaking down into smaller and smaller rays, layered like the fractal of waves of Hokusai's famous print.

It was the same fate-portrait I'd started tracing in the pizza oil a few days back, only a thousand times more complex.

Her fate-portrait.

The light sun represented the possibility that her visit to our house was benign. Each ray represented a different reason she might have been in the neighborhood. *Looking for someone else's house. Trying to find someone to ask directions from. Was intrigued by our garden and wanted a closer look.* Branching off from each of those were the many different choices that might follow. A hundred different fates, neatly ordered.

And the dark sun represented—well, darker possibilities. Every nefarious purpose I had been able to imagine had its own ray. Some of the ideas were pretty crazy, but I'd wanted the number of rays on each side to be the same. Positive and negative energy in perfect balance: a yin-yang of fate. A thin line of footprints wandered between the solar disks, weaving in and out of the zig-zag channel that the rays created. That represented my own search for meaning in Tommy's report. No beginning, no end, no clear destination: just me wandering among the facts.

I called the drawing *Stalker*.

The woman was looking down at it now, and I felt a strange sickness come over me as her long finger, tipped in blood-red nails, stroked my work gently. It was strangely intimate.

"Mrs. Fletcher was telling me that you base some of your work on dreams," she said, breaking the moment's spell.

I nodded.

"It reminds me of Australian dream art. Very similar in form." She looked up at me. "Are you familiar with that tradition?"

I shook my head.

"Aboriginal mythology speaks of a time called The Dreaming. The source of all creation." She looked back at my drawing; her finger traced the thin line of footprints. "Some speak of a network of mystical paths called songlines, where the creator-beings once walked. Material reality and dreaming reality intricately intertwined, and their art reflects that union."

"My artwork isn't all that complex," I stammered. "I just dream about geometric shapes. If I like the way they look, I paint them."

The look she shot me from under her jet-black lashes made it crystal clear she knew I was lying. "And yet your end product echoes much more complex forms," she said. "Which is why it interests me." She glanced briefly at Mrs. Fletcher, who by now was beaming with all the pride of a mother whose kid was just accepted by Harvard. "Your teacher told you I would like to buy a piece of your work?"

"Yeah." If I hadn't been totally comfortable with the idea before, I *really* wasn't comfortable with it now. "I'm not sure I want to do that."

"I'm willing to offer you a hundred dollars for a drawing. More than that for a painting, if you're willing to part with one of those. There's one on display in the corridor that I find particularly appealing."

A hundred dollars. Jeez, that was real money.

I felt a lump come into my throat.

"I'm sorry . . . I can't. This stuff is too personal."

Her dark eyes fixed on me, and for a moment—just a moment—it was as if I could feel her thoughts piercing into my mind. Vivisecting my soul. Sickness welled up inside me, and for a second I was afraid I was going to vomit.

"I'm so sorry about that," she said softly. The illusion released me. "Will you tell me something of the inspiration behind your art, then? I would love to know more about that."

I shrugged stiffly and looked down at the table again. Anywhere but those eyes. "There's not much to tell."

"Jessica . . . ." Mrs. Fletcher began. She seemed both confused and disturbed by my response.

"Really." I said it more firmly this time. "There's nothing to talk about."

For a moment there was silence. Then, with a silvery laugh of false humor, the visitor turned to my teacher. "Well, that's it, then. I do thank you so much for your assistance." She took out a business card and handed it to Mrs. Fletcher. "Please call me if Ms. Drake changes her mind."

Her path out of the room took her right past me. Almost close enough to touch.

"You have a rare gift," she said softly, as she walked by. "Make the most of it."

I nodded dully.

And then she was gone.

"Is something wrong?" Mrs. Fletcher's voice was filled with concern. "You usually love to talk about your work."

"I ate something bad at lunch," I said. Not looking up at her. "Just not feeling well."

Someone else might have pressed me for more information, but Mrs. Fletcher wasn't that type. She just reached across the table to gather up my art, and asked nothing more.

I watched her for a moment, then said, "Mrs. Fletcher? Could I take my work home with me?" I hesitated. "All of it."

She looked at me curiously. "School lets out in a week. You'll get everything back then. What's the rush?"

"My father is coming this weekend," I said quickly. It was the only excuse I could come up with that fast; I prayed she didn't know what my relationship with my father really was. "I'd like to show him my work." When she did not respond I added, in a pleading voice, "I hardly ever see him."

She hesitated, then sighed. "I suppose it would be all right."

"And the stuff in the exhibit," I said quickly. "I'd like to take that, too."

She raised one carefully plucked eyebrow. I thought for a moment she might ask me why I was so anxious about all this, and I started rehearsing answers in my head. But she was not the sort to seek confrontation, and in the end she just said, "Well, then. I can hardly deny your father the chance to see your talent, can I?" She pushed the pile of drawings toward me. "Come on. I'll help you pack everything up."

We took down all of my sketches that were taped to the glass wall, and the painting that was on display by the door, and then I wrapped my nascent sculpture in a plastic garbage bag—it was still wet—and headed out the door. I knew that I was acting strangely, and Mrs. Fletcher might well contact the guidance counselor after I left and ask her to get involved in my life in some intrusive way, but if that was the price I had to pay to claim all my work, so be it. The stalker-woman had wanted a piece of my art very badly, and for some reason it seemed very important that I not let her have it.

The bike ride home was difficult, what with carrying all that stuff, but I stopped halfway to mash the clay sculpture into an unrecognizable lump, and left it behind in a dumpster. That helped.

Mom loved seeing my artwork. She never questioned the fact that I'd brought it home before the end of the quarter; she was just happy that I was sharing it with her. She made me spread everything out on the kitchen island and tell her about each piece, which seemed to take hours. But I guess that was a good thing, as it gave me a chance to focus my mind on something other than the weird soap opera my life had suddenly become.

I couldn't bring myself to tell her about the goth woman. I mean, what would I say? *A strange woman liked my art and offered to buy some of it. But I didn't trust her because she'd stopped by our house last week, which could just have been because she was trying to figure out how to get in touch with me, but Tommy thought it looked odd, and besides, she was asking about my dreams.* Yeah, it all *felt* wrong, but in the actual measure of events it wasn't. That's what Mom would tell me.

Finally the long night was over, and I gathered up my artwork and headed up to my room. It was good to know that all my paintings were there with me in the house, where no mysterious stranger could get at them. Pieces of one's soul should be properly safeguarded.

I wondered what Tommy would make of Seyer's visit, once I finally told him about it.

⸺⸺⸺

Texting and Facebook and Twitter and email. It was my nightly ritual, as sacred as tooth-brushing. I generally took care of it while curled up in bed, scrolling through site after site with methodical determination, making sure that all waiting texts were answered, all contacts acknowledged, and all posts on my Facebook page read and commented upon.

Finally I got to my email. There was one new letter, from an address I didn't recognize, *thetruthisoutthere99@gmail.com.* Cute, if not original. I opened it. And I guess if I had to identify the one moment when the course of my life changed forever, that was it.

Saw your posts, the letter said. *Look for changelings.* Below that was a URL for some social network I'd never heard of. No signature.

I stared at it for a long while, not quite sure why it made me so uneasy. I wanted answers, right? If this email was going to lead me to them, that was a good thing, wasn't it?

My nerves were probably just on edge from the meeting with Miriam Seyer.

Shutting down my email program, I headed to the networking site to look for changelings. So much for getting a good night's sleep.

5

SOUTHERN TIER EXPRESSWAY
UPSTATE NEW YORK

STANDING BY THE SIDE OF THE ROAD, the deer was all but invisible in the darkness. A sharp outcropping of rock shielded it from the view of cars heading north, while cars heading south were perilously close to a steep drop-off, and were too busy watching the road itself to look for wildlife. This close to the river driving could be treacherous, and one wrong move coming around the sharp turn on the mountainside could send a car hurtling down to the water.

Had anyone stopped to look at the deer they might have wondered at its presence there. Sandwiched between a steady stream of cars and the jagged cliff face, it barely had room to stand. Further north the slope was gentler and led to sheltering woods, the kind of place that deer normally preferred. Here there was only danger.

The deer did not look afraid.

It watched as the cars sped by, glancing briefly to the side as each one passed, as if to keep its reflective eyes from revealing its presence. Some of the vehicles whizzed by so close that the wind from their passage bristled the deer's fur, but it did not shy away.

It waited.

A blue Corolla came into sight; the deer tensed as it approached. For a moment the vehicle disappeared behind the bulk of the mountain, but its headlights continued to scour the valley like a searchlight, and the deer watched the twin beams of light, tracking the car's position. Then it came around the final turn and was visible again.

The deer leapt into the road.

The car swerved to the left to avoid hitting it.

The deer rushed directly at it, forcing the driver to swing wide to avoid collision. But on this stretch of road there was no such thing as "wide." The blue car skidded, crashed into the low metal guard rail head-on, and smashed through. Shattered glass flew through the air like hail as it hurtled down the rocky slope, flipping end over end, the sound of each new impact resounding through the valley like a gunshot.

And then there was a splash.

And all was still.

The deer picked its way carefully across the road and started down toward the car. The mountainside was steep, and a keen observer might have noted that the deer's footing was not as steady as one would expect from a member of its species. But at last it reached the narrow river, and the wreck that was half-submerged in it.

The driver's window had shattered. The deer could see that there was a body inside, that of a young woman strapped into the driver's seat. She wasn't moving. The deflated airbag that hung sadly from the steering wheel was splattered with her blood, a monument to the limits of technology. Her skull had been crushed against the side of the car.

The deer reached its head into the window and pressed its nose against her neck.

No pulse.

As it drew back from the car, then, a strange light entered its eyes. Or perhaps it would be more accurate to say that a strange light *left* its eyes.

Suddenly the deer looked confused. Its nostrils flared as it smelled the blood in the air. The fur around its neck stiffened as it whipped its head about, checking for predators.

There were none.

It looked at the car one last time and then bounded off to the north, seeking the safety of the deep woods.

6

FOUND THEM.

I took a while, but not for the reasons one would expect. Turned out there were a thousand pages with *changeling* in the name; the trick was finding one that didn't refer to a game, novel, movie, or fairy legend. There was no search engine that could help me, so I had to scan every single page by eye, one by one, rejecting any that were focused on popular culture. I didn't know what my page should look like, exactly, but I did know what it *shouldn't* look like.

It was a slow and frustrating process, and I was nearing the point where I was ready to give up for the night and just go to sleep, when I finally came across a page description that looked promising.

> If you aren't your parents' child, but you can't be anything else, then this is your page.
>
> If you don't have a clue what that means, it isn't.

It was a members-only page, so I sent a request to join. Ten minutes later I got a message back, asking about my changeling experience. I gave them the bare bones: DNA didn't match, babies weren't switched, who the hell knew what was going on? Heart pounding, I pushed the *send* button. Five minute later I was in.

And . . . holy crap.

I wandered in awe through forests of data—posts, files, pictures, even a video—from over two hundred people. Apparently my situation wasn't as uncommon as I'd thought. I got the impression from some of the comments that there were a lot more of us out there, who had never joined the online community; apparently some of the "DNA orphans" (as they called themselves) weren't comfortable posting their stories on a public web page. I could certainly understand that. The last thing you wanted, if you were a chimera who defied the laws of science, was to wake up one morning and find your life story featured in a *Weirdest Stuff On The Internet* blog.

Most of the page's activity seemed to center around the mystery of our existence, but there was a smattering of personal items, including a notice that one of the list members had just died. I scanned the major discussion threads but discovered nothing new or insightful. Alien invasion, supernatural influence, government conspiracy, covert medical experiments . . . there weren't all that many entities you could blame for a global conspiracy to switch babies in their cradles. Sadly, I realized I was not going to find answers there. But the sense of community was refreshing, and it was good to talk to people who understood what I was going through. So I stayed. I chatted. Long into the night and past sunrise, I typed.

Mom had to call me three times to get me to come down to breakfast. When she saw the shadows of sleeplessness under my eyes she asked if I had caught Tommy's internet bug, and would she now have to pry me loose from the computer with a crowbar, too? She was smiling, but in her eyes I could see concern. I assured her I was fine.

When she turned away to get some more orange juice, Tommy looked at me, a question in his eyes. I nodded. He grinned and gave me a thumbs-up.

School was maddening that day. Even art class was intolerable. I wanted to be home, on my computer, exploring the great mystery of my life—not stuck in a classroom listening to a teacher drone on about how we should attempt to make the summer "academically enriching." As soon as the final bell rang I rushed home to see if there were any new messages waiting. There were. Nearly a hundred of them. Mostly from people who wanted to tell me their life stories, or wanted to hear about mine. Or commenting on my comments about their comments. Or inviting me to join another discussion group.

One stood out from the crowd.

You're in Manassas? Rita and I are right next door. We should all get together and chat live. Devon.

I paused for a moment, trying to remember if I'd told anyone where I lived. Usually I was more circumspect than that online—you never knew who you were talking to. But I'd been very tired last night, and maybe I slipped up. Not to mention I probably had a few online profiles with the name of my school on them. Everything was interconnected these days, and sometimes profiles followed you around like stray puppy dogs. So the information was out there for the finding.

Still. Call me paranoid.

I stared at the keyboard for a few minutes, then typed,

How do I know you're not some crazy psychopathic killer? Jesse.

The answer came immediately.

This isn't Craigslist. :-P

I grinned, then typed,

Seriously.

I expected another smart-ass comment in return. Or maybe he would try to reassure me. I figured I could learn a lot about him from how he went about that.

What I got was a name and number. Dr. Jason Tilford. The number was an extension in Fairfax Hospital.

Ask my dad.

I blinked. References. This guy had just given me references.
That was . . . strangely classy.
How could you not want to meet someone like that?

иппппппп

The IHOP was nearly empty when I arrived, the worst of the dinner traffic having died down long ago. I looked the place over to see if my contacts were there yet, but it didn't appear so.

Mom had actually called Devon's dad. Turned out he was a doctor of estimable rank and reputation, and no, of course he didn't mind that she'd called, because you couldn't be too careful about people on the internet, right? He assured her that his son was a good kid, then she assured him that I was a good kid, and everyone agreed that two good kids meeting for the first time should do so in a public place.

I chose a table at the back of the IHOP and sat facing the door. A waitress came by several times to ask if I was ready to order yet, and "I'm waiting for someone" didn't seem to be an acceptable answer, so eventually I ordered a lemonade. Truth be told, I was too nervous to eat or drink anything, but it made me feel less guilty about taking up space there.

I put my book on the table. I waited.

Two couples wandered in, then a family with kids. They all found seats and ordered food.

I waited.

Maybe they're not really coming, I told myself nervously. *Maybe they chickened out.* Or maybe they would show up, and I was about to share my worst insecurities with strangers.

I spilled some sugar on the table and started sketching patterns of fate in it. My version of a nervous twitch.

Then a mismatched pair of teens walked in, and I knew as soon as I saw them that it was my contacts. You could have guessed just from the way they carried themselves—clearly they'd come here for something more significant than pancakes—but the flower the guy was carrying made it a no-brainer. I'd suggested we both carry books with flowers tucked into them so that we could identify each other on sight; it was a trick I'd seen in a play once. My own copy of *The Hunger Games* was sitting on the table in pain view, with a dandelion sticking out the top. This guy was carrying something book-sized that had a flower tucked into its cover, but it wasn't a real book. It took me a minute to identify it, but when I did I smiled. A Kindle. Cute.

When they looked my way I pointed to my own book on the table and gestured for them to come join me.

I'm not sure why it surprised me that Devon turned out to be black. He was a good-looking guy, with dark skin and long, lean features. He was also tall—very tall—and his height was all in his legs, which gave him the look of a marathon runner. Although he was dressed in a simple T-shirt and jeans, something about the cut of them suggested money, and I noted that his Nikes were brand new. Mom always said that you could tell a lot about a person from two things: the condition of his shoes and how he tips in a restaurant.

Rita was a small, wiry girl, with dark hair, piercing eyes, and an aura of barely suppressed energy about her. Though she seemed to be roughly my age, there was something about her that hinted at more life experience than teenagers usually had, the majority of it probably not pleasant. There was a wariness about her, almost feral in essence, like a cat trapped in an unfamiliar environment. I saw her glance at both exits as she entered, as if taking note of where they were. I guessed that she'd had to bolt for an exit more than once in her life.

Devon smiled as they approached me. The expression seemed genuine enough. "Jessica?"

I nodded, and shook the hand that he offered me. "Jesse is fine."

"I'm Devon. This is Rita."

Rita said "Hi," but didn't offer any physical contact. She glanced around the room one last time as she slid into the booth, tucking herself into the corner of the seat with her back to the wall. Devon followed. A waitress came over with menus as they settled in, but Devon said that they wouldn't need any, as they already knew what they wanted. He ordered a milk shake for himself and nachos for the table. Rita just wanted a soda.

Then we were alone together. There was a moment of awkward silence in which we all sized each other up, wondering how you were supposed to start a conversation in a situation like this. Finally Devon broke the ice. "So, my father's a doctor, you know that already. He found out about a genetic condition that ran in my mother's family and wanted to screen me for it. Turned out I didn't have that condition . . . or anything else that runs in the family. So then he checked my birth records, looking for a breach of protocol, but everything was clean. There's no explanation for why I'm not who I'm supposed to be. Right now we're all pretending nothing's wrong, while he tries to think of some new angle to test." He shook his head and added in a sober tone, "Creepy thing is I look just like him. Dead ringer."

He looked at Rita. She had one foot on the seat and her knee was drawn up to her chest. "Paternity case," she said quietly. "I was just a little kid when the test was done, and they never told me any more than I had to know, so I don't have any details. I do know I was a home birth, so there was never any question about who my mother was. Until that test." She shrugged stiffly. "I don't think anyone cared enough to follow up on it."

Devon said gently, "Rita wound up in foster care."

"No great loss." Rita snorted. "My birth family was nothing to write home about."

It was my turn. I drew in a deep breath and said, "My dad left us years ago. He's a bit crazy, and when he started raging about how I wasn't really his daughter, Mom offered a paternity test to shut him up." I was aware of an echo of pain in my voice. "So . . . the test said I wasn't his kid, or Mom's. But the hospital has told me that I can't be anyone else's kid, so right now I'm in limbo. They're redoing the DNA test just in case there was some kind of mistake, and we should get the results on Monday. But I expect they'll be the same as the first time."

"Sheesh," Devon said, shaking his head. "How's your mother taking it?"

I sighed. "As well as can be expected. She's not going to disown me or anything." I thought I saw Rita flinch. "Beyond that . . . I don't know."

So there we were. Three genetic anomalies. Teenagers who should not exist. It made for a surreal sense of connection, like I hadn't just met these guys ten minutes ago. Somehow, in a way I didn't totally understand, I felt as if we'd been connected for years.

"How many of us do you think there are?" I asked. "I mean all together, not just the ones who joined that page?"

Devon shook his head. "No way to know. My father works with an Indian doctor, who says that babies get switched pretty often in his country. State hospitals there are large, overcrowded, and under-staffed. Mistakes happen. But when one of those mistakes is discovered, doctors assume the real parents are out there somewhere, waiting to be tracked down. No one is looking for . . ." He floundered for the proper word.

"Chimeras?" I offered.

"Changelings," Rita counteroffered.

The waitress brought over our food. We were silent until she left.

"I've seen some other groups on the internet," Rita said. She pulled a nacho from the cheese-covered heap in the middle of the table with practiced dexterity. "Mostly young people. I'm not sure if adults don't get tested as often, or if their lives are just so settled that when they find out about something like this they figure it's best to just pretend it never happened."

"They may not spend as much time online as we do," I offered.

But I knew that was a lame explanation. Tommy knew adults who spent more time playing World of Warcraft than he did.

"I've talked to folks from all over the world," Devon said. "US, Canada, Europe, Australia, Russia . . . it's amazing how similar all the stories are. Whatever is going on appears to be global."

"Tell her about the Chinese guy," Rita said.

"Taiwanese," he corrected her, then he said to me, "Chen's father was a geneticist. Supposedly he assigned a whole government lab to his kid's case. Found all sorts of anomalies, Chen said. Stuff that *should* have been in any human DNA, but wasn't in his. He wasn't allowed to give us details, but he did tell us that, thus far, they'd found no good explanation for it."

"I'm kind of surprised that didn't make the news," I said. "The tabloids would have loved it."

"You may not see anything about it in the popular press, but my dad has the right connections, and he told me there's a network of scientists who are pooling their resources to determine just how widespread the problem is. They want to get some solid data before they reveal anything to the public."

"Can you imagine the panic there'll be when that happens?" Rita whistled softly. "The alien abduction crowd will have a field day."

I stirred the ice in my lemonade without responding. I'm sure we were all thinking the same thing, but no one wanted to say it out loud. What if the nutjobs were right? What if we really weren't human?

That was just too crazy to think about. There had to be a simpler—and more reasonable—explanation. "So what happened to the Taiwanese guy?" I asked.

"Out of touch now." A shadow passed fleetingly across Devon's face. "Chen warned us that might happen. He said that if his dad's people started asking too many questions, he would cut off contact with us so that we wouldn't get dragged into things. A little while after he said that, he cancelled his Gmail account; no one's heard from him since."

His voice trailed off into silence. The kind of silence where you know that important things are not being said.

"Tell her," Rita said softly.

"Tell me what?" I asked.

For a moment Devon said nothing. Then he reached into his pocket and pulled out an iPhone. I could see the logo flash as he brought up the Changelings page, then he scrolled down to one of the more recent posts and handed the phone to me. "Here," he said. His expression was solemn. "Read for yourself."

To all Sarah's friends: I'm sorry to have to tell you that my daughter died in a car accident yesterday. They think she lost control of the car while trying to avoid something in the road. I'm told she died on impact. If any of you were close enough to her that you'd like to attend the funeral, message me through this account and I'll send you directions. We are located in upstate New York. —Sarah's mom.

"I saw that earlier," I said, handing him back the phone.

He shook his head. "No, you didn't."

"Yes," I insisted. "When I first joined the page. I remember thinking, 'Wow, that's one hell of a welcome message.'"

"Check the timestamp," he said quietly.

I took the phone from him again and did so.

The message he'd just shown me had been posted while I was driving to the restaurant.

Perplexed, I scrolled down the page, looking for another post I remembered reading. I didn't have to go far.

This is Di's father. I regret to inform you that we lost our daughter today. She was struck by a hit-and-run driver and died before she could make it to the hospital. She once asked me to let her friends know if anything bad ever happened to her, so I'm doing that. She said to send her love, and to tell you all to stay safe.

Slowly I put the phone down. For a moment I just stared at it, not saying anything. For as long as I didn't ask questions I could pretend this didn't mean what it seemed to.

"There've been other deaths in the group," Rita said quietly.

I finally found my voice. "How many?"

"Eight so far." Devon said. "There are probably more we don't know about. Not everyone's family thinks to post notices to their friends."

He took the phone back and put it in his pocket. Then he waited. They both waited. Respectfully silent, mercifully silent, while I struggled to digest the terrible implications of what they had just told me.

"Do the police know?" I finally asked.

Rita shrugged stiffly. "What are the cops going to do? Every death has a different cause, and they're spread out all across the world. No one's going to believe they're connected."

"These two were both car accidents," I pointed out.

"And Yuri dove into a concrete pool the wrong way and broke his neck on the incline," Devon said. "Tam was bitten by a snake while hiking with her family, and the hospital they carried her to was out of antivenom. Andrew Billings—he was one of our older members—he went in for routine surgery and died three days later from a staph infection. And you remember the big storm they had on the west coast a couple of weeks ago? Mario went surfing in it. It was a stupid thing to do, and everyone was begging him not to, but he said the waves were 'too rad to resist,' so he did it anyway. Never came home. And then there's Samara. You remember the *E. coli* thing last week, out in Idaho? She was the first victim." He looked at Rita. "That's seven. Who am I forgetting?"

"Mike."

"Oh, yeah." Devon shook his head grimly. "Guy had a run-in with a swarm of bees. He was deathly allergic. Of course he always carried epi on him, but the doctors said there was so much venom in his system he never had a chance."

"Africanized bees?" I asked.

"It happened in Canada, so I doubt it."

Normal bees rarely stung human beings. Generally people only got swarmed like that when they disturbed a hive. And people who were allergic to bees were fastidiously careful about never doing that.

The more I learned about this situation, the more bizarre it got.

"There've been other deaths," Rita said. "Outside our circle."

"All of them DNA orphans?"

She nodded.

"Someone's killing us off one by one," Devon said grimly. "And they do it in a different way every time, so that no one will make the connection. That's why we wanted to talk to you live, instead of by email. To warn you about it."

My head was spinning. Bees. Snakes. Germs. Drunk drivers. Teen recklessness. What kind of organization had the power to orchestrate deaths like that? And *why* would they do it? Were we really the product of some secret scientific experiment, like one of the discussion threads had suggested, and now the people responsible for our existence were trying to erase all evidence of their work? It seemed pretty far-fetched to me, but compared to the alien abduction idea it sounded downright reasonable.

And of course there was one thing these two didn't know about. A thing that sent chills down my spine, now that I suspected its true significance.

I told them about Miriam Seyer. How my brother had caught her casing our house. How she had come to my school to buy my art, then started questioning me about my dreams. It seemed an unlikely coincidence that someone just happened to start stalking me the same time all this was going on, but try as we might we couldn't fit the pieces together. Had the other kids been approached before they died?

I sketched Seyer's face on a napkin for them. It was hard to do; my hands were trembling now. It wasn't every day you were told you might be on someone's hit list. When I handed it over to them they stared at it for a long time, and I knew they were committing every detail to memory.

"So," I said, trying to sound calmer than I felt. "What happens now?"

Devon hesitated. "We trade phone numbers and addresses, so that we can talk to each other offline. No more meaningful discussions online. It probably would be safest if we all quit the group. Though, then we wouldn't be able to keep an eye on things." He paused. "I should come meet your mother in person, so that if someday you need to get away from your house for a while I can offer you a safe place to stay without everyone getting all paranoid about it."

Jeez. I hadn't even considered the possibility that I might have to flee my home. "What makes your place any safer than mine?" I demanded. "The fact that you haven't caught anyone casing your place doesn't mean you're not being watched."

"My folks own a cabin out by Front Royal. It's a last resort, but I can get the keys to it if I need to."

Would it really come to that? Running away from home so that our families would be safe, hiding in the woods so that a mysterious cabal of murderers wouldn't be able to find us?

"What about your dad?" I asked, my voice shaking slightly. "You said he knows the truth about us. Did you tell him about the killings?"

Devon hesitated. "Yeah, I told him. He said I was reading too much meaning into purely random accidents. And that if there was any trouble heading our way he would hear about it in advance, and he had enough friends in high places to make it go away." A shadow crossed his face "That said, he did arrange to have our security system upgraded. Not very reassuring."

Rita stared at me. "Are you going to tell your mom?"

For a moment I was silent. There were so many discordant emotions colliding in my head at that moment that I felt strangely numb. Love, fear, hope, desperation, despair . . . not the kind of mess you could sort out over lemonade at IHOP.

"I don't know," I said softly. "Are you going to tell yours?"

She snorted. "Yeah. Right. Like fostermom would give a damn if I disappeared."

Devon pushed a napkin toward me; it had a number and address on it. I wrote down my own and gave a copy to each of them. The act was strangely liberating. We would be proactive, take control of our fates, rather than just wait for unnamed enemies to strike.

As I headed up front to pay for my drink I saw that Devon was leaving a really big tip on the table.

ıııııııııııı

Mom didn't get home until late that night; evidently the Koontz monster had put her in charge of closing. By the time she finally arrived I'd been pacing around nervously for so long that I'd worn a rut in the carpet, and Tommy—who fluttered about me like a crazy moth all that time—had offered every bribe at his disposal to get me to tell him what was going on. But this story would be hard enough to tell one time; I didn't want to have to do it twice.

Shortly after eleven o'clock Mom arrived. She looked exhausted—mentally and physically—but as soon as she saw me she knew that something was wrong, and that became her top priority. She sat me down in the living room and asked me what had happened.

So I told them both everything. Because when you get to the point where you're talking to strangers about running away from home in order to stay alive, it's time to come clean. Mom took it all pretty calmly, but it was clear that she had her doubts about the global teen-murdering conspiracy. So I took them to the computer to show them the death notices online. To my horror, I saw that two more had appeared since our meeting in IHOP. One was for a kid in Montana who had run into an angry bear while taking out the garbage. The other was for an older guy in Perth, Australia. Car accident. Those must be the easiest to arrange.

When she was done reading I sat there in silence, waiting for the axe of judgment to fall. A knot in my chest was making it hard to breathe.

"Tomorrow," my mother said quietly, "first thing in the morning, we're going to the police."

I felt a wave of relief so powerful it made me dizzy. "They're not going to believe us," I whispered. "They'll think we're crazy."

"Hush." She pushed back a stray lock of hair from my face. "I'm not going to tell them about the bears and the bees and how a global conspiracy of scientists is targeting my daughter and her friends because of their genetic code. To be honest, I'm not yet sure how I feel about all that myself. But I *am* going to tell them that a strange woman is stalking my children, and that I'm afraid for your safety. They'll listen to that. I'll *make* them listen."

I fought the urge to cry. "Thanks, Mom."

She looked at Tommy. "They'll want to question you about what you saw. You good with that?"

He nodded. There was a spark of pride in his eyes now, crowding out the fear. The crazy little kid with the video games was needed to protect his family.

"C'mon," she said, taking my hand in hers, patting Tommy on the back to set him in motion. "Let's make this place safe for the night."

We made the rounds of the house together, window by window, door by door, making sure that every possible entrance was securely shut, and that everything that could be locked was locked. It wasn't so much an act of protection as a ritual of purification, banishing malign influences from our home.

And it seemed to work, for when I climbed into bed, my heart wasn't pounding any more, and the knot in my chest was gone. The last thought I had before I fell asleep was gentle and reassuring. *It's going to be all right*, I told myself. *Everything's going to be all right.*

7

MANASSAS
VIRGINIA

*T*HE BLACK GLASS PLAIN *beneath my feet is hot. So hot! I have to walk quickly if I don't want my feet to burn. The doors are back, but now they're made of metal, and they're round, like bank vault doors. A dry heat radiates from them, sullen and stifling.*

The heat is significant. That awareness comes to me viscerally, born of animal instinct rather than intellect. In the same primitive manner, I know there are clues behind those doors that could tell me why it matters so much, but when I reach out to touch one of the handles—gingerly, like you might test an iron to see if it's heating up properly—the metal is so hot that I pull back with a yelp of pain. Not my brightest idea.

A disembodied voice in the darkness cries, "Jesse!"

I begin to run. Not because I have anywhere to go, or because there is anything specific to run away from, but because the heat of the ground is less painful if I'm moving. The air sears my lungs with every breath. Where is all this heat coming from? Why are the doors impassable? The answers matter, they matter so much, it's a question of life or death that I must figure out before it's too late—

"Jesse!"

Golden flames flicker around the edges of the doors; the circular

handles are glowing bright red now, and smoke is filling the air. I
cough, barely able to breathe.

"Wake up, damn it! Jesse! Wake up!"

||||||||||||

Suddenly the dream was gone. For a moment I was totally disoriented. The room I was in looked like my bedroom, but the smell of it
was wrong, all wrong, and light flickered weirdly at the window. Rita
was there, leaning over the bed and shaking me fiercely by the shoulders. What was going on?

As soon as Rita saw that I was awake she gripped me by the arm
and tried to drag me out of bed. There was fear in her eyes. "We need
to get out of here, Jesse!"

Suddenly the room came into clear focus, and with it an understanding of just what was happening. Outside my window, fierce yellow light was flickering. All around me the house was sputtering,
snapping and popping like wood in a fireplace. I could see tendrils of
smoke seeping in over the top of the door, and I could smell the stink
of melted carpet and broiled plastic. The air was warm. Too warm.
Way too warm.

The house was on fire.

I struggled to get out of bed as quickly as I could. As soon as my
bare feet hit the floor I could feel how hot the wood was, which sent a
wave of panic surging through my veins. I looked toward the window,
hoping to escape that way, but flames from the first floor were already
licking at the bottom of the wooden frame. No way out there. Rita
called for me to join her at the door, where she stood with her hand
poised over the knob, tendrils of smoke coiling over her head like
snakes from Hell.

Mom's bedroom was downstairs, I realized suddenly. Right in the
middle of that inferno.

"JESSE!" Rita screamed.

I stumbled to the door, and heard her mutter a prayer under her
breath as she pulled the door open. A thick layer of black smoke

gushed into my bedroom. We ducked down as low as we could and darted out beneath it. There was a window at one end of the hallway and through it, the flickering orange glow picked out highlights along the roiling black smoke-clouds overhead, lending them an almost animate aspect. The whole lower floor was being consumed.

It was hot. So hot. Impossible to breathe in such heat. Impossible to think clearly.

"This way!" Rita cried. She grabbed my hand, and we sprinted toward the center of the house together, covering our mouths with our shirts, keeping our heads as low as we could. A ribbon of fire suddenly shot out of the dark cloud overhead, terrifying in its abruptness. We kept on running. The smoke stung my eyes, and I could feel tears streaming down my cheeks as I struggled to keep them open. I knew that, in fact, it was only a few yards to the central staircase, but in those terrifying moments it felt like a thousand miles. All we could see ahead of us were black clouds, streamers of fire, and the ominous orange glow that seemed to be coming from somewhere beneath it all. The closer we got, the worse it looked.

The staircase was located in the center of the house. We headed toward it in the desperate hope that it was still passable. But when we came to the place where the hallway opened out onto a landing, we could see it was already too late. The fire itself was downstairs, and long tongues of flame licked out through the living room's wide archway, spewing flames and soot and sparks up into the stairwell. The smoke was so thick that the stairs themselves were all but invisible; here and there you could see sparks of yellow flame where the banister had caught fire, but otherwise, the way out had effectively ceased to exist.

Sweat pouring down my face, I crouched down low to the floor, gasping for clean air and trying to think clearly. It was a nearly impossible task. I suddenly understood why animals trapped in a fire might bolt in the wrong direction or even freeze in place, unable to move at all. It took all my mental fortitude to overcome the raw animal panic that was flooding my brain, to do something other than turn around and run screaming back the way I had come. But I knew if I did not focus—if I did not *think*—we were both going to die.

The fire was coming from our side of the house, and it felt like the floor beneath us might collapse into it at any moment. But the other side of the house didn't appear to be burning yet, so that side of the landing should still be stable. Tommy's room was on that side of the house, with a roofed patio right beneath his window. Assuming we could get there before the fire did, we might all make it out alive. Including Tommy.

I put my hand on Rita's arm, nodding toward the column of churning black smoke in front of us. Her eyes grew wide and she mouthed something like *you're friggin crazy*—but then she looked at it again and nodded. She might not know or care about Tommy, but it was clear we weren't getting out the front door.

And so we leaned down low and filled our lungs with as much clean air as we could, and then we ran. Or crawled. Or some desperate stumbling motion midway between the two, that involved trying to keep our heads as low as possible while getting across the landing before our flesh was cooked. The heat was like nothing I'd ever felt before—like someone had thrown us into a blast furnace and slammed the door shut behind us—and I tried not to breathe at all, afraid that my lungs would burn if I did. I closed my eyes to protect them from the smoke, which made the journey twice as terrifying. But at least it would protect my vision for later.

It seemed like an eternity that we were stumbling through hell-fire, but in reality it must have been no more than a few seconds. As soon as I felt the temperature drop I fell gasping to the carpet, and Rita collapsed beside me. Coughing, we struggled immediately back to our feet and began to move down the hallway again, desperate to put as much space between us and the burning staircase as we possibly could. I coughed up black spittle as we ran.

Tommy's room was at the far end of the hall. His door was closed—thank God!—which meant that the air in his room should still be breathable. We opened the door, rushed inside, and then slammed it shut behind us. There was a thin grey haze hanging about the ceiling, but otherwise no overt sign that anything was wrong. The air in his room was blissfully cool.

I looked around for my brother.

He wasn't there.

My first thought was one of utter relief. He must have woken up in time. He must have gotten out. I could see that one of the windows in his room had been shattered; if he'd climbed out through it he could have dropped down onto the patio roof. There was a tree in the backyard whose branches reached to the edge of that roof; maybe it was strong enough to bear a young boy's weight, allowing him to descend safely.

But something about the room was all wrong for that. Maybe in a calmer moment I could have figured out what, but right then all I could do was stare at the broken glass with my mouth gaping as Rita headed toward the window. She grabbed my arm and tried to get me to come with her, but I yanked myself loose from her grasp. "Check the closet!" I yelled, while I ran over to the bed. We had to make sure Tommy wasn't cowering in some dark corner, too overwhelmed by fear to respond to us. Grabbing hold of the blankets, I jerked them off the bed and threw them to one side. An assortment of socks, cookie wrappers, and several small electronic devices went flying along with them. The usual. No brother there. I knelt down and looked under the bed. No brother there either.

I was no longer sure if that was a good thing or a bad thing.

I looked up and saw Rita standing by the closet door, shaking her head. No Tommy. The smoke seeping in over the door had gone from grey to black, and I could taste soot on my tongue. There was panic in her eyes. I nodded toward the window, then caught sight of Tommy's desk. His laptop was open and it was on; he'd probably been online when the fire started. I grabbed it as I passed, yanking the power cord loose from the wall. Whatever was wrong here, his computer might offer a clue.

And then we were at the window, and Rita shoved it open and

climbed through. I could hear her land with a resounding bang on the patio roof six feet down. I tried to follow, but it was hard to maneuver through the narrow window with a laptop in my arms, especially with glass shards sticking out of the frame. I wound up losing my grip and falling straight down to the patio roof, one arm clutching the laptop to my chest. It wasn't a long drop, but under the circumstances, it was terrifying. All the air was knocked out of my lungs as I landed beside Rita, and I could feel the lightweight roofing shudder beneath our weight. Overhead, smoke was now pouring out of Tommy's window, and the hellish light of a hungry fire blazed right behind it. We had made it out just in time.

We slid down the patio roof as quickly as we could, desperate to get to safety before it collapsed beneath us. The tree branch was thinner than I remembered it, not strong enough to bear the weight of one frightened teenager, much less two. Rita and I grabbed for it anyway, hoping it would at least slow our fall. No such luck. The only thing I got hold of was a handful of leaves, and they came loose with a tearing sound as I tumbled over the edge of the roof and hurtled toward the ground. I tried to brace myself as the earth rushed up at me, but it was all happening too quickly. I hit the ground hard, and for a moment just lay there, breathless and stunned, pain resonating in every inch of my body. Then a piece of burning shingle landed right by my head and I struggled to my feet again, hoping I hadn't broken anything important. The world around me suddenly looked strangely colorless, and the ground seemed to sway beneath my feet as Rita and I ran across the open yard, to a thick stand of trees that backed on the park. I still had the laptop clutched in my arms, but had no way to know if it had been damaged.

Not until we reached the tree line, and I could grab hold of a trunk to steady myself, did we stop to catch our breath.

The entire house was engulfed in flames, its terrible light transforming midnight into day. Anyone who hadn't gotten out by now wouldn't stand a chance, and the full horror of that was just starting to sink in. My brother was missing, but at least he might still be alive somewhere. My mother . . . her bedroom was downstairs, in the very part of the house where the fire had started. There was no way she could have gotten out in time.

Tears started to run down my face, stinging my cheeks. Rita tried hug me, but I was numb, and it was probably like hugging a statue. I began to shake violently, and despite the heat from the nearby fire I felt strangely chilled, as if we were standing outside in the dead of winter rather than on a warm June night. "Mom," I whispered hoarsely. "Please don't leave me. Please don't die. I need you . . . !"

Sirens were approaching now; their piercing wail made my head feel like it was splitting open. The whole world was full of spotlights and crackling flames and doors slamming open and fire trucks wailing, all of it pounded in my head in fearsome chaos, too bright and terrible for any sane mind to absorb. I could see people leaving their houses and gathering in the street, some of them with pets or possessions clutched in their arms. Terrified that the fire would spread to their houses as well. I saw the faces of my neighbors, and they looked like the faces of demons, with the burning house reflected in their eyes. And then I saw *her.*

I froze in place, and something about my expression must have frightened Rita. "What?" she demanded hoarsely. "What is it?"

I pointed.

The goth woman stood across from our driveway, her demon-eyes taking in the whole scene. Her long black hair shimmered with sparks of reflected fire as she turned her head from side to side, not staring at the house like everyone else, but studying the neighborhood around it. As if she was looking for something in the shadows. Or for *someone.*

For a moment my heart forgot how to beat.

"Is that her?" Rita asked.

I nodded.

A strong hand gripped my shoulder. "We need to get out of here," she said. "Fast." I wanted to argue with her, to tell her that we couldn't leave yet, but no words would come. I wanted to explain to her that my mother needed me, that this fire had been my fault, and I needed to go to her and apologize and make it all better. Mom was waiting for me, didn't Rita realize that? But the words wouldn't come out of my mouth. Because they were wrong, all wrong. Suddenly I started crying about words I didn't understand, and a terrible loss I couldn't put a name to. While the whole earth swayed beneath my feet, and the world I had lived in for sixteen years came crashing down around my head in a rain of hot embers.

"Come on," Rita urged gently. With a steady hand she encouraged me to move further into the woods with her. There were shadows there, I knew, deep enough and dark enough for two girls to hide in, even with the fire nearby. "I saw a place where you can wait by the road without being seen. I'll go get the car and bring it around. No one will know you're there." And she added, as an afterthought, "You'll be okay."

I wondered if she really believed that.

As we left, I looked back one last time. There were flashing lights coming up the road, and the sirens were so loud they made my ears hurt. The bonfire that had once been my house was as bright as the sun. Numbed by grief and confusion, I let Rita lead me into the shadowy depths of the park.

8

BLUE RIDGE MOUNTAINS
VIRGINIA

IN MY DREAMS I saw my house consumed in flames again, and its heat was a personal accusation. I embraced the guilt and walked into the fire until my clothing and my hair began to burn. I deserved to burn. I deserved far worse than burning. Our house was gone because of me. My mother had died because of me. My little brother was missing—perhaps also dead—because of me.

Then a door opened somewhere, and I could hear a wooden floorboard creak as someone approached me. I cracked open my eyes with effort, blinking away the crust of dried tears.

It was Devon. He crouched down by the side of my bed and waited until my eyes focused on him before speaking.

"She got out," he said. He touched me gently on the cheek; the tenderness of it made me want to cry. "Your mom. She got out in time. It was on the news. She's in the hospital now, in stable condition."

I trembled, and I wept, and he waited silently by my bedside, allowing the tears to flow. I wanted to ask him where I was now, what had happened after the fire, but I couldn't gather my thoughts enough to form words. One thing mattered more than everything else, though, and finally I managed, "Tommy. Is he . . . ?"

He hesitated. "No one's seen him since the fire, Jesse. I'm so sorry." He eased himself to his feet once more. "We can talk more about it when you get up."

"His computer," I pressed. "Did it have any clues on it? So we can find him?"

He shook his head. "We'll talk about it when you get up."

I wanted to ask more questions, but I didn't have the strength for it. My body ached from a thousand small wounds; my soul had been bled dry of all vitality. But at least the serpent of guilt that had been crushing my heart was finally easing its death-grip. My mother had survived the fire, and as soon as I got on my feet again I would find my brother. Wherever he was, whatever had happened to him, I would find him, and I would bring him safely home.

Somewhere in the middle of that thought, sleep claimed me again.

⁕⁕⁕⁕⁕⁕⁕⁕⁕⁕

When I next awoke, I was alone. I wiped a crusted layer of dried tears from my eyes and looked around the room. It was a small but well-appointed space, with neat modern furniture and a few pieces of tasteful but impersonal art on the walls. Totally unfamiliar. The thin bars of sunlight streaming in between the blinds were low-angled, which could have meant it was late afternoon or early morning. I had no sense of time.

As I got out of the narrow bed—which took an amazing amount of effort—I struggled to get my physical and emotional bearings. The events of the night before were now a blur of fear and exhaustion, and judging from the way the room wavered around the edges, I must have hit my head pretty hard. One thing I remembered clearly: Devon telling me that my mother had survived the fire. The rest was a chaos of fragmentary memories: sharp rocks, broken glass, a barefoot flight through the woods, tears shed in the back seat of a car while we sped through the mountains, heading . . . where? My skin throbbed from a thousand small cuts, my body ached from a thousand bruises. Never run through a forest barefoot. And never climb through a broken window with nothing but a tank top and sleep shorts to protect you.

Lessons to be remembered for the next time someone tried to burn me to death.

A pile of clothing lay neatly folded on a chair by the door. I figured it had been left for me, but I didn't feel coordinated enough to manage the task of dressing. Or perhaps it just didn't seem as important as other things. I needed to know what had happened since the fire more than I needed clean clothing.

I approached the door and waited until the room stopped swaying and my legs felt reasonably steady, then I opened it.

Outside was a long, L-shaped room, with a half-circle of couches and chairs surrounding a fireplace at the near end and a combination kitchen and dining area at the other. The furniture was crisp and neat, straight off the showroom floor, with glass-topped tables like you see in home decorating magazines. Except for one end table with half-eaten fast food items on it, the whole place was spotlessly clean, which made me acutely aware of my current sooty state. One wall of the room was made of glass, and it looked out over a steep green hillside. No other houses were in sight.

Where the hell was I?

Devon and Rita were sitting next to the messy table; they jumped up as soon as I entered. Both looked like they hadn't slept in days. "Jesse!"

"Where are we?" I whispered hoarsely. "What time is it?"

"Sunday afternoon," Devon said. "You're in my family's cabin. Rita brought you here last night. We figured it was the safest place to hide out while we figured out what to do next."

A place to hide out. Because there were people trying to kill us, I thought. That's what the fire had been about. Someone tried to burn me to death. I swallowed back hard on a rising tide of fear. *Stay focused, girl.*

"We got you food," Rita said, indicating the messy end table.

Hunger growled in my stomach, but I didn't feel up to eating just yet, so I waved the offer aside. "What happened after we left?" I asked. My voice was so dry I could barely force words out.

My house was completely gone, they told me. It had burned so quickly that by the time the fire department managed to put the flames out there was pretty much nothing left. Mom had gotten out through a window in time to save herself, but barely. She was in Manassas Hospital, her condition serious but stable. Devon had tried to get more information on her, but the hospital said they would only give that out to family members, and he thought that pretending to be related to me was a bad idea. I totally understood. Whoever had tried to kill me and my family might target anyone claiming to be my relative.

Assuming Devon and Rita weren't in their crosshairs already.

I fought back a sick wave of fear that accompanied that thought and asked hoarsely, "What about Tommy?"

"MIA," Devon said. "Local news says they're searching the woods for both of you."

So much for hoping that Tommy would magically show up after the fire died down. Not that I'd really expected him to. The minute I'd seen the broken glass in his room I'd known that something was seriously wrong, though I still couldn't put my finger on what gave it away. But I knew deep in my gut that this was about something far more complicated than *little kid escapes a house fire.*

"What about his computer?" I asked. I'd grabbed it that night without really thinking, but now that my brain cells were starting to function again I realized just how important it might turn out to be. If Tommy had been online when the fire started—playing a game, chatting with his friends, whatever—he might have said something to someone that would give us a clue to his whereabouts. That was, assuming we could track down whoever he'd been talking to, and drag them back to reality long enough to get intelligible answers from them. . . .

"Locked up tight." Devon's response scattered my thoughts. "We were hoping you knew his password."

"Shouldn't need one. It was on when I grabbed it."

"Except that somewhere between Manassas and Front Royal it ran out of power. And when we finally plugged it in again, it rebooted. Hence . . ." He spread his hands in the universal gesture of helplessness.

Did I know Tommy's password? Good question. He had told it to me once, while he was off visiting relatives, so that I could post something for him, but it was a good bet he changed it as soon as he got home. What thirteen-year-old wouldn't? But that did give me an idea about what kind of password he preferred, so I might have a shot at guessing the new one. "Where is it? I'll see what I can do."

Evidently the laptop was charging in the kitchen. While Devon went to fetch it I picked up a lukewarm hamburger and tried to eat it. It had been sitting around way too long to be appetizing, but at least it filled the void in my stomach. Rita handed me a can of soda, and I downed half of it without pausing to see what it was. My body soaked up the moisture with painful desperation, though I tasted nothing.

"Maybe he just got spooked," Rita offered. "Ran scared when the fire started, and is just too shaken to come out of hiding now. When things calm down, he'll show up again."

I wanted so much to believe that! But even as she spoke I could see his room again, the way it had looked that night. Glass shards littering the floor. Blankets a tangled mass on the bed. I had sensed at the time that something about the arrangement was wrong—terribly wrong—but I hadn't known what it was. Now, suddenly, it came to me, and the revelation shook me to my core. "Someone took him," I muttered.

Devon was on his way back with the laptop, its power cord trailing behind like a forgotten dog leash. "How do you know that?"

"The broken glass. It was all *inside* the room." I wiped my eyes dry with the back of my hand. Everything about me felt gritty. Filthy. "If he'd broken the window himself it would have shattered *outward*, not inward. And he wouldn't have to do that, anyway; he could just open it from the inside." I paused. "Which means someone broke it coming in."

"Jesus." Rita shook her head in amazement. "I would never have thought of that."

"Saw it on *Law and Order* once." I almost added: *My whole damn life looks like one of their episodes right now.*

"But why would they want him?" Devon put down the computer in front of me and looked for a place to plug it in. Apparently there was no outlet close enough, so he coiled the cord and set it on the glass table. "He's not one of us, is he?"

Us. Changelings. Fugitives.

I shook my head. "Maybe they broke in upstairs to avoid the alarm system on the first floor. Then when they found him there they had to do something to keep him quiet."

But even as I said that, I knew it wasn't the right answer. If all they had wanted was to keep Tommy quiet, wouldn't they have just killed him on the spot? Count on the fire to destroy the evidence? No, there was something more than that going on, something way more complicated than simple arson.

His body hasn't been found yet, I comforted myself. *So he's not necessarily dead.* I knew it was a slim hope, but I clung to it with all my might. The thought of Tommy being kidnapped was something I could *almost* deal with. The thought of Tommy lying dead in a ditch somewhere, his body being picked over by wild animals, wasn't.

Shutting all those thoughts out of my mind, I sat down in front of the laptop. In the back of my mind I was aware that I was leaving sooty streaks all over the pristine couch, but it was a distant fact, without the power to move me. All that mattered now was the data on this computer, and what it might reveal.

The password he'd given me previously was the name of one of his favorite gaming characters. God knows I'd heard enough stories about Tommy's online adventures to fill a phone book, so one by one I entered all the fantasy names I could remember him ever mentioning, my heart skipping a beat each time I hit the "enter" key. But no matter how many I tried, nothing worked. Character names, quest locations, guild titles, you name it. I even tried three or four versions of a few names, just to make sure I had the spelling right, and substituted numbers for letters in every variation I could think of. But still nothing worked.

Leaning back on the couch, I wiped a film of sweat from my brow as I struggled to come up with a new idea. I had to get into my brother's head, to sort out all the crazy gaming stuff that must be swimming around in there. What was he proudest of? Which tidbit of data would matter the most to him? I started to enter stuff from his Australian game—not only names this time, but every combination of elements I could think of. It was a long shot, since that game had only taken place a few days before, and I couldn't imagine he'd changed his password since then. But either Seyer's visit to our house had really spooked him, or else maybe he'd known those players longer than I thought. When I finally typed AUSSIE25 and hit *enter*, the system let me in.

Trembling with anticipation, I watched as the desktop loaded, colorful gaming icons popping into existence one by one. Given that his wallpaper was an illustration of two dragons spouting neon fire at each other, it was hard to see anything. I focused on each icon as it appeared, searching for anything that would give me a clue as to what Tommy had been doing that night. But I wasn't a computer person and really didn't have a clue how to look for that kind of information. When the desktop finished loading I was no closer to an answer than when it had started.

Tears of frustration welled up in my eyes, making them sting. I wiped them away with the back of a sooty hand. Which made them sting worse.

"Here," Devon said gently. "Let me try."

He came around the couch, and I moved over to let him have the driver's seat. You could tell immediately that he knew what he was doing. His typing was lightning fast, pure geek style, and screen after screen flashed by, some of it stuff I'd never seen before. While he worked, his expression was so intense you'd think it was *his* little brother at risk. I would have hugged him for that, if I hadn't been afraid it would screw with his concentration.

Finally he saw something on the screen that seemed to be of particular interest to him. He hit a few more keys, watched as a few more pages of data flashed by, then asked, "Your brother was into video?"

"He uploaded things to YouTube, if that's what you mean. Clips from his games, mostly. Sometimes speeches. Every time one of his games changed something in its design he uploaded hours of bitching. Which his friends responded to with videos of them bitching." Suddenly it sank in why Devon would ask me that. "You think he might have been recording something when all this went down?"

"Looks that way." He started typing again. "Let me see if anything was saved when the power went out."

I think we were all holding our breath in that moment. I know that I was.

After a few seconds a video box appeared on the screen, and we saw Tommy's face. The room behind him was achingly familiar, books and toys and posters on the wall that now were no more than ash. I took another swallow of soda, trying to wash down the lump in my throat. His computer hadn't been facing the window, which was frustrating, but you could see most of the room clearly enough. A small desk lamp had been turned on, but not the ceiling light; Tommy hadn't wanted anyone to realize he was awake.

With an expression so solemn you'd think he was speaking at a funeral, my little brother addressed the camera. "I'm sorry, I just can't agree with that review. Yeah, the new module is really flashy. Lots of bells and whistles. But at its heart it's just the same old story line, and there comes to a point where new graphics can't save—oh, crap!" A wave of his hand had hit something off screen; I heard a thunk and a splash as it struck the floor. "Hell," he muttered, as he slid out of his chair. I could see him looking around the room, probably searching for something to wipe up the mess with. Finally he scurried out of camera range, presumably to go fetch a towel or something. We heard the door to his room open, then close.

And we watched the screen in silence. I was so intent on listening that I hardly dared breathe; I didn't want some subtle clue to be drowned out by the sound of my respiration. But when the clue finally came, it wasn't subtle. Glass shattered loudly somewhere off-camera, and I found myself leaning forward, as if getting closer to the screen would somehow bring the cause of it into view. Then there was the sound of glass crunching underfoot as someone walked across the room, louder and louder as it approached the computer . . . and just when I thought I was going to scream from sheer frustration, a shadowy figure appeared on the screen. He was wearing some kind of hood, so we couldn't see his face, and he crossed the camera's field and disappeared on the other side without turning.

Then there was silence again. It didn't take a genius to deduce that the intruder was probably waiting beside the door, ready to grab hold of my brother the minute he returned. My hands balled into fists as I waited. I was maddened by my own impotence. It's a terrible thing to watch a video of someone you love about to be hurt and not be able to do a damn thing about it.

We heard the door open again, followed by a brief scuffle. *Don't let him be killed. Please, God, anything but that.*

The dark figure returned to our field of view. He had Tommy's small body thrown over his shoulders like a sack of potatoes. "You want me to wait?" he asked someone off-screen. He had an odd accent: almost British but with a hint of a southern twang.

"No." The voice that responded had a similar accent. "Head back to the caverns. I'll finish up here."

The guy carrying Tommy nodded and started toward the window. Our brief show was about to end, and we had learned nothing useful.

But just before the man left the camera's range he glanced back briefly over his shoulder, and for an instant—just an instant—we could see his face.

"Holy crap . . ." Rita whispered.

I was speechless.

It was a slender face, delicate in bone structure, with high cheekbones and a narrow, feminine chin. The eyes were large and dark, vast almond-shaped orbs that reflected the shadows in the room.

Maybe those eyes were impossibly huge, or maybe it was just the tiny size of his nose and mouth that made them seem that way, but the end result was that the face looked . . . well, not human. And the color of his skin wasn't human either, but a weird grey hue with some kind of mottled pattern. *It's the lighting,* I told myself. *Or the monitor's got the color wrong.* But as an artist I was pretty alert to cues of lighting and color, so those excuses fell flat. Everything else in the room looked perfectly normal, which meant that both the lighting and the monitor settings were close to true. We were seeing what this guy had really looked like.

The figure walked off-screen. We heard more glass crunching. Then there was the sound of a window opening, a few muffled comments I couldn't make out, and finally a heavy wooden thud as the window fell shut again. A faint tinkling of glass followed that, as if someone had brushed against a wind chime. Then silence.

For a full minute, none of us said anything. English didn't have the kind of words you needed to respond to a video like that.

Rita was the first to find her voice. "What the hell *was* that?"

"A hoax," Devon croaked. "Some kind of video hoax. Kids do things like that all the time."

"Someone tried to *burn down my house,*" I said sharply. "Two people nearly died. That's hardly the kind of practical joke my brother would play." My head was pounding fiercely now, and not from physical pain this time.

"We should tell someone," Devon said, without conviction.

"Tell them what?" Rita snapped. "Jesse's brother was kidnapped by a space alien? Or by some kind of . . . Jesus Christ, what *was* that thing?"

Maybe this is all just a bad dream, I told myself. Wishful thinking. A dream was something you could wake up from. This was worse than any nightmare I'd ever had.

Rita got up from the couch and started pacing. Back and forth, back and forth, movements jerky and quick like those of a nervous animal. "We can't show this to anyone. Anyone! You all understand that, right?"

Devon opened his mouth to protest . . . then just shut it and nodded. Because Rita was right. If we showed this crazy video to the police they would just accuse us of having altered it digitally—perhaps even staging the whole scene ourselves, as some sick kind of teenage prank—and then not only would we not get any help, we'd probably be arrested for falsifying evidence. Maybe they'd even suspect us of having started the fire, because why else would we make up such a crazy story? I'd seen people on cop shows arrested over less.

No one would believe what was in this video. No one.

Which meant we were completely on our own. And that was more scary than all the rest combined.

"He mentioned caverns," Devon told me. "That's where they were taking your brother."

"There are a million caverns around here," I reminded him. The karst mountains flanking the Shenandoah Valley were like Swiss cheese—I remembered that much from Geology. "So that's not much to go on."

Rita looked at me. "He said it like it was the name of a place. Or part of a name, anyway. Aren't there caverns with names around here?"

Devon nodded. "Half a dozen, at least. Shenandoah, Endless, Skyline, Luray . . . but they're all open to the public. Not the kind of place kidnappers would use for a hideout."

Least of all kidnappers who don't look human, I thought darkly.

But his words sparked a memory of something that had happened back when I was a kid. Fifth, maybe sixth grade. My science teacher had booked a tour for us at one of the big caverns: special lecture for young people, private tour, the whole nine yards. Only it got cancelled at the last minute. Apparently the caverns we'd planned to visit had come under new ownership and would no longer be open to the public. It all happened so fast there wasn't time for our teacher to book an alternative tour before year's end. Man, we were angry. Really angry. You never forget that kind of thing. "Mystic Caverns," I said. "Closed about six years ago."

Without saying a word, Devon returned to the laptop. I saw him pull up a browser and start scrolling through web pages. I rescued the remains of my soda from the table and tried to wash down the lump in my throat as I watched him. Rita went back to pacing.

"Got it," he muttered at last. He leaned back on the couch and began to read aloud.

> ". . . *Shoponi tradition says it is home to powerful spirits, and that if a shaman sleeps there after proper ritual prepara-tion, he can enter the spirit world in his dreams. In the early 19th century the caverns were used as a way station for es-caped slaves, and during Prohibition private parties were often held in its depths. In 1936 the owners revamped the tourist facilities, adding steel walkways, an electrical system, and a new and larger entrance at the southern end. Mystic Caverns remained a popular tourist destination until it closed in 2007 . . . ."*

"Of course," Devon cautioned, "we don't know for sure that's where Tommy is."

But I knew in my gut that it was. All that stuff about spirits and dreams, and visiting other worlds . . . it fit too well. Something strange was going on, and this place was at the center of it.

I felt a flutter of excitement in the pit of my stomach. Like you feel when you are about to step off a high diving board for the first time. Fear and elation all tangled up together.

"You're going to go there," Rita said. Not a question.

I didn't respond.

"Whatever's going on there probably won't be aboveground," she warned. "And we can hardly just wander in the main entrance with-out being noticed."

"They built a new entrance in 1936," Devon reminded her. "That means that somewhere there may be an old one that's still accessible. If we can locate that . . ." He turned back to the computer and started typing again.

"You two don't have to go," I said quietly. "He's not your brother."

"Hey." Rita glared at me. "This isn't just about your brother, okay? Devon and I are on the same hit list you are. So are a lot of our friends. So on the off chance there's something out there that will tell us what's going on—and why—I sure as hell want to be there when you find it."

Devon nodded as he typed. "This may take a while, Jesse. Why don't you go take a shower, get changed . . ." The words trailed off as he focused on the computer.

Get ready to leave this place of safety. Get ready to invade dark places where dangerous people—dangerous creatures—might reside.

I started to protest, but then stopped myself. There was nothing I could do in this living room right now that would make our situation any better, and meanwhile, I wanted to get clean so badly I could taste it. So I went and collected the clothes they'd left out for me, and a fluffy white guest towel, and headed off to the bathroom to wash off the mixture of soot and sweat and fear that clung to my skin. A lot of fear.

The latter didn't wash away completely, but I tried my best.

‖‖‖‖‖‖‖‖‖‖

Night was falling; the woods surrounding us were dim, like a photo that had faded over time. A breeze stirred my newly washed hair, scattering droplets of water across the shoulders of my camo T-shirt. Yeah, camo: the kind of thing you wear when you want to hide out in the woods. That tells you something about what those two were thinking when they shopped for me.

Prescient of them.

Devon came out onto the narrow deck and joined me at the railing.

"Find anything useful?" I asked.

"An old map. Won't know how accurate it is until we get there. I cached a satellite image of the local terrain."

I hesitated. "Do your parents know we're here?"

"My dad knows *I'm* here. He thinks I'm off hiking this week, using the cabin as a base of operations. Hopefully we'll be back before he realizes that isn't the case. My mother . . ." He paused. "She died a few years ago."

"I'm so sorry."

He shrugged stiffly. "Beltway collision. Still hard to accept." He offered me the phone. "You want to try your mom?"

I hesitated. I did want to talk to my mother, more than anything in the world. She must have been going crazy not knowing where I was. But the mere thought of taking the phone from him made my hand start shaking, as the full implications of our situation hit home: Whoever wanted to kill me must surely have realized by now that the fire had failed, and they'd be looking for me, to try again. If they were smart they'd be watching my mother's every move, possibly even tapping her phone. The one sure way to find me.

I might have been willing to take a chance with my own life, but they'd proven they were willing to kill my family to get to me, and I didn't want to put her in danger.

I'm sorry, Mom. I blinked back tears as I waved off Devon's offer. *I'm sorry I can't tell you that I'm okay. I know it must be tearing you to pieces inside, not to know what happened to me.*

"Hey," he said gently. "It's okay. We'll be back soon enough. Maybe with enough solid evidence to give to the police. That's the goal, right?"

"And what if something goes wrong along the way?" I whispered. "What if we don't come back? No one will ever know what happened to us."

He nodded, and I got the sense that this was something he'd already considered. "We can leave a note in the cabin. If I don't check in for a few days my dad will start to worry, and eventually he'll come out here and find it. That'll give us enough time to check out the caverns without interference, but also guarantee that we get backup eventually, in case anything goes wrong."

I nodded dully. It wasn't a perfect plan, but it was the best we were likely to come up with.

"You could leave a letter for your mother," he offered. "I'm sure my dad would deliver it."

"Thanks," I whispered.

He hesitated, then put his hand over mine. It felt strong and certain and it vibrated with positive energy. I tried to draw strength from it.

"C'mon," he said. "We need to head out to Front Royal while the Walmart is still open."

ııııııııııı

In my letter, I told Mom everything. Never mind how crazy some of it sounded when you put it in writing; if she got this letter it would mean that the worst had happened, in which case she had to know it all. I even drew her a picture of Tommy's kidnapper. I tried to make him look realistic, but he still came out looking like a space alien in a hoodie. My hand shook as I drew Tommy's small body draped over his shoulder.

I hope you never have to read this, I thought, as I sealed my letter and put it beside Devon's. *I hope we come back soon enough that no one even knows we were gone.*

Rita didn't leave a letter for anyone.

9

FRONT ROYAL
VIRGINIA

RITA'S CAR WAS A SLEEK BLACK AUDI, which was not what I'd expected. Turned out it wasn't her car after all. I figured that out when we stopped in a bad neighborhood in Front Royal so she could leave it on the street with the key in the ignition. She wiped the steering wheel down carefully first, then the door handles and gear shift, removing her fingerprints with a thoroughness that suggested she'd done that kind of thing before. Maybe her prints were "in the system."

She caught my eye as she slid into the back seat of Devon's SUV, apparently reading some kind of challenge in my expression. "I was worried about you that night," she said defiantly. "I wanted to see if anyone was casing your house. What was I supposed to do, walk?"

I muttered something that I hoped was appropriate. I honestly didn't know what to say to someone who would steal a car just to take a trip across town, though I was certainly grateful she'd done it.

The trip to Walmart was apparently so we could stock up on bottled water. And backpacks to put the water in. And flashlights. And rope. And chalk. And three of those folding utility knives that have all sorts of household tools tucked into them.

"Are you expecting to get lost in a cavern?" I asked Devon, trying to keep my tone light.

"No one ever *expects* to get lost in a cavern," he pointed out reasonably.

He told us that if there was anything Rita and I thought we should pack, that he'd left out, we should go get it. So I headed over to the hardware department, because, as every fan of *Mythbusters* knows, the single most important thing to have with you in unfamiliar territory is duct tape. Rita disappeared into Housewares and soon returned with three large kitchen knives. They were the kind you see in horror movies, when the heroine is being hunted by a killer inside her own house, and she searches in the kitchen drawer for the deadliest looking weapon she can find. They were long and triangular and surely would scare off the most hardened serial killer.

We also picked up a set of children's walkie-talkies (Devon's idea), pocket-sized first aid kits (my idea), and a box of breakfast bars (Rita's idea). We bought everything in threes, which was actually kind of disturbing, as it meant we were planning to get separated. That was a possibility I was trying hard not to think about.

Devon's parents had given him a credit card for emergencies, but he'd intentionally left it at the cabin, not wanting to risk it getting into the hands of the wrong people. That left him only with the cash he'd withdrawn from his personal bank account when we'd arrived in Front Royal. After all our stuff was paid for, there wasn't much left. Hopefully, whatever emergencies lay ahead wouldn't be expensive ones.

It was dark by the time we finally pulled back onto Route 340, heading south. Rita sat in the back seat, trying to cut up the clamshell packaging from her kitchen knives so that we could use them as sheathes. I munched on a breakfast bar without tasting it, trying not to think about what kind of creatures might be waiting for us just down the road.

They're human beings, I told myself stubbornly. *The one that took Tommy was probably wearing some kind of disguise, to fool security cameras.*

But try as I might, I couldn't get those alien eyes out of my head.

Devon was using the car's GPS to navigate, and after about half an hour it directed him to turn left, onto a narrow dirt road. Soon after that he killed the lights, which made the last part of the drive somewhat harrowing; tree branches seemed to jump out of nowhere, and giant potholes were all but invisible until you were right on top of them. Once we bottomed out so hard I feared the axle might get broken. My nerves hadn't been all that calm to start with, and this wasn't helping.

Finally he stopped and parked. We were in the middle of nowhere.

"I don't see a cave," Rita said.

Devon nodded. "I don't want to bring the car too close to it, they might hear us coming. We can walk from here."

Even with our flashlights, visibility was poor. The ground was rocky and uneven and the trees looming overhead blocked most of the moonlight. More than once I stubbed my toe on some unseen obstacle, or heard Rita curse as she did the same. Devon had brought his smartphone along, complete with a GPS app and some cavern maps that he'd cached, so at least there was no chance of us getting lost. But it was one hell of a walk.

Finally the ground leveled out and the trees gave way to a plain of tall wild grass. Devon glanced at his device again and nodded; by unspoken agreement, we all turned off our flashlights. We were getting close to *something* and couldn't take the risk that we might be seen.

Silently we skirted the grassy area, moving as quietly as we could manage. Then we came over a rise and saw what must once have been the Mystic Caverns tourist center. A semi-circle of small buildings flanked one large one at the center, all of them designed to look like log cabins. Whatever signs might once have identified them were missing, and the buildings were so weathered and aged that the whole place looked like a ghost town. But the surrounding grass had been neatly mowed, and near the main building there were tire tracks plainly visible. My heart skipped a beat when I saw them. Had the vehicle that made those brought my brother here?

We skirted the compound with care, which, as it turned out, was a really good idea, because someone had strung up barbed wire around the place. It was nearly invisible in the moonlight, and Devon almost walked right into it. Whoever owned this place *really* didn't want visitors. Which, when you were searching for kidnappers and arsonists who were trying to kill you, was a pretty good sign you were in the right place.

When we got to the far side of the compound we could see that there were several vehicles parked behind the main building, including a small shuttle van. But the compound was silent, and there wasn't any light visible in or around the buildings; whoever owned those vehicles was probably underground.

As we moved past the entrance the trees closed in on us again, and Devon checked his GPS app. "That way," he whispered, pointing southwest. We moved as quietly as we could in the thick underbrush. I kept looking behind me as I walked, straining to see if we were being followed. Thus far, it seemed, we were unobserved.

Then Devon whispered "There!" and pointed to something directly ahead of us.

In the dim moonlight I could make out a small cabin, its weathered planks green with mildew. At one time, the surrounding land must have been cleared, because there were no large trees near it, though dozens of smaller ones had sprouted up, and a thick carpet of tangled brush covered the ground. I was willing to bet that no one had come here in a long time. If we were lucky, the new owners didn't even know this place existed.

The cabin had no door, just a simple rectangular archway like you might find at the opening of a mine. Someone had nailed wooden planks across it, and while the job wasn't neat, it was thorough; there were enough nails in the wood to keep a recycling center busy for a week.

"Jeez," Devon muttered. "I didn't think to bring a crowbar." He considered the problem for a moment, then took his utility knife out of his backpack and began prying loose fibers of wood from the edge of one of the planks. Rita and I couldn't help him without getting in his way, so we stood watch. Finally, when he had made a hole big enough to fit his hand into, he grasped the upper edge of the plank, braced his foot against the door frame, and pulled. At first the plank didn't budge, and it looked like we would have to figure out some other way to break inside. But then suddenly it gave way, and fragments of moldy wood went flying in every direction as he jerked the plank away from the archway and threw it into the brush.

Now there was room for all three of us to grab the next plank down, and we made short work of it. Two more gave way after that, until we had an opening large enough for a person to climb through.

Pausing to catch our breath—dismantling an eighty-year-old shack is surprisingly hard work—we shined our flashlights into the small building, to see what was there.

The interior was empty, and most of the floor was just flattened dirt. But near the rear of the building the ground looked darker, and when we swung our flashlights that way we could see the opening of a deep black pit. Inside, it looked like there might be some kind of staircase leading down. Devon's research had come through for us.

I stared at the hole for a moment, and my hand trembled, making the beam from my flashlight jerk around a bit. The reality of what we were doing—and the sheer danger of it—was sinking in. If anyone other than Tommy had been kidnapped by aliens, I might have turned around and headed home right then and there. Only for family did you do something like this.

But we can't go home, I reminded myself. I could see in my companions' eyes that the same thought was running through their heads. If we returned home now, without answers, we'd just be putting our families at risk. No one was going to investigate this place for us based on the kind of evidence we currently had, so we'd wind up sitting at home helplessly, just waiting for someone to come kill us.

Better to take our chances with the unknown.

Deciding that since this was my venture I really should go first, I started to climb inside, working my way gingerly over the remaining planks. But the rotting wood gave way beneath me and sent me crashing to the ground inside the cabin. I fell full length, which mean that my head wound up less than a foot from the gaping pit. For a moment

I just lay frozen, fear surging through my veins, while tendrils of cool air from the netherworld chilled the sweat on my skin.

"Are you okay?" Devon asked.

"Yeah," I muttered. "I think so."

Slowly, carefully, I edged myself away from the pit. It took me a minute to catch my breath and to still the wild beating of my heart; then I crawled over to where my flashlight had fallen and retrieved it. Devon and Rita were climbing through the entrance—more carefully than I had done—and by the time I was back on my feet, they were standing beside me.

Now we had a better angle on the pit and could shine our lights straight down into it. There was indeed a flight of stairs, carved out of the bedrock itself. The steps were narrow, steep, and uneven, and it went without saying there was no handrail. They went down as far as our light could reach and then were swallowed up by the darkness of the pit. Nameless malevolence seemed to waft up from the depths.

"Just when you need an elevator the most," Devon muttered.

"Should have picked one up at Walmart," Rita chided him.

"Next time," he promised.

The banter steadied my nerves a bit. I felt ready for this. Taking a deep breath, I started to descend into the earth. It wasn't easy. The treads weren't wide enough to accommodate my feet in a normal walking position; I had to turn them sideways and work my way down the staircase like a crab. The stairs were damp, too, which meant they were slippery. I tried to find handholds on the rock wall to steady myself, but there were very few, and the descent was pretty scary. Flashlight beams played about my feet as Rita and Devon descended behind me, balancing precariously on stairs that had not felt the weight of a human foot for eight decades. If either of them slipped, we'd all go down.

But I finally reached the bottom, and moments later the two of them joined me. As I waited for them I swung my flashlight beam around the long, narrow cavern that we were now standing in. The nearer end appeared to have been hewn from the rock by some sort of hand tool; deep gouges criss-crossed the wall in parallel groupings, as if a giant cat had sharpened its claws there. A few yards beyond that the space opened up into a natural chamber, the kind they call a "live cave," whose walls were slick with moisture from recent rains. There were small calcite icicles hanging down from the ceiling, and ripples of glistening stone seemed to be have been frozen in place as they trickled from cracks in the walls. This place had been famous in its time, I recalled, and with caverns like Luray and Skyline right down the road, that meant it must have some pretty impressive formations.

There was only one direction to go in, so we started walking, following a path of rough bricks half-covered in mud. The original tourist route? Running along one wall I saw a horizontal ridge that looked man-made, no doubt disguising an electrical line. There were probably lights down here somewhere, disguised as cave formations so as not to distract tourists. But even if we found functional lights, and they were still hooked up to a power source, we could hardly risk turning them on.

Devon turned his phone off as we walked, to conserve its power. Our flashlights provided some light, but not nearly enough to drive back the oppressive cave darkness. As we walked, their narrow beams made the formations flanking our path look like stuff out of a horror movie. Spires would suddenly appear overhead, from nowhere; waterfall-shaped cascades of limestone seemed to shift position as we passed by, and curtains of translucent calcite rippled like jellyfish. My parents had taken me to visit Luray Caverns back when I was a kid, and I remembered how beautiful such formations could be, when viewed in the proper lighting. But when viewed this way they were unsettling, and we were all acutely aware of how many hiding places there were in the darkness surrounding us, that might shelter any manner of enemy or trap.

But thus far, no one seemed to know we were there.

Suddenly I thought I heard something other than our footsteps, and I motioned for everyone to stop moving. Straining my ears, I could just barely make out a sound in the distance.

I looked at my companions to see if they had heard it too. They both nodded. Someone else—or something else—was down here.

Rita and Devon switched off their flashlights, and I kept mine pointed downward as much as possible; it barely gave us enough light to walk safely, but we had to minimize the chance that anyone ahead would see us coming. Periodically we stopped to listen again; each time the distant sound seemed louder. It was beginning to sound like human speech, though the echo from the caverns made it hard to pick out individual words. We seemed to be heading right toward it, and I wondered if we would really be so lucky as to have our path lead straight to the kidnappers we sought.

But then we came to a place were the line of bricks turned off to the right, while the voices were coming from the left. There seemed to be no way to continue walking in the direction we needed to go. Anxiously, we searched the left wall of the chamber for any kind of passage, and Devon finally found a narrow crevice hidden in the shadows. Little more than a crack in the wall, it looked like something no man in his right mind would enter; but then I saw the thin line of concrete running down one of its walls, and realized it must have been used as a maintenance tunnel. Good enough.

One by one we squeezed ourselves into the narrow space. Devon went last, and before he committed himself to the crevice he took out a piece of chalk and marked the ceiling overhead. Always the organized one. Rita had her knife in her hand again. I wondered what it would feel like to stab someone. I wondered, if circumstances called for it, if I would be able to. I wondered if Rita ever had done so.

The floor of the passageway was covered with a thick layer of mud, and our feet made soft squelching sounds as we worked our way through the narrow space. Way too conspicuous for my taste, but there was no helping it. Sometimes the ceiling dropped so low that Devon couldn't get through without crouching, and at one point the passage grew so narrow that I had to slip off my backpack to squeeze through it sideways. Meanwhile the light was growing brighter by the moment, so we knew we were headed in the right direction. The voices were gone, though; even when we stopped our mud-squelching to listen for them, we could hear nothing.

Eventually it grew bright enough that I shut my flashlight off. Soon after that the tunnel opened out into a small chamber, just large enough for the three of us to stand in. Through a narrow slit at the far end we could see there was a much larger chamber beyond, and the light seemed to be coming from there.

Slowly, warily, we approached that final opening, and for a moment we all stood as still as the rock itself, listening for any sign of danger. But all we could hear was the distant drip of water, the music of a living cave. So I took the lead and squeezed through the narrow slit.

I emerged into a massive chamber. I didn't need a guidebook to tell me that this was the crown jewel of Mystic Caverns, the point where all tours converged. The ceiling was so far overhead I couldn't make out its limits, and a thick forest of columns and stalagmites surrounded me, making it hard to see what else was in the chamber. All about the room, inside crevices and behind formations, the light cast deep black shadows. God alone knew what might be hiding in any one of them.

As I crept warily forward I thought I could make out a large open area ahead of us, surrounded by a waist-high railing. The light we'd detected was coming from a series of lamps affixed to its support posts, and though the illumination must have been pretty dim by aboveground standards, it was nigh on blinding to us in our current state. I blinked as tiny purple spots swam before my eyes, as my eyes slowly adjusted. Then I got to where I could see what was in the central part of the chamber. And I froze.

Rita came up behind me. I heard her gasp.

Facing us was an arch. It was twice as tall as Devon and wide enough that he could not have touched both sides at once. The underlying shape of it was perfectly regular, but its surface was coated with flower-like clusters of cave crystals—anthodites—some of them so tiny I could hardly make out their details, others more than a foot long. The needle-like blossoms glittered as we shifted position, crystalline spines seeming to shift and sway as if they were living things.

The caverns hadn't made this thing. Nor had human hands. It was . . . unearthly.

Beside the arch was a row of steel tables on wheels, the kind you might see in a morgue. Atop each one was a white sheet draped over what appeared to be a human body. I was about to move toward them when suddenly there was a loud metallic sound from the far end of the chamber. The lamps flared to sudden brightness, blinding us. From behind we could hear a large metal thing approaching . . . or maybe human feet pounding on metal.

"Hide!" Devon whispered fiercely.

As if we needed to be told that.

I looked about feverishly for cover and spotted a broad column near our entrance point that looked wide enough to hide behind. Fear lent fire to my muscles as I sprinted toward it. Rita and Devon ran off in other directions, presumably toward hiding places of their own. There were certainly enough of them in the chamber.

I dove into a thick black shadow behind the column, and I prayed that no one entering the main chamber would be able to see me. I leaned back against the wet rock and tried to stay calm, my heart pounding so hard I thought it would burst out of my chest. The metallic sounds were louder now, and yes, they clearly were footsteps. Curiosity warred with fear in my heart, and after a brief stalemate the former won out by a narrow margin; I peeked gingerly around the edge of the column to see who was coming.

In our fixation on the crystal arch we hadn't noticed a suspended walkway leading away from the far end of the chamber. I could see two figures there, talking to one another as they walked along the metal grate toward us. On the left was a woman dressed in a navy skirt-and-jacket ensemble, a neat and conservative figure with hair coiffed to meticulous perfection. The other figure was thinner and taller, and the voice sounded male, but I couldn't get a clear view of him.

"We don't have the facilities for this," the woman was saying. Her accent reflected the same odd cultural mix as that of my brother's kidnappers, and she was clearly annoyed. "This party should have been broken up into two. At least."

"This is the way the Shadows want it done, so this is the way it will be done." The man's voice was quiet, resigned. "Arguing with them is a bad career move, Delilah."

She snorted lightly. The sound was derisive and delicate at the same time, and I got the impression it was something she'd rehearsed. "We wouldn't be in the mess we're in now if they would let the other Guilds counsel them."

"I strongly suggest you don't let them hear you say that."

"Of course, Malik. I'm not a fool. But they're not here right now, are they?"

Then they passed out of sight behind the column. I inched my way around the back of it, seeking a safe vantage point on the other side.

"Are you sure of that?" the man said.

"Please. I can smell their undead presence from two spheres away. Maybe you've been around them too much if you can't."

If the man responded, I didn't hear it. The woman's words rang in my head, sending a wave of fear up my spine. No other focus was possible.

I can smell their undead presence.

For all our nervous banter about aliens and changelings and animal-controlling powers, I knew in that moment that I hadn't believed any of it. Deep in my heart I'd clung to the belief that there was a rational explanation for everything we'd seen, and if we just looked in the right places and asked the right questions we would figure it out. That was why we'd come down into the caverns, right? To search for rational explanations.

I can smell their undead presence from two spheres away.

Maybe this was all a dream. Maybe I'd wake up soon, and I'd go into Tommy's room and tell him all about it, and we'd have a good laugh together about how crazy my dreams were.

When the voices were audible once more, it sounded like the man was near the crystal arch. "Given how many people will be coming through today, you might want to stand back a bit."

Heart pounding wildly, I dared another peek around the edge of the column. The two of them were in front of the arch, waiting silently and expectantly for . . . what? I could see the man more clearly now. His skin was a mottled grey, the same color as the stone behind him. His eyes were large and dark and the outer corners were angled slightly upward, like a cat's. His clothing was normal enough, but all of it was the same shade of grey as his skin, which made it hard to pick him out from the limestone background. I couldn't tell if he was the same person who had carried Tommy out of our house or not, but he was definitely of the same type.

Then the archway began to glow. I pressed back into the shadows as far as I could without losing sight of it. I had the impression of a complex geometric design filling its interior, though it wasn't something I *saw*, exactly, more like something that I knew in my gut was there, even though there was no visible evidence of it.

A man stepped through the arch.

His face was pale, and it had an unnatural sheen to it. His body was solid enough in the center but its edges looked strangely insubstantial, as if someone had begun to erase him. Wisps of shadowy mist played about him, and for a moment it looked as if they were about to coalesce into some sort of creature—or creatures—but instead they faded into nothingness before any features became recognizable. The long grey robe that he wore lent him a vaguely medieval air, a jarring contrast to the very modern clipboard he was carrying. For some reason that last item made him seem even creepier.

He took a few steps away from the arch, looked down at his clipboard, and started to read. His voice was a thin tenor that sounded . . . empty.

"Arianna Withersham, Apprentice of Elementals. Naomi Balfort, Master of Weavers. Nicholas Tull, Journeyman of Seers." He recited maybe eight names in all, each with a title.

The grey man, meanwhile, had pulled out a smartphone and was checking those names against a list of his own. He nodded his approval as each name was spoken, and when the recital was done he said "Good to go," and gestured toward the row of gurneys.

The man with the clipboard looked around the chamber, and I realized with a start that he was about to turn in my direction. I fell back into the shadows as quickly as I could, nearly slipping on the wet floor in my haste. My heart almost stopped. *Oh God, please don't let him see me!* I couldn't even imagine what would happen if these people realized I was in the room spying on them.

One second passed. Two. In all my life I've never felt time move as slowly as it did at that moment.

Then I heard the sound of gurneys being wheeled across the stone floor. People walking back and forth. Suddenly there seemed to be many more people than had been there a moment before. I heard a lot of voices, mostly young, murmuring and laughing in the quiet way that students do when class is about to begin.

The woman in the suit started speaking, and all the other voices subsided. "Ladies and Gentlemen, Masters and Apprentices, Journeymen and Aspirants: welcome to Terra Colonna. My name is Delilah Mason, and I will be your docent for this visit. If you would all be so good as to follow me, I will see to your orientation."

I could hear a number of people follow the sharp click of her heels as they moved across the room; the steel walkway thrummed as they stepped onto it one by one, their footsteps becoming less and less audible as they moved away from the main chamber. There was a bit of giggling in the distance, and then they were gone.

The grey man said quietly, "You said there would be fourteen."

"The others were delayed." The voice of his pale companion sent shivers up my spine.

"I have a schedule to keep. When are they expected?"

"Half an hour."

I heard a sigh of exasperation. "What about the Drake boy? Did he make it through all right?"

I felt my heart lurch in my chest.

"He arrived intact and in the right time sequence. But I'm told the exchange wasn't well balanced. If he ever attempts to return home there could be consequences."

"Well. That's not going to be an issue, is it?"

Silence.

"What do the Shadows want with him, anyway?"

Silence.

The grey man snorted. "All right. Have it your way. I'll return in half an hour. Make sure the transfers are ready by then."

I heard someone leave the chamber. A moment later the strange geometric vision flared again, then faded, dissipating like golden smoke.

And they were gone.

I leaned back against the column, heart pounding, struggling to make some kind of sense of what I'd just heard. It sounded like my brother was still alive, so there was still hope. But why had they taken him?

"Jesse!" The call was only whispered, but the place was like an echo chamber, magnifying the sound.

I peeked out from around the column, and saw Rita and Devon standing out in the open. After a brief glance around the place to see for myself that the visitors were really gone, I joined them.

For a moment we just stared at each other in silence.

"How much did you see?" Devon said at last. I could hear in his voice how hard he was struggling to stay calm.

I drew in a shaky breath. "The grey guy and the woman. And that *undead* thing, that came through the arch."

"I saw people come through it." Rita's voice was a haunted whisper. "The grey man pushed a trolley through the archway each time one of them arrived, and it . . ." she drew in a deep breath, "it *disappeared*."

"The timing of it seemed important," Devon added.

A balanced exchange, I remembered.

I walked over to the nearest gurney, paused for a moment to gather my courage, then folded the top of the sheet back to see what was underneath.

The body on the steel surface was that of a teenage boy. He looked dead, but when I put my hand on his cheek I could feel living warmth. So I took out my phone and held the screen to his lips. There was no fog from his breath, or any other sign of life.

Devon and Rita uncovered the other bodies. Two adults and four teens. Most of them looked as if they were sleeping peacefully, until you noticed they weren't breathing. One of them was a girl exactly my age; seeing her lying there like that made me queasy.

"Caucasian male, 43," Rita was reading from a form clipped to the end of one of the carts. "Blood type A+, 180 pounds, muscle tone 6. Single, no offspring, no siblings. Diabetes, allergy to dust mites. College professor. Musical talent." She raised an eyebrow. "Conservative Republican."

"Creepier and creepier," Devon muttered.

Rita looked at me. "The Drake boy they were talking about. That's your brother?"

Lips tight, I nodded.

Soon the grey man and his pale companion would return. More people would emerge from the crystal arch, ready to tour *Terra Colonna*. Our world. And meanwhile these unconscious bodies would be exchanged for them, and transported to . . . where?

Wherever my brother is, I thought. A tremor of fear ran up my spine.

"They came this way," I murmured. "The ones who are hunting us. The ones who burned my house to the ground, trying to kill me. This is how they got here."

And this is how they will go home.

I walked over to the body that looked so much like mine. In a short while this girl would be wheeled through that portal, into another world. A place where alien-looking grey men and undead tour guides—and God alone knew what other kinds of monsters—took little boys prisoners. A place where my death, and many other deaths, had been planned.

There comes a point when so many crazy things have happened

that your mind just can't process them any more. Insane things start
to sound reasonable.

"We could go there," I said quietly. I put my hand to the girl's
cheek. It was warm, so warm.

"You mean . . . take their place?" Rita clearly thought I had gone
insane.

"You said the exchange was one-for-one. We know more visitors
are about to arrive." I paused. "They'll send these bodies through to
the other side, won't they?"

"Jesse . . ." From her tone of voice you could tell she thought she was
arguing with a crazy person. "We don't have a clue what's out there."

"No," I said softly. "We don't. But we know what's here." I indicated the bodies. "And when will we have a chance like this again?
Maybe never."

And what about these people? an inner voice demanded. *Where
will you hide them while you make your substitution? And what will
happen to them once you're gone?*

I looked down at the girl on the table. So still, so helpless. But she
wasn't hooked up to any kind of machine or IV, I noted. Which meant
that whatever strange suspended animation state she was in, removing her from the gurney wasn't likely to make a difference. We could
hide her body behind one of the formations, where people passing
through the crystal arch were unlikely to see her. Later on, when the
aliens who ran this place discovered our empty gurneys on the other
side of the arch and realized what we'd done, they would find her.

And then what?

My brother is gone, I told myself. *How else can we find him, if we
don't do this?*

Devon put a hand on my shoulder; I could tell from his expression
that the same thoughts had been running though his mind. "We could
call in some outside help," he said quietly. "Now that we know there's
stuff down here for them to see. There are people far better equipped
than we are to figure all this out."

"And what will happen when they get here?" I demanded, turning on him. "They'll cordon this place off. Seal all the entrances, station guards outside, do whatever it takes to keep the public from ever finding out about this place. Then the government will bring in its scientists, and they'll study this arch molecule by molecule, write papers about it and conduct experiments and hold conferences and maybe, after years of that, start sending people through. One lost boy will be the least of their concerns." I shook my head. "You think we'll be able to sneak down here again, once that starts? We'll lose access to this place. Forever. A sacrifice to science, nothing more."

Devon said nothing, but I could see the uncertainty in his eyes. I couldn't read Rita at all.

"Aren't you the least bit curious?" I asked her. "Don't you want to know what's out there?" I looked back at Devon. "Don't you want to be the one who discovers a new world? Instead of reading about how someone else did it?" I was trying desperately to appeal to the science geek in him. Devon was the practical one, always thinking ahead. The guy who had thought to make chalk marks so we could find our way home. If I was going to dive headfirst into an unknown world, I definitely wanted him with me.

But to my surprise it was Rita who spoke first. "Crap," she muttered. "I've got nowhere better to go."

I looked at Devon. Still he said nothing.

"We left notes at your house," I pressed. "If we don't come back in the next few days our parents will know where we went. They'll send people down here, figure out what's going on, and make sure someone comes after us." I wasn't actually sure that was true—once the government found out about this operation, three missing teens might be pretty low on their list of priorities—but it seemed to be the telling argument. Lips tight, he finally nodded.

Moving inert human bodies turned out to be a lot harder than you'd think, especially when you're trying not to bang them against tables or rock. As we positioned them behind a cluster of thick formations, Rita pointed out that our backpacks couldn't ride on the gurneys with us without being visible. We didn't want to leave them behind, so I jury-rigged a quick support line to hang mine underneath the tabletop, and the others followed suit. Thank God for duct tape. The sheets were just long enough to hide our packs from sight, assuming the fabric stayed in place.

Then, one by one, we laid down on the sleek steel slabs, arranging ourselves like corpses. Rita covered Devon and me with our sheets, taking care to make sure they were arranged the same as the ones covering the other bodies. She had to arrange her own after that, and I prayed it would be convincing. The things these people might do to us if they discovered our little trick didn't bear thinking about.

No sooner were we settled in when we heard footsteps again. I tried to minimize my breathing as they approached, so that the rise and fall of my chest wouldn't give me away.

People walked around us. They talked. I concentrated on my heartbeat, my breathing, listing in my mind the thousand and one things we probably should have talked about before doing this . . . anything but what was happening in the world beyond my sheet. I couldn't afford to react to events in the room, even reflexively.

Then the strange pattern filled my brain again. Golden lines, dancing and weaving all about me. This time they felt familiar, as though I had seen them somewhere before. As though I should know what they meant.

Suddenly the steel table beneath me jerked into motion. I held my breath for a moment—and then reconsidered, and risked one deep, slow inhalation to fill my lungs. You never knew when you might need air.

The golden patterns surrounded me, caressed me, penetrated me. For a moment I was an integral part of them, and nothing else in the universe mattered.

Then suddenly everything was gone, save my fear and my sweat and the cold touch of steel beneath my fingertips. We had left our world behind.

Hang on Tommy! I'm coming for you.

10

BLUE RIDGE MOUNTAINS
VIRGINIA

MOONLIGHT SHIMMERED ACROSS the polished wooden floor of the mountain cabin, mottled leaf-shadows dancing along the polished planks as the wind shifted outside. Had there been anyone present, he might have heard the soft chirping of crickets, their normally shrill song muted to a low musical throbbing by the thick plate glass. Almost peaceful. After that he might have heard a rustling overhead, the quick patter of animal feet across the roof, and a scratching sound at the top of the chimney. Then movement inside the chimney itself, and the sound of something slowly descending. Then a pause, and a dull thunk as the metal flue opened.

A large raccoon dropped down into the fireplace.

It sat there for a moment, dark eyes alert, nose vibrating as it drank in the smells of the place. Then, when it had verified that the cabin was empty, it pushed past the fire screen and entered the living area.

It began to search. Not as an animal normally does, instinctively following scent cues to their source, but methodically, geometrically, studying every inch of the place with its piercing black eyes, lowering its nose to test any item that seemed out of place.

It paused at a side table and savored the trace aroma of hamburgers and french fries. A chicken nugget had fallen onto the floor when the table had been hurriedly cleaned. The raccoon glanced at it briefly, but otherwise showed no interest. It paused at the couch, its nose wrinkling as it drank in the traces of sweat, fear, and fire that clung to the crisp chintz.

It paused in each bedroom, tasting the human scents that lingered on the sheets.

It jumped up onto the dining room table and walked over to where two neatly folded papers were standing upright, tucked between a vase of artificial flowers and a marble napkin-holder. For a moment it cocked its head to one side, and a fanciful observer might have imagined that it was trying to read who they were addressed to.

Then, with small and dainty hands, it drew the papers out.

For Dad, said one.

For Evelyn Drake, said the other. *Currently in Manassas Hospital. Pls deliver. Tx!*

Opening the letters, the raccoon glanced briefly at their contents. Then it folded them again, took them in its mouth, and carried them back to the fireplace.

And up the chimney.

And out into the night.

Other than the chirping of crickets, the cabin was silent once more.

11

WHEN TOMMY'S MIND FINALLY CLEARED, he found himself in what appeared to be a prison cell. The narrow metal bed he was lying on was bolted to the floor. A toilet seat without a lid was in one corner, and a sink and shelf table were bolted to the wall near another. There was a narrow horizontal slit in one wall through which a sliver of sunlight was visible, but it was too high up for him see anything other than sky. The walls were made of stone, so he wasn't going to be breaking out that way any time soon. Ditto that note for the door, which was made of metal, with a mail slot in the center. The flap was on the outside.

He didn't know where he was.

He didn't know who had brought him there.

He didn't know what they wanted with him.

He *did* know he must have been drugged with something pretty powerful, probably hallucinogenic in nature. Crazy, disjointed visions from the night before were still reverberating in his mind: a soaring arch with crystals exploding from its surface, a corpse-like man who trailed ghosts in his wake, a glowing pattern of golden lines that filled the air all around him. It seemed to be slowly clearing out of his head now, but the real world was still a little hazy around the edges. Whatever drug they'd given him, it had been a doozy.

But that didn't explain what he'd seen *before* he was drugged. He remembered with unnerving clarity the moment when he'd looked into the face of his attacker and seen something other than human features. It was the kind of face that belonged in a fantasy game, not a teenager's bedroom. Was it possible that memory was real? He couldn't even consider it without trembling.

What the hell *was* that thing?

Suddenly he heard footsteps outside his door: dull and heavy, a man's stride. He levered himself up to a sitting position and then stood, trying not to look as anxious as he felt. His balance was a bit shaky, so he leaned against the bed frame to steady himself. As the door opened he drew in a deep breath, readying himself to run, or scream, or do whatever else the moment required.

Two men were visible in the doorway. One was tall and pale and wearing a knee-length black coat that buttoned up to the neck, like a priest's cassock. The other looked like a guard of some kind, and indeed, as the first man stepped into the room the second remained at the threshold, glaring at Tommy as if he expected some sort of trouble from him.

As his visitor came into the light Tommy gasped and backed away, until the stone wall at his back made it impossible to move any further.

The man wasn't human!

He had the same shape as a human being, and the same general arrangement of features, but there the resemblance ended. His eyes were too large for his head and they had slit pupils, like a cat's. His nose was tiny and he had almost no lips, which made the cat-eyes seem even larger by contrast. His skin was a strange mottled grey, and the fingers peeking out from the long arms of his coat were considerably longer than fingers should be.

Tommy recognized him. Not just from a thousand horror movies. This was what his kidnapper had looked like.

His heart pounding wildly, he felt a powerful urge to flee, but there was nowhere to go. "Who are you?" he demanded, trying to sound braver than he felt. "Why am I here?"

The creature looked at him curiously, as if Tommy was some strange kind of bug that had just crawled in the window, and he wanted to figure out what it was before he squashed it. "I am Alistair Wells, Master of the Guild of Obfuscates. I'm the one who ordered that you be brought here, and I'm the one who will ultimately determine your fate. So I suggest you do your best to remain on my good side."

The utter mundanity of the creature's name, combined with its quasi-British accent, threw Tommy completely off his guard. "What . . . what do you want?" he stammered.

"Ah. The cooperative approach." The creature nodded. "Very good."

He nodded to the guard, who closed the door from the outside. "I have an interest in your dreams, Mister Drake. If you would be so good as to describe some of them for me, I might find myself well-disposed toward you."

Tommy blinked in astonishment. "My dreams? That's what you want from me? My *dreams?*"

The grey man nodded. "Specifically, the ones that inspired several gaming modules you designed. Let's begin with *Demon World, The Seven-Fold Path,* and *Passage to Hell.* Please describe to me exactly which elements in those modules were inspired by your dreams and what the dreams themselves were like."

This is too friggin' surreal, Tommy thought. Here he'd suffered what seemed to be a genuine alien abduction, and all they wanted was to know about his dreams? What happened to prodding him with giant needles and stealing his bodily fluids? What made this even crazier was that it wasn't *his* dreams this guy was asking about; those three modules had been based on stories that Jesse had told him, about *her* dreams.

Oh.

Understanding hit him like a bucket of ice water.

Oh!

They wanted *Jesse's* dreams. That what this was all about! She'd told Tommy he could use them for his games if he claimed them as his own, so he'd done that, and now . . . holy crap.

They think I'm Jesse.

He started to talk, but very slowly. Forcing words out—any words—to buy himself time to think. The first thing he needed to do was confirm to this guy that they'd grabbed the right dreamer, to buy himself some time to evaluate the situation. So he started talking about his dreams, but he deliberately mixed up the details. Some bits were from Jesse's dreams, some from his own, and some was stuff he just made up on the spot. He did rip off a few ideas from World of Warcraft, but despite the fact that the grey man was the one who had brought up the subject of game modules, Tommy suspected he wasn't enough of a player to catch the references.

His captor listened to all of it with no change of expression, but Tommy could tell from the questions the grey guy asked which parts of the recitation interested him the most. And that was all stuff from Jesse's dreams. Tommy tested that theory out with a few more story twists, and soon there was no doubt about it: She was the dreamer they'd meant to kidnap, not him.

The revelation both elated and terrified him. Whatever they'd been planning to do to Jesse, it surely wouldn't accomplish their purpose to do it to him instead. So that was a good thing, right? Only here he was, trapped in this cell, and they couldn't just let him go now that he'd seen these aliens with undrugged eyes. So as soon as they realized that they'd made a mistake, and that he was of no possible use to them, they'd probably dispose of him. And so he struggled to sound useful, feeding the grey man the stories he seemed to want to hear, presenting each dream as his own.

After about a half hour of that the grey man finally held up a hand and said, "Enough for now." Which was a good thing, because at that point Tommy was mentally exhausted, and he was running out of dreams to talk about.

"Can I go home now?" he asked in his most plaintive naïve-little-boy voice. He was sure the answer would be *No,* but he figured that the more scared and helpless he looked, the less likely it was that this guy would think him capable of misleading anyone.

The huge cat-eyes fixed on him. "Not yet," their owner said, without a hint of emotion. *Not ever,* his eyes proclaimed. Then the alien called for the door to be opened, and he exited without further word, leaving Tommy alone with his thoughts, and his fears.

Enough for now. Did that mean that this guy would be coming back later, to hear more dream stories? If so, then Tommy would need to come up with some new ones, and fast. He would include details from Jesse's dreams to keep the grey man engaged, but mix in enough nonsense from gaming scenarios to make it hard for his captors to be sure which parts mattered. The longer they were uncertain, the longer they would need to keep Tommy around to feed them information.

Always keep them wanting more, he thought grimly.

He remembered a story he'd read once, about a princess whose husband wanted to behead her after their wedding night, but she had talked her way out of it. What was it called—1001 Nights? She told him a story that night but left off the ending, so he had to let her live another night to finish it. Then the next night, after she finished that story, she started a new one, which also had the ending missing. And again the next night. And the night after that. Eventually he just gave up on the whole beheading idea and let her live on as his wife. Happily ever after. True, it hadn't sounded like a very healthy marriage to Tommy, but who was he to judge?

He was pretty sure that his captors wouldn't give him a total reprieve like that. But as long as he kept telling stories they wanted to hear, they'd probably keep him around. And meanwhile, maybe Jesse would find him. Or someone else would. Or he'd figure out a way to get out of here by himself.

Lying back on his bed, trembling, he shut his eyes and began to weave suspense-filled fantasies in his head.

Hell, he thought dryly, *at least I'm playing to my strengths.*

12

YOU KNOW HOW YOU FEEL when you jump off a high diving board for the very first time? There you are, suspended in midair with nothing to hold on to, and suddenly it hits you just how far down the water really is, which you never really understood until that minute. You have this long, terrible moment where you're falling—just falling—and the whole world seems to slow down around you, so you have time to analyze every flaw in your diving technique and calculate just how bad the pain is going to be when you hit the water belly-first, because empty air doesn't offer any handholds and gravity doesn't allow do-overs.

Going through the archway was like that.

One minute I was lying like a corpse in my cloth-and-steel coffin, trying to ignore everything that was going on around me, and the next minute I was moving. The cavern floor that had seemed so smooth when I was walking on it turned out to be anything but, and a few times the gurney got jolted so badly I was afraid my backpack would come loose and fall to the floor.

Trust the duct tape, I told myself. *Trust the duct tape.* A mantra of serenity. *Trust the duct tape.*

Then strange patterns filled my head again, and this time they were ten times brighter than before. Glowing lines swept around me in seemingly chaotic abandon, but I could sense that there was a greater pattern to them, and that the pattern mattered. I tried not to think about what it could mean, for fear of getting so distracted that I would turn my head to look at some part of it.

We must have entered the archway then, because suddenly the ground was level and everything else was gone. Just gone. I'm not sure how I knew that, from under my sheet, or how I knew that there were a thousand different directions we could go in—a hundred thousand—and only one of them would bring us safely to the other side. Assuming there was anything on the other side that a Manassas gal would call *safe*. It was a terrifying ride, smooth on the outside but roller-coaster scary on the inside, and I had to fight not to reach out and grab the edges of my gurney, just to have something to hold on to.

And then, as quickly as it had begun, it was over. The gurney jolted as one of its wheels bumped into something solid. The sound of human voices—or maybe non-human voices—filled the air and the bits and pieces of conversation I overheard were so unexpectedly mundane that they served as an anchor, grounding my soul as the strange patterns faded from my mind.

Is this the last group for today?

Paula asked if you could take her shift.

No, I don't know when Sanderson will be finished. Why don't you just ask him yourself?

I was shaking pretty badly by that point, which was dangerous. I tried to hold my body rigid so that its trembling wouldn't be visible, but trembling doesn't work like that. Luckily no one was looking too closely.

There was a sudden jerk as my gurney started moving again. The floor was perfectly smooth, which at least told me that we were no longer in the cavern. Then the table stopped moving, and I heard other gurneys wheeled into position beside me, five in all. Footsteps moved away from us. Snatches of conversation fluttered about my head like anxious insects, then moved off into the distance and were gone.

Silence.

For the first time in what seemed like eternity, I dared to draw in a deep breath. My chest ached as clean-smelling air filled my lungs. I had the sudden crazy vision of a *Star Trek* landing party reporting back to Captain Kirk: *"The aliens breathe oxygen, sir."*

Then the lights went out.

I listened for a moment just to make sure no one was still around then pushed the sheet to one side and reached for my flashlight. But Rita got to hers first. We had been wheeled into a small room that looked like a storage closet of some kind. There were shelves on three sides of us, with boxes and piles of folded fabric and what looked like cleaning supplies. Not until we got to the doorway could we see what was outside.

It was a cavern, similar in form to the one we'd just left. But this one had been upgraded considerably. The central portion of the floor was covered with colorful tiling, and slatted benches were positioned at regular intervals along its periphery. The tunnel where the steel walkway had been was now framed with a decorative archway labeled "Victoria Passage," and further down were two smaller archways labeled with symbols I'd never seen before.

All it needed was a ticket booth and it could pass for Union Station.

"We need to get out of here," Rita said. I could hear fear rising in her voice. "I don't like being trapped underground on a good day, and throwing those Shadows into the mix doesn't make it better. Let's get out of this deathtrap first, then figure out what to do about Tommy." She looked at the arches. "We've got three options, so we can't just flip a coin. Unless someone packed D&D dice." She glanced at Devon.

"Four options," he corrected her. "Assuming this cavern really is the same as the one we left."

We took a few minutes to stow supplies from the closet under our sheets, creating what we hoped were reasonable simulacra of comatose bodies. Then we went searching among the formations to see if the crevice we'd come out of in our own cave existed in this one too. It did. Which at least answered the question of how we were going to get out of there without being seen.

Apparently the locals never used this crevice for anything, so they'd never bothered cleaning it out, which meant it was muddy as hell. And of course there was no neat brick path at the other end. Our former route was still in its natural state, which meant that much of it was covered in mud, some of it ankle-deep.

We sloshed and mucked and squelched our way through quasi-familiar chambers and tunnels, all too aware that we were leaving behind a trail of footprints deep enough for a blind man to follow. But what had seemed like a simple enough journey when following a brick path wasn't nearly as simple without one. Devon marked every turning point with his chalk, and one time we discovered that we had circled back to a previous mark. But eventually we managed to locate the place where a narrow tunnel cut up through the rock, leading to the surface.

There were no stairs this time, and no one had expanded the tunnel to facilitate climbing, but we were pretty damned determined, and nothing short of solid rock would have stopped us at that point. Eventually, we reached the surface, and we exited onto the grass one after the other, collapsing underneath a black sky filled with stars. For a handful of minutes we just lay there, utterly exhausted. Every muscle in my body ached, and the night wind chilled me through mud-soaked clothing as I took my first good look around.

The mountain behind us was familiar enough, but there was some kind of large building perched up on the crest. By the light of a slender moon we could make out the shape of a Victorian-style mansion, looming over the surrounding landscape like a hungry vulture. Anyone walking its ramparts would be able to see for miles in the moonlight . . . which meant that for as long as we were out in the open we were vulnerable. We had to find cover, and find it fast.

We started to walk. And we walked. And we walked. We came to a place where the trees were dense enough to shield us from observation, but that was too close, Devon said. Sooner or later the locals would discover our trick with the gurneys, and we had to be far enough away by then that a basic search of the area wouldn't find us. Much as it pained me to travel away from the place where my brother was most likely to be, I knew he was right. We'd be more use to Tommy if we weren't caught by a search team.

Sometime during the walk that followed, the last of my energy finally faded, and if not for Devon I don't think I could have kept going. He lifted my arm and wrapped it around his shoulders, encouraging me to lean on him. I put up a token protest, but I was grateful for the physical support; I don't know how long I could have gone on without it. The fire had been only a day ago, and the muddy trek out of the caverns had been exhausting. Fear can only sustain you for so long.

"We need rest," Rita said, voicing my thoughts.

At one point I caught her watching us. She turned away quickly when I looked in her direction but not quickly enough. I suddenly realized that I knew nothing about her relationship with Devon. They were such different people, I'd assumed they were just friends, strangers from opposites sides of the track who'd been drawn together by a common threat, and who had established a friendship of convenience. Which was pretty naïve of me, really. The world was full of lovers who had nothing in common. Playwrights wrote whole plays about them . . . and about their jealousy.

I kept a wary eye on her for the rest of the night, but she never looked my way again.

13

WHEN TOMMY WOKE UP in the morning, a fresh shirt and jeans were on the little table, along with a washcloth, sponge, and towel. He was genuinely grateful for the clothing; surely there was nothing more humiliating than being interrogated while wearing Star Wars pajamas. The bath supplies seemed kind of pointless as there was no bathtub in the room, but he took the hint and cleaned up the best he could by the sink.

Keep the kidnappers happy, right?

Soon after that he discovered the purpose of the mail slot, when a food tray came sliding through it. It had been a day since he'd eaten, so he devoured its offerings in record time. No sooner had he swallowed the last bite then he heard the steady rhythm of footsteps approaching his cell once more. This time there was a high pitched tap-tap sound in the mix. High heels, maybe? Sure enough, when the door opened he saw that the grey man had brought a woman with him, and she was ushered into the room with such an air of formality that Tommy guessed she must be a very important person.

She was a striking woman, and—to Tommy's relief—she appeared to be human. Her clothing was white, and it seemed to glow in the shadowy confines of the small room, drawing his eyes to her.

White silk blouse, white waistcoat, flowing white evening pants. Her face was pale gold, sun-kissed, with a hint of coral in her cheeks, and her blond hair was dressed up in a complex arrangements of coils and braids that must have taken a hairdresser hours to arrange. Her eyes shifted from grey-blue to grey-green as she looked around the room, and they might not have seemed remarkable on their own, but the thick bands of eyeliner that extended far past the outer corners of her eyes—black on top, gold on bottom—made her look like an ancient Egyptian queen.

"This is Her Ladyship Alia Morgana, Mistress of the Guild of Seers," the grey man announced. "You will cooperate with her in all that she requires."

The woman smiled; it seemed a well-rehearsed expression. "Tommy Drake, is it?" When he said nothing she asked, "Are you the dreamer?"

He flushed. "If you mean, am I the one who's been telling this guy all about my dreams? Yeah, I guess so."

"No," she said quietly. "That was not what I asked."

He felt a flutter of unease in his stomach. The woman's gaze made him feel like an insect pinned to a collection board. "I'm sorry, I'm not sure what the question is."

"On the contrary, Tommy. I think you are far sharper than this gentleman makes you out to be"—she nodded toward the grey man—"and I think you know exactly what I'm asking."

There were no safe words, so he said nothing.

She walked toward the bed and sat down on the end of it, then patted the mattress beside her. He shook his head quickly in refusal. He didn't want to get any closer to her than he had to.

"Do you know what it means to be a Seer, Tommy?"

"No, ma'am."

The grey man interrupted. "She is to be addressed as Your Ladyship, or Your Grace."

Tommy whispered "No, Your Grace."

"It means I know how to read people," the woman told him. "It means I can tell when they're lying to me, or even when they're just trying to hold something back. It means I can sense their emotions, so I know which questions make them afraid. Which ones they don't really want to answer. Do you understand what that means?"

He nodded miserably. What a fool he'd been, to think that he could have any kind of control over this situation! Never before had he felt so utterly helpless. And she knew it, too. She could read him like a book. He saw it in her eyes.

"Do you know why we're so interested in your dreams, Tommy?"

He shook his head.

"There are some people in the world who have special abilities. For example, I can sense a person's spiritual essence." She nodded toward the grey man. "Master Wells here can walk through a crowded room without anyone noticing him. We call them Gifts, and they come in many varieties. We try to identify the people who have such abilities while they're still young, so that we can arrange for them to have proper teachers."

Wary of where this was leading, Tommy nodded again.

"There is one very special ability that few people have mastered. Can you guess what that is?"

His throat was dry; it took effort to force the words out. "Something to do with dreams?"

"Exactly. That's why we watch for young people who have certain types of dreams, because it tells us that they may have this Gift." She paused. "Your dreams suggest you're one of those people, Tommy."

A tremor of foreboding ran through him. "I . . . I don't know anything about that. . . ."

"Well, you are only thirteen, so even if you had this Gift, it wouldn't be apparent for a few more years. We call it 'manifesting,' when a Gift first appears. Most people can't tell whether someone has a particular Gift until that happens. But a Seer can detect it much earlier. For instance, I can tell right now if you have the dreamer's Gift."

But I don't, he thought desperately. *Jesse's the one who has the special dreams. If anyone has this Gift it's her, not me.*

"There's no reason to be afraid, Tommy. You won't feel a thing. It'll be just like when someone looks at you from across the street. That doesn't hurt at all, does it? Except that I'll be looking at the inside of you, instead of the outside." She paused. "It will be much easier if you cooperate with me. That's why I've told you all this, you see. In the hopes that you'll understand the value of this examination, and cooperate."

He tried to swallow the lump that was in his throat. "What . . . what do you want me to do?"

She smiled. "Just relax. Think about dreams you've had in the past. Think about how much you'd like to understand them better. How much you'd like me to help you with that."

But I don't want you to help me, he thought. And for one crazy moment he thought about trying to fight her off. But he had no clue how to do that, and he was pretty sure that even if he tried, she'd blow away his best effort in a heartbeat.

He was doomed. Totally, painfully, irrevocably doomed.

Maybe if I cooperate, they'll be less angry at me when they find out the truth.

Biting his lip so hard he nearly drew blood, he nodded.

She told him to lie down, but he was way too nervous for that, so they settled for him leaning against the wall. *Shut your eyes, now. Take deep breaths. Imagine a pleasant dream you once had . . .* Her voice was hypnotic, compelling. He couldn't have resisted her if he'd wanted to.

It seemed to him that he fell asleep for a moment. When he opened his eyes again it took effort to focus them; everything was blurry.

And then her eyes came into focus, and he saw what was in them: She knew.

She *knew.*

So much for his secret. So much for his kidnappers' thinking he was useful. So much for them having any further reason to keep him alive.

"Well?" said the grey man, somewhat impatiently. "What's the verdict? Is he a dreamwalker?"

Tommy shut his eyes, bracing himself for the storm that was about to break over him.

"It appears so," the Seer said.

His eyes shot open. *What the hell—?*

"Which means he has the potential, nothing more. Whether that Gift will ever fully manifest is something no Seer can tell you. We can only read the potential of a soul; its true destiny is always in flux."

She stood up and smoothed the creases out of her white pants. "Keep him under observation for now. Have him record all his dreams. We still have much to learn about how this Gift works. He can help us."

Her grey eyes fixed on Tommy. "You'll cooperate with Master Wells, won't you? In whatever he asks you to do?"

Dazed, he nodded.

Without further word the two visitors turned and exited the room. The steel door closed behind them, and Tommy heard the heavy lock slide into place. He was alone once more.

He didn't move. He just sat there, stunned. Something subtle and complicated had just happened, but he lacked the mental resources—or perhaps the experience—to interpret it.

At least I'm safe for now, he comforted himself. They would have to keep him alive if they wanted a record of his dreams, right? By giving that order, the woman in white had probably saved his life.

But then he remembered how she had looked at him, right after her examination. The clear and certain knowledge in her eyes. He wasn't the dreamer they'd been searching for, and she knew it.

Why did you lie for me? he wondered.

⸬⸬⸬⸬⸬⸬

"Tea, your Grace?"

"Please."

Wells waved to his menial, who went to the sideboard and filled two cups, straining out the tea leaves as she poured. As she stirred sugar into one of the cups, she looked at the Seer and made a hand signal: *Instructions?*

"Just one, please."

A minute later Alia Morgana was handed a cup of tea with a biscuit neatly tucked beside it. She lifted the porcelain cup from the saucer and sipped from it delicately as the servant withdrew. "How delicious, Master Wells! Some sort of Darjeeling?"

Wells nodded. "From Terra Marcella. Spring rains are unusually constant there; it makes for a unique bouquet."

"You will have to let me know next time a shipment comes in." She smiled pleasantly. "Provided your Guild doesn't keep it all for themselves."

Wells chuckled softly. "There's a limit to how much tea one Guild can drink, your Grace. I'm sure we can set aside a few leaves for you."

They drank their tea in companionable silence for a few moments. Finally the Seer put her cup aside and said, "The boy needs to die, you know that."

The grey man sipped from his own teacup without responding.

"I realize there are things we could learn from him, but his Gift is too dangerous to have around. Whole cities have been destroyed by it in the past. That's why we kill all potential dreamers as soon as they're born, rather than waiting to see if the Gift will manifest. The risk is just too high."

"I'm aware of the culling," Wells said, "but aren't you exaggerating the risk just a tad?"

She leaned forward in her chair; her gaze was intense. "When this particular Gift manifests, the first thing it does is drive its host mad. Then it spreads that madness to everyone in the surrounding area, through their dreams. And yes, we have records of whole populations succumbing. Prosperous cities falling to chaos, all because of one so-called *dreamwalker* in their midst." She leaned back in her chair again. Her expression was as controlled as ever, but something hard and cold flashed in her eyes. "That's the reason we eradicated them centuries ago. That's the reason that now, any time we find a child with the potential for that Gift, we remove him from the gene pool. Immediately. No matter what world he was born on, or who his parents were. There are no exceptions."

"Except that this one got past you," he pointed out.

"Since we can't stand guard over every birth on every human world," she said irritably, "there's always the chance that will happen. We deal with such children when we find them."

"But this one's only thirteen. You said yourself it would be a few years before his Gift matured. The matter hardly seems urgent."

"That's what I said to *him*, Master Wells. In truth, we know very little about how this Gift manifests—only that once it does the madness comes on quickly and consumes every mind in its vicinity." A delicately painted eyebrow arched upward. "So what is it you want this boy for, that's worth risking a whole city?"

"Not me. The Shadows want him. I'm to send him to the Crest tomorrow."

She drew in a sharp breath. "That is . . . very foolish of them."

"Take it up with Guildmaster Virilian, then. It's his call." A faint smile twitched across his thin lips. "I hear he welcomes constructive criticism."

She snorted delicately. "He might well do so, once his precious Shadows start going mad."

"As opposed to their normal state?" He chuckled softly. "Remember, we're talking about certifiably insane people here. If you can even call them people. One wonders if a dreamwalker's influence would even be noticed in such crowd."

"Madmen in charge of all the human worlds," she mused. "Or at least the passage between them. How did we allow ourselves to be brought to such a pass?"

Wells shrugged. "No one but a madman would be willing to do what they do. And our own Guilds profit handsomely enough from the arrangement, so we're hardly ones to complain." He gazed at her in silence for a moment, as the fleeting spark of humor faded from his eyes. "Rumor has it—rumor, mind you—that the Shadows suspect the boy isn't from Terra Colonna at all. They think someone from our world may have planted him there. Now that you've confirmed their suspicions about his Gift, they'll want to get enough information out of him to identify the guilty party."

The startled look on the Seer's face morphed quickly into one of suspicion. "Why in all the worlds would anyone do that? There'd be no mercy shown if such treachery were ever discovered. The fury of all the Guilds would come down on their heads."

"That's the big question, isn't it? Unfortunately I'm not on His Lordship's need-to-know list, so I can't help you answer it. All I know is, tomorrow I'm supposed to deliver the boy to the Shadows, then he's their problem, not mine." He nodded. "I will deliver your warning to His Lordship, though . . . for what little good it will do."

Getting up from his chair, he headed over to the sidebar. "This kind of talk calls for a drink. Can I get you something, Your Grace? Scotch, perhaps?" He lifted up a bottle to show her the label. "I've got some thirty-year-old from Terra Nkosi."

"Please." She smiled. "I remember that world fondly. They did produce good scotch. And very fine cocoa." She sighed as he handed her a glass. "Too bad about the asteroid, though."

"Indeed. That one was a little too close for comfort." He raised his own glass in a toast. "Death to all dreamwalkers?"

"Death to all dreamwalkers," she agreed.

It was indeed very good scotch.

14

BLUE RIDGE MOUNTAINS
VIRGINIA PRIME

I DON'T KNOW HOW LONG we walked that night. Blindly we staggered through the darkness, fleeing enemies whose powers and motives we could not begin to guess. We didn't even know where we were, in the larger sense. Parallel universe? Alternate timestream? Somewhere in the *Twilight Zone*? It's not like there were maps for this kind of thing.

All we knew for sure was that we couldn't head back to where we'd left the car, because that would require passing by the entrance to the caverns again. Way too risky. Not that we expected the car to actually be there, mind you, but when you're cast adrift in a strange universe, you grasp at any straw.

Since all the known dangers were north of us, we headed south. Once we found a safe place to rest we could discuss more concrete plans. But the terrain was rough and it took us a while to locate a promising campsite. By the time we found a flat bit of ground comfortably far from the vulture citadel, even Devon seemed to have exhausted his final reserves of energy.

It had been a long night.

We made our camp there, heedless of any lesser dangers nature might throw at us. Which, when you didn't have tents, blankets, or any other camping supplies, pretty much meant pushing together a pile of vegetation—living and dead—and going to sleep on it. Fortunately it was summer, which meant that no blankets were needed. We were so exhausted that we probably could have slept on naked rock.

As to the details of our sleeping arrangements, that was another matter. I don't think I was imagining the looks that were going back and forth between Devon and Rita as we picked out our spots, or the sense of unresolved tension in the air. For a while it looked like Devon would settle down very close to me, and I found myself hoping for that. (Because his stable presence was so comforting, I told myself.) But after a glance at Rita, he wound up making his bed on the opposite side of the campsite, as far away from me as a person could possibly get. Which was, in its own way, a pretty powerful statement of interest.

Be careful, I cautioned myself. *This three-way partnership is fragile. Don't do anything that might upset it.*

We arranged for a watch schedule. I don't remember who was supposed to go first, but whoever it was failed to stay awake, and no one else took over.

A small and furry creature sniffed my nose just as I drifted off. I muttered something incoherent along the lines of *Please don't eat my face,* and then I was gone.

⸺⸺⸺

The morning sun was comfortingly yellow, and there was only one of it, so that much was good.

As we slowly got up from our leafy beds, I took mental stock of the situation. I couldn't speak for the others, but the previous night was mostly a blur to me at that point. I tried to sort out the details in my mind as best I could, but some of them defied rational analysis.

At one point I asked, "You don't think that guy in the cave was really undead, do you?"

Rita shrugged. "He *looked* undead. And someone *called* him undead. Who really knows?"

Devon winced as he rubbed a knotted muscle in his neck. "I was hoping someone would tell me I'd dreamed that part."

We shared a meager breakfast of bottled water and breakfast bars, and then Rita and I went off into the woods to find a private spot where we could fertilize the trees. Yeah, I know, it's when the girls go off alone to pee that the serial killer always attacks . . . but it wasn't like there was any real alternative. A girl's gotta do what a girl's gotta do.

On the way back I added clean underwear to the list of things to pack next time I went rushing off into an alien world.

"So what's the goal here?" Devon asked. "Do we have a more concrete objective than just 'running away'? Not that I have an issue with that as a general guideline, mind you."

"Find out where we are," Rita said. "Figure out exactly what that gate is, and how it works, so we can get back home when we want to. Figure out why people from this world are coming across to ours and killing our friends and family. Because until we find a way to stop that, there's no point in going home."

"Find my brother," I reminded them.

Devon nodded. "It sounded like the Shadows are the ones who took him. Any idea why they would do that?"

That's the million dollar question, isn't it? "Maybe he heard something he shouldn't have. I can see that if stories from this place ever made it into his gaming circuit they'd spread like wildfire. Maybe they want to use him to track down the source of a leak."

"Well," Rita said, "if the Shadows want information from him, they'll keep him alive until they get it."

Yeah, I thought darkly, *but what are the odds they're just going to ask for it nicely?* History was full of tales of the kinds of horrific tortures that people used to get information or to enforce obedience. Or sometimes just because they thought a display of ruthless ferocity would make them look good. And that was *human* society—now we had *inhuman* motives to consider.

But with all that said, there was a spark of hope within me that refused to die. Because my little brother wasn't stupid. Crazy, yes, and game-obsessed, and half a dozen other adjectives that might be delivered with disdain, but never stupid. And twisted stories in which supernatural creatures with unknown powers were threatening to kill him, and he had to solve convoluted mental puzzles in order to stay alive, were second nature to him. If any kid could stay afloat in this crazy situation, it was Tommy.

"What we need right now," Devon said, "is information. Which we're not going to get by hanging out here in the woods. As I see it, we have a choice between going back the way we came—not my personal preference—or finding some locals to talk to. Since it's unlikely we can gather information without that."

I shuddered at the suggestion we talk to anyone. I didn't want to interact with this world any more than I had to. But in my gut I knew he was right. We couldn't just run around blindly, hoping to trip over Tommy.

He pulled out his iPhone and turned it on. I gaped in astonishment as one of his maps appeared on the screen. "You have *reception* here?"

"No," he said calmly. "I have maps that I cached when there *was* reception. Since I figured once we entered the caverns there wouldn't be." He thumbed through several screens' worth of data. "Looks like Luray is only a few miles south of us. Assuming it even exists in this world. That seems the most likely place to find people." He hesitated. "Not to mention the best chance to lose ourselves in a crowd."

Just in case someone comes looking for us, I thought darkly. None of us really had a clue what would happen when the Shadows figured out that we'd snuck into their world, or how much they would care about coming after us, but we needed to prepare for the worst.

We packed up our half empty water bottles and extra energy bars, took one last look at the vulture citadel as we left the shelter of the trees—it was marginally less ominous by daylight—and then shouldered our packs and headed resolutely south.

15

THE SKINNY MAN walked through the halls of the Shadows' citadel with a catlike tread, toe-balanced and silent. His features
were lean and angular, and his eyes were focused straight ahead with
predatory intensity, unblinking. The scents of the forest clung to his skin
and trailed in his wake down the hallway: pine trees, musk, and decay.
They seemed to be natural scents, rather than something acquired.

A person who crossed his path at that moment might have jumped
back in fright, sensing the animal essence in him before the human
essence was apparent. Such a reaction would not be wholly inappro-
priate or unwise.

At the man's side walked a wolf. It was taller by half than the normal specimen, and as lean and angular as the man was. It didn't look
at all pleased to be in such an enclosed space, and now and then it
growled softly in the back of its throat, but when that happened the
man would reach out and stroke its hackles, causing it to subside into
a sullen but wary silence.

A casual observer might have said that the two of them were
walking in lockstep. A more savvy observer might note that there was
no way a man and a wolf really could do that, given their anatomy, but
the impression of it was strong.

At last they reached their destination. A man was waiting for them there, dressed in the livery of an *umbra mina*. The skinny man nodded his head slightly in respect. The wolf, out of respect, did not eat him.

"He's waiting for you," the Shadow said. He opened a pair of heavy wooden doors with the symbols of a hundred worlds emblazoned on them, and ushered them inside.

The chamber beyond the doors was immense, with a vast open space in its center. The audience chambers of the *umbrae majae* were always like that. Visitors generally wanted to keep space between them and the scent of death.

At the far end of the room the Guildmaster of Shadows waited. The skinny man walked toward him, heedless of the ghostly voices that whispered on all sides. The wolf's hackles rose and it growled a bit more loudly, but it stayed by his side.

The Shadowlord waited until the skinny man approached within normal speaking distance. It was something few men would do voluntarily "I'm told you have news for me."

The skinny man took two pieces of folded paper from his pocket and handed them over. The Shadow opened them and read.

"Jessica. Jessica Drake." He looked at his visitor. "This is the matter from Terra Colonna? The changeling problem?"

"Aye, Master Virilian."

His eyes narrowed. "This is the girl you supposedly killed?"

"The girl the Greys tried to kill," the skinny man corrected testily. "If I'd done the job she'd be dead."

"So instead she is . . . where?"

He indicated the notes in the Shadowlord's hand. "The letters they left behind suggest they were headed toward the Gate. Three empty trolleys have been found on our side. So logic suggests they came over with the last set of transfers."

"Indeed." The Shadow's displeasure was an ice-edged razor. "The Greys' security is unimpressive."

"So it would seem, Your Lordship." He paused. "They offered me a bribe not to report this."

"Of course they did. Of course they did." The Shadow looked down at the letters again; his expression was thoughtful. "And you took the bribe and promised them secrecy. How fortunate, then, that I discovered the truth by other means."

The skinny man bowed his head. "You are a wise and insightful man, Your Lordship."

"I have loyal servants. That is every bit as important as wisdom." He indicated the letters. "You said there were three trolleys found. I see only two notes. Who was on the third?"

"We don't know that yet, Your Lordship. Probably another changeling. There's evidence some of them were working together right before the Cleansing began."

"Yesss . . ." The word ended in a cold hiss. "A Cleansing that should have begun long ago. The Greys will pay for the delay."

The skinny man said nothing.

"You say they came across on the gurneys. Does this mean you have their scent?"

The skinny man hesitated. "Regretfully, Your Lordship, no. By the time I was informed about the situation the gurneys had been cleaned, and new bodies placed on them. The scents we need could no longer be isolated." The corner of his mouth twitched; a faint note of scorn crept into his voice. "No doubt the Greys were concerned that if their error was discovered it might distract you from more important concerns. They are very loyal and hardworking creatures, Your Lordship."

"Indeed," the Shadow said dryly. "I must remember to praise them as they deserve."

The skinny man's smile bared teeth that had been filed to sharp points, making him seem as feral as the wolf by his side. "There are other ways to hunt, Your Lordship."

The Shadow nodded sharply. "Then do so. Track down these invaders, kill them, and bring me back the bodies so I can personally verify their deaths. It shouldn't be too hard a task. They're primitive creatures from an unenlightened world, and they lack the knowledge

they need to survive here, much less hide themselves so well that that
the Guild of Soulriders can't find them."

The skinny man's eyebrow raised slightly. "I thought you needed
the girl for something."

"We have her brother. He's the one that matters." The Shadowlord waved a hand dismissively. "Kill her, kill any changelings who are
with her, kill anyone who tries to protect them. You have my full
sanction."

"You don't think the Lord Governor will have issue with that?"

The Shadow scowled. "No mere *politician* would dare contest my
orders. Not when the prosperity of his city depends upon the commerce that flows through my Gate." He nodded sharply toward the
door. "Go. Now. Bring me news. And bodies."

The skinny man bowed his head deeply. "Yes, Your Lordship."

"Meanwhile . . ." The Shadow's expression darkened. Given what
it had looked like to begin with, the result was uniquely disquieting.
"I will deal with the Greys," he promised.

16

WE DECIDED TO KEEP TO THE WOODS, though that meant climbing up and down some hills along the way. We all agreed that we didn't want to come out into the open until there were more people around, at which point it would be harder for observers in the looming citadel to pick us out. But really, I think that we just didn't want to walk to where Route 340 was supposed to be, and find out it wasn't there. We all had this visceral need to pretend things were normal for as long as we could, and staying away from familiar landmarks helped us do that.

At one point we came to a narrow stream, and we all bathed. Not in the normal sense of the word but full immersion, clothes and all. We figured we were better off looking like drowned rats than covered in flaking mud. We ate some more energy bars and continued on. Soon the slope grew much steeper, and the going became more difficult. Devon brought out his cached maps and assured us that this ridge was the last major obstacle before we reached Luray. Once we got to the top, we should have a good view of the city, he said. So we climbed with newfound energy.

But when we finally reached the crest, gasping for breath from the last steep bit of climbing, we looked out over the valley and . . . well, like I said, this wasn't our world.

Apparently Luray was so expansive here that it had extended civic tendrils up and down the Shenandoah Valley, swallowing up all the peaceful little towns nearby, turning them into tightly packed suburbs. From our hillside perch we could see the heart of the city to the south of us, and it looked as crowded and congested as any urban jungle, its narrow, twisting streets running like rat burrows between looming walls of brick and concrete. There were a few green islands here and there in the urban sea, great mansions with trees and grassy lawns surrounding them, with walls or tall fences to protect them from the rest of the city. One had a slender tower several stories high, with an observation deck running around the top. From it, one would be able to see most of the city. The streets surrounding each mansion radiated outward like the spokes of a spider's web, with wealthier residences spaced along them at neat and perfect intervals . . . until those streets collided with the pattern radiating from some other mansion, and the whole pattern devolved into chaos.

I wondered if the urban planners responsible for this place had helped L'Enfant design Washington DC.

On the outskirts of town the houses thinned out, and wherever a rising slope rendered the ground so inhospitable that only the poor would live there, I saw shantytowns, crowded with shacks precariously constructed from cast-off wood and bits of rusted metal. I'd seen such things in movies, of course, but usually in a Third World setting. Never had I stood this close to so much poverty.

Nothing in the view looked so drastically unfamiliar that it should have made my skin crawl, and yet crawl it did. There was something wrong here; I sensed it viscerally but couldn't identify the cause. Something made the place seem utterly alien to me, despite the fact that many of its streets looked so mundane that they could have been set down in Manassas without drawing notice. Devon was the one who finally gave it a name.

"There are no cars," he said quietly.

I realized with a start that he was right. There were houses, shopping plazas, parks, and even playgrounds, all so very familiar in form . . . but nowhere was there a single car, or truck, or gas station, or even a paved road with lines down the center. I did see a railroad track running north-south, right where Route 340 should have been, and there were boats on the river, albeit small ones. So it wasn't like there were no transportation vehicles. Cars were the only thing missing. I shook my head, unable to make sense of it all.

Then Rita gasped and pointed skyward. I shielded my eyes against the sun and followed her gesture to where a bullet-shaped silver object was edging its way over the mountain ridge west of the city. It was coming in low over the trees and seemed to be headed for a tower on the far side of the river.

"Is that a blimp?" I asked.

"I think it's a zeppelin," Devon offered.

"Jesus." Rita shook her head. "This place is seriously screwy."

Understatement of the day.

We began to climb carefully down the steep, rocky slope. Along the way we had to surrender our view of the city as the trees closed over our heads, but it was worth it to have cover again. Soon enough we would be out in the open, and I was already feeling exposed and vulnerable.

About halfway down the hillside we came to a sudden steep drop, twenty feet of sheer rock that stretched in both directions as far as the eye could see. We started looking for the best way to hike down and were so focused on that task that it took us a few minutes to realize there was some kind of encampment at the base.

Twenty, maybe thirty, ramshackle shelters had been jury-rigged from tree branches, ragged blankets, and trash. It took no great insight to recognize it as a transient camp for the homeless; the architecture of despair didn't differ much from world to world. And though I recognized what the camp was, it felt, once more, strangely alien. I squinted as I tried to make out enough detail to figure out why.

And suddenly it came to me.

There was no plastic. No strips of tarp had been used to rainproof the tents, no sheets of corrugated roofing had served as construction materials, no plastic bottles had even been used to haul water to the site. Even the piles of trash at one end of the camp had no plastic in them. Not even those ubiquitous six-pack holders you're supposed to slice open so wildlife can't get their heads stuck in the holes. Nothing.

Suddenly a small figure emerged from one of the tents. Startled, we all froze, praying that he hadn't seen us. He was small and dark and hunched over, and at first glance I wasn't even sure he was human. At first he seemed wary, even afraid, but when he saw there was no immediate danger nearby he straightened up to his full height, and I realized that he was indeed human . . . assuming your definition of that word is a bit flexible.

He wasn't much taller than Tommy, and the combination of narrow shoulders and a thick torso gave him an ungainly aspect. Everything about him seemed just slightly off: arms too long, skin too hairy, feet not arched quite right. His toes dug into the ground as he walked in that odd way they do when you're trying to hold a thong sandal in place, making his gait awkward. As for his face, I realized that I'd seen the type before, though not on a living person. Jutting brows, arched cheekbones, heavy jaw . . . it was hard to deny what that all added up to. Or accept that a world so similar to mine would have such a creature walking around in it.

Rita whispered, "*Planet of the Apes,* anyone?"

"Early hominid," Devon whispered back. "The kind that died out hundreds of thousands of years ago." He paused, then said with less certainty, "At least that's what it looks like."

Whatever species the man was, his large, protruding ears had evidently caught wind of our conversation. Fear flared in his eyes as he scanned the landscape anxiously, searching for its source. We ducked low behind a fallen tree as he looked our way, and stayed down until we heard him moving around again. Then we heard even more movement coming from the camp, and we peeked gingerly over the top of the tree trunk to see what was happening about.

Several other hominids had joined the first one. They were all of the same body type, though some had more human-looking features than others. Their clothing was simple: either a sleeveless shift of some heavy natural fabric, or else a shirt or dress of more complicated construction, with its sleeves torn off. The loose garments hid all the body parts I would normally have used to determine gender, so it was hard to pick out the men from the women, other than by size. Nobody was wearing anything akin to pants. Or shoes, for that matter.

I was about to turn to Devon and risk another whispered comment when suddenly there was a loud cracking sound from downhill. The hominids froze like deer in headlights. The primitive fear in their eyes was a terrible thing to witness. They started running. Not in any organized way, as in running *to* or *from* something in particular. Raw animal panic had taken over, and they simply ran. You could smell fear in the air. But it was too late for them to flee.

A moment before there had been no other people on the mountainside; now, suddenly, there were men on all sides of the camp. Three teams of soldiers in mottled green uniforms—clearly some kind of camouflage—moved in from the east, west, and south, leaving only our steep escarpment unaccounted for. Several of the hominids actually tried to scramble up the cliff in sheer panic, but by the time they managed to find good handholds the soldiers were upon them, and they pulled them back with enough force to send their bodies reeling to the ground. I heard a sickening thud as one of the hominids hit his forehead on a rock, and a trickle of blood seeped out from beneath his hair as he lay still upon the dirt.

Some of the soldiers had drawn sabers, but the majority were carrying a weapon I'd never seen before. It looked like a crossbow, but rigged to fire small spheres instead of bolts. I watched as one man fired at a couple of the fleeing hominids. Halfway to its target the sphere broke apart in mid-air, dividing up into slices that shot out in all directions. As the slices fell to the ground the hominids fell also, and they began to thrash desperately, like rabbits in a snare. It took me a few seconds to realize that a fine net had entangled them.

I felt a cold sickness growing in the pit of my stomach as I realized what was happening.

Very few of the hominids tried to fight back. Maybe they felt it
was a lost cause. Those who did try were ruthlessly cut down. They
had no weapons and no defense other than flight, so killing them was
easy. At one point the scene got so bloody that I had to look away.
Devon put an arm around me and drew me close to him, letting me
bury my face in his chest. I could feel him trembling deep inside, but
his expression was steady, and his arm around me was strong and
comforting. Always the brave one.

And then, as quickly as the raid had begun, it was over. The hominids trapped in the nets were untangled and brought together in the
center of camp, where thick steel collars were locked around their
necks. Each collar was connected to a heavy chain, and you didn't have
to be a professor of American History to recognize what was going on.

As the bulk of the soldiers started to lead the long chain of cap-
tives down the mountainside, you could see just how defeated the
small hominids were. Their lanky arms hung low about their legs as
their backs bowed in defeat, and they were so submissive in aspect—so
spiritually broken—that the leather whip one of the soldiers carried
hardly had to be used at all. Meanwhile a few soldiers who had remained behind gathered up all the hominids' abandoned possessions.
Blankets, food, clothing, and whatever pitiful tools or mementos they
might once have treasured: all went into the central fire pit, covered
over with handfuls of dry leaves and clumps of dead grass. And the
bodies that had fallen in battle were thrown on top of all that, like
they were just more pieces of garbage. Then one of the soldiers started
walking around the fire pit, lighting matches one by one and throwing
them onto the pile. Some of them landed on clumps of dried vegetation, and fire spread quickly from there. Within minutes the pit was
filled with roaring flames, and the sickening smell of burning wool
and roasting flesh enveloped us along with the smoke. Eyes tearing,
we had no option but to keep our heads low and try not to cough; we
didn't dare leave our cover to try to get out of the way.

After a while the fire died down. The soldiers prodded it a few last times, then kicked some dirt over the glowing ashes and left. Tendrils of smoke were still rising from the center of the mound, but even they died down as the final embers slowly turned to ash.

With shaking hands we took bottles of water and tried to wash the taste of ash and burning flesh out of our mouths. Which is when my stomach decided it had finally had enough, and I leaned over the edge of the escarpment and vomited. Afterward, I just lay there, drained, my body draped over the dead tree, too exhausted by emotion even to cry.

"We need to wait here for a while." Devon's voice sounded hollow, like it was coming from far away. "We need to give them time to put distance between us."

No one felt like arguing with him.

"Why does this stuff scare me more than the undead guy?" I whispered hoarsely. "More than the gate, and the aliens, all of it . . ."

"Because none of that connected to you emotionally," Rita said. "It all felt like a fantasy. A dream. This—this was *real*. People used to do this in our world. In some places, they still do. Our own ancestors probably—"

She stopped herself suddenly and glanced at Devon. For the first time since meeting him I was aware of the color of his skin as something more than pigmentation, and I didn't know quite how to deal with that. My ancestors had been among the *huddled masses yearning to be free*, for whom America had been a precious dream, a place of hope. While for Devon's ancestors the journey had been the end of freedom.

I took his hand, and I held it, and I know from the way he squeezed my fingers back that it was the right gesture at the right moment.

We gave the soldiers enough time to march their line of slaves down the mountainside, and then some more time than that, just to be sure—after which, we rose unsteadily and started moving downhill again.

‖‖‖‖‖‖‖‖‖‖

We reached one of the poorer districts of Luray first. Our presence raised more than a few eyebrows, and at first we thought it was our clothing. My jeans had seemed pretty basic back home, but the slim cut and embroidered pocket details made them stand out like a sore thumb here. Rita had on cargo pants with a zillion pockets, and there was nothing remotely like them that we could see. As for Devon, whatever subtle elements had made his normal clothes look expensive back home were ten times more conspicuous in this environment. A business man in an Armani suit driving down the street in a Rolls Royce couldn't have appeared more out of place than he did.

So, after deciding that Devon and I had no clue about how to steal laundry from clotheslines without getting caught—a pretty accurate appraisal—Rita pilfered new wardrobes for all three of us. Simple woven shirts and loose denim pants, not stylish but comfortable. We found a narrow alley in which to change our clothes, each of us taking a turn at guarding the entrance. Rita had grabbed a few dingy sheets for us, too, so we wrapped up our backpacks hobo-style to disguise them, then shoved our original clothes inside.

But when we got back on the street, we realized we had a bigger problem than clothing.

Back home in the DC suburbs there was so much ethnic diversity that you just took it for granted. Last year in English class I'd had a Korean kid sitting to my right, a Somali kid to my left, and the class as a whole could have hosted World Culture Day without needing to import anyone. After a while you just stopped noticing that kind of thing. Rita and Devon came from similar settings, and they didn't notice either.

But this place didn't have any Korean, Vietnamese, Pakistani, or African kids running around.

Special stress on the *African*.

No one in sight was black except for Devon. And he was pretty aggressively black, not some coffee-and-cream biracial who could pass for a suntanned white guy. Add to that the fact that he towered over most of the local kids, and it was damned hard not to notice him. Which meant that while we were with him, we were all damned hard to overlook.

None of us dared say anything about that. Such a conversation would have inevitably led to the question none of us wanted to ask out loud: *What if the hominids are the only people here with dark skin? What if the locals are staring at Devon not just because he looks different, but because they think he's one of them?* Instead we just hiked on in silence, our makeshift packs slung over our shoulders. You could feel Devon's anxiety radiating from his body like a heat wave, but we knew there was nothing we could do about that, so we didn't try. Sometimes silence is best.

Eventually the wretched slums gave way to the city proper, and we began to see more familiar features: glass storefronts, street vendors hawking their wares, even a few small parks tucked between tall brick houses. There were beggars all over the place, and most of them seemed to be children. Dirty, ragged children, all different ages, weaving in and out of the crowd in search of a brief sympathetic nod and a handout. Some looked injured, and they huddled against the brick walls of apartment buildings, tin cups in front of them, begging for charity with their eyes. I tried not to think about whether their injuries were real or feigned, or maybe imposed upon them by someone who would take a cut of their profits later that night. It wasn't the kind of thing that a Manassas teenager normally had to deal with, but I knew that it happened.

There were horses moving up and down the streets; apparently that was the favored means of transportation in this place. Most were hitched to some kind of wagon or carriage, and the resulting traffic was pretty chaotic; at times it was hard to cross the street without getting trampled. Evidently the locals were used to it, because we saw kids dash across the street without sparing a glance either way to see what was coming at them. I wondered how many of them got trampled each day.

Devon—font of trivia that he was—noted that there were no horse droppings in the streets. As he started to explain why that was significant, we spotted a small dark-skinned figure coming down the street toward us. One of the hominids. He was dressed more neatly than the ones we'd seen in the woods, but otherwise his appearance was much the same. He walked with his eyes cast downward, quickly scurrying out of the path of any larger person headed toward him. I could sense Devon stiffen by my side as he watched the ballet of submission, but he said nothing. Ultimately the hominid ducked into a butcher shop, and we lost sight of him.

There were fruit stands all around us and a sausage stand at the end of one block, so the air was filled with luscious and inviting smells. After a day of eating nothing but energy bars, it made my stomach growl. But with all the street urchins running around, the outdoor vendors were watching their wares like hawks, and I didn't see how we were going to manage to take anything. I started to go through a mental list of my supplies, wondering if I had anything I could barter for food, when Rita nudged me from behind. "You two go over there," she said, pointing to a café halfway down the block. "Hand in hand. Then kiss." She pushed us gently forward. "Make it look good," she urged.

I hesitated, then I thought, *what the hell,* and I caught up Devon's hand, and we both started to walk to the spot she'd indicated. But when we reached the café I was suddenly so embarrassed I couldn't look him in the eye. But he touched a finger softly under my chin and tipped my face up, until my eyes met his. Such gentle eyes! There was a touch of humor in them, like he knew just how awkward this moment was, and it was okay if we laughed about it together. There was also a touch of gravity in them as well, because we were lost in a strange world, and we were all more scared than we were going to admit. But that was okay, too, as long as we faced that fear together. So I closed my eyes, went up on tip-toe, and kissed him.

I hadn't kissed a lot of boys in my life. I certainly had never kissed anyone who made my heart speed up the way he did, or who made my legs tremble so much that I had to put a hand on his chest to steady myself. Maybe the kiss wasn't objectively that great, and it was just the power of that *two-lost-souls-connecting* moment . . . but for whatever reason, it shook me to the core of my soul.

You could feel that every eye in the place was on us—mostly because of Devon—but I didn't care. It no longer mattered who was standing around us, or what world we were on, or anything else. The really great kisses of the world are like that.

"Jeez, guys." Rita's voice was pitched too low for anyone else to hear it. "Get a room."

Startled and embarrassed, we quickly broke apart. She put a hand on each of our shoulders and pushed us gently forward. "To the corner, then turn right." She seemed to have some kind of plan in mind, and we didn't, so we obeyed. Then she had us go another short block and make another turn, and we had gone far enough from her, and we stopped.

We had reached a pretty quiet street, with a little park just ahead of us. She motioned for us to sit down on its low retaining wall, in the shadow of a large tree. Then she reached into her hobo bag and brought out three apples, one for each of us. And then warm pastry wraps with some kind of meat in them. And three twisted pieces of warm bread that looked vaguely like pretzels.

"You guys were good," she appraised, as she started eating. "I could have put that that whole damned fruit stand in my bag, and no one would have noticed."

I was glad that Devon and Rita were focused on their food, so they wouldn't see me blushing.

It was the first real food we'd had since leaving home, and it seemed pretty delicious, but after a diet of dry energy bars and distilled water, that wasn't a very high bar. For a few minutes we all concentrated on eating—which, in hindsight, was not our brightest move. As I wiped my greasy hands on my hobo bag, I realized that someone was watching us.

He was a thin boy, roughly our own age, and he was lounging

against a storefront across the street. His pose was casual enough, but there was something about his expression that warned us not to take his relaxed posture at face value. And there was no missing the fact that we were the focus of his attention.

We tensed as he started to walk toward us; something about his stride suggested that he wasn't alone, but I didn't want to look away from him long enough to check for his allies. Out of the corner of my eye I saw Rita's hand creep to where she had her kitchen knife hidden.

He came up to a spot about five feet from us and stopped. He looked us over, his gaze fixing finally on Devon. "You Maasai?"

Devon blinked. I could tell he was having a hard time transitioning from *no one here has ever seen a black person* to *this guy knows the name of an East African tribe*. So he opted for just staring at him and saying nothing.

"I saw the Maasai ambassador once," the boy explained. "You look like him."

The Maasai ambassador? Half the assumptions I'd made about the place of black people in this world suddenly went flying out the window, and I could see that Devon was equally startled. But he just nodded slowly, as if he knew exactly what was going on. I made a mental note never to play poker with him. "Others have said that to me," he offered warily.

The boy's eyes narrowed suspiciously. "You Guild?"

"Do I look Guild?" Devon's voice had a disdainful edge that could be interpreted as either, *"Of course I'm Guild, why are you asking such me such a stupid question?"* or *"Of course I'm not Guild, why are you insulting me with such a stupid question?"* Damn, he was good!

"Are we on someone's turf?" Rita asked suddenly. Plainly, she'd gotten something out of this bizarre exchange that Devon and I had missed.

The boy's expression shifted slightly. It was a subtle change, and I sensed I was missing nine tenths of its meaning, but Rita looked as if she understood him perfectly.

"You were pretty good back there," he told her. "But taking so much at one time gets you noticed. Security will be tighter tomorrow. The locals won't be happy about that."

She was about to respond when a dark shape suddenly passed overhead. Muttering a curse under his breath, the boy moved quickly into the shade of our tree. The shadow of something with broad wings swept down the center of the street, heading east. He shielded his eyes with one hand as he gazed up into the sky.

"Shit," he muttered. "Shit. That's a Hunter, for sure." He eyed us suspiciously. "Is it one of you he's after?"

"How do you know it's a Hunter?" Devon asked.

He jerked a thumb toward the east. "Those lazy Guild bastards don't come into town to do their dirty work, they just grab a host from wherever they are and hitch a ride. Nine times out of ten if you see an animal that doesn't belong here, it's one of theirs." He gestured toward the sky. "That one was a mountain hawk, which means—"

His expression darkened suddenly. "You didn't answer my question," he challenged Devon.

"No," Devon agreed calmly. "I didn't."

For a moment they just stared at each other, like two dogs trying to figure out if they needed to fight. I saw Rita's hand close around the grip of her knife, though I wasn't sure what she thought she'd do with it in the middle of a city street.

"Shit," the boy muttered. "If the Hunters really are after you, then we should talk. But not here, with the whole world watching."

Without another word he started to walk away from us. The three of us looked at each other in confusion, no one quite sure what to do. Then Rita nodded slightly, and since she seemed to understand the situation better than anyone else, that was good enough for Devon and me. We grabbed up the last of our food, threw our packs over our shoulders, and hurried off after the boy.

Somewhere in the distance a mountain hawk screeched.

17

WHEN THE WOLF REACHED the edge of the clearing, it stopped. For a long moment it stood still, its nostrils flaring as it drank in the layered scents of the place. Then it began to pick its way forward, its sharp eyes taking in every detail of its surroundings. Many animals had passed through here recently, leaving behind a host of traces for him to detect. Over there, to the far left, a wild cat had sharpened its claws on a tree. Over there to the right, several deer had foraged. On the ground directly beneath, a rutting squirrel had rested for several moments, leaving the damp grass perfumed with its lust. There was another scent here as well. Not animal. The wolf felt its heartbeat quicken.

Human.

Slowly it turned its head about, tasting the air in every direction, seeking the source of that smell. In one corner of the clearing was a mound of leaves and grasses that did not appear natural in formation. The wolf walked over and sniffed, its indrawn breath strong enough to make the leaves stir. A human male had lain here recently. Beneath his scent was another subtle sign, deliciously familiar. Fear. Whoever had stopped here to rest had not slept easily.

But who, exactly, did the scent belong to? Many humans hiked through these woods during the summer, with the result that a thousand scent trails could be found along the moist, pine-laden trails. Under such circumstances, the wolf's chances of identifying the one trail it was looking for were low. The only memory it had of its quarry's scent had been passed from species to species, and then dulled by passage through the Gate, so it was all but worthless for comparison. The wolf needed to locate a clear, strong trace, before it could track its quarry properly. But would it recognize that trace when it found it?

It had to. There was no other option. The hawk had been unable to locate the fugitives, which meant they were likely under cover somewhere. If so, a thousand more flights would not root them out. A scent trail, on the other hand, could lead a Hunter directly to them, regardless of what path they had taken.

Circling the clearing, the wolf found two more carefully arranged beds of vegetation, each bearing the scent of a young woman. That was a good sign. Three empty gurneys had been found at the Gate, implying that there were three fugitives, and the letters from Terra Colonna suggested that a boy and a girl would be among them. So the numbers were right. And the location made sense: far enough from the Gate that three young people fleeing pursuit might have pushed themselves to get this far, yet not so far that exhaustion would have crippled them.

A lesser Hunter might have declared victory at that point and set off after his prey, but the one that was soulriding this wolf hadn't risen as high as he had in the world of the Shadows by jumping to conclusions. Following the wrong trail now could result in precious hours wasted, during which time the quarry might put enough distance between them that pursuit was no longer possible. The Hunter needed to be sure this was the right scent.

Around and around the clearing the wolf circled and sniffed, looking for more clues. It found a place where the humans had defecated, and a few crumbs of nuts and honey that ants were diligently dismembering. All of which neither confirmed nor denied the identity of these particular humans.

Then, just past one of the bed-mounds, the wolf thought it saw something glistening in the brush. At first it looked like a scrap of silver foil that had gotten lodged between two rocks. But as the wolf drew closer, it could see that its movement wasn't right for metal foil. Despite its mirrored surface it looked strangely lightweight, and it fluttered like fine tissue in the breeze.

As the wolf drew closer it could make out words, apparently the end of a sentence. Bright red block letters, shiny as glass.

AND REAL CHERRY FILLING!

The wolf stared at the torn plastic wrapper for a moment, then pushed it down further between the rocks and covered it over with dirt, so that no one else would find it. It didn't need to have the nature of the thing explained to it, because the Soulrider who was sharing its body had seen such things before, and the wolf had access to all those memories.

It had found its prey.

Together they began to search for the place where the scent trails of the three humans exited the clearing, so the real hunt could begin.

18

THE WARRENS

WE FOLLOWED THE BOY through a dizzying maze of alleys, past broken fences and through a few half-collapsed buildings. The neighborhood grew more and more slum-like as we progressed, and our route grew less and less comprehensible.

Now and then our guide would pause, look about intently, then suddenly change direction. At first it seemed he was leading us in a bizarre serpentine route just to skew our sense of direction, but as I observed more closely, I soon realized the truth: he was trying to keep us under some kind of cover at all times, to protect us from overhead observation. It was an unnerving discovery.

From what he'd said, it sounded like the bird that had been looking for us was possessed by some kind of hunter. Could that be the explanation behind the animal murders back in our own world? Had the deer, bees, and bears that killed DNA orphans been under the same kind of control? It would certainly explain a lot. But it raised many new questions also . . . like what those hunters wanted, or whether they were even human.

Now and then our guide would pause, cup his hands before his mouth, and utter a bird-like warble. I couldn't have picked it out from all the natural noise around us if I hadn't been listening for it, but apparently others could, for similar cries soon started answering him. Some kind of signal. After a few repetitions he added new notes to his bird-song, and the answering cries also became more complex.

After picking our way through a final garbage-strewn alley, we came to what looked like an abandoned building. He scanned the sky warily, then directed us to scurry quickly across an open street, to a basement window that had been masked by a carefully arranged pile of debris. The frame had been cleared of glass, but wooden planks had been nailed across it. Apparently those were just camouflage, for they pivoted on the anchoring nails as our guide pulled them to one side, and he motioned for us to climb in.

We looked at each other. I was less than certain about this new development. Then Devon shrugged: *What the hell.*

He went first so he could help the rest of us scramble down, into what turned out to be a large, dusty basement. A line of metal cabinets stood along one wall, most of them open, all of them rusted and battered. The doors of one were shut, and had been secured with a chain and padlock that looked newer. And there were crates filled with cans and jars stacked up nearby. Wooden crates, of course. I still had yet to see any plastic in this place. There were no other objects or items of furniture around, though the floor was littered with broken bits and pieces of things that might once have been meaningful.

There were people there, waiting for us. Half a dozen of them. They were all my age or a bit younger, and they watched suspiciously as we lowered ourselves down into the dark, dirty space. I could sense a wound-up tension in them, like wary animals ready to bolt for safety, but also a readiness for violence that set my own nerves on edge. Right now they were all staring at Devon. Of course. I would have given my right arm at that moment to understand why everyone did that.

"What's this about, then?" one of them asked. He was the tallest of the lot, a lanky, olive-skinned boy with tangled hair down to his shoulders, almost but not quite dreadlocked. "Who are these people?"

"No clue," said our guide. "But there's a Hunter might be looking for 'em, and I figured we should find out why."

A blonde girl with short-cropped hair and a worn leather vest stepped forward aggressively. "Who are you?" she demanded. Though she was speaking to all of us, her eyes were fixed on Devon. "What do the *Shadows* want with you?" You could taste the hatred in her voice when she referred to them . . . and maybe an echo of fear. That was a good sign, I told myself. We might not be among friends yet, but at least we weren't among enemies.

I figured the best strategy was to let them know that we hated the Shadows also, to establish some common ground, so I took a big gamble. "They kidnapped my brother."

The six of them looked at each other, startled.

"Shit." A stocky redheaded boy, a deep scar running across one cheek, was the first to speak. "Shit. If they took your brother, it's all over for him. Probably a vegetable by now. Or worse."

"What do you mean?" Despite my determination to sound confident, I could hear my voice start to tremble. "Why would they do that?"

"Same reason they always do," said one of the younger kids. "Bodies to feed to the Gate." He was the only one wearing a visible weapon, a long hunting knife tucked into his boot, but they were probably all armed. They looked like kids who expected trouble and were ready to confront it. "That's what it's always, yeah? Merchants and thieves and spoiled fat cats need bodies to go world-hopping, so who's gonna miss a few kids from the slums?"

"Meat don't need brains," the blonde girl snarled.

For a moment I was so horrified by the suggestion of Tommy becoming a mindless body on a gurney somewhere that I failed for a moment to catch the significance of his other words.

A moment later it hit me: *World-hopping*, he'd said. *Gates*.

These people knew about the Gate we'd come through! Did everyone here? Was the whole setup common knowledge, or had these kids somehow stumbled on a closely guarded secret? The latter would certainly explain why they were so wary of strangers. But the casual manner in which the boy talked about "Gates" and "world-hopping" suggested that common knowledge was more likely. Certainly no one seemed surprised by such references.

My stomach churned with fear for Tommy. My mind reeled from trying to sort it all out.

"Doesn't make sense," Devon challenged. "Who would expend that much effort to steal away one particular boy, just for *meat*?"

"Yeah," our guide agreed. "They do prefer the big roundup."

"Or donations," the blonde girl said sharply.

Donations? I blinked, hoping I was mistaking her meaning.

There was an Asian-looking boy in the group, with sharp cheekbones and hungry eyes. He glared at Devon with naked hostility. "So come off the intro now, tell us what a Guild aristo's doing in the middle of this? No brother of *yours* has been culled, I'm sure. What are you getting out of all this?"

Rita took a small step toward Devon, as if ready to get between him and trouble. I saw her hand twitch toward her knife. "What makes you think he's aristo?"

The redhead snorted. "The only time you see Africaners around here is when they come on business. Which costs money, yeah? When's the last time you knew an indie with the pocket cash for a transatlantic trip?"

The blonde girl turned to him. "You've got some Zulu in Boston. Might be some indies up there."

"Yeah, but when's the last time you saw one of them come down to Luray?"

I shook my head, trying to clear out some of the craziness. One thing at a time. "What did you mean, *donations*?"

The blonde girl turned back to me. "Kids with no potential." She said it definitively, as if that one phrase should explain everything I needed to know.

"The aristos don't like to waste time or money on deadheads," the young one explained. There was no mistaking the edge of bitterness in his voice.

"Or it's a Guild thing," the redhead said. "If you're born into a Guild House and you don't have their Gift, you won't last till your first birthday."

"Not always," the Asian boy said. "They could just trade you out."

"Like meat," the blonde girl agreed.

Gift. Guild. Deadhead. Meat. The terms were beginning to connect in my mind, but I still couldn't get a handle on the bigger picture. My confusion must have been visible, for our guide's eyes narrowed in sudden suspicion and asked, "Where are you all from, that you don't know this stuff?"

You could tell from his tone that there was a right answer and a wrong answer, but I was damned if I knew which was which, so I said nothing. Finally Rita dared, "Not here."

"Shit." The redhead spat on the ground again. "They're transfers. SHIT!"

Suddenly the Asian boy had a knife in his hand. I saw Rita stiffen in readiness, and I wondered how fast I could get to my own knife. Or if I could bring myself to use it on a living person. High school doesn't exactly prepare you for that kind of thing.

But then our guide held up his hand and everyone froze in place.

"If you came through the Gate," he challenged us, "Then you already know about the Shadows. They're the only ones who can bring people across." There was no mistaking the accusation in his eyes: *You're working with them.*

A distant part of my brain registered that this was actually a good sign. If these kids hated the Shadows so much that they'd kill anyone who cooperated with them, they might prove valuable allies. Assuming, of course, that we could win them over before they stabbed us to death.

"Unless you sneak past them," Rita riposted. There was scorn in her voice, but mostly for show. I was sure she was every bit as scared as I was.

Our guide stared at her for a few seconds, weighing her words. We all held our breaths.

"Was it your first crossing?" he demanded.

Devon said, "Yes."

You could see them all looking at each other, but in the dim light it was hard to read their expressions.

"Why does that matter?" I demanded.

A girl who'd been silent up to that point, snorted lightly; strands of dirty shoulder-length hair bobbed about her thin and hungry face. "If you'd sneaked across twice you wouldn't need to ask that."

"Shit," the redhead said. He nodded sharply toward Devon. *"He* already knows all this. Why are we playing word games with him?"

Devon opened his mouth to protest, but our guide spoke up first. "Don't you get it, Ron? He's not Guild. He's not aristo. He's not Zulu. *He's not from this friggin' world at all."* He looked at Devon. "Right?"

A muscle along the line of Devon's jaw twitched. "Yeah," he said. "That's right."

Rita offered, "We're *all* from another world."

"As is my brother," I added.

Our guide's jaw flexed slightly as he digested the information. It was as though he was actually chewing on our words, tasting them. Clearly this new revelation surprised him, but not as much as you'd think. Evidently the concept of someone from another world showing up on his doorstep was not as alien to him as one would expect.

"You need to meet the others," he said at last.

The blonde girl looked at him sharply. "You *trust* them?"

Our guide looked at us, each one in turn. When his gaze met mine, I returned it without flinching. *Read me,* I dared him. *Read what I'm really about. Read what lengths I would go through to get my brother back.*

"Yeah," he said. "Yeah, I trust them. More important, I think Ethan would trust them."

"Shit," the redhead muttered. He spat on the floor again. Apparently that comprised the bulk of his vocabulary.

"So what now?" the blonde girl asked. "We take them to the Warrens?"

Our guide nodded solemnly.

And so, with no further courtesy or explanation, they headed toward the window, clearly expecting us to join them. After a moment's hesitation, we did. One by one we helped each other up through the narrow wooden frame, and in that moment of mutual aid the tension in the group seemed to ease a bit. But only a little bit.

Devon went last. Perhaps because he was tallest, so it just made sense. Or perhaps because he was afraid to have any of these people behind his back.

That's how I would have felt, in his shoes.

⸻

The Warrens turned out to be down in the city's sewers. Or in its storm drains, more accurately. They didn't smell as bad as the actual sewers would have—or so we were told—and the rancid water that flowed down the center of the brick-lined tunnels had very little human waste matter in it. But that was a pretty fine distinction when you were stumbling on the slick ground along the edge of it, trying not to fall in. The air was foul, the walls were slimy, and rats the size of house cats glared at us with naked hostility before scurrying out away from our lamplight. The tunnel ceiling was low enough that even I had to walk hunched over, and I couldn't begin to imagine how bad it was for Devon. Compared to this place, the muddy passages of Mystic Caverns seemed like a five-star hotel.

But at least we were safe from surveillance, right? That was what mattered most right now.

Devon stayed at the rear of the party, and occasionally I could hear the soft scritch-scritch of his chalk on the brickwork overhead, though God alone knew how he was finding spots dry enough to mark. Our guide was the only one carrying a lamp, which meant that the back of our group was in shadow, and Devon's actions went unnoticed. But I was deathly afraid that one of the locals would hear his activity, check it out, and wind up erasing all the marks. Those tiny bits of color were much more than directional markings right now;

they were our spiritual anchor, our last link to the aboveground world as we struggled to proceed with courage in this fetid, claustrophobic setting.

Just as it seemed to me that I couldn't stand another moment without either screaming or vomiting, we entered a large open chamber. It was a circular space, perhaps thirty feet across, with other tunnel openings radiating out from it at regular intervals, and a shadowy ceiling high above us. Sort of a Grand Central Station of storm drainage. Some of the tunnels must have led to cleaner and cooler places, because the air here was almost palatable. There seemed to be a narrow walkway running high around the wall of the chamber, with a rusty ladder leading up to it, but the light from a single oil lamp wasn't conducive to making out any details.

Yes, that's right, an *oil* lamp. Our guide was carrying an open flame through a place that probably had clouds of methane swirling down every corridor. Obviously he wouldn't be doing that if there was any reasonable alternative, which led to so many questions it made my head spin. Every time I tried to figure out the technology of this world it threw me another curve.

I was sorely tempted to pull out my Walmart flashlight, just to see what the reaction was. Probably a bad idea. If producing light without a visible source didn't get me labeled a witch and burned at the stake or something, having it come out of a tube made of an unknown substance—i.e., plastic—probably would. I wouldn't put anything past the people of this world.

Up the ladder we climbed, lamplight dancing along the walls, until we were all perched on the walkway. Our guide led us halfway around the circumference of the chamber, to a heavy wooden door reinforced with iron bands. It looked like something out of a medieval dungeon. There was a rusty knocker that he rapped twice, and sharp cracks resonated through the empty space like gunfire. After awhile we heard footsteps approaching from the other side, and a heavy bolt slid back. Then the door swung open, and the light from the other side seemed so bright after the gloomy tunnels that for a moment it

blinded us. We stood there until the blaze of visual pain had subsided, and we could see where we were, then a boy motioned for us to
enter.

Apparently this place had been a utility station once; you could
see where enormous pipes had been affixed to the walls, and a few
rusted segments were still in place. You could smell the age of the
place. There were a few battered light fixtures on the wall that looked
like candleholders at first glance, but then I realized they were oil
lamps too. By their flickering light we could see that there were people all over the place.

Children.

I couldn't count them because most ran for cover as soon as they
saw us, but there were at least two dozen. From the shadows they
watched us warily, their glistening eyes floating disembodied in the
darkness. Probably the sight of Devon in all his Maasai glory scared
them half to death.

At least the smell was a little bit better here; there must have been
a source of fresh air somewhere nearby. And I didn't see any rats.

A boy stepped forward to meet us, but he didn't say anything
right off, just looked us over. Which gave us time to do the same to
him. He was thin—but not excessively so—and I guessed that he was
about our age. He looked cleaner than the others, which said a lot—
staying clean would require monumental effort in a place like this.
Even in the amber glow from the oil lamp you could see that his skin
had a hint of tan to it, and the flush of a sunburn was blazoned across
his forehead and cheeks. So he didn't stay down here all the time. His
thick brown hair was close-cropped, and eyes of the same color had a
spark of humor in their depths, even though his expression at that
moment was serious. Something about his carriage communicated
confidence and authority, and you could see from the way the others
responded to him that he was what people sometimes call a "natural
leader."

Our guide spoke first. "Found these guys upstairs working our
turf. Figured you'd like to meet 'em."

The blonde girl said, "There's a Hunter after them."

"Really?" The leader-boy looked at us. "Why is that?"

I opened my mouth to answer him, but before I could get any words out our guide pointed to me and said, "This one claims her brother was snatched by the Shadows. She wants to get him back." His tone of voice made it clear how little chance he thought I had of succeeding.

The other boy nodded slowly, his eyes narrowing slightly as he processed that information. "I only know one person who ever got away from the Shadows," he said. "And it's rumored the cost of that was pretty high. You want to take a chance like that?"

"He's my brother," I said stubbornly. Meanwhile I filed away the precious new fact he had just revealed: someone else had escaped the Shadows. If we found that person, could he tell us how to rescue Tommy? For the first time since we'd arrived in this godforsaken world I felt a ray of hope.

"They're from another world," the blonde girl announced.

"*Maybe*," our guide corrected her.

Children whispered in the shadows as the leader-boy digested all that. "Well," he said at last. "That's quite an introduction." He held out his hand in our direction, leaving us to decide who would take it first. "I'm Ethan."

It was Devon who reached forward and shook his hand, offering his name. Then Rita. Then me. You could feel this boy's confidence in his grip; I tried to return it in kind. After that, the group that had brought us to the Warrens all introduced themselves. Our guide was named Kurt, the redheaded boy who liked to spit was Ron, and the Asian-looking boy was Seth. The younger kids had taken on names from the animal kingdom: the boy who was Tommy's age called himself Hawk and the tough little blonde girl was Moth. Her tone was defiant when she introduced herself, as if she was daring us to ask for a more traditional name.

Others began to come out of the shadows as we spoke, some our age, most younger. In some cases *much* younger. Dirt and dim lighting had reduced their clothing to a uniform mud color, and most of the faces that stared at us in undisguised curiosity were layered in grime. They reminded me of the street urchins in *Oliver Twist*.

There seemed to be no adults around.

Now that we had been officially accepted into the Warrens, the youngest children clustered around us with undisguised curiosity, and they followed as Ethan led us through a shadowy archway at the far end of the chamber, into a large, irregularly shaped room. It looked like it had once been a control center of some kind, but with valves and levers in place of switches. Like something out of an old science fiction movie. Trinkets were strewn across every square inch of open surface, a crazy mix of items that seemed to have no common theme. Tidbits snatched from the world above us, maybe? I saw china cups, bits of broken jewelry, ragged dolls, tarnished silverware. The place reminded me of a giant magpie's nest.

In the center of the floor was a circle of mismatched cushions, all of them well-worn. Those who entered the room first claimed seats for themselves, leaving three cushions for us on one side of the circle and one for Ethan across from us. My cushion was a colorless, shapeless thing that looked like it had come from the dusty attic of someone's grandmother, but it was comfortable, and after all that walking through slums and sewers I was glad to get off my feet.

When we'd all settled down on our cushions and the children without seats had arranged themselves in a circle around us, Ethan said, "Tell us about your world."

That was the last thing I wanted to begin with—I was so anxious to get more information about the person who had escaped from the Shadows that I could barely sit still—but it was clear that if we wanted to get information from these people, we were going to have to put down a deposit first. So Rita started telling them about our home world. But soon it became clear from the questions the children asked that for all their casual talk of "other worlds," they envisioned our Earth—*Terra Colonna*—as nothing more than an exotic foreign country. Further away than Europe perhaps, but no more alien to their understanding than the town next door. The concept that there might actually be two different versions of the same Earth inhabiting the same space wasn't even in their lexicon. As for the mysterious Gate . . . yes, that seemed magical to them, but it was a kind of magic they were used to. There were people with Gifts who could do all sorts of things like that, they informed us.

I was dying to learn more about those Gifts, but it wasn't our turn to ask questions yet.

Eventually it became clear that what these children really wanted from us wasn't scientific information as much as simple entertainment. So Rita started telling them adventure stories set in our world, and she kept them enthralled that way for a good hour or two. They probably would have demanded she go on like that forever if she hadn't started inserting long, boring descriptions. It was a brilliant strategy, and it soon bore fruit. One by one most of the youngest kids either fell asleep or wandered off, until all that remained in the magpie room was a small group of older teens, and the team that first found us.

Then it was our turn.

I wanted to start by asking about Gifts right off, but Devon wanted to know about the Guilds, and he talked louder and faster, so he won. As it turned out, the two things were connected, Gifts being mental powers that came in a number of distinct varieties, while the Guilds were organizations that trained and protected the Gifted, one Guild for each specialization. Since they controlled the most powerful people in this world, they also controlled most of its commerce, either directly or indirectly. Which meant that cities had to keep the Guilds happy if they wanted to prosper. Which meant that politicians needed to keep the Guilds happy, as did businessmen, law enforcement . . . you get the idea. Basically, if you pissed off the Guilds in this world, you were seriously screwed.

So now the foraging team's reaction to Devon made sense. If these kids had been concerned that he might belong to a Guild, it was because that would make him an agent of the vast, Gift-driven network of authority that controlled their world—what folks back home called *The Man*.

Okay. It was starting to make sense now.

Ethan named some of the most powerful Guilds, and sure enough, the *Guild of Shadows* topped the list, followed by *Seers, Weavers, Elementals,* and a few scary-sounding ones like *Soulriders* and *Fleshcrafters*. Some of the names sounded like they came right out of one of Tommy's fantasy games, which made me miss my little brother even more. Then Devon described the weird grey aliens we'd seen, and Ethan said that yeah, those were the Greys. People called them that because their actual Guild name was a pain to pronounce. Their Gift was sneaking around, so they did most of the Shadows' dirty work, and they inbred a lot to keep their Gift in-house.

Because true Gifts were so rare, Ethan told us, the Guilds were constantly on the lookout for children who had the seeds of power inside them. That's what the Seers were for; they could tell if a child had the potential to become Gifted, and if so, what form his Gift would likely take. Babies in this world were presented to the Seers soon after birth, and if a Gifted one was discovered it was taken from its family and adopted into one of the Guilds.

"Wait," I interrupted. "Don't the parents object to that?"

"Not if they're paid enough," our former guide muttered. His tone was bitter.

Ethan nodded grimly. "A Gifted baby can bring in enough money to raise a whole family up out of poverty." And he went on to explain how some poor families would give birth to a slew of kids just to increase their chances of producing a Gifted one to sell. Which was a long shot, those being very rare, so the result was a lot of extra kids wandering around whom no one wanted. Meanwhile, any child born into a Guild family who had no discernible Gift was considered an embarrassment and risked being abandoned. . . .

I didn't actually hear what Ethan said next. Because suddenly I grasped who and what our hosts were, and the revelation was so stunning—and so horrifying—that for a moment I couldn't hear anything at all.

All these children were rejects. Giftless kids who'd been abandoned when they were young, or maybe just so badly abused in the name of parental resentment that they'd run away from home. Some might have been children from lower-class families who'd failed to manifest the one precious commodity that could lift their families out of poverty, so they'd been shoved aside to make room for their parents' next attempt at profitable reproduction. Others might have been upper-class children who'd proven unworthy of their lineage, and were driven out to spare their relatives shame.

The revelation sickened me so much I didn't dare look into the eyes of any of them, for fear that they would think the horror in my expression was directed at them. What kind of a world was this, that would do such things to its children?

"Some are sold to the Shadows, to be used for the Gates," Ethan continued, oblivious to my reaction. "Others are sent to labor farms. A few are sent to other worlds—"

"Hold on," Devon interrupted. "What do you mean, *sent to other worlds?*"

"As replacements," Ethan explained. "When the Shadows steal a Gifted baby from another world, they leave an unGifted one in its place."

I saw the look on Devon's face, and I suddenly remembered what he'd told me back at the IHOP, about the DNA orphan in Taiwan. *There was stuff that should have been in any human DNA, that wasn't in his.*

Suddenly my earthly identity was falling to pieces, and there was nothing stable to hold on to. Was this the world we were originally from, Rita and Devon and I, and all the other "DNA orphans"? Were these our real people? The concept was so insane that I wanted to laugh and cry at the same time. But there was no denying the logic of it. Add this piece to the puzzle of our lives and everything fit together perfectly. That's why the genetic code of the Taiwanese orphan had been lacking the most basic human elements: he wasn't human. Neither were we.

"Why?" I whispered, trembling. "Why would they do that? Why not just let people think the stolen babies had been lost, or kidnapped? It's not like anyone would guess why they were being taken. Why leave your own kids behind on an alien world—?" I couldn't bring myself to finish the sentence aloud: *so they would grow up ignorant of who and what they really were.*

A voice from behind me said, "Genetic investment."

I twisted around to see who was talking. In a dark corner of the room a boy was tucked into the shadows, barely visible. His face was ghost-like in the darkness, his eyes so black they seemed to suck in the lamplight.

"Meaning what?" I demanded.

"Meaning that it helps keep foreign gene pools compatible with ours, so that when Gifted children appear in other spheres we can claim them."

Rita glared at him. "So it's like—what?—crop fertilization?"

It seemed to me that one corner of the boy's mouth twitched slightly, but whether that was a smile or a smirk I couldn't tell. "That's the general idea, yes."

Before I could find the words to respond to that bombshell he stepped back into the shadows, so that I could no longer see his face. I sensed a dark shape moving toward the exit, and an instant later he was gone.

"Seriously?" Rita demanded, turning back to our hosts. "Is that how you all see us? Crops to be harvested?"

"Isaac's an aristo," Kurt said apologetically. "And yeah, that's how his kind sees our world. Everything in the universe exists for their benefit, human beings included."

Ethan nodded bitterly. "They claim the ones they want, use the rest for breeding experiments. Not only on other worlds. They breed their own children like livestock sometimes, trying to produce kids with particularly valuable Gifts."

"So what's he doing here?" I demanded. "I thought this was a refuge for—" I stopped myself just in time. *For rejects,* I'd almost said.

"He's fleeing an arranged marriage," Ethan explained. "It isn't the usual reason people come here, but it's good enough. He's our age, he's outcast, he pulls his weight on foraging expeditions . . . maybe he's not always as diplomatic as he could be, but who is?" He shot a warning look at Kurt. "He had a formal education, which is more than most of us can claim. It's useful sometimes. So if you want more detailed information about the Shadows or the Gates, or anything else, you might want to talk to him."

"Assuming he'll talk to you," Kurt muttered. "Not exactly the friendliest guy in town."

I asked, "Is he the one who escaped from the Shadows?"

Ethan shook his head. "No, that's the Green Man. We can put out a call for him if you want, but there's no telling if he'll answer it. He comes and goes as he pleases."

"If he hears there are visitors from another world he'll come," Kurt said.

"He lives in the forest," Moth offered. "He can merge into trees, so the Shadows can't find him."

"He trades in knowledge," Ethan said. "So if you want information from him you'll have to offer something in exchange. He's already collected stories from a hundred different worlds, so finding something he doesn't already know won't be easy. Most of the people who try to bargain with him walk away empty-handed."

"We'd like to try," Devon said quietly. "Would you put out the call for us?"

"If you want." He shrugged. "Just remember, there are no guarantees."

I twisted around on my cushion, looking after the strange pale boy they called Isaac. He understood the concept of *other worlds* in a way that the others didn't. And if what Ethan said about his education was true, he might be able to shed some light on the situation with

Tommy. If we could figure out why the Shadows had kidnapped my brother, maybe we'd know how to retrieve him.

I glanced at Devon and Rita. They saw the question in my eyes and nodded.

Quietly, I got to my feet and headed after pale aristo boy, while the group conversation continued on behind me. The exit that he'd taken led to a tunnel with very little light in it, so I had to be especially careful not to walk into anything. It was hard while peering down lightless side passages, and one time I struck my head against a pipe so hard that the noise of it resonated down the length of the tunnel.

When I found him at last, in a little nook leading from one of the main conduits, I almost walked right past him. Apparently he'd heard me following and waited. From up close he looked a little less like a ghost, but only a little. There was a haunted quality to his gaze that made me shiver, and the shadows cast by the small lamp at his feet gave his lean and elegant features an eerie cast. In the full light of day he would have turned heads in any high school. In this light he looked . . . well, damned creepy.

For a moment we just stared at each other. Then he nodded ever so slightly and said, "I'm Isaac."

"I'm Jessica," I responded, with equal formality. "Jesse, to most."

The dark eyes studied me in silence for a few seconds. It was impossible to read his expression.

"You followed me," he said at last. "Why?"

I decided to go for the direct approach. "They said you might have information for me."

Again a moment of silence. "Why does he matter to you?" he said at last.

I blinked. "Sorry, what?"

"Your brother. You crossed into another world to save him. That was very brave of you, but it was also very foolish. Why do it?"

I didn't know quite what to say. "He's family."

"Which means what to you?" he pressed.

"Same thing it means to everyone, I'd expect." But as soon as those words left my lips I knew I'd made a mistake. This was a boy who'd run away from home because his family wanted to breed him like a prize farm animal. I had no way to know how much he still loved them—or didn't—or what had led him to that terrible decision. "I'm sorry."

He didn't look upset. He didn't look anything. His face could have been carved from marble for all the emotion it revealed. "How did you get through the Gate?" he asked.

I felt a twinge of frustration. It had made sense that in the group interview we'd had to answer endless questions before being given any information, but now that was over. The game was getting old. "We took the place of some bodies on tables. The Shadows wheeled us across."

This time there was emotion visible: A flicker of surprise. "Clever. Though I imagine when the Shadows decide who to blame for that, there'll be hell to pay."

Damn. I hadn't thought about what would happen to whoever had been in charge of security that night. Probably the grey guy. Damn.

"It bothers you?" he pressed.

"Shouldn't it?" I snapped.

He shrugged. "The security of a Gate isn't something to take lightly. Imagine all the terrible things that might happen if the wrong person came through one of them. Or the wrong *thing*."

Suddenly I was tired of providing amusement and getting nothing in return. "Listen, you want to ask me questions? Then you answer some of mine, okay? One for one."

He stared at me for a long moment, but I'd been through enough staring contests with Tommy to know how to hold my own. No one could do a better eerie stare than I could.

Finally he nodded. "Okay."

I exhaled sharply. "Then yes, it bothers me. It bothers me a lot."

"Why?"

"That's a second question," I pointed out.

I thought I saw a spark of humor in those dark eyes. It made him seem a bit more human. "Very well. Go ahead."

"What are the Shadows?" I asked.

A black eyebrow arched upward in surprise. "That's a rather big question, isn't it?"

"I don't recall a size limit."

I thought I saw a smile flicker briefly across his lips. "Their Gift allows them to see the pathways between the worlds. Their sacrifice allows them to travel them safely."

"What kind of sacrifice—"

He smiled slightly as he held up a finger, reminding me of our bargain.

Despite myself I smiled.

"Why did they take your brother?" he asked.

"I was hoping you could help answer that."

He shrugged. "I have no special insight into Shadow business. The things I'm telling you can be found in any high school textbook."

"Not in ours," I said. "Our textbooks are full of things like electricity, polymer chemistry, rocket science . . ."

I thought I saw a flicker of recognition in his eyes. Were the *aristos* familiar with our technology? It stood to reason they would be, if tourists from this world were constantly crossing over to visit mine. But then why hadn't anyone done the obvious, like, oh, bringing back a flashlight from Walmart? Or better yet, a high school science textbook? The more I learned about this world, the less sense it made.

"If your brother was a changeling," he said thoughtfully, "and it turned out he was Gifted after all, that might have drawn their interest. It happens sometimes."

"He isn't the changeling—" I began. Then suddenly I realized I'd been tricked into giving him more information than I'd intended. *Screw you*, I thought, *I'm counting that as a question.* "How does the Gate work?"

I thought he might try to evade the question, but he didn't. "There are places where the barrier between worlds is naturally weak, and things from one sphere can leak into another. Mostly it's insubstantial stuff, dreams and the like. Few people even notice it. But sometimes it's possible for physical matter to cross over, and even living creatures. The Gate doesn't create such a phenomenon, it just stabilizes it. Otherwise things might not line up quite right, and you could lose time during the crossing, arrive at your destination a hundred years later than when you left. Or wind up in the wrong sphere altogether. It's a pretty unstable system. Sometimes things go wrong even when the proper precautions are taken."

"Like fairy abductions," I mused aloud, and when he looked curious I explained, "There are legends in my homeworld of people who travel to a magical land for a short time, but when they return home they find that decades have passed in their absence." *And the fairies leave changelings behind,* I remembered suddenly. That was where the concept came from in the first place. Fairy children exchanged for humans in the cradle, left behind for the human mothers to raise as their own. They looked like the real kids in every way, and their mothers rarely caught on to the switch, but they didn't belong in our world, and they never really fit in.

Like us.

"You understand now, don't you?" His words were soft in the darkness "Shadows of alien realities are glimpsed through invisible portals. Dreams bleed over from one world to the next. Tourists with magical Gifts show up in places where those Gifts don't exist, doing things that the natives think are impossible. So the natives make up stories to explain it. They anchor their religion in places where the visions are strongest, they train their seers to listen for the echo of other worlds, they weave fictions to try to make sense of the unexplainable . . ." He paused. "We are the legends of your world, Jessica."

I wrapped my arms around myself, but they had no power to banish the chill that had suddenly invaded my soul. I looked away from him but couldn't banish unwanted images from my mind.

"You want to see what the Guilds are about?" he asked. "Their summer assessment fair is going on right now. I'll take you there tomorrow, you can see them in action."

"The Green Man may come," I whispered. "We have to wait for him."

"It will take him a while to get here. If he comes at all. You have time."

But did my brother have time? I wondered. Would the Shadows put off whatever they were going to do to him, until we showed up? Tears of frustration welled up in my eyes. It wasn't this hard in the movies. You showed up, you located the evil castle, you invaded it. Good won out over evil in the end—though a few good people might get hurt along the way—because that was the way such stories always ended. Then you got to go home. The house lights came on. Everyone lived happily ever after.

What those stories didn't tell you about was the *waiting*. How it bled you of strength, drop by drop. How it wound your nerves so tight that you wondered if, when the time came to act at last, you'd be able to trust your own judgment. *Focus, Jessica*. I drew in a deep breath. *Focus*.

Isaac said that dreams could cross over from one world to another. Was that what my door dreams were all about? Were they visions from another world? I remembered Miriam Seyer showing particular interest in my art. No, in my dreams. That's why she came to me, I realized suddenly. Not to buy my art. To learn about my dreams.

I chose my words very carefully, not wanting to reveal too much to someone whose primary identity was still *creepy stranger*. "You said something about dreams crossing over. Are there people who are especially sensitive to that?"

His eyes narrowed. "There was a Gift related to dreaming, once. Centuries ago. It drove its users insane, and ultimately was judged to be so dangerous that anyone who showed signs of having it was destroyed on sight. They called them dreamwalkers." He looked at me curiously. "Why do you ask?"

"Just trying to make sense of it all," I muttered. My heart was pounding in my chest so loudly I was afraid he could hear it. "So much to absorb at once."

"Come with me tomorrow, then. You'll understand more of how it all works once you see it with your own eyes."

I managed to nod in a casual manner. Or tried to, anyway. "When?"

"Early morning. There'll be a wake-up call. They try to keep the Warrens in sync with the world above. Makes foraging easier."

I looked up at his face in the darkness. Skin pale as alabaster. Eyes black as midnight. From somewhere I managed to dredge up a fraction of a smile. "You go out in the sunlight?"

He looked startled for a moment, then smiled broadly. "Yeah. I go out in the sunlight. Don't tan worth a damn, though."

Do you sparkle? I wanted to ask him. But I wasn't sure he'd get the reference. Or consider it funny if he did.

We are the legends of your world, he'd said.

So what did that make me?

||||||||||||||

After I left him, I wandered for awhile in the dimly lit corridors. No guide, no chalk marks, no sense of self-preservation. Fortunately the larger tunnels all connected to the main chamber eventually, and I was able to use the echo of distant conversation to orient myself. But it was awhile before I was ready to rejoin human company.

All kids have a secret fear of discovering that they aren't who they're supposed to be. Maybe they were adopted, or abducted from their parents at birth, or else their dad wasn't really their dad; those are normal childhood nightmares. Everyone has them. But even the worst of those fears couldn't compare to our reality. Not only weren't our parents our parents, but the world we'd grown up in wasn't really our world.

My little brother wasn't really my brother.

I remembered what I had promised Tommy that night while he was sleeping. And suddenly the tears I had been fighting so hard to repress while I was with Isaac, started to flow, and my heart ached with a pain so vast it felt like it would swallow me whole.

You will always be my brother, I promised him silently. *Always.*

19

LURAY
VIRGINIA PRIME

THE WOLF WALKED through the city without looking up. People who saw it coming quickly got out of the way, and a few riders pulled their horses over to the far side of the street, afraid that their mounts might panic if it came too close. One pedestrian, too preoccupied to pay attention to where he was going, almost bumped into it. The wolf raised its head long enough to bare its teeth and growl, sending that person fleeing for safety. But it had no interest in pursuing human prey. It watched the man long enough to be sure that he wouldn't get in the way again, then put its nose to the ground again, striving to distinguish three specific scent trails from the thousands that clung to the street.

Everyone in Luray knew what it meant when a creature from the wild behaved like that, and they steered clear. No one wanted to tangle with a Hunter.

The scent of its quarry was fresh enough that it was still strong, and despite the hundreds of people who had walked down the same street since then, the wolf had no trouble identifying the trail of its prey. The smells of the surrounding city failed to distract it, though it looked up briefly as it neared a sausage stand and watched the owner quickly put a few links on the ground. But it did not accept the offering, and the vendor moved hurriedly out of the way as it resumed the task at hand.

The wolf paused outside a cafe, where two of its targets had lingered for awhile, then followed their trail down a side street, away from the heart of the business district. There it discovered a place where the three of them had rested on a wall, leaving behind trace scents of food, sweat, and fear.

It was there that a fourth scent trail joined them, one that the wolf knew from previous hunts. It growled low in its throat as it continued moving.

Children in the slums ran away when they saw the wolf coming.

Cats and small dogs bolted for cover.

Rats pissed themselves in terror.

Finally it came to a narrow alley strewn with garbage, in the center of which was a manhole leading down into the city's drainage system. The wolf sniffed the cast iron lid just long enough to confirm that the fourth scent was all over it. Its three targets had come here, led by someone who had opened the manhole for them then led them down into the undercity.

Into the Warrens.

With a huff of satisfaction, the wolf set out at a loping pace to rejoin its human handler.

20

THE SUNLIGHT HURT. It must have been a psychological effect, since we'd only been in the Warrens for a day, but knowing that didn't make it hurt any less. The sudden exposure to the blinding light made my eyes burn, sunbeams rasping like steel wool on my flesh. Is this what the locals went through each time they emerged from their underground haven?

At least our hosts had decided that we were trustworthy enough to travel the route that their foraging teams used, a path infinitely more direct (and less odiferous) than the one we'd taken on the way down. No smelly sewers this time, or streams of muck thick enough for creepy things to hide in, just a quick trip through several abandoned utility tunnels and one short climb up a steel ladder. That brought us to a hidden door, which in turn led into someone's abandoned cellar. It was a messy place, and we picked our way across a floor littered with broken bottles and rusted cans that looked like they'd been there since the beginning of time, finally reaching a pair of battered storm doors. They were locked from the inside. Isaac had the key, and after a few seconds of fumbling with the rusty lock he managed to get the doors open. Sunlight suddenly flooded the small space, its searing intensity hitting us in the face like a physical blow.

Like I said: Ouch.

Once my eyes stopped stinging, and I could see clearly again, I discovered that Isaac didn't look nearly as disturbing in the full light of day as he had underground. His pale skin actually had a healthy undertone to it; give him a few days at the beach and he'd probably tan up nicely. The eyes that had seemed so ominous in the Warrens were still compelling, but now in a different way. I felt a warmth when he looked at me that raised a flush of guilt in my cheek, and for some reason I thought of Devon. It didn't really make any sense. The kiss he and I had staged to distract the locals had no real meaning. There was no reason for me *not* to look at other guys. But I guess when you're a fugitive in an unfamiliar world, you feel a sense of loyalty to those who are fugitives along with you. Something about being chased by aliens together.

But Devon wasn't with us right now. Despite our best efforts to get him to come along with us, he'd opted to stay behind in the Warrens. He said that his skin color made him too conspicuous, and his being with us would put the whole operation at risk. But neither Rita nor I was fooled by that. Something the locals told him the night before had shaken him badly, and he needed time alone to digest it.

Last night when I'd come back from meeting Isaac, I'd found Devon sitting off in a corner, just staring at the wall. He wouldn't tell me what was wrong, and Rita just shook her head in a kind of *don't ask* way, when I looked at her. Later on he came back to life a bit and helped us arrange our borrowed blankets into makeshift beds, but every now and then I caught a glimpse of terrible emptiness in his eyes. Haunting. Frightening.

Finally we all settled down to sleep, with only a small night lamp left alight to ward off the terrifying cave-blackness of the place. When my sight adjusted I could see Devon staring into space, its tiny flame reflected in his eyes, and I knew that whatever had shaken him so badly was not going to allow him to sleep peacefully.

Rita scrunched over to me, close enough that we could whisper in each other's ears. Not that Devon was likely to hear us anyway; he looked as if some circuit in his brain had disconnected, leaving his body unoccupied while his brain wandered down roads of nightmare, alone. My heart ached to see him like that, but I didn't have a clue how to comfort him. Maybe I was afraid I'd make things worse if I tried.

"It's the abbies," Rita whispered.

"What about them?" I whispered back.

It turned out that while I was gone the locals had explained to Rita and Devon about the diminutive hominids we'd seen in the woods. Turns out they weren't from around here at all. And by *here*, I mean *this world*. Someone had discovered them on a parallel earth and decided they had good market value, so he brought back some specimens for mating stock, established a local population, and then sold them off. They turned out to be the perfect servitors—human but not human, intelligent but not *too* intelligent—and a few dozen generations of selective breeding had guaranteed the proper submissive spirit. End result: the perfect slave species.

That's why there were so few black people in this version of America. The millions of Africans who'd been brought across the ocean in shackles in my own reality had never arrived in this one. They hadn't been needed. Stocky abbies from one hominid species labored in southern fields beneath the blazing sun, while their more diminutive cousins served as housemaids and manservants in the halls of the northern aristocracy. Meanwhile slave traders continued to scour the worlds for proto-humans to breed and sell; there were at least five types in common service now.

What was it the Declaration of Independence said? *All men are created equal.* Only here they weren't equal, and no mere document could ever change that.

I could understand why that revelation hit Devon so much harder than the rest of us. I also understood why he didn't feel comfortable talking about his feelings with any of us, and just wanted to be alone for a while. Sometimes guys are like that.

Most of the time, actually.

"You okay?" Isaac asked.

Startled back to the present moment, I blinked and nodded.

He'd dug up a pair of wide-brimmed sunhats for Rita and me and a visored cap for himself, for protection from overhead scrutiny. He pulled his own hat down until the visor rested right above his eyes, casting them into shadow. The brim of mine drooped low enough that someone talking to me would have had to lift up the edge to see my eyes, but even so I felt dangerously exposed. As we stepped out into the sunlit street I had a sudden impulse to dive back underground, to bury myself in the womblike safety of the Warrens while enemies scoured the city looking for me. Maybe in a few days they'd stop searching for me. Maybe in a month.

Maybe not ever.

Pull yourself together, girl. Tommy's depending on you.

Isaac explained that for a few weeks during the summer the Guilds camped out in Luray's main plaza, providing testing stations where any child who showed signs of Talent could be evaluated. Mostly this was a service for the lower classes. Aristo families arranged for private viewings for their own kids soon after birth, and apparently they were big social events, to which all the leading families in town were invited. Gifts were exchanged, food and wine flowed freely, and at the end an infant swaddled in pure white cloth was given over to the Seers to evaluate. The aristos had been interbreeding with the Guilds for centuries, so the odds of one of their offspring being born with a substantial Gift were reasonably high. Among the poorer classes such births were one in a million.

Yet such children, when they were born, were worth their weight in gold. A poor family whose child was accepted for apprenticeship in a Guild would be richly rewarded, and if the child eventually earned the title of Master, they'd be set for life. So every summer families made pilgrimages to the Guild Fair in Luray, to present their children for assessment and set the dice rolling.

Isaac glossed over the part of the story where the children with potential were taken away from their parents and given to strangers to raise. Depending on the nature of the apprenticeship contract, they might never see their birth families again. Because if you call it *fostering* it's all right, yes?

The whole system seemed so dismal to me that the festive smells that wafted toward us as we approached Guildmaster's Plaza were totally unexpected. Roasted pork, fried chicken, honey and butter and fresh lemonade . . . it smelled as if we were approaching a county fair rather than a place where children were bartered like livestock.

Then we turned the last corner and the Plaza was spread out before us—and indeed, it looked exactly like a county fair. There were colorful little kiosks all over the place, some offering games of chance, others serving up the kind of junk food you only find at a fairground. Never mind that there were no giant polyester pandas anywhere, no Mylar pinwheels, no plastic balloons. What the locals lacked in polymer technology they made up for in architectural excess: every available surface was decorated with arabesques and scrollwork, painted in festive colors.

On the surface it was all quite cheery, but there was a disconcerting sense of artificiality to the place, and I half expected stagehands to come in and start peeling away the colorful facade, exposing its rotten armature. Evidently Rita was also uneasy, for she stayed close by my side as Isaac led us on a cursory tour, pointing out items of interest as we wended our way slowly through the crowd.

The plaza was filled with people. Families, mostly, with a few lone children darting in and out between the kiosks, playing games. At first glance they all seemed happy enough. But if you looked closely, you got the sense that, for some of them, it was just a facade. One family that passed us had obviously come from a very poor quarter of town, and probably spent their last dime to get here. What I saw in their eyes was not joy, relaxation, or any variety of happiness. It was desperation. I caught sight of a boy who had tucked himself into the shadow of a kiosk, and his eyes were filled with a haunting sadness that made my heart lurch in sympathy. Had he failed his assessment? Been forced to stand by as a beloved brother or sister was handed over to strangers? Or was there some other misery associated with this place?

None of this bothered Isaac at all. He led us past those kiosks without stopping, and Rita and I followed in solemn silence. Soon we came to a place where the colors were a bit more muted and the crowd a bit less noisy. Families walked quietly here, and the children who trailed behind them made no attempt to play. This was the place where Guild business was conducted, Isaac told us.

It was also the place where magic was performed.

The first time I saw it, a little girl was responsible. She was standing in the shadow of a great tree with an older woman—her mother?— and holding her hands out in front of her, palms cupped toward each other as if she were holding an invisible sphere. It was hard to say whether the strained look on her face reflected great effort or great pain. The woman was urging her on, but her manner wasn't encouraging so much as demanding. You could see the girl's hands trembling as she strained desperately to satisfy her, to do—what?

Then, suddenly, fire appeared between her hands. There was only a tiny spark of it, that flickered for a moment and was gone, but the implications of it were mind-blowing. I stopped walking and just stared at her, struggling to come to terms with what I'd just seen.

"Longer!" her mother snapped angrily. "You have to hold it longer!" For a moment my sense of wonder was overwhelmed by sheer indignation. I wanted to walk over and smack the mother. Not just because of how she was treating the little girl, but for the sake of every kid in the universe who had ever brought home an A on a test, only to have angry parents demand to know why it wasn't an A+.

Without turning, I stammered to Isaac, "What . . . what is that?"

"Elemental control," he said. His tone was totally casual, as if people conjuring fire out of thin air was something he saw every day. "Pyromancy's a lucrative Gift, and it rarely manifests so young; the Guild of Elementals will snap her up." He pointed. "They're over there."

I didn't want to stop watching the little girl, but there was nothing

I could do to make the situation with her mother better, and Isaac was urging us to move on. Eventually I let him guide us away.

Each Guild that participated in this event had its own encampment where it received candidates and admirers. He led us to the one belonging to the Guild of Elementals. Along the way I caught sight of other children struggling to accomplish strange mental tasks, staring at cups of lemonade or handfuls of leaves or invisible objects with an intensity that made my heart quiver. But would I have struggled any less hard, if I had been in their place?

The Guild of Elementals was operating out of a colorful pavilion, with some kind of heraldic banner flying from the center pole. Very Renaissance Faire. The surrounding area had been marked off with velvet ropes, and people lined up at each of several openings, waiting their turns to enter. Servants in matching livery moved back and forth between the lines, taking down names and information, occasionally moving a visitor from one queue to another. Central to the whole arrangement was a grand fountain, with four stone angels pouring water down into a wide basin, in which flames burned brightly.

Yes, that's right. There was a ring of fire surrounding the angels, and though water was being poured directly onto it, the flames didn't even flicker. At first I thought it might be some kind of chemical fire that water couldn't extinguish—dramatic but plausible—but then I saw that the water wasn't affected by the fire at all. Droplets passed through the flames and then splashed down into the basin as if nothing unusual was going on. Shouldn't they have turned to steam, or . . . or . . . or something?

"The Elementals like to show off," Isaac said. The look on my face seemed to amuse him.

"But how . . . ? I mean . . . is that a Gift?" I shook my head incredulously. "You can't just change the laws of nature like that. This isn't a videogame—"

I stopped myself, but too late. I held my breath, dreading the questions that were sure to come. But if my use of a high-tech Earth term drew Isaac's notice, he didn't remark upon it. "Natural laws are never suspended," he said, "though I've heard there are spheres where they function differently. Gifts simply channel energy into the natural system, giving it form."

"But energy from where?" I demanded. *What about the second law of thermodynamics?* I wanted to ask him. But that sounded way too geeky, so I settled for, "What's the source?"

He shrugged. "Where does any energy come from? You eat food, you digest it, you store the results as chemical energy, then use it to fuel physical movement, mental processing, whatever. Same as with any human effort."

But . . . but . . . I looked at the fountain again. "Are you telling me that making something like that fountain is no more strenuous than— what? Picking up a rock?"

He laughed. "Hardly. Holding a single drop of water steady in a candle flame for a few minutes might be like picking up a rock. But *that,*" he indicated the fountain, "that's more like building a ten-foot wall that stretches across the entire city. I'd be surprised if fewer than a hundred people were involved in making it. And since the Guild will probably keep it running all week, constant energy will be needed to sustain it. Thousands of people might wind up contributing to it by the time this event is over. Like I said . . . Elementals like to show off."

Somehow it had been easier to think of these Gifts as alien magic than to try and fit them into a scientific framework. I struggled to make the adjustment. "You say people provide the energy for this thing, no one's even paying attention to it. So where is the energy coming from?"

Isaac nodded. "That's the Weavers' job. They bind mental energy to physical objects." He gestured off to the left. "Their setup is nearby, if you want to take a look."

I did. But when we arrived there, so many people were crowded around their pavilion that we couldn't get close enough to see any- thing. That was because this was the Guild that made *fetters,* Isaac explained—small objects to which a tiny bit of Gifted energy had been bound. Common types—such as *glows*, which were lamps with a Lightbringer's Gift affixed to them, or *harmonies*, which were crystals used for communication—could be purchased just about anywhere, but some of the more esoteric varieties could only be obtained at events like this. Hence the crowds.

So these people had their own version of high tech, but it was powered by mental exertion rather than electricity. Wow. Imagine what a flashlight would cost if someone had to spend time running on a treadmill every time you used it. Suddenly the whole class system of this world came into sharp focus. Electricity was an equalizer on my Earth: easy to obtain, adaptable to many uses, and minimal in cost. But the technology that came from Gifts was none of those things. Its rarity and expense divided human society into three distinct classes: *those who have, those who have not,* and *those who suck up to the ones who have in order to better their lot.*

I wondered what our Walmart flashlights would bring on the open market.

Rita asked if the Greys had an encampment, and Isaac said that yes, they did, but we wouldn't be able to see it, because that was the whole point. If you couldn't locate the Guild of Obfuscates, then you didn't have the Gift needed to join. I asked about the Shadows, and he said they didn't come to this event. Their Gift was passed down from person to person, and was usually kept in-house, so they had no need to recruit. He didn't offer any further details, but I suspected the Shadows were just so damn creepy that no one wanted to go near them. Even our smooth aristo guide seemed reluctant to talk about them.

The Seers did have a camp, and we headed there next. I wanted to see the arrogant bastards who controlled the fates of so many children and their families. Their setup was located at the western end of the park, where all the public walkways seemed to converge. Fitting. A narrow, minaret-like tower loomed overhead, and I realized that must be the one we'd seen when we first scoped out the city. Isaac said it was part of their Guild headquarters, situated a short distance away. The slender tower lined up perfectly with their pavilion, lending the encampment a sense of architectural majesty that none of the others had.

There were dozens of mothers with infants in their arms, lined up next to crowd-control barriers, waiting patiently for their turn to enter the Seers' pavilion. They were mostly poor women, of course; aristo mothers didn't have to wait in line for stuff like this. I saw one woman exit the tent with a nursing blanket thrown over her shoulder, but no baby in her arms. She was smiling and accepted the congratulations of the others with a gracious nod, though the tears in her eyes didn't look like the product of happiness, and the tightness of her mouth suggested she was struggling not to cry.

What kind of sick world rewarded a mother for abandoning her child?

Suddenly a figure dressed in white emerged from the pavilion, and a hush swept over the crowd. She was a tall woman, striking in appearance, with golden hair swept up into a complex arrangement of curls and twists and braids, pearls tucked into the larger curls as if they had formed there naturally. Every twist of hair was perfectly controlled, every ornament perfectly placed. The style reminded me of something I'd once seen in a movie about ancient Rome. But her eyes looked more Egyptian than Roman, with thick bands of eyeliner that extended past the outer corners, drawing the gaze to them. Black on top, gold on bottom. The irises were a misty grey-green, the color of ocean waves right before a storm. Her fingernails were burnished gold, to match her eyeliner. Her gaze was arresting, and I instinctively stepped back into the shadows as she looked around the encampment, not wanting it to rest on me.

"That's Alia Morgana," Isaac whispered. "GuildMistress of the Seers. It's said nothing happens in Luray that she doesn't have a hand in." He paused, then added in a conspiratorial tone, "It's rumored even the Shadows are afraid of her."

We watched as the woman in white made her rounds of the encampment; the people waiting for assessments moved out of her way like the Red Sea parting for Moses. This was the woman who would ultimately determine which families graduated to a new station in life, and which went home disappointed. The sycophancy was so thick in the air you could choke on it.

At one point she stopped to study a little girl. The child was too fearful to look up at her, but Morgana reached out, and with a touch beneath the girl's chin, tipped her head back till their eyes met. For a moment there was silence. The girl's eyes widened slightly in wonder.

"Ah," the woman in white murmured. "Very good." She motioned for one of the attendants to come take the girl away, and whispered a few words to the mother that I could not hear. The latter's grateful tears raised a knot in my throat. Was there any reward on Earth for which my mother would have abandoned me like that?

This isn't the real Earth, a stern inner voice reminded me. *And these aren't your people. Never forget that.*

But they *were* my people. I'd been born here. Some mother just like this one had chosen to hand me over to strangers, in exchange for a more promising child. Had I originally been born aristo, I wondered, or destitute? Had I been abandoned for greed, social ambition, or some other, as-yet-unimagined motive?

I felt tears rising in my eyes, and hurriedly wiped them away. *If you'd been raised here you wouldn't ever have known your mom,* I told myself. *You'd never have known Tommy.*

Suddenly there was a flurry of activity at the far end of the pavilion; a thin woman with black hair broke through one of the lines and headed directly toward Morgana.

I gasped when I saw her.

"What?" Rita said. "What is it?"

This woman's face was angular and thin. Her thick black hair gleamed in a smooth Cleopatra cut. She had on more eyeliner than when I'd last seen her, but that face was one I would never forget. Never.

"It's *her,*" I muttered. Backing into the crowd a bit more, just to make sure she couldn't see me.

It took Rita a second to put the pieces together. "Jesus. The one who watched your house burn down? You're sure?"

I nodded. My throat was so tight I could barely the force words out. "She asked about my art. My dreams." Out of one corner of my eye I saw Isaac look sharply at me, but my attention remained fixed on the woman. "She said that her name was Miriam Seyer—"

That's when it hit me.

Seyer.

Seer.

Oh, my God. What idiots we'd been. She'd all but announced her true identity.

Heart beating wildly, I watched as the two women talked. Their voices were pitched too low for me to hear, but whatever they were discussing was clearly weighty business.

Morgana looked over the crowd, shook her head sharply, and then gestured toward the tower. Seyer nodded. They started to walk in that direction together.

I trembled, but not just from fear. From exhilaration. Miriam Seyer was part of the conspiracy that connected me to this world . . . which meant she was also connected to Tommy. She might know where he was, and how I could rescue him. Right now, she was the only lead I had.

Without further thought I started after them. But hands from both sides grabbed my arms, stopping me abruptly in my tracks. "Don't," Isaac warned sharply.

I tried to pull away from them, but though I slipped out of Isaac's grasp, Rita continued to hold on tightly.

I lowered my voice to a fierce whisper. "That woman has information we need. That's what we came here for, right? To get information?" I glared at him. "I can't just let her walk away."

Isaac started to voice an objection, but I was no longer listening to him. I jerked myself free of Rita's grip and looked to see which way the two women had gone. The woman in white was no longer visible, and Seyer was about to pass out of sight as well, behind the Seer's pavilion.

I didn't dare lose her.

My instinct was to shove the milling sightseers out of my way and just run after the two women, but I knew that would be foolish. If Seyer heard a commotion and looked my way, the whole game was over. So I forced myself to walk at a pace that wouldn't set me apart from the crowd. It was agonizing. I had to swing wide around the pavilion, out past long lines of people waiting to learn their destiny. It cost me time. Precious time. By the time I reached the back side of the pavilion the women were gone. A knot of pure despair clenched in my gut: I'd lost them! But then I saw a flash of white from an intersection nearby, where a local street met the park, and I hurried in that direction.

Rita and Isaac followed in silence, making no further attempt to stop me. I guess they accepted that I was going to follow Miriam Seyer no matter what they said, and they didn't want me to do it alone. And they were right. I would have jumped off a cliff with no parachute if that's what it took to find out where my little brother was.

The street the two women had entered was a broad flagstone promenade flanked by ritzy boutiques, and it was crowded with window shoppers enjoying the midday sunshine. Back in the plaza the crowds had been an obstacle, but here they provided a valuable blind. I tried to remember everything I'd seen on cop shows about using passers-by to mask your stalking, but I could have saved myself the trouble. The two women were totally engrossed in their conversation, and neither spared a glance for the world around them. Least of all the three teenagers following behind them.

How I hungered to listen to what they were saying! It had been less than forty-eight hours since we'd arrived in this godforsaken world, so this might well be Seyer's first opportunity to report the details of the fire. She might be talking about us right now. It was maddening not to be able to hear her. But the women were speaking too softly for me to eavesdrop without getting much closer, and I didn't dare do that. Not yet.

I trailed them from a safe distance while they walked, watching

for any opportunity to close the gap between us without being noticed. Rita and Isaac followed, deliberately lagging behind me so that
our group movement was less likely to draw notice. Soon shops grew
scarce and the promenade gave way to a wealthy residential neighborhood, with well-maintained townhouses lining both sides of the
street. There were fewer people in this part of town, and by the time
we reached the main entrance of the Seers' estate it was getting hard
to find cover. Fuming in frustration, I was forced to fall back as I
watched them approach the gate.

The estate was large and surrounded by an aggressive black iron
fence, with several close-set rows of junipers planted right inside it, to
serve as a privacy screen. The only thing I could make out through
the wall of branches was a single large building. Overhead the tower
loomed, and I could see there was an observation deck circling the
top of it. From there one could probably look out over most of the city.

A pair of uniformed guards stood at attention on each side of the
gate, as motionless as the guards outside Buckingham Palace. When
they saw the two Seers they moved in perfect synch to open the ornate lattice-work doors, waited motionlessly for the women to pass
through, then closed them again.

And just like that, my quarry was out of reach.

Damn.

I couldn't even see where they had gone; a cluster of junipers
blocked my sightline.

I wanted to scream in frustration. Or break things.

Or maybe just cry.

"Let's go back," Isaac quietly. His voice made me jump; I hadn't
heard him coming up behind me. I looked at him and saw sympathy
in his eyes, but also a kind of wariness that hadn't been there before.
This place clearly made him uneasy.

"I want to hear what they're saying," I told him.

"I know," Rita said gently, "but we can't do that now. We just can't.
I'm sorry, Jesse."

She tried to put a comforting hand on my shoulder, but I shook it off. Maybe she was ready to give up, but I wasn't. The frustration of the last two days was a wildfire in my veins, and I had to give it outlet or I would explode.

I started to circle wide around the estate, to see if there was a break in the privacy screen that would at least allow me to peek inside. But the juniper barrier was several rows thick and there was no gap in it anywhere. I felt despair welling up inside me. To have someone who knew the truth about my situation so close by, and yet so inaccessible, was maddening. But whoever had designed this place had done it well; I was not going to be able to spy on Seyer from outside. Which meant . . .

I stopped walking. Yes, there was one course of action that would allow me to spy on her, but it was unspeakably dangerous. How much was I willing to risk?

Rita must have read my mind at that moment. "Jesse . . . no."

The bars of the fence were simple and smooth, with nothing to brace a foot on. The sharp, spear-like finials at the top were closely placed, allowing little room for a person to maneuver. I saw nothing in the immediate vicinity that I could push up against the fence, to help me climb.

Even thinking about what I wanted to do was crazy. Absolute, no-holds-barred, batshit crazy. Only a lunatic would try to sneak into a walled estate like this, to spy on women who had unknown mental powers. Maybe the stress of this whole experience had finally driven me insane. But I had to do *something* or I would explode.

I couldn't climb the fence without help.

I looked at Isaac. He was taller than Rita and probably stronger. Besides which, I was willing to bet money *she* wouldn't help me climb this thing, while he . . . he was an unknown quantity.

His face betrayed no emotion. "Unbelievably foolish," he said quietly.

"You have a better idea?"

"You understand how bad it will be if you're caught? Excuse me . . . *when* you're caught?"

"Worse than it is for Tommy right now?" I demanded.

The dark eyes fixed on me. They were disturbingly unreadable. *He's alien,* I reminded myself. *And aristo, to boot. He has motives I can't begin to guess at.*

"He means that much to you," he said at last. A question.

"He's *family,*" I told him. But how much did that mean to a guy who had abandoned his own family for the company of strangers? Was there anyone he cared about enough that he would risk the wrath of the Seers for them? After a moment he nodded grimly and gestured toward the fence.

I handed over my bag and hat to Rita and looked for a suitable spot. She muttered something under her breath about the stunning magnitude of my idiocy, but took the items. The look in her eyes was plain to read: *God help you if we have to go in there and rescue you.*

God help us all, in that case.

I found a place where the landscaping outside the fence offered some cover, so that my act of insanity wouldn't be in plain view of everyone walking down the street. There was a cluster of trees with thick, heavy branches near the fence, and only if you ducked down low could you see past them. It was as good as I was likely to get.

The fact that I'd decided to do something crazy didn't mean my body was happy about it. There was a knot of fear in my gut, clenched so tightly I thought I was going to vomit. I'd been in a pretty constant state of dread since coming to this world, but this was a whole new level. When you are actively fleeing alien pursuit and being hunted by shapechangers and diving into unknown worlds, you don't have any choice about the matter. They're coming after you, so you run. End of story. It all feels unreal while you're doing it, like everything is just a bad dream, and any minute now you'll wake up and find yourself home safe in bed. But this was different. This was *real.* This was a conscious choice that I was making, and if anything bad came of it, I'd have no one to blame but myself. This fear was an abyss that I was daring to vault across, without safety net or harness.

But it had to be done.

Drawing in a last deep breath for courage, I wiped nervous sweat from my palms and looked at Isaac. With a grim look on his face he crouched down by my side and offered me his cupped hands to step into. He managed to hoist me up high enough that I was able to get a firm grip on the top rail of the fence, and I swung my right leg over it. Then I struggled to achieve the precarious ballet needed to turn around without impaling myself on any of the spikes. Rita and Isaac watched in silence as I finally managed it, lowering myself down on the other side of the fence as far as I could, and then—muttering a prayer under my breath—dropping the rest of the way.

It wasn't far, but I landed on rocks that shifted beneath my feet, and my ankle twisted, throwing me to the ground with a loud *thwunk*. We all froze in place, and I waited breathlessly for the sound of some-one coming to investigate. But seconds passed, and no one did. Fi-nally I struggled back to my feet. My ankle throbbed but it wasn't broken; I could still walk on it, thank God. I winced slightly as I stepped forward to part the wall of branches—slowly, oh so slowly—hoping that anyone who saw the motion would ascribe it to the wind.

The estate I could now see was mostly open land, with a single imposing building at its center. It was a large structure, temple-like, with broad marble stairs leading up to a columned porch. A pair of golden statues of Egyptian cats anchored the lower corners of the staircase, and some of the carved figures in the frieze over the en-trance looked Egyptian as well. It reminded me of a Masonic Temple I'd once seen in DC. From the center of the roof rose the tower we had seen from the park. Thank God there was no one out on the ob-servation deck right now, because anyone up there would have a bird's eye view of the entire estate . . . and me.

The open land surrounding the building was meticulously land-scaped, and tall flowering hedges of at least a dozen different types crisscrossed the grounds in complicated patterns. I wondered if, when viewed from overhead, those designs had some special significance.

Suddenly I caught sight of two people off to my right, talking be-neath a vine-covered trellis. Their faces moved in and out of shadow as they spoke, but there was no missing the gleaming white of Morgana's ensemble or the intensity of their conversation.

They were still too far away for me to hear what they were saying. Heart pounding, I studied the terrain between us, wondering if I could get any closer without being detected. The hedges between us were tall enough to conceal me, at least from the two women. But if someone looked out an upper-story window all bets were off.

Time was running out. Every minute that passed meant they were more likely to wrap up their discussion of the issues that interested me, after which spying on them would have little value. If I was going to do this insane thing, I needed to do it now.

I started to creep forward, keeping as low to the ground as possible. For the first few yards there was no cover, so all I could do was crouch-trot to the nearest hedge as quickly as I could, praying that neither of them would look in my direction. My heart was pounding so loudly I was surprised no one inside the house could hear it. Or maybe they could. Maybe there was a Seer watching me right now, like a hawk watches a hare as it moves out into the meadow to forage, waiting to choose the right moment to strike.

Focus, girl. Focus.

Once I reached the first line of hedges the tension in my body eased a bit, and I took a moment to breathe deeply and stretch out a nascent cramp in my leg. Then I began to edge forward once more. My progress was blind, as I didn't dare raise my head over the top of the shrubbery to see where I was going. I just tried to head in the general direction of the women's voices, by whatever path allowed me to do so safely. Now and then I could hear tantalizing bits of their conversation, though still not enough to make sense of it.

. . . not a good move . . .

. . . yes, but who . . . ?

. . . and maybe tell them . . .

. . . not interested in excuses . . .

Suddenly there was a sharp sound from above. Startled, I looked up and saw that a man was standing on the observation deck of the tower. *No!* I despaired. *Not now!* I pressed myself close to the nearest hedge, trying desperately to sink into its foliage, but the dense evergreen branches were too closely packed for that to work. If he looked down he was sure to see me. And then I would have to do—what? What on earth could I do to save myself?

Nothing. Nothing at all.

Heart pounding, I watched as he began to circle the tower. When he passed out of sight behind it I had a sudden mad impulse to dash for better cover. But that kind of movement might draw the attention of those on the ground, so I just waited, breath held, body shaking, until he appeared again on the other side.

He paused to look out toward the main gate for a few seconds, and *almost* looked my way, then disappeared through a door leading back into the tower. It shut behind him with a thud.

I allowed myself to breathe again.

Slowly, my whole body trembling, I began to move once more, struggling to focus on the women's conversation. I was getting close enough to make out most of what they were saying, though now and then a phrase was voiced too quietly for me to hear. Finally I found a good hiding spot behind a bank of laurels, and I crouched down to eavesdrop.

". . . not like it hasn't been done before." That was Miriam Seyer's voice. Hearing it again invoked chilling memories of the night my house had burned to the ground.

"But not for so weak a cause." The other woman's accent was the liquid, elegant drawl of Virginian aristocracy, with just a faint hint of *Masterpiece Theater*. It was a voice rich in confidence and power, suggesting a speaker who could get others to do her bidding without ever needing to raise her voice.

"Master Virilian might not agree with that," Seyer responded.

An edge of scorn crept into Morgana's voice. "The Shadowlord is a man of passion. Sometimes that outweighs his judgment."

"Which is why he answers to the Council."

"Who are less and less willing to rein him in."

"Because they fear his power, or his madness?"

"Anyone with a brain would fear such madness," Morgana said quietly. "But that's true for all the *umbrae majae,* isn't it? There's no way a Shadowlord could be anything other than stark-raving mad, given what Communion requires of them."

"You really think he would call for a full Cleansing?"

"Why not? He's already called for a partial one. And the Shadows who called for genocide in the past may still be around, whispering advice into the depths of Virilian's soul. That's the true curse of their kind, that even death can't free them from the madness of their predecessors."

Cleansing? Genocide? The words hit me like electric shocks. What the hell had I stumbled into?

"At least Jessica is on this side of the Gate now." I gasped as Seyer spoke my name. "So whatever happens on Terra Colonna won't affect her."

"Yes." There was a pause. "She seems to be quite resourceful, doesn't she?"

Seyer chuckled softly. "She takes after her mother."

My mother! Too much, too much! Bits of information were pouring into my brain at such a pace that I had no time to assemble them into a meaningful picture. Only one thing stood out, bright and clear: Whatever the mystery was that tied me to this world, these two women were at the heart of it. They knew who I was and why I'd been abandoned on a foreign world.

They knew who my real mother was.

"I'm impressed by how quickly she got her bearings," Morgana continued. "I feared for a while we might lose her." She paused. "Of course, with the Shadows hunting her, we still might."

"They don't suspect what she is, do they?"

"Heavens, no. They called me in for an official Assessment, and I told them what they wanted to hear: that the boy was a latent dreamwalker. Who among them would dare doubt the word of the Mistress of the Guild of Seers? I even tried to convince them to kill the boy—the neatest solution from our standpoint—but I doubt they'll do that. Most likely they'll study him for a while, seeking insight into the ancient curse he supposedly carries. The boy's mind is filled with wild fantasies, so if he's resourceful enough to figure out what they want, he may be able to last for a while. Meanwhile, he's a true Colonnan by birth, so nothing they find out about him is going to put our project at risk."

"Unless they get hold of Jessica herself."

"Ah." Morgana's voice dropped to a murmur. "Then we'll see how resourceful she really is, won't we?" There was a pause. "You're sure she's outside the Warrens right now?"

"Yes, your Grace."

"The Lord Governor told me he's going to 'flush out that rat's nest once and for all.' I smell Virilian's hand in it. Let's keep her out of there for as long as we can."

I heard Seyer hesitate. "You know that my methods don't lend themselves to guarantees. If you want me to act more directly—"

"No. No. You're right; we can't risk her catching on. Try to keep her aboveground until nightfall, if you can. The worst should all be over by then. Though if she returns after that, what she finds may be . . . disturbing."

I didn't hear what they said next. Something about dreams and strong negative emotions and how trauma might open a door for me. Fear could be a good thing.

They were going to raid the Warrens. Right now.

Devon was still down there. So were all those children. Orphans of this heartless culture, cast adrift to live in squalor, now due to be exterminated like rats—or maybe something worse. In this crazy place even death wasn't certain.

I hesitated only an instant. True, I'd learned more in the last half hour than in all my previous time on this world. These women clearly knew the answers to my most burning questions, and once I left here I might never have another chance to get them. But. . . .

Devon.

Ethan.

Moth.

I had to go back. I had to warn them all.

I started to head back the way I'd come. My limbs felt numb, as if the informational overload had somehow seeped into my arms and legs and clogged my veins. I tried to focus on moving quietly, keeping my head low, and not thinking too hard about what I'd just heard, but the last was impossible. The women's words echoed and remixed in my head, drowning out all other thoughts.

I tried to convince them to kill the boy . . .

Those who called for genocide are still around . . .

She takes after her mother . . .

When I finally got to the open stretch just before the fence, I peeked up over the bushes one last time to make sure the two women were turned away from me, and then I bolted. Or tried to bolt, anyway. The damage to my ankle turned the motion into a feverish stumble, and my attempt to dive neatly into the juniper branches nearly turned into a belly-flop. That kind of stunt isn't as easy as it looks in the movies. I saved myself at the last moment by grabbing on to a handful of scratchy branches, and I didn't stop to listen for pursuit, just kept going. If someone was following me, I wanted to at least pass a warning on to Isaac and Rita before any pursuer caught up with me.

I didn't emerge at the same location where I had entered the estate, but my companions saw me through the fence and came running. I almost blurted out something about the raid then and there, but I realized that if I did, Isaac might not want to wait for me to climb the fence again, just run off to warn his people. I wasn't sure I could manage the climb with only Rita to help me, and even if I did, that would still leave us in the middle of this strange city without a guide. So may God forgive me for my selfishness: I kept my silence while he thrust his hands between the bars and cupped them to give me purchase. Rita grabbed hold of whatever part of me was within reach, to help steady me as I climbed. My hands were shaking so badly I could barely hold onto the bars, and as I pulled myself over the top of the fence I felt one of the iron finials scrape across my stomach. I didn't dare look down to see if I was bleeding but fell heavily on the other side, taking Rita and Isaac down with me.

"There's going to be a raid," I gasped. "The Warrens. They're going to clean it all out . . ."

They helped me to my feet, and then Isaac looked in my eyes and said, "I'll take care of this. You head back to the plaza for now; the crowds will keep you safe. We can meet up at the Elemental's pavilion"

I knew he meant it well, and was just trying to protect me, but he had no personal investment in Devon's safety and I doubted he would take personal risks to save him. I had to go myself.

"We have people down there too," I reminded him. *Not to mention I don't want to be left up here without a guide. What if you don't come back?*

We started running. Or rather, they started running, and I started lurching quickly. Each time my left foot hit the ground there was a sharp pain; what would happen if it got so bad I couldn't keep up with them? In my mind's eye I could see Devon peering out from the shadows of the Warrens, and the thought that he might be swept up in some terrible pogrom was more than I could handle. Not to mention that the thought of dividing our party terrified me. In the movies that's always when disaster strikes, when people split up. Driven by fear I struggled on, trying not to let the others see how injured I was.

But Isaac could see that I was having a hard time. He hooked an arm around me, letting me throw my left arm over his shoulder so that I could transfer some of my weight to him. With his support I was able to move more quickly, and the pain muted slightly. His body was warm and firm against mine, and the contact was comforting. It shouldn't have been. Nothing should have been comforting at a time like this. But he was strong and confident, and he seemed to know what he was doing, and some of his certainty seeped into me through the contact.

Everything is going to be all right, I told myself. Over and over again. *Everything is going to be all right. Everything is going to be all right.*

But try as I might, I couldn't make myself believe it.

21

The Warrens

RUN TO THE WARRENS AND WARN EVERYONE turned out to be a task more easily described than accomplished.

Isaac led us to the nearest entrance he knew of, which turned out to be a manhole in a dingy alley. He stopped a block away from it, ostensibly so we could catch our breath, but also because he wanted to get the lay of the land before moving in closer. I wasn't about to complain. The pain in my ankle was becoming more intense with every step, and it was getting harder and harder to keep up with my companions. It helped to have a few moments to hang my head and catch a deep breath, while he went on ahead to scout our route.

Soon he returned, and his dour expression said it all. "Too many people around," he told us. "More than should be here. I don't like it."

"They're covering the exits," Rita said quietly.

I remembered how alert she was when we first met at IHOP. I remembered the look in her eyes as she checked out all the exits in the place, before committing herself to a defensive position at the table. Always wary. Always ready to run.

She looked like that now.

Isaac led us to several other access points. The story was the same at each one: too many people nearby, an unexpected obstacle in our path, or something else unexpected and ominous. Clearly, people and equipment were being moved into place so that when the raid went down any kids who tried to escape would run straight into a trap. Or maybe the raid was meant to drive them topside, so they could be scooped up more easily.

Flush them out, Morgana had said.

I felt sick inside, and not just from pain.

What if the raid had already begun, deep underground? Isaac told us he didn't think that was the case, because the people standing near the access points didn't look particularly alert. They hadn't yet been cued to spread their nets. But that could change at any moment.

Devon, please tell me you haven't wandered off somewhere. Please tell me you're sitting in the middle of the magpie room, bag packed and ready to go . . .

Finally Isaac found a route that the raiders didn't seem to know about. We had to burrow under a collapsed storage shed to an uncovered drainage pipe, which headed down into the earth at a steep angle. It would serve us as an entrance, Isaac warned us, but not an exit. That's probably why no one was watching it.

"Are you sure you want to do this?" he asked. His eyes were fixed on me.

I nodded. But in truth, I was no longer sure of anything. The pain in my ankle was growing so intense that I was beginning to wonder if I could keep my footing in the treacherous labyrinth. But what was the alternative? Let Isaac go down alone, and entrust Devon's fate to him? Send Rita down with him while I waited up here, defenseless and alone? Each option was worse than the last.

No, I had to remain with them. Whatever that required of me.

Rita and I sent our bags sliding down the pipe, then followed them. It was a tight fit. The inside of the pipe was covered in slime, and while the lubrication was helpful, it was also unspeakably gross. Slime-slicked, we slid down the steeply angled pipe with no visibility and no control. I wondered if I was going to hit something hard at the bottom, and break both my legs. Or maybe splash down in some reeking, garbage-filled dumpster, like in *Star Wars*.

The answer, as it turned out, was neither. One minute I was whizzing down the pipe, and the next I was flying through open air, and then: *thwump!* I landed on a thick pile of mattresses. Fortunately I managed to draw up my left leg just before landing so that my injured ankle wouldn't have to absorb the shock. I landed hard on my butt and tiny winged creatures flitted off in all directions, chittering as they flew off into the darkness. Probably complaining about how I had messed up their nice home.

When all three of us were safely down the chute, Isaac produced a small blue lamp from his pocket, so that we could finally see our surroundings. I could spend a week with a thesaurus and still not find the words needed to capture how filthy, wet, and disgusting that place was. But at least there were no guards here, ready to capture us.

I fell in behind Isaac as he led us through the putrid labyrinth. He salvaged a broken pole from a heap of garbage for me to use as a walking stick, which helped take some of the weight off my wounded ankle. But there was a hot pain spreading across my belly now, where the finials from the fence had scraped me, and I was afraid to lift my shirt and look at it. If I had any kind of an open wound I'd need to clean and bandage it immediately, lest it get infected in this dismal place. But that would require a delay, which meant Devon might not be warned in time, which meant the raid might catch him. What was I supposed to do? With pain lancing through my leg at every step I couldn't think clearly enough to weigh the options, so I just stumbled behind Isaac, focusing on keeping my footing.

After awhile we climbed a ladder that brought us to cleaner tunnels, and soon after that we came across one of the residents. The little girl started to run away as soon as she saw us—hardly a wonder, with us looking more like swamp monsters than people—but Isaac got her to stand still long enough for him to warn her about the coming raid. I watched as the color drained from her face, and before he could ask her to help tell the others she bolted off into the darkness. So much for that plan.

Isaac did seem unusually calm, through all this. On some level of my pain-hazed brain, I recognized that was odd. But maybe he figured that his aristo background would protect him. He wasn't one of the common sewer rats that the raid was meant to eradicate. He *mattered*.

Soon, we came to an area that looked familiar, though that was due more to a nebulous sense of *déjà vu* than any concrete recognition of detail. We started passing the tiny lamps that the denizens of the Warrens kept burning to drive back the darkness in the outer tunnels, then the larger lamps that were used in the Warrens proper. When there was finally enough light to see by, Isaac put his own lamp away. I hadn't paid attention to it before, but as he shut it off and put it in his pocket I saw that it was simply a large glass marble, with no visible markings. A fetter? Since I knew that he came from an aristo family it shouldn't have surprised me that he possessed something like that, but for some reason it did. I guess I'd pictured him running away from home with nothing but the shirt on his back, as he left behind all the trappings of his former life. It was, in hindsight, a foolish vision. One could be rebellious without being stupid.

As soon as we reached the magpie room, the children there realized that something was wrong; they gathered closely about us, anxious to hear the news. I was distantly aware of Isaac's filling them in, but I was no longer listening to him. My attention was wholly fixed on seeking Devon in the shadows.

He wasn't there.

Once the children understood the Warrens were about to be raided, they began to scatter. I still had no clue where Devon was, and in a few seconds there would be no one left to ask. I caught sight of a young boy I'd been introduced to the night before and called out his name. He ignored me. I called to him more loudly, and when he tried to run past me without acknowledging my existence I grabbed his arm and jerked him to a stop, forcing him to turn and look at me.

"Where's Devon?" I demanded.

"Dunno," he said, and there was panic in his eyes as tried to break loose from my grip. But I was damned if I was letting him go before he gave me an answer.

Finally he said, "In the gallery. Maybe."

I let go. A moment later he was gone, swallowed by the shadows of the underworld.

I turned to Isaac, but before I could speak I was interrupted by a sudden metallic clanging. It took me a second to realize that someone must be banging on the pipes elsewhere in the Warrens, and the sound was resonating throughout the underground sanctuary.

"It's started," Isaac whispered. I could hear a note of fear in his voice now. Maybe he'd counted on getting out of the Warrens before the raid began in earnest.

Too late now.

"We need to find Devon," I said. "Where's the gallery?"

"This way," Isaac said, pointing to a tunnel opening across from us.

We followed him into the depths of the labyrinth. The clanging had ceased now, leaving the abandoned halls tomb-like and silent. When we passed the last of the guide lamps he took out his glowing blue sphere again. By its light we finally reached a chamber where a series of rectangular items had once been attached to the wall. They were gone now, but they'd left behind ghosts outlined in grime, as neatly ordered as the paintings in an art museum.

Devon wasn't there, so we called out his name, though not so loudly that distant raiders would hear us. For one terrifying moment it seemed that he wasn't going to answer. But then he stepped around a corner, and if I'd been standing closer to him I would have hugged him. "Thank God," I whispered. "Thank God." He had his backpack with him, I noticed. Even in this refuge he had never felt confident enough to leave it behind. Yet another thing to give thanks for.

He opened his mouth to speak—and then the screaming started. It was impossible to tell how far from us the source was, as the stark tunnels echoed and amplified every cry. There were at least three different voices, however, and they all sounded young.

And then suddenly they fell silent, which was even more terrifying.

"We need to get far away from here," Isaac muttered, and none of us felt like arguing with him.

I won't catalog all the twists and turns we took, trying to find a way out of that deathtrap. The rusted pipes we squeezed through, the rotting ladders that shattered beneath our feet, the abandoned corridors that led nowhere. My ankle was getting worse and worse, and pain shot through my leg every time I put pressure on it. But whenever we stopped to listen, the noise of the raid was still too close. The screaming had begun again and it seemed to be coming from all sides. One time we emerged from a narrow crawl space to see a half-dozen lanterns coming toward us, and we barely got out of their way in time.

But eventually we reached a place where there was relative silence. We paused in a narrow tunnel to catch our breath, though it was not a comfortable respite. Ankle-deep water rushed past our feet, heading from nowhere to nowhere, and when we started moving again the current was so strong that it nearly knocked me down. Rita grabbed me and kept me from falling, then let me rest an arm across her shoulders for support, like Isaac had done earlier. But it was hard to maneuver through the narrow tunnels in such a posture, and soon I had to go back to stumbling along by myself, terrified that a fall would land me face down in that lightless soup.

"Do you know where we are?" Rita asked Isaac at one point.

His grim silence was an eloquent response.

"Great," she muttered. "Just great."

"So how are we going to get out of here?" I asked him. I was starting to feel feverish, and I hoped that was a consequence of fear and exhaustion, and not something more ominous. "We'll have to do that eventually."

No one said anything for a moment. A long moment.

"We have compasses," Rita offered.

"That'll tell us direction," Isaac said. "Not which way is out."

"No," Devon said, "but the water will do that."

I looked at him. In the bluish light of Isaac's glow lamp Devon's dark skin glistened eerily, like some fearsome obsidian statue. Since my expression could not possibly capture the full extent of my confusion, I offered, "Huh?"

He pointed to the water coursing about our feet. "It's moving." A rotting bit of something that might once have been food floated into our field of light, and we watched as it made its way past us, moving down the tunnel until it was swallowed by darkness again on the other side. "It's heading toward some kind of exit."

"Or some kind of underground cesspool," Rita muttered.

Devon shook his head. "Luray flanks the river. I'll bet you ten to one that this system empties into it. And where the water exits, we may be able to."

"Shades of Harrison Ford," Rita muttered.

"Well, we're not nearly that high above water level, and we'll probably be wading in raw sewage by the time we get there . . . but otherwise, yeah, something like that."

It sounded like a respectable plan, so we let him lead the way, following the flow of the water. Honestly, it could have been a bad plan, and we would have still followed it. When given a choice between, "I have a plan" and "I will sit in the darkness waiting to starve to death" there's not much to think about.

Soon we started hearing noises again, like someone was headed our way. I felt my stomach tighten in dread. If the raiders had thought to block off access to the river, there would be no way out . . . but we couldn't know if that was the case until we got there, so onward we trekked. Other tunnels and pipes emptied into the one we were following, and the water level began to rise around us. It was a good sign, but it made walking difficult. I was starting to get dizzy, and there were moments when I couldn't feel the ground beneath my feet.

Then Devon turned back and gestured to Isaac. "Turn off the lamp," he whispered.

Isaac did whatever you do to turn a fetter lamp off.

For a moment we were plunged into total darkness. In my exhausted state I was acutely aware of the tons of rock over our heads, and a combination of panic and nausea threatened to overwhelm me. But then I realized that it wasn't as dark as I'd thought. Indeed, as our eyes slowly adjusted, we could see there was something ahead of us.

Light. Very faint, very distant, but unmistakable.

Isaac turned his lamp back on, and we began to move forward as fast as the slippery tunnel would allow. *Just let us make it to the river,* I prayed. *Then I can collapse.* The ambient light grew brighter and brighter, and soon we got to the point where Isaac's lamp was no longer needed. That was a great moment, when he finally stuck the fetter back in his pocket. Our horrific journey was almost over.

Finally we reached the place where the storm system dumped its waste water into the river. We could see that beyond the large circular opening was clear sky above and free-flowing water below, with tree-covered mountains in the distance. The river was only a few yards beneath us: an easy drop.

All that stood between us and freedom was an iron grate with inch-thick bars, secured by a padlock as big as my fist.

"Shit," Rita muttered.

I leaned against the slimy wall in sheer exhaustion, fighting the urge to cry. Black water rushed around my knees, threatening to drag me under. *Don't give up,* I told myself. *Not yet. We'll find a way out. Hang in there.*

Isaac grabbed hold of the grate and shook it, testing its strength. After a moment Devon joined him. Together they banged on it and pushed it and pulled it and shook it, trying everything they could think of to force it to give way. But it didn't budge. Rita then offered to try to pick the lock, but the mechanism was so clogged with rust and filth that the tools she pulled out weren't strong enough for the job. When one of them finally snapped in her hand she, too, sagged against the wall, too frustrated even to curse.

For a moment all of us were silent, wondering what on earth we should do next. That's when we heard a rhythmic splashing that could only mean one thing: someone was coming toward us. It wasn't a distant sound, subtly alerting us to the fact that enemies were somewhere on the same level, but intimately close, disconcertingly clear. Maybe only a tunnel or two away. And coming toward us quickly.

There was nowhere to run. Nowhere to hide. We didn't even have darkness for cover any more. *Is this how I'm going to die?* I thought feverishly. Despair welled up in my gut, not only for myself but for all the people who depended on me. *Tommy, I'm sorry, I failed you . . . .*

Suddenly we heard new footsteps, out of sync with the splashing. Someone was coming toward us from another direction, where the water wasn't as deep. I braced my back against the wall for support—my legs were so weak they could barely support me anymore—and wished I believed in the kind of God who saved people from being attacked in the sewers. Maybe I should have gone to church more often.

The man who finally came into view wasn't dressed like a tunnel raider, which was marginally reassuring. He was an older man, with gleaming white hair pulled back into a short ponytail and a close-clipped beard to match. His face was weathered and fine lines fanned out from his mouth and his eyes. The latter were a piercing blue, and his gaze as he studied us was intense. Overall he wasn't large, but he bore himself in a way that implied confidence and strength—a stark contrast to how we all were feeling. His long brown leather duster reminded me of an Australian trench coat, and it had small metal ornaments arranged haphazardly down one side. My vision was too blurry for me to make out any more detail than that. In fact, everything was getting a bit blurry. I shook my head to try to clear it.

"You are the visitors?" he asked.

We all just stared at him. No one knew what to say.

"From Terra Colonna?" he pressed.

I nodded to him. To both of him. Or maybe there was only one of him, but it had four eyes. I suddenly wasn't sure.

Dimly I realized that I was becoming delirious.

"Yeah," Devon croaked. "That's us."

The man was about to say something more when the splashing sounds suddenly grew louder; the raiders must have turned a corner nearby. "Come!" he whispered, and he gestured for us to gather by his side. We figured he was going to lead us away or something, so we all obeyed. I think deep inside we were all glad to have someone tell us what to do. I wasn't quite strong enough to make it across the current to get to him, but when I fell he stepped forward and caught me under the arms, before I hit the water. He was surprisingly strong.

And then we all were there, standing next to him, ready for him to lead us . . . nowhere. Seriously. He didn't move. We just all stood there in a huddle, our backs pressed against the wall of the tunnel, while the ominous splashing footsteps came closer and closer. Totally exposed.

If there was a Guinness Book of World Records award for hiding badly, this would have nailed it.

"But—" Rita began.

"Shhh!" he whispered fiercely. "Stay close to me. Don't move. Don't say anything!"

Before any of us had a chance to respond, four men turned the corner. They were classic goons, exactly the type you'd hire to crawl around in sewers beating up small children. I trembled as they approached the grate.

"Looks like we missed 'em," one of them said. He was a stocky man with the face of a bulldog.

One of the others stepped forward. He stared at the grate for a moment, then reached out and shook it, to see if it was solid. Then he grabbed the lock and tugged it a few times to see if it would come loose. When it didn't, he grunted. "They'll be back. That or topside. There's no other way out."

He looked down at the water flowing around his feet. "Not gonna find a trail in this place." He looked up at his men. "Fall back. Give 'em room to think they're safe. If we can corner them in here they'll have nowhere to run."

Then they turned to leave.

Seriously. They all turned to leave. As if we weren't there, right in front of them.

Maybe that was a delusion, too.

The bulldog man turned back for one last look. I stiffened as his eyes scanned the water, the grating, the mildew-covered walls, bracing myself for what would happen when he finally saw us. But he never did. It wasn't like we were invisible or anything, more like he looked *around* us.

Then, with a final dog-like grunt, he followed his fellow goons into the shadows.

"What the hell—?" Rita began to whisper, but the man with the white ponytail clamped a hand over her mouth to shut her up. Normally I'd have expected her to bite the hand of anyone who tried that— especially a stranger—but I guess she figured he'd earned the right.

We waited in silence, listening to the splashing of the goons slowly fade away. Only when we could no longer hear them did the man in the leather coat release Rita and wade back to the grate.

"Damn," Devon muttered shaking his head. "What was that all about? Some kind of cloak of invisibility?"

"Nothing so simple," the man responded. "And it's very costly. So don't count on my using it again."

He took out a ring of heavy brass keys from his pocket, chose one, and inserted it into the lock. "Used to come this way," he said. He strained to turn the key, but it didn't budge. "Long time ago," he muttered.

Then, with a sudden snap, the key moved. He pulled the lock open and swung the grate back a bit, just far enough for us to get past it. There was a low creaking sound as it moved, and we all flinched, worried that our enemies were listening.

"Move fast," he said, gesturing for us to squeeze past him. Rita was the first to go, and as she was the smallest, it was an easy fit. "Get down to the shore," he told her, "somewhere out of the line of sight from here. Wait for me."

She walked a few feet, looked over the edge, then jumped. A few seconds later I heard a deep splash.

Devon went next.

I tried to approach the grate, but my leg had stiffened up in the last few minutes, and I found I could barely move it. The grate seemed to be moving around a bit. Rippling, like water. I hoped it would stand still long enough for me to squeeze past it.

The white-haired man looked at me with concern, then reached out and pressed the back of his hand briefly against my forehead. The fine white lines between his eyebrows deepened.

"I'll take her," he said.

Isaac hesitated, then nodded. With a strong arm the white-haired man drew me close to him, holding me tightly against him as he urged Isaac through the opening. His coat smelled of things that were not raw sewage, which was nice.

"I apologize for what is going to seem an undignified exit," he said to me, as Isaac went over the edge. Holding me close to him, he squeezed through the narrow opening. Barbs of rusty iron scraped my skin as he pulled me along with him. Great. Tetanus too. This trip just got better and better.

He closed the gate carefully behind us and reached in through the bars to lock it again. Then without warning he picked me up and threw me over his shoulder, head first, so that I wound up hanging down his back. I grabbed onto his coat, dimly aware that if we jumped down into the river like this it would be really hard for me to swim. But he didn't jump. He walked to the edge of the tunnel, grabbed hold of something off to one side, then swung himself around the opening. It didn't look like there was anything next to the pipe but a pretty steep hillside, but apparently he found some kind of foothold.

And then we stood very still. Well, *he* stood very still. I hung with my butt in the air, very still.

Over the sound of the water I could hear people approaching. The goons must have had heard the gate open, and they were coming to investigate. I prayed my companions had gotten out of sight in time.

I heard people moving around inside the pipe. Saying things I couldn't make out. Then they left. We waited until we could no longer hear them, and then we waited some more. And some more. The blood rushing to my head, meanwhile, made for an interesting sensation. Kind of like an internal roller coaster.

Finally he began to move again. I was aware of him climbing down the embankment, then carrying me a short way along the shore. We came to a big canoe, and he laid me down inside it. Then he pushed off, and we were on the river. The sun warmed my skin. Nice, very nice. I shut my eyes for a minute then felt the canoe jostle as more people climbed into it. Three in all. I opened my eyes but couldn't see anything clearly. Feet pressed against me on all sides as my companions packed themselves into the narrow space. Not such a big canoe after all.

And then the strange man with the white ponytail pushed us away from the shore and let the current carry us south. Away from Luray. Away from pursuit.

Away from Tommy.

No! I screamed inwardly. *No! This isn't what's supposed to happen!*

I opened my mouth to protest, but no sound would come out. My tongue was hot and swollen.

"When we get to where the water's clear," the man said, "the three of you are going to take a dip. I won't bring someone who smells like fresh manure into my home."

But I smelled like fresh manure, too. Didn't that matter? Wasn't I going home with them?

"Who are you?" I heard Isaac ask him. "Why are you helping us?"

There was silence for a moment. Then soft laughter.

"I thought you'd have guessed that by now," he said. "They call me the Green Man."

That's when I passed out.

22

Obfuscate Guildhouse In Luray
Virginia Prime

THEY PUT A BAG over Tommy's head when they moved him. But that was a good thing, he told himself. You put a bag over someone's head when you didn't want him to see things he might report on later. There was no point in doing that if you intended to kill him. Right?

He kept telling himself that. Over and over again. But it wasn't enough to fend off a tide of raw panic as they dragged him from his cell, blind and bound, and carted him off to unknown places. He probably would have pissed his pants in terror if he hadn't just emptied his bladder before they arrived; as it was, the more sensitive bits of his anatomy pulled up so tightly against his body that it felt like they were trying to take shelter inside him.

Where were they taking him? He asked, but they wouldn't say. He might as well be whimpering questions to the wind.

He knew he should pay attention to the world around him, memorizing whatever details of sound or smell he could identify, in case he needed to find this place later . . . but that was easier said than done. And besides, what good would it do? He hadn't been hooded when the aliens brought him through the crystal gate, so he wasn't under any illusion about where he was. Or, more accurately, where he wasn't.

Even if he managed to get away from these people, it was going to take a lot more to get him home than a brisk walk through a bad neighborhood.

He knew when they took him outside, because the heat of the sun started to turn his head-bag into an oven. Then he was led up a couple of steps into an enclosure that was marginally cooler. From the echo of his movements, it sounded like he was in a small space. A van, maybe? No, because when it started moving he heard the clip-clop of horse hooves on pavement. For a moment the sheer incongruity of it distracted him from his fear. Was he was being transported from one alien stronghold to another in a *horse-drawn carriage?* Seriously? What kind of low budget aliens were these, anyway?

The noise of the surrounding city was muffled by carriage walls and the bag, but it sounded like a crowded place. He thought briefly about screaming for help, but then he figured that the odds of someone responding to a muffled cry from inside a vehicle in the middle of a crowded city were not nearly as high as the odds of his captors hurting him if he tried it. The last thing he wanted to do right now, bound and helpless, was piss them off.

Eventually the outside noises faded, and the carriage began to move uphill. After a while Tommy could tell it was entering a cool, dark space. Then it stopped.

He heard the door open. "Is this the boy?" someone asked.

"It's *a* boy," someone else responded gruffly. "Are you the one who signs for him?"

They pulled him from the carriage, and there was more walking. More stumbling. They were indoors now, and once or twice he had to go down a staircase, a precarious feat that required he feel for each stair with his toes.

Then they put him in something that felt like an elevator, but didn't sound like an elevator. Heading down.

The air in the lower level was chilly. As the sweat of fear evaporated on Tommy's skin he shivered, and the bag was finally removed from his head. He blinked as his eyes adjusted to the dim blue light.

He was standing in a cave. Well, mostly a cave. Someone had laid down a smooth concrete floor and stuck eerie glowing balls to the ceiling, then put metal bars across the openings of several natural alcoves. Call it the world's creepiest jail. The door to one of the alcoves was open and Tommy didn't need a degree in rocket science to know that they wanted him to go in there.

Were they going to lock him up and leave him alone down here? It was a scarier thought in this surreal environment than it would have been aboveground. Despairing, he tried to come up with an alternative to entering the cell—any alternative—but he couldn't think of any option that these guys were likely to accept.

They untied his hands and let him walk into the alcove of his own accord. It was a long and narrow space, with black, ominous shadows at the far end. The short walk through the door felt like a death march.

The door clanged shut.

"There's a journal on the table," came a voice from behind him. He turned around and saw a man with a deathly pale face, whose eyes and voice were devoid of any emotion. Two men stood behind him, equally dispassionate. Clearly scaring the hell out Tommy was just a job to them. "You will record your dreams every day. For so long as your information has value to us, you will be kept alive."

"What if I don't dream anything?" he asked. Not because he thought the answer would enlighten him, but as a stalling mechanism. Every minute he kept the man talking was one less minute he had to be alone down here. "This place isn't exactly conducive to sound sleep."

The cold eyes stared at him, unblinking. A lizard's gaze. "Then we will turn off the lights until you do dream. Do I need to demonstrate what that would be like?"

"No," he whispered. "I'll take your word for it."

As the man began to turn away from him, something flitted in between them. A wisp of smoke, that moved against the air currents in the room. A hint of shadow, that didn't have the shape of a shadow.

"Wait!" Tommy cried. "What was that?" He grabbed the bars, his heart pounding wildly. "What's down here?"

The lizard-man looked back at him. "Spirits of the dead. They're immaterial, and cannot hurt you."

"Ghosts?" he demanded, aghast. "You're leaving me down here with *ghosts*?"

"Fragments of ghosts," the man corrected. "Echoes of shattered lives, granted brief autonomy and the illusion of purpose. Some call them soul shards. Don't worry, few men can see them in any detail, and fewer still can make sense of their whispering. I don't expect they'll bother you much." A faint, cold smile spread across his face. "Surely not enough to disturb your sleep."

He motioned to the other two men, who followed him out of the chamber. A few seconds after they rounded a natural turn that took them out of Tommy's line of sight, he heard the strange elevator sound again.

Then there was silence.

No, not silence.

Whispers.

. . . scared . . .

The disembodied voice was so soft it was almost inaudible. A shadow wisped across the front of Tommy's cell, then vanished.

. . . so scared . . .

Shaking, he slid down the bars of his cell to the concrete floor. The courage he'd been clinging to so desperately up to now was beginning to crumble. A handful of blue light bulbs in the ceiling was all that stood between him and a nervous breakdown.

Jesse, he swore, *if you don't come find me soon, I'm gonna go crazy. Not gamer-crazy. The real thing.*

A few of the soul shards began to circle around him. They seemed to find him interesting.

But the lights were still on. So things could be worse.

Right?

23

THERE WAS A PTERODACTYL sitting on my chest.

Not a big one. Parrot-sized. Its head was turned to one side, and its little black eye was staring at me. There was no mistaking the profile. A pterodactyl.

"Ah. You're awake." A man's voice filtered into my awareness. I tried to turn my head toward him, but the motion hurt. Everything hurt.

"Here," he said, to someone other than me. "I saved one for you."

A small fish came flying in my direction. The pterodactyl reached up and snapped it out of the air. One gulp later the fish was gone. The pterodactyl went back to staring at me.

"Brought over from a world where the great asteroid never hit. They were popular pets among the elites for a while. Then the aristos tired of them, like they tire of everything. Here." He knelt down by my side. "This will help."

My chest burned like fire as he helped me to a sitting position. The pterodactyl squawked as it was dislodged, and fluttered off to take up a post on a nearby chair. My left leg, I saw, was swathed in thick bandages. It smelled of herbs. Every inch of my body was sore.

He lifted a cup to my lips.

"What is it?" I whispered hoarsely.

"Chicken soup. A thousand worlds have yet to come up with anything better. Drink."

I did so. Its heat soothed my throat, and my stomach soaked up the nourishment like a sponge. As I handed him back the cup I looked around, ready to face whatever my next trial was to be.

We were in a narrow cave, lit by flickering candles that were lined up in a neat row along a natural ledge at the far end. The chamber had been outfitted as a living space, albeit a spartan one. The bed I was now sitting on had a rough-hewn frame, and next to it stood a matching table with a single chair. In a dark recess far from the candlelight I saw some rough wooden shelves with a collection of items arranged on them, but I couldn't make out any details. A curtain had been hung across the mouth of the cave, made from some coarsely textured cloth. Burlap? There was no light bleeding through it from the outside.

"Where are the others?" I asked. The previous day's events were coming back to me now, along with bodily echoes of fear and exhaustion.

"Waiting outside. Very anxiously, I might add. Which is appropriate, given the condition you were in."

I put my hand up to my stomach and felt a thick swath of bandages there. My leg was wrapped in linen, with some kind of coin strapped to it. I ached in some places and burned in others, but it was nothing compared to the pain I'd been in the day before. I felt . . . better.

"You're a costly guest," the Green Man told me, as he saw my eye fall upon the coin. "The fetters that I used to heal you were worth their weight in gold. Not the sort of thing I usually part with for strangers."

"Was it necessary?" I asked.

He chuckled softly. "My dear, you swam in sewage with an open wound across your stomach, not to mention a day spent walking, jumping, and climbing on an ankle which, while not broken, was sorely damaged. Had I a month to heal you, then no, I would not need a Gift to do it. But your friends said that you wouldn't be willing to wait that long—that in fact you would want to jump up to go raid a Shadow's citadel as soon as you were capable of moving again. So other means were required."

"I didn't swim in sewage," I muttered.

"But you *are* planning to raid a Shadow's citadel."

I flushed a bit. "Well . . . yeah. Sort of."

"Then we should get you on your feet right away." He motioned toward the niche with the shelves. "There are some clean clothes over there. I regret that none are likely to fit you, but your own clothing is still damp, so choose whatever works the best. I'll let your friends know you're up and about."

He started toward the burlap curtain, but before he could push it aside, I said, "Have I . . . have I missed much?"

He looked back at me; the piercing blue eyes seemed to take my measure. "Several hours of your companions bringing me up to date on American history, punctuated by complaints that I was not answering enough of their questions. The information had enough value to me that it paid for the use of my healing fetter, but nothing you should worry about missing." He smiled slightly, indicating the coin that was on my leg.

"American history." I blinked. "From . . . my America? My world?"

There was a pause. The smile faded. A haunting sadness veiled his expression.

"It was my world once," he said softly.

Then he pushed the burlap curtain aside—I saw that the world outside was dark, with a tiny fire in the distance—and left me alone in the chamber.

Easing myself off the bed, I gingerly tested my left foot against the ground. The worst of the pain was gone, but my ankle still didn't feel strong; I would have to be careful with it.

I suddenly realized I was clean, which mean that someone had washed me while I slept. And I was dressed only in a loose smock of some kind, so someone had changed my clothing as well. Not that I wasn't glad to be rid of all that filth, but I dearly hoped Rita was the only one who had seen me naked.

I walked over to the shelves, and discovered a collection of items that reminded me of the mementos in the magpie room—that chamber in the Warrens that had reminded me of a magpie's nest. Aside from basic supplies like food and clothing there were books, charms, small pieces of pottery in seemingly random shapes, and a few personal items that didn't look like they would belong to my host. There were a few things I couldn't identify at all.

I saw there was a pen on one of the shelves, but it seemed so normal, so insignificant, that I just looked past it without thinking. A few seconds later it hit me just how significant it was.

It was plastic. One of those cheap pens you buy by the dozen, with a clear plastic shaft and a ball-point tip that always clogs. Totally unremarkable in my normal context. But it wasn't a normal context, and this was a world with no plastic in it.

He says he's from my world originally, I reminded myself. *So maybe he brought it with him.*

The clothing on the shelves was too large for me, as he'd warned, but I managed to find an off-white linen shirt that was wearable. It hung down to my thighs, so I figured I didn't need to go through the effort of trying on pants. I'd worn dresses shorter than that.

As I finally headed toward the cave entrance, I realized there was one other thing of significance in the cave, resting on a narrow ledge near the curtain.

A gun.

It was a heavy piece, shaped like a rifle but much longer than any I'd seen before. Below the age-blackened barrel was a slender ramrod, and when I looked at the trigger mechanism I saw a fragment of stone in a metal clamp, arching over a small, flat pan.

A flintlock. Next to a ball point pen. Guarded by a pterodactyl.

Maybe I should just give up trying to make sense of this world.

Pushing my way past the curtain, I found myself standing on a smooth natural shelf jutting out from the side of a steep hill. The surrounding view was magnificent. Overhead the sky was a vast black pool of blackness, filled with thousands of stars and a brilliant quarter moon. Richly forested mountains surrounded us, their crests gleaming in the starlight. Summer's heat had given way to a breeze that was blissfully cool, and it stirred the folds of my borrowed shirt and soothed my skin. For a few seconds I just stood there and drank it all in, a precious moment of peace.

I saw the flicker of a fire coming from a short distance down the path and began to walk toward it, my bare feet reveling in the delicious chill of the dirt beneath my feet.

In a place where the shelf widened out a bit a small campfire burned, around which my companions were sitting and talking. As soon as they saw me they jumped to their feet, and Rita squealed and ran over to hug me in relief, which was not a response I would ever have expected from her. Devon and Isaac waited for me to come to them, but you could see from their faces how relieved they were to see that I was okay. Their clothes were clean now, though it looked as if Devon's shirt was still damp. I saw that our bags had been piled up at the far side of the campfire, and next to them was all the stuff I'd been carrying in my pockets. Further down the path I saw a rope strung between two trees, with a shirt and jeans clipped to it.

The Green Man watched our reunion in silence. When we finally sat down, using various rocks and logs for makeshift chairs, he remained standing.

"Where are we?" I asked him.

"You would call this place West Virginia," the Green Man said. "But the state never divided in this world, so that name does not exist."

"And all of this?" I nodded back toward the cave. "This is your home?"

He chuckled. "Hardly. Call it a waystation. A place where I entertain guests who aren't yet ready to learn where I live."

So many questions were filling my head that I didn't know which ones to ask first. "You said you were from Terra Colonna."

He nodded. "Yes."

"From what time period?"

Devon and Rita were startled by the question. They hadn't seen the gun.

The Green Man just smiled. "Born in the year of our Lord 1747. In a small town northwest of Richmond, Virginia. I'm guessing that was your next question."

I'd expected some answer like that, but even so it was hard to absorb. "Do people not age normally in this world?"

"They live and die at the normal pace here. As they do in most worlds. Though I've heard there are a few exceptions."

I opened my mouth to ask another question, but he raised up a hand to silence me. Then he reached forward with a long stick and stirred the embers at the base of the fire. Orange sparks went floating up into the night. "You want my story. You want all the Shadows' secrets. You want to understand this world well enough to get home safely, after you take advantage of those secrets. Those things do not come free."

"We've been giving you information for hours," Rita said testily. "Shouldn't it be our turn now?"

"That has paid the bill thus far," he told her. "And you're getting off rather cheaply, in that I saved all your lives. So if you want more from me, you will have to offer more."

"What is it you value?" I asked.

His sharp eyes fixed on me. In the firelight they were a steely grey, shadowy and ominous. "I trade in information, my dear, and not just for my amusement. Information is what keeps one alive in a hostile environment. Now, it happens that because I am from your world, I value news of its progress—as your friends have discovered. But they've already covered that ground. Otherwise?" He stabbed the stick into the dirt by his side; it remained upright when he released it. "Secrets, artifacts, innovations . . . the more rare things I collect, the more likely people will seek me out when there is something unusual they want."

"What about an update on technological developments?" Devon suggested. "There's so much that's happened in the last few years, and we didn't tell you about that at all." He pulled out his iPhone, turned it on, and showed it to him. The Green Man glanced at it for a moment. A faint smile flickered across his lips. He shook his head. Devon shut the phone off and put it back in his pocket.

I remembered the items that I'd seen on his shelves. *Artifacts. Innovations. Rarities.*

I walked over to our backpacks and began to dig through mine. Everything I'd brought with me was necessary for survival—that's why I'd packed it all in the first place—but most of our supplies had been purchased in triplicate, so as long as I didn't get separated from my companions, I could afford to part with something.

I considered what would have the most value here, reflected upon the artifacts he already owned, and finally took out my flashlight. One of his eyebrows rose a bit, but he said nothing. I switched it on and off to show him how it worked, then put it down on a flat rock next to him. An offering.

He still said nothing, but I thought I saw a gleam of interest in his eyes.

Rita headed over to her backpack, and after a moment of rummaging she withdrew something round and silver: her roll of duct tape. She peeled off a short length to demonstrate its stickiness, ripped it to reveal its texture, then walked over to him and put the roll down on what had become our official offering rock.

Devon's turn. He hesitated, clearly uncertain about what to offer. Finally he reached into his bag and pulled out a couple of water bottles. At first that struck me as pretty lame—the last thing the Green Man was likely to need in a land of rivers and streams was water—but as the Green Man nodded in thoughtful approval, I realized the brilliance of Devon's choice. Lightweight plastic bottles, flexible and watertight, had a thousand possible uses. And in a world without plastic they were a true rarity.

We all looked at Isaac. You could tell from his surprised expression that he hadn't expected to be included in our little ritual. But then his eyes met mine, and I pleaded with him silently: *please*. I thought there would be a dramatic value in all us making this offering together, as a group, that might outweigh the value of the items themselves.

Finally he took out his little glow lamp and put it on the offering rock.

Thank you, I mouthed silently.

The Green Man studied the items before him for a few seconds in silence, then nodded. He walked over to where a fallen tree trunk lay in a bed of weeds and sat down on it. I felt the knot in my chest loosen a bit. Hopefully we were about to get one step closer to our end goal: rescuing Tommy.

"My name is Sebastian Hayes," he told us. "And yes, I fought in the War of Independence. After the city of my birth was burned to the ground by a traitor, I signed up. Fought till the end. It wasn't glorious, like they tell you in history books, just . . . necessary. And damn bloody." A shadow of pain crossed his face. "When it was over I hurried home, anxious to see my wife and daughter again."

There was a long pause, during which he stared into the fire without speaking.

"The places where the boundaries of a world grow thin aren't stable," he said at last, "and they usually aren't passable in any physical sense. The vast majority of such breaches only allow dreams to slip through, or at best, fragmented whispers. Native shamans back home held their dream-quests at such locations, weaving narratives from the fleeting impressions they received from other worlds. But eventually such a breach heals, or shifts location, and dreams stop coming.

"Rarely, a breach becomes so wide that for a short while physical objects can pass through it. This is what the Shadows call a *portal*. They are volatile things, unstable and unpredictable. One day a portal might become wide enough for a man on horseback to gallop through it. The next day there will be no sign that it was ever there.

"The year that war ended, North Anna River was running low due to a recent drought, and on my way home I cut across a tributary that would normally have been impassable. And I ran into such a portal. Never saw it coming. There was a fleeting moment of dread as I approached, and my horse was clearly anxious—you can sense a breach when you get that close—and then suddenly I was swallowed up by the most fearsome darkness a man can imagine. I understand now that what lies between the worlds is a more terrible emptiness than that which separates the stars . . . but back then, all I knew was that I was lost and terrified. So was my horse. She bucked and threw me, and I fell to earth a few yards from where the darkness had first enveloped us. Or so I thought. But the land that had been dry a moment before was now knee-deep in water, and even as I struggled to my feet, coughing up the water I'd inhaled when I landed, I knew that something was terribly wrong.

"I soon learned the truth, which was that I wasn't in my world any longer, but a dark and terrible simulacrum, where people and things looked familiar but their essences were twisted beyond all recognition. In this new world the war hadn't ended yet, and Richmond was controlled by Loyalists, so showing up in a Continental uniform did not make for an auspicious start. By the time I learned enough of what was going on to save my neck from the gallows, the Shadows had gotten wind of my arrival. They despise anything they can't control—that is a part of their nature—and the thought that a man might dare to cross between the worlds without their say-so was deeply offensive to them. The Shadowlord of Richmond became my nemesis, and I spent months dodging his Hunters, unable to get back to my arrival point. By the time I finally managed it, the breach had disappeared. I had to travel hundreds of miles to find another one, hidden deep within the woods where native shamans gathered. Which is a story unto itself.

"After crossing back to my world I headed straight for home, feverish with the desire to be reunited with my family. But when I arrived, I discovered that my house had been burned to the ground.

Oddly, it appeared to have happened some time ago; there was already a few years' worth of vegetative growth rooted in the ashes. But how could that be? And where were my wife and daughter?

"I scoured the countryside in panic, but there was no sign of them anywhere. Then I headed into Richmond proper, where I learned the terrible truth. In the months that I'd spent struggling to stay alive in this godforsaken world, striving to evade the Shadows long enough to find my way to an unguarded portal, five years had passed back home. One night brigands had fallen upon my house, and—"

He shut his eyes, his brow creasing in pain as he remembered. We waited in respectful silence.

"I should have been there to protect them," he whispered. "And if I'd come back the right way I *could* have been there in time. I know that now." His voice trailed off into silence.

Quietly I asked, "What do you mean, *the right way?*"

He opened his eyes; the agony in their depths made my heart lurch. "You are part of the world you were born into. Your body knows it, your mind and soul know it . . . the whole universe knows it. When you leave your homeworld, you leave a gaping wound behind. And when you arrive in a new one, you're bringing a foreign element into a perfectly balanced system. The first time you cross the disturbance is minimal, but after that each passage becomes more difficult, and more damaging. In time even your own home world may reject you, no longer recognizing you as its own. Thus, with each crossing, there is a greater danger of lost time, scrambled memories, the chance of arriving in the wrong sphere altogether . . . even of being trapped between the worlds, unable to enter any sphere ever again.

"The Shadows long ago discovered that if they sent people in both directions at once, binding the two passages together, a safe crossing could be stabilized. I don't really know how it works. No one outside their Guild does. All we know is that they've perfected the art of orchestrating balanced transfers, to the point where it's rare for any traveler to suffer a time dilation of more than a few days, provided they pass through one of the Shadows' Gates. And mental damage is very, very rare." He paused. "Hence their monopoly over interworld commerce."

"But if all that's needed is to trade bodies back and forth," Devon said, "Why can't anyone do that? Why do they need the Shadows?"

"Because it's impossible to coordinate such a thing without being able to communicate freely between two worlds. And the Shadows are the only ones who can manage that."

"Why can they do it, when no one else can?" I asked.

The pale eyes fixed on me. "Whatever the metaphysical mark we bear, that connects us to our homeworld, does not exist for inanimate objects. So they can be carried back and forth with no issue. Dead bodies, likewise, can move from sphere to sphere without adverse consequences."

I breathed in sharply. "Are you saying the Shadows are . . . dead?"

He nodded. "Dead, and also alive. Trapped halfway between the two states, they belong to no world, and thus are accepted by all. It's a gruesome and unnatural existence, but without them interworld commerce could not exist. So I suppose you could say they've earned their right to power." There was bitterness in his voice.

I said it softly: "You don't believe that."

He shrugged. "I was a revolutionary. This is a world where revolutions rarely succeed. France, America, Russia . . . the popular uprisings that reshaped Terra Colonna all failed in this world. Here, it's Gifts that make or break a war, and once the nobility get enough of a chokehold on society to harvest all Gifted children for their own ranks, common men don't stand a chance. When the worlds finally go to war with each other—as I believe they will some day—it will be a similar story, only on a cosmic scale. Eventually the Shadowlords will rule everything. And you see what kind of social order they prefer."

I thought about the abbies, the children being torn from their parents' arms, the two Seers who had spoken so casually of cleansing a world. I shivered.

Then Isaac spoke. "You said that you arrived home five years after you left. But now you're back here, what, three centuries later? How did that happen?"

Sebastian sighed. "I was mad with grief. To the point where I could no longer stand to live in the world where my wife and daughter had died. And I wanted revenge. So I found a way to cross back. I told myself I would kill the Master Shadow of Richmond, he who had prevented me from going home. And if I died in that attempt, so be it. No one who had failed his family so miserably as I had deserved to live.

"But I didn't understand how the portals worked, back then. How the negative effect intensifies with each crossing. It cost me twenty-three years to return here. By then the Shadowlord I'd come to kill had been promoted to the regional Guildmastership in Luray. So I went there." He paused. "Looking back, I think I hungered for my own death even more than for vengeance."

"You killed Guildmaster Durand," Isaac said.

The Green Man looked at him for a long moment. Something passed between them that I could not interpret. Like when two people take out their cellphones and transfer pictures to each other, while no one around them has any idea what they're looking at.

"Master Durand died," he said steadily. "I was in Luray when it happened."

"Did you ever try going home again?" Devon asked, trying to steer the conversation back to safer ground.

Sebastian nodded solemnly as he turned back to us. "Once. By then I understood the price I would have to pay. But it no longer mattered. There was nothing in either world that I cared about enough to fear the loss of it." He paused. "I arrived in 1865. Richmond was alight again. Only this time her own people had set the fire. I walked through fields of blood-soaked mud where brother had fought brother, striving to tear apart the very nation I had risked my life to build.

"I had thought I could know no greater pain than the loss of my wife and child. I discovered I was wrong."

"But the secession failed." Rita's tone was unusually gentle. "The nation wasn't torn apart."

"I know." He nodded. "I get news from home whenever I can. That's why I came when Ethan sent word that you were here. Fortuitous, as it turned out."

"Do you think you'd ever go back home?" I asked.

He shook his head. "I doubt I would survive it. The last trip cost me far more than time. My presence has become an offense to this world. That will be true anywhere I go. The day might come when I exited one world and would not be able to enter another. Which would leave me . . . well, you've seen what lies *between*."

I remembered the darkness I had sensed when we passed through the arch, and I shuddered.

"What else did it cost you?" Rita asked. "Besides time?" When he didn't answer right away she added hurriedly, "It's all right if you don't want to talk about it—"

"No. I do. I do. You need to know these things. No one should travel between the worlds without knowing the risk."

He gestured down toward the ground by his feet. It took me a moment to realize why.

I heard Rita gasp.

The grass beneath his feet had wilted and browned while he was talking to us. The plants climbing up the log had been reduced to shriveled black ribbons. All around him, in a circle a yard wide, every single living thing had died.

A chill ran up my spine.

"I am no longer compatible with this world," he said in a hollow voice. "Or any other. Animals can hold their own in my presence, but plants are more primitive, and easily succumb. Next time . . . it's possible men will not fare so well when they are near me."

I looked back at the area surrounding his cave. How stark it was! Not a single tree grew near the entrance. Not a single plant flanked the path he and I had walked together, nor were there seedlings struggling to take root in the dirt near his fire. Surrounded by a sea of life, Sebastian's home was an island of death.

Suddenly a lot of things came into focus. The strange title he had adopted. The legends about his supernatural affinity with the forest, his ability to meld into trees. He'd probably spread those legends himself. Camouflage. Where would you go looking, if you wanted to hunt a man who was one with the forest? Not on a barren mountainside devoid of foliage.

"Come," he said suddenly, rising to his feet. "Enough for tonight. Jessica has had some sleep, but the rest of you haven't. You don't want to go into battle without being well-rested: Trust me on that." He indicated the cave. "There are blankets in there; take whatever you need to make yourselves comfortable. I'll wake you in the morning."

I got up to follow the others, but before I took my first step Sebastian said, "Jessica, your clothes should be dry by now. Why don't you help me take them down?"

Help him take two pieces of clothing down from a clothesline? Was he serious? I glanced at where my things were hanging, so far from the fire one could barely make out the outline of them. And then I got it.

"Sure," I said, and I followed him in that direction.

My clothes, as it turned out, were not completely dry yet, but with the others rummaging in the cave for blankets and the darkness of midnight closing in, we had as much privacy as was possible in this place.

He took out a folded piece of paper from his coat. It was a large piece when opened out, and drawn on it in red and black ink were a series of diagrams. The first few looked like the floor plans of a building. Beneath that were some spider-like sketches that reminded me of a metro map. Everything was labeled, but in the darkness I couldn't read it. *Should have kept my flashlight*, I thought dryly.

"Those are the plans for Shadowcrest," he said, "as best my memory serves. The route labeled in black is the way I travelled when I escaped my own imprisonment there. Follow my steps back to their source and you will come to the place where your brother is likely being held. The details in red indicate things that others have reported to me since then. I can't vouch for their accuracy, but I included them in case you are forced to choose another path. Better unverified information than none at all." He paused. "This is what you wanted from me, yes?"

I suddenly had a lump in my throat, that made it hard to speak. "Yes," I whispered. "It's . . . more than I dared hope for. Thank you." I looked up at him. "But why talk to me alone? We're all in this together."

He shook his head. "Three of you are in this together. One is a boy you picked up en route, whom you know nothing about. And yes, I know your instinct is telling you to trust him—that's clear from the way you look at him—but trust *me*, people from this world may look just like the folks back home, and we may want them to be like the folks back home, but there's more dividing our two worlds than a mystical barrier. You have no idea where his loyalties lie. You can't begin to name the prejudices that drive him. You don't know his real feelings about what you're planning to do. So for your safety, and that of your friends, you should part from him as soon as possible. And until that time, share no information with him upon which your life might depend." When I said nothing, he put a finger beneath my chin and tipped my face up until I was looking in his eyes. "Promise me that, Jessica." When I was still silent he pressed, "for Tommy's sake."

Tears welled up in the corners of my eyes. Finally I nodded, because he was right. I didn't *want* him to be right, but I knew in my heart that he was.

"Good, then." He glanced back to make sure we were still alone, then took a small object out of his pocket. It was a glass sphere, maybe an inch in diameter, hanging from a thin chain. Clear glass with tiny golden threads running through it, that glittered in the moonlight. "I want you to have this. Guard it with your life, because if the Shadows find out you have it that will indeed be the price."

"What is it?" I murmured.

Silently he placed the marble in the center of his open palm and focused his attention on it. After a few seconds, ribbons of golden light began to swirl out from the depths of the glass. A glowing pattern perhaps three feet across took shape in the air above his palm. Familiar, it was so familiar . . . could it be the pattern I had seen at the Gate? No, not quite that, but something similar.

Then he closed his hand about the marble and the light disappeared.

"The portals don't actually transport you from one world to another; they simply allow you to enter the formless chaos that lies between the worlds, from which you exit elsewhere. Some worlds, like this one, have a powerful attraction, and tend to draw travelers to them, but if you want to go anywhere else the journey is much more precarious. Many have become lost between the worlds, trapped in a terrible darkness from which there is no return." He held up the marble before me. "This is a codex. It's a kind of fetter the Shadows create to facilitate travel between the worlds. Activate this one when you step through the Gate and it will help you reach Terra Colonna safely." A corner of his mouth twitched. "No guarantee on the time frame."

He took my hand, pressed the marble into my palm, and closed my fingers over it. "I risked much to obtain this," he said, a tremor of emotion in his voice. "Now I give it to you, for your brother's sake. Guard it well."

I stared at him. For a moment I was speechless. "I can't," I said finally. "I can't take this from you."

"I want you to have it."

"But if you did want to go home someday . . . wouldn't you need it?"

He touched a hand gently to my cheek. There was a terrible sadness in his eyes. "I told you before: I'll never walk that road again. Better this should be in the hands of someone who can use it. Someone whose family is still alive, and needs them." His hand fell away from my face. "I failed to rescue my loved ones, Jessica. Let me seek my redemption in helping yours."

Tears welled up in my eyes. "Sebastian, I can't ever—"

"Shhh." He put a finger to my lips to silence me. "Just say thank you. I ask for nothing more."

I whispered it from the depths of my heart: "Thank you."

He turned away before I could say anything more, and probably that was a good thing. My throat had become so tight from emotion I couldn't have gotten another word out.

After he left me I stood there for a long while, feeling the weight of the codex in my hand. The weight of this whole mission on my shoulders. Tears began to flow freely down my face, but they were good tears. The kind that wash away pain.

Tomorrow the final leg of this journey would begin. Tomorrow I would rescue my brother or die trying.

Slipping the chain over my head, I dropped the codex inside my shirt so no one would see it. Then I headed back to the cave to see if I could get a few more hours of sleep before we started back to Luray.

24

*T*HE BLACK PLAIN *beneath my feet feels solid enough, but this time I know that it isn't. Beneath my toes I can sense the thrumming of a terrible chaos, that measureless void where nothing is real, which my dreaming mind has frozen into solid form. The realm between the worlds. That's what my dreams have always been about. I sensed the truth without understanding it. I witnessed a multiplicity of worlds without knowing their names.*

How much of what I see is real, how much is metaphor, how much is just illusion? The glassy surface beneath my feet feels solid enough, but I sense that's just a feature of the dreamscape, an image my mind supplied to mask a reality I can't yet comprehend. Now that I don't need the mask as much as I once did, it's becoming less substantial. Reality is seeping into my dreams. I recall the darkness that engulfed me as we passed through the Gate, and I shudder. Will it come to the point where my dreams deposit me directly into that void, without any familiar images to serve as anchor?

All about me I see doors. This time they all look like the entrance to the Green Man's cave, burlap curtains hung from stone archways. The stone surrounding them doesn't end suddenly, but bleeds off into the darkness on all sides. And the curtains waver as I look at them, as if they are fading in and out of existence. It's as if the whole place is becoming less solid as I look at it. Less real. Clearly the constructs of my dreaming mind are beginning to break down. But what lies behind them: reality or madness?

I walk to the nearest curtain and pull it aside. Beyond it I see a dark room with a small boy huddled inside. Tommy. I watch him for a moment as he sleeps, his body twitching like a kitten's as some unseen nightmare wracks his brain, and my heart aches. Is this a world that is merely possible, or one that actually exists? If I had the right codex and a Gate to transport me, could I travel to the place where he's sleeping, right now, take him up in my arms and bring him home? Or am I only dreaming things that might come to pass, but which, like Schrodinger's cat, are not yet realized?

I walk to another curtain, but I don't open it. I don't need to. The worlds that are clustered together will all be similar; the ones that are farthest from me show the greatest variance. So if I walk for miles in this place, what will I find? A world where Australopithecus Afarensis *rules supreme? Where soaring pterodactyls still fill the sky? Or perhaps where the landscape is so alien and the life forms so incomprehensible that I won't be able to make any sense of it at all. Behind me I can see that I've left a thin trail of golden fire, marking the path I have been walking. It reminds me of the pattern I sensed within the arch back home, just before the Shadow passed through it. Are the two connected? Will manipulating one affect the other? Or is the similarity a fantasy, conjured by a mind that is desperate to discover meaning in such things?*

Too many questions. Too many questions. I sense that the truth is out there, waiting for me to discover it, but I'm not sure that I can face it and still remain anchored in reality. A world needs boundaries. A soul needs limits. In a place where everything is possible, nothing can exist.

No wonder dreamers go mad.

||||||||||||

I woke trembling; it took me a minute to remember where I was. Fortunately Sebastian had brought some embers into the cave just before we all retired, so we weren't in total darkness. By their dim orange light I could see three dark, blanket-swathed bundles on the floor. It took my sleep-addled brain a few seconds to remember that Sebastian had insisted I take the bed. I'd been wounded, he said, and needed it more than he did.

The pterodactyl was asleep on my chest. Apparently it liked me.

As I looked around the room, it struck me that something was wrong. Why were there only three people on the floor? I could see the spot where a fourth blanket was lying, but there was no one underneath it. Who was missing?

I pushed aside my blanket gently, nudging the snoozing creature (bird? reptile? dinosaur?) off my chest as gently as possible, then sat up and looked around. Everything looked normal, except for the missing person.

I got up and padded out of the cave as softly as I could, trying not to trip over any sleeping bodies. Maybe Sebastian had just gone off to do some hermit-type errand. He'd probably berate me for worrying, when I finally found him.

Hopefully that's all it was.

Most of the sky was still ink-black, stars glittering overhead like diamonds. But to the east the first light of dawn was rising, and a thin line of pale blue was edging up from behind the mountains, outlining them in dramatic silhouette. As a city girl I wasn't used to such sights, and for a moment I was so entranced I almost forgot what I had come out here for.

Almost.

I headed to the campfire area to see if anyone was there. Along the way I caught sight of a figure standing off to one side of the path, near the edge of the shelf. He was staring at the sunrise, so focused in his observation that he seemed unaware of my presence.

Isaac.

Conflicting emotions churned in the pit of my stomach. On the one hand I felt overwhelming gratitude toward him. Without him,

Devon would have probably been killed in the raid, and God alone knew where Rita and I would have wound up after that. On the other hand, Morgana had talked about things she could only know if there was a spy reporting to her, and how many people in our party were in a position to fill that role? Seyer had suggested that she could influence whether I went back to the Warrens or not, and wasn't it Isaac who had tried to talk me out of doing that? It was too much coincidence for comfort.

A cold sadness filled my heart. I liked him. I wanted more than anything to be able to trust him. But if he really was spying on me for the Seers, how much of our relationship was even real? Maybe the chemistry I'd imagined between us was just a game to him, something he was fostering in order to manipulate me more easily. How much did I really know about him?

"Why are you doing all this?" He spoke so suddenly, so unexpectedly, that it made me jump.

"Say what?" I stammered inelegantly.

Slowly he turned to look at me. "This trip. Crossing over into an alien world without any real preparation, taking crazy chances once you get here . . . why do you do it?"

"You know the answer to that," I said. "I'm trying to find Tommy."

"Why?"

I wasn't sure what his point was, but the intensity of his expression told me that it wasn't just a casual question. "Like I told you before. He's family." I shrugged. What more could you say? All my hope, dreams, motives, and fears were wrapped up in that one statement. "I know you had a falling-out with your family, but if you heard they were in trouble, wouldn't you want to help?"

He hesitated. "Crossing over into an unknown world, knowing I might never come back?" He shook his head. "I don't know," he muttered. "I don't know."

"Of course you'd do it." I was trying not to think about the "knowing I might never come back" part. *Of course* I'd go back home when this was all over. And Tommy would come with me. Someday soon,

God willing. "It's natural to doubt that now, especially with what's happened to you. But you still love them, right? So I'm sure you'd do whatever was necessary to keep them safe."

A haunting sadness filled his eyes. There were volumes of things not being said, and I sensed behind them a sea of sorrow so vast and deep you could drown in it. Just for a moment, and then they returned to their usual unreadable state.

"Love isn't the same for us as it is for you," he told me. "Passion isn't valued by my—" he hesitated. "By my family."

"How can loving your family be bad? Other than when it makes you run off to strange worlds to rescue your kid brother. . . ." I forced a smile to my face, trying to ease the mood.

He shook his head tightly. "It's not just family. Any strong attachment is bad. To people, to things . . . even a love of beauty can betray you. Anything that makes you lose focus."

He turned away from me, back toward the sunrise. A thin band of gold was creeping into the sky. Soon the sun would breach the mountaintop and molten light would flood the valley. Maybe he didn't want to miss that sight. Or maybe he didn't want me to look in his eyes any more, for fear of what I would discover there.

"What's it like to care that deeply about someone?" His voice was little louder than a whisper. "Does it change who you are?"

I wasn't totally sure I understood the question. "Why would it? Nature meant us to love. It's part of being human. Look at how long Sebastian has held onto his passion, even though his family passed away long ago. When we connect to other people. . . it's what makes us real. It's what keeps us alive."

I thought I saw his shoulders tremble slightly.

"Is everything okay?" I asked softly. When he said nothing I dared, "Do you miss your family? Is that it?"

I knew nothing about his background save what Ethan had told me—that he'd left home to escape an arranged marriage. I couldn't imagine anything my own family would ask of me that would cause me to abandon them for so long.

"You don't understand," he whispered. "You *can't* understand."

"Maybe not . . . but I do know that it's okay if you're conflicted about it. You left home for a reason, right? Not because you didn't care about your family. And I'm sure that deep down inside they know that. Maybe someday you'll go home, and things will work out. If you showed up on their doorstep tomorrow—"

Suddenly the words caught in my throat. I was remembering that terrible day when my dad left us. Years later I came to understand why that had happened, and the rational half of me recognized that it had been coming for a long time. But we're not purely rational beings. There was a part of me that would never understand or accept it.

As far as I knew, Isaac didn't hate his family or his home life. He left because his parents had wanted him to do something he found untenable, and he thought that was the only way out. But there had to be another way. No family on the face of the earth—any earth—wants to lose a kid over something like that. Oh, sure, they'd yell and scream if he showed up on their doorstep without warning, and he'd probably be grounded until Doomsday, but they'd get the message. When a kid cares so much about something that he's willing to give up everything he loves for it, parents have to listen. Right?

But I couldn't tell him that. No one could tell him that. It was the kind of thing you had to discover for yourself.

Quietly, I walked up to him. He stared out at the sunrise in silence and said nothing, but I knew that he was aware of me. He had that look on his face that guys sometimes do when they're feeling so much emotion they don't know how to process it. At times like that there's nothing you can do but stand by their side, share their space, and just let them know they're not alone.

At one point I took his hand, or maybe he took mine. I'm not sure. We watched the dawn together, sharing the beauty of a world being revealed to us inch by inch, mile by mile, as golden sunlight flowed across it, purifying and awakening every living thing in its path.

I still didn't know how I felt about the spy issue. But the chemistry was real.

25

SHADOWCREST

WHEN THE SHADOWLORD ARRIVED Tommy was at the far end of his cell, looking as miserable and forlorn as it was possible for a thirteen-year-old boy to look. He was tucked into a rocky niche barely larger than he was, with his knees drawn up to his chin and his arms wrapped tightly around them, staring into space and muttering inaudible things to himself. Soul-shards flitted about him like flies near rotting meat, and occasionally he lifted a hand to swat at them. On those rare moments when he connected with one, his hand passed right through it.

The tall figure stood before the bars for a few minutes, watching him in silence. Tommy was so wrapped up his own mental world he wasn't aware of his presence.

"Tommy."

The voice echoed emptily in the dank chamber. It was not a human sound.

Blinking, Tommy slowly looked up.

The thing standing outside his cell was human in shape, but not human in essence. Its face was pale, with translucent skin and seemingly bloodless flesh, and the bluish halo that the light-spheres cast down about its head and shoulders only made it look more eerie. Its eyes were black and empty.

The figure gestured. "Come here."

Slowly, Tommy got up. His limbs were stiff after sitting in a cramped position for so long, and he was clearly less than enthusiastic about coming close to the visitor. He walked halfway across the chamber and then stopped.

"Do you know what I am?" the ghastly figure asked.

"A Shadowlord," Tommy said hoarsely. "Your people run things here." He'd picked up that much from comments made by the servants who brought him food. They never talked to him, but they talked to each other despite him. Like he didn't exist.

That the spooky creature had authority here did not need to be explained. Power hung about him like a dark cloud, fearsome and compelling. The Shadowlord held out a sheaf of papers: pages from Tommy's dream journal. "What are these?"

"Dreams. You told me to record them."

"Barely legible. Incoherent in places. These are not the quality of what you produced before."

Tommy shrugged stiffly, in the manner of someone who was so physically and emotionally exhausted that he no longer had the energy to care about anything. Inside, his heart was pounding. "It's harder in this place."

"Your duty is no different," the Shadowlord said. "Your life will be spared as long as you are useful to us, and not a moment longer. Was that not made clear to you?"

He whispered it: "Yes, sir. It was."

"Do you wish to die?"

"No, sir."

"So the problem is not motive. What, then?"

Tommy hesitated, then looked anxiously at the shades surrounding him. The fear he was exuding was real enough, even if the source of it wasn't quite what he was pretending. "The shades," he whispered. "They show up in my dreams, whispering to me. It . . . it disturbs everything."

The Shadowlord's eyes narrowed. "You can hear the voices of the dead?"

Oh hell, Tommy thought. *Was I not supposed to?* "Sometimes," he hedged. "Maybe it's my imagination. I . . . I don't know."

"Can you make out what they say?"

He was aware that he was totally out of his depth, lost in a name-less mine field. There was no safe answer to give. So he just looked down at his feet in terrified silence and trembled. Let the undead bastard read into that whatever he wanted to.

There was silence for a moment. Then: "I do not think you are a dreamwalker." The chill in his voice made Tommy's skin crawl. "Some others believe that you are, but they have never met the dream-cursed. I have. I know how they think. You do not show the signs."

Tommy's heart skipped a beat. "The Seer said that I was one."

"She said you had the *potential* to become one, nothing more. A thousand children with such potential are born every day, of which perhaps one will manifest the dreamer's curse. If even one. The fact that we take in such children doesn't mean we expect them to be-come dreamwalkers. It is simply a safeguard."

It is simply a safeguard.

The dreamwalker Gift wasn't something these people valued, Tommy realized suddenly. Not something they wanted him to mani-fest. It was something they wanted to *isolate.* To destroy. They were using him right now as a scientist would use a mouse in a lab, studying him in order to learn how to make a better mousetrap. That's what the dream reports were all about.

If these people decided that he lacked the Gift, they would have no reason to keep him alive. That much he'd known all along. But even if he did have the Gift, he realized now, they would *still* kill him. As a "safeguard."

There was no way out.

The empty eyes were fixed on him. Not an ounce of humanity in their depths.

"It's the ghosts," Tommy whispered hoarsely. Clinging to his original strategy like a lifeline, though it was rapidly fraying beneath his grasp. "They get into my dreams. It changes things." He spread his hands helplessly.

The Shadowlord glanced down at the journal pages in his hand. Tommy held his breath. This plan had seemed clever enough when he'd come up with it, but now that he was putting it into action he could see gaping holes in it, a mile wide. Had this creature spotted them as well?

The Shadowlord looked at him. The empty eyes flashed green in the darkness, like a cat's. Then he whispered something incomprehensible, breathing wordless sounds into the dank chamber. The spirits that had been hovering around Tommy left him, drawn to the pale creature as if to a magnet. Soon all the broken souls that were in the chamber were circling about the Shadowlord.

"Now there are no ghosts to distract you," the creature said coldly. "I will read your next set of dreams tomorrow evening. If they lack the signs I'm looking for, this experiment will end. Do we understand each other?"

Tommy didn't dare meet his eyes. "Yes, sir," he whispered, looking down. "I understand."

Then the Shadowlord turned and left the chamber without another word, ghostly soul fragments fluttering behind him. A moment later the entire retinue all passed out of Tommy's sight, living and dead, and he heard the elevator carry them all away.

And he was alone. At last!

Reaching out with a trembling hand to a squat stalagmite nearby, he lowered himself slowly down onto it. His legs were so weak they could not have supported him a moment longer, and his chest was so tight he could hardly draw a breath. But . . . the ghosts were gone. He'd taken a terrible chance in order to get rid of them, but it had paid off in the end. No one was spying on him any more. And even more important, he'd proven that the Shadowlords weren't omniscient. They could be fooled, just like anyone. There was some hope in that, right?

One more day, he reminded himself grimly. *That's all I have left, before this guy declares me a fraud.*

Shutting his eyes, he drank in the wonderful silence, trying to transform it into hope.

26

"**W**E'RE GOING TO HAVE TO destroy the Gate ," I said.
Sebastian didn't respond.

I was sitting in the boat with my legs stuck out straight in front of me, grateful to have a moment to stretch them while my traveling companions were answering the call of nature. Sebastian's canoe was big enough for the five of us to travel in it, but once his equipment and provisions were packed inside it was a tight fit.

He'd served us a quick breakfast at daybreak—flatbread with honey, strips of smoked rabbit, surprisingly good coffee—and then we'd set off down the river. I'd been too nervous to eat much, and now the hunger pangs in my stomach were getting intense. But I still didn't think I'd be able to keep anything down.

"That would be unspeakably dangerous," he responded.

I looked at him sharply. "But you know how it could be done?"

Rita emerged from a thick clump of bushes some distance down the riverbank and started back toward us. The guys still weren't visible. Which was pretty ironic, when you think about it. If Rita and I hadn't been present they probably would have just pissed over the side of the boat, maybe even placed bets on who could shoot the furthest. But put two girls in the vicinity and suddenly they needed enough trees around them to reforest the Amazon.

If Rita heard our conversation, that was fine. Sooner or later I'd fill her and Devon in anyway. Isaac was another matter.

"You can't use simple explosives," Sebastian said. "That would only destroy the physical arch. You're talking about closing the portal itself, yes? Or at least making it harder to access?"

I nodded. "Is there a way to do that?"

Devon emerged from the woods. A moment later Isaac joined him. Sebastian lowered his voice to a conspiratorial whisper.

"It won't stop them, you know. There are other portals on Terra Colonna. If the Shadows want to come after you, they'll find a way."

"But what if they thought we were dead? Or lost somewhere in time or space? They don't know that I have a codex, right? What would they expect to happen if we entered the Gate without one?"

"They'd expect you to be lost forever." he whispered solemnly. He held up a hand to forestall any response; Isaac was getting too close now for us to talk privately.

Between the worlds. That's what he meant. I remembered the chaos that had churned beneath my feet during my last dream. That was only a pale shadow of what we would have to deal with if we failed in our crossing. And we could wind up stuck in there forever.

Don't think about the risk. You'll go crazy if you do. Just deal with this step by step, and wherever that leads us, we'll face it when we get there.

The canoe bobbed in the water as Rita and Isaac climbed inside, and I tucked in my legs to give them room. Devon resumed his station near the front of the canoe, ready to help Sebastian with the rowing. Yes, our tech geek knew how to paddle a canoe. Go figure. Meanwhile the little pterodactyl, who had followed us from camp, returned from its hunting expedition with a small struggling fish in its jaws. Settling down on my left shoulder, it held the prize in front of my face for a minute. I wasn't sure if I was being invited to eat it, or if the pterodactyl just wanted me to admire its hunting prowess. A moment later it tipped its head back and flipped the fish neatly down its throat, making the question irrelevant.

I had the codex tucked into my bra and the map was in the back pocket of my jeans. I wanted those two things on me at all times, so that if anything separated us from our backpacks we'd still have access to them. I hoped that Isaac wouldn't take note of the chain around my neck and ask what it was. It made me feel sick inside to distrust him, after all he'd done for us. You didn't want to believe that someone who helped rescue your friends and led you through a network of sewers to safety would betray you. But Sebastian was right. We didn't know anything about who Isaac really was, where he came from, or what he wanted. And there was way too much at stake here to take chances.

Of course he chose that moment to smile reassuringly at me, and my face flushed in guilt. I tried to smile back.

The river brought us to the King's Canal, which cut straight across the valley, saving us from having to follow all the twists and turns of the river's natural course. Even so, the trip took too long for my liking. I tried not to think about Tommy too much, because that only increased my anxiety. But the closer we got to Luray, the harder it was for me to think about anything else. I began to shift position so often in my restlessness that the pterodactyl finally squawked and fluttered away, perching on the edge of the canoe next to its master.

We're coming for you, I promised my brother. *Only a little while longer.*

⁓⁓⁓⁓⁓⁓⁓⁓

We dropped Isaac off just south of Luray. We had explained to him about how Tommy was our responsibility, not his, and we couldn't ask him to help us break into a Shadowlord's stronghold for the sake of a kid he hadn't even met, and really, he'd be safer without us, since Hunters might still looking for us. But Isaac knew what was really going on. You could see it in his eyes. It hurt him, but he understood why it had to be that way. You could see that in his eyes, too.

I wanted a moment alone with him to say goodbye, to squeeze his hand and murmur something meaningful about the sunrise we'd shared and reassure him that in time the issues between him and his family would work themselves out. But circumstances were unobliging. As we approached the southern end of Luray, a few miles past the point where the canal and the river rejoined, Sebastian steered the canoe over toward some docks, and that's where we said goodbye to him. We thanked him for his help, he wished us all good luck, and Sebastian offered him a bit of money to help him get home. Isaac hesitated, then took it. And that was it. Nothing I wanted to say to him would have sounded right in front of the others, and there was no way to go off with him alone without the others being suspicious. Or was I just worried about what Devon would think? It was hard not to be aware of him as I said goodbye to Isaac. Devon seemed to be relieved that Isaac was leaving, but was that because, like Sebastian, he didn't trust him, or was there something more personal involved? As we got back into the canoe Devon put his hand on my shoulder and squeezed gently. Was that for my benefit or Isaac's?

As we pushed off into the river, Isaac caught my eye and held it for a moment. Then the current began to carry us away from him, and he turned away. Tucking the money into his pocket, he headed toward the city at a stiff trot. If he looked back at us again I didn't see it.

Probably best that way.

॥॥॥॥॥॥॥॥॥

Sebastian took us as far as he could by canoe, but once we passed into the foothills of the Blue Ridge Mountains the stream we were following became a series of rocky waterfalls, all flowing in the wrong direction, and he finally declared an end to our aquatic journey. We were close enough to the Shadows' citadel that we could see it looming in the distance. Now that we knew more about who and what controlled it, it seemed ten times more ominous.

From here we would have to walk.

We had a last meal together by the side of the stream, rabbit jerky and breakfast bars washed down by bottled water. In between mouthfuls, Sebastian told us what little he knew about how the Gate worked. Apparently there were fetters embedded within the arch itself that served as locational markers, and that's what a codex focused in on when you activated it. While that helped provide a bridge between worlds, he said that it was a shaky one at best, as unsteady as a rope bridge slung over a windy chasm. The fact that the breaches were constantly shifting meant they could never be stabilized perfectly, and Sebastian thought that if we destroyed the codex as we passed through the Gate, it might set off a chain reaction that would collapse the whole system.

He didn't actually say *chain reaction*, of course. His own understanding of the matter was more metaphysical in nature, and he even referenced Purgatory at one point. But that's what I derived from it.

Of course, to achieve this chain reaction, we'd have to be inside the arch itself. Generally it's not a good idea to destroy a rope bridge while you're still in the process of crossing it, so hopefully we could make it to the other side first. The alternative was just too scary to think about.

Devon had made copies of Sebastian's map so that each of us could carry one. We'd gone over our intended route at least a dozen times, and identified several places inside Shadowcrest where we could meet up if anyone got separated from the group. I think we were more afraid of that possibility than we were of the Shadows themselves. To be isolated inside the enemy stronghold, facing all the horrors this world had to offer with no friends by your side, was the most terrible fate I could imagine. *And it's what Tommy is going through right now,* I thought darkly.

Hopefully we would make it down to the prison level without running into anyone, but there was no guarantee of that. Which meant that we might have to fight. I tested that concept in my mind as I chewed on a stiff piece of rabbit jerky. Soon I might have to stab someone. I still wasn't comfortable with the thought—or sure that I'd able to do it—but the mere suggestion of it wasn't as shocking as it once had been. Journeying through this strange and callous world had hardened me, and I wasn't sure if that was a good thing or a bad thing.

Sebastian gave us two more things before we left him, fetters that he'd been wearing on his coat. One was a small silver charm with a symbol inscribed in it, that he called a *stealth ward*. He said that if we were seen by anyone it would help deflect suspicion.

"Is that what you used in the sewers?" Devon asked him.

Sebastian shook his head. "This one won't blind a man to something that's right in front of his face, only cause him to think that what he is looking at is of no concern. How well it works depends upon you. If you act as if there is no reason for people to be wary of you, this will help turn their attention away. But if you act in a manner that would normally raise an alarm, or go where no people should be, it will not be as effective." It also had a finite charge, he warned, so we should save it for when we really needed it.

The second fetter was a disk of hammered brass with no markings at all. "This will open any lock," he said, "but it can only be used once. Apply it judiciously."

My hand trembled as I took it from him. For the first time in this misbegotten adventure I was beginning to feel a spark of real hope. We knew how to get to Tommy. We had a fetter to help us reach him safely, and a means of springing him from whatever prison he might be in. And we had a codex to help bring him home. All thanks to the Green Man.

Sebastian gave us Isaac's glow lamp as well, and then handed me an envelope sealed with resin. "For you," he said softly, "when you get home."

When, not *if*. The choice of adjective brought grateful tears to my eyes. *We can do this*, I thought.

Parting from him was painful. With all he'd told me about his own family, and how Tommy's rescue would provide him with personal redemption, I wondered if he might not offer to come with us in the end. I prayed that he would. His quiet and confident spirit had provided an anchor of sanity in this crazy world, and I wasn't sure how well we would do without him. But you could see in his eyes when he looked up at the citadel that such a course would be unbearable. Whatever tortures he had endured in that place had left his soul deeply scarred, and return was unthinkable. So we all just hugged him, one after the other, and when it was my turn I held him so tightly that eventually he chuckled softly and had to pry me loose. As he did so my eyes met his, and the depths of pain that I sensed behind his gaze made my heart ache in sympathy.

"Thank you," I whispered. A thousand other sentiments were left unvoiced, but you could see in his eyes that he heard them all.

"May God protect you," he murmured, and he kissed me on the forehead. Tenderly, like a man might do with his own child.

Then, with a terrible heaviness in our hearts, we started eastward.

As we began to work our way slowly up the steep slope, I remembered the warning he'd given to us over breakfast.

The Shadowlords are insane. Never forget that. Their Gift is handed down from person to person, and it carries with it all the memories of its past owners. All their prejudices and obsessions, their hatreds and fears and uncertainties, poured into the brain of one who was born and bred to receive it, and who has been told from childhood that he must submit . . . think what that would do to a man! I've been told that some become lost in the process, that they wander about in a haze, unable to fix on a single identity or even a single time. Others appear to be more rational. But even with the latter, there's still madness at the core of them. Dozens of ancestral voices clamoring inside their heads every waking moment, each derived from a Shadow who was himself insane. Madness layered upon madness, all of it trapped within a soul that must walk the borderline between life and death, committed to neither. Never forget what they are. Never forget that no matter how human they may appear to be, they ceased to be human long ago.

Little wonder Sebastian expected the worlds they controlled to rise up against them some day.

Hopefully we'd still be alive when that happened.

27

SHADOWCREST

TWO YEARS HAD PASSED since Isaac last approached the Guild-master's audience chamber, and he had forgotten just how long that final hallway was. The walk gave him enough time to reconsider his decision, though, and wonder about whether he should turn back before it was too late. Once the Guildmaster saw him that option would be lost forever.

At the end of the hallway was a pair of heavy wooden doors whose design he had studied in his childhood. There was a time when he could have identified every symbol carved into them, and recited the particulars of each world those symbols represented. Now, after two years of self-imposed exile, he found that his school memories were getting hazy. Or perhaps he was just so nervous about this interview that it was hard to focus on anything else.

The *umbra mina* who had arranged for his audience lifted the knocker and rapped down sharply; even from outside the doors one could hear how the sound echoed emptily in the chamber beyond. Isaac didn't hear any signal come back from inside the room, but evidently his escort did, for the man pulled upon the heavy doors and gestured for Isaac to enter.

A tremor of nervous anticipation ran through him as he stepped forward. The audience chamber was vast—cavernous—and the sound of the doors shutting behind him resonated as if the place were a tomb. There was nothing in the room save a throne-like chair at the far end, adorned with images of ghosts and tormented souls . . . and of course, the man who was seated upon it.

Augustus Virilian, Guildmaster of Shadows, had been an impressive man even during his natural life. Now, with his black undead gaze fixed upon Isaac, fragments of lost souls circling about his head like an unholy halo, he transcended such simple adjectives as *powerful* and *intimidating.* Isaac had seen the Shadowlord a few times before, but never so close and never without family surrounding him. It took all his self-control not to turn around and flee from the room.

"Isaac Antonin." The Shadowlord's voice was a hollow, inhuman thing. For all of Isaac's experience in dealing with the *umbrae majae,* the sound of it sent chills up his spine. "Your father said you would return some day. I told him he was a fool."

Isaac bowed his head slightly but said nothing. He didn't trust his voice to be steady.

"Why do you come to me, instead of him? Do you fear facing your family as an outcast? Do you come here to be reinstated first, so that they won't reject you outright?"

"If it so pleases Your Lordship," he whispered.

"And if it doesn't please me? What then?"

When Isaac said nothing the Shadowlord stood up from the throne and approached him. A faint moaning sound seemed to ripple in his wake. "You're the son of a prestigious bloodline, Isaac Antonin, and could have risen to be a great Shadowlord. Your family had high hopes for you. In time, the fate of a hundred worlds might have been placed into your hands—to guide, to protect, to assimilate. Few men could ever dream of more. But you ran from your duty like a frightened sheep, and in doing so shamed not only yourself but the entire Antonin line. So tell me now: Why should the Guild want you back? Why should those who share your lineage ever want to see your face again?"

Isaac drew in a long, slow breath; it bought him a moment to steady his spirit. He understood that the Shadowlord was testing him, and that any overt show of emotion now would be viewed as a sign of weakness, but that didn't make this confrontation any easier. "I couldn't have served the Guild properly back then. Not like everyone wanted me to. Yes, I went where I was told to go, and said and did all the things I was supposed to, and in that sense I did my duty . . . but my heart wasn't in it."

"And it would be now?"

He drew in another deep breath. "Yes, Your Lordship. If you allow me return."

"I see." The black gaze was merciless. "And what prompted this miraculous change of heart?"

Isaac had rehearsed the answer to that question all the way here, hoping he could make the words sound as if they flowed from him naturally rather than as something he'd spent hours preparing. "I needed to figure out who I was, before I could commit myself to serving others. I needed to learn what I wanted for myself, to know if I truly belonged here. I needed to know that if I dedicated my life to this Guild it wasn't just because I was born into it, or because everyone expected me to follow in my parents' footsteps, but because this was where I *wanted* to be."

"Passion," the Shadowlord observed dryly. "You wanted passion."

Isaac felt color rise to his face.

"Strong emotions are natural for a boy your age, but that doesn't make them any less of a weakness. So: for two years you wandered the world without discipline or responsibility, indulging every teenage impulse, chasing every rainbow that crossed your path . . . do you feel that experience will make you a better Shadow? Or a weaker one?"

"It will make me a more confident one," he said sharply. Though he'd promised himself he wouldn't let this man get under his skin, the characterization of his time in the Warrens as *chasing rainbows* raised his hackles. "Would you rather have a Shadow who hides his emotions from you but is tormented by inner doubts, or one who has faced his own strengths and weaknesses and knows what he's capable of?"

For a moment the Shadowlord was silent. A thousand ancient voices might be clamoring for attention, for all Isaac knew, but in appearance the man was as quiet and still as a frozen lake. Even the whispers of the dead that normally surrounded him had grown silent, which was surprisingly disconcerting.

"There's a reason we live as we do," the Guildmaster said at last. "A practical reason. Preparing one's soul for First Communion is no easy task. The less attached one is to this life, the more likely one is to be able to embrace other lives without tragedy."

The words spilled out before Isaac could stop them. "I won't be seeking Communion, sir."

For a moment there was silence. The shadows surrounding Virilian grew agitated, spirits stirring in distress as they sensed a sudden change in his mood.

"There is no other way you can fully awaken your Gift," he replied in an icy tone.

"I know that, sir."

"Without Communion, your Gift will never mature. At best, you will have a stunted capacity. At worst . . . it might drive you mad."

"I understand that," Isaac said. The steadiness of his own voice surprised him. Inside, his heart was beating wildly.

"You will never hear the music of the spheres within your soul. You may continue to hear the cries of the dead, but you will never fully comprehend them. You will never know the freedom of stepping through a Gate at a moment's notice, without need for physical transfer or support teams. You will never know what it feels like to be the first to set foot upon a virgin world, to assess its value for our Guild, to have it bear your name forever. Some of our greatest explorers have come from your bloodline. Some of our greatest leaders, also. You would be abandoning their legacy, trading all that for the life of an animal in a cage. Albeit a gilded one."

"I understand," he said tautly.

"Is it that you're afraid of what will happen to you if Communion fails? The Antonin bloodline is strong in that regard; I can't recall the last time we lost one."

"Fear is part of what drove me away originally," Isaac said frankly. "But if I really wanted to be an *umbra maja*, I wouldn't let that stop me."

The Shadowlord's expression didn't soften, but Isaac sensed that the answer had pleased him. "Your family won't approve of such a choice."

He felt a knot within his chest ease slightly, as he realized he'd just gotten past the first hurdle. "That was why I ran away, sir. I didn't have the courage to tell my parents how I felt, so I chose a coward's course. Now I've come back to own up to my responsibility, and have that conversation. The question is whether I return to them as a Shadow in good standing, or as an outcast." As if from a distance, he heard an edge of pain come into his voice; his hands balled into fists by his sides as he struggled to suppress it. "Family pride being what it is, that matters."

"So you seek the sanction of my office first. Not for the honor that sanction would bring you, but to start you on your new path . . . the humble duty of an *umbra mina*." There was a faint edge of scorn to his voice.

"Yes, sir. That's what I came here for." And then he added, in a slightly more humble tone, "If it please Your Lordship."

The seconds that passed while the Guildmaster stared at him in silence were endless. Isaac tried not to think about Jesse. Tried not to remember the beauty of the mountain dawn he had shared with her, the caress of morning sunlight on his face, the strange, unaccustomed warmth he'd felt holding her hand. He didn't want to lose those memories. And he would indeed lose them, if he ever accepted Communion. They'd be crowded out of his brain by a million colder, more "relevant" memories. The Isaac Antonin who had existed that morning in the mountains would effectively cease to exist, replaced by someone more knowledgeable and more powerful, but less *him*. He would never allow that to that happen, he swore. No matter what his family did.

"Very well," Virilian said. "I accept your petition to return to the Guild of Shadows. Let me know when you are reconciled with your family, and I will speak to them about changing your course of study to reflect your new path."

"And if they don't take me back?" he asked quickly.

The Shadowlord shrugged stiffly. "You're past the age of majority. Other arrangements will be made." He paused. "Is that all, Apprentice Antonin?"

Isaac shut his eyes for a moment. "No," he said quietly. "No, it's not."

Forgive me, Jesse. If you understood our ways, you would know why I have to do this.

He opened his eyes and met the Shadowlord's undead gaze without flinching. "I have some information to give you. . . ."

28

SHADOWCREST

SHADOWCREST WAS EVERY BIT as creepy as I had imagined it would be. It was also considerably larger than Sebastian's map suggested, which was not reassuring. Clearly the Shadows had expanded their stronghold since Sebastian had last been there, which meant that some of the areas he'd originally passed through might have been changed. Which meant that his escape route might no longer exist.

Another thing not to think about.

There were several buildings clustered along the ridge, the largest of them an immense stone Victorian Gothic structure whose every inch was dedicated to architectural excess. Arches within arches within arches. Emaciated spires thrusting up aggressively through the steeply angled roof, surrounded by smaller sub-spires. Thorn-like finials adorning every possible corner and edge. Narrow windows staring out at us with an anthropomorphic intensity that made my skin crawl. If you were looking for the perfect place to set a horror movie, this was it.

Or maybe it was just your average Victorian Gothic mansion. Maybe the fact that we knew what kind of horrors it represented made it seem more intimidating.

There were other buildings nearby, smaller and less opulent but built in the same general style. Two of those were on Sebastian's map, so we knew them for servant dormitories, linked to the main building by underground passageways. The others must have been constructed more recently; their grey stone exteriors were of simple design, built for function rather than aesthetics. A volleyball net had been staked out in front of one, a disconcertingly frivolous note in an otherwise forbidding landscape. Of course, for all we knew the Shadows played volleyball with severed human heads. All this we observed by the low-angled light of the setting sun, which sent stark shadows lancing across the close-cropped lawn and turned the smallest, most innocuous tree into a sprawling, black-limbed monster.

We had taken shelter behind a low rise, which was as close as we could get to the complex without leaving the cover of the surrounding forest, and we lay full length upon the ground to stay out of sight as we studied the place. Never had I been so grateful for a chance to stop moving. The hike up to the crest had been long and strenuous, and there wasn't a muscle in my body that didn't ache. As for my injured ankle . . . well, it was still supporting my weight, which was a good thing, but the limitations of Sebastian's healing fetter were becoming painfully obvious. I knew that if we got out of here alive I'd be off my feet for at least a week, and I'd probably need to sleep for at least twice that long.

Never had convalescence sounded so appealing.

We decided to wait until nightfall before trying to enter the citadel. The Shadowlords were sensitive to sunlight, and most of them spent their daylight hours underground. The prison facilities were located in the lowest level of an underground complex dedicated to their use, and during the day all the resident Shadowlords would likely be present. Once darkness fell, however, some of them would emerge to deal with aboveground business. We figured that every enemy who wasn't underground was one less enemy we might run into.

Now the sun was setting, and soon it would be time to move. For the first time since we'd arrived in this world the magnitude of what we were planning to do truly hit home. Suddenly I realized how small the odds were that we'd come out of this alive, much less with Tommy in tow. Yeah, I'd known that all along, in a theoretical sense, but until now it had been possible to hold the knowledge at arm's length. Like it was something I was reading about in a book, or watching on TV. The mind focuses on small details instead: the map in your pocket, the wards you've been given, your innate faith that the good guys will win out because, well, the good guys always win out. But now all of a sudden it was real. And there were no guarantees that anything would go the way we'd planned. Glancing at my companions, I realized I wasn't the only one experiencing such a revelation. The color had drained from Rita's face, and even Devon looked a little grey around the edges.

Suddenly we saw a pair of abbies heading our way, each one carrying a long wooden rod with a thin metal spike on one end. I tensed as they headed in our direction, afraid we'd been spotted. But then one of them stabbed his pole into the ground, and when he brought it back up it had a piece of crumpled paper was stuck to it. He plucked it off the stick and stuck it in the bag by his side. Trash collectors.

As they moved away, Rita whispered, "I want one of those sticks."

"Yeah," Devon whispered back. "Carrying those wouldn't draw attention to us at all."

The abbies went on their way and were soon gone from sight. The sun dropped below the horizon right after that, providing us with a brief but spectacular sunset view across the valley. Night quickly followed. A low-lying fog moved in, swallowing most of the stars and draping the surrounding mountains in mist, isolating us from the rest of the universe. We could see lights flicker on in a few windows— amber in the outbuildings, pale blue inside Shadowcrest itself—but fog blurred their edges, making them seem as if they were will-o'-the-wisps hovering in midair. The volleyball net flapped loosely in the breeze and for an instant its upper edge caught a stray beam of light, giving the motion a surreal quality, like the wing of giant bat.

"All right," Rita muttered. "Time to get this show on the road."

We rose to our feet and brushed the dirt from our clothing. Sebastian had given us burlap sacks to carry our stuff in, and we slung them over our shoulders in what we hoped was the proper manner for servants delivering supplies. The more we looked like people who belonged in Shadowcrest, the better the stealth ward would work. Of all of us Rita seemed to be the best at bluffing her way past trouble, so she pinned the silver fetter to her shirt, while I kept the brass one affixed to my own. I wasn't letting the key to Tommy's cell out of my sight.

Like all good Victorian mansions, Shadowcrest had been designed to allow its owners to go about their business without ever having to see a servant. That meant there were hidden passageways through which housemaids might carry fresh linens to the guest rooms, hidden staircases by which food could magically make its way from kitchen to dining room without a guest seeing it pass by, and below the service level, a veritable labyrinth of secret tunnels that extended into every wing of the Shadowlords' private space, offering discrete access to nearly every corner of the underground complex.

Sebastian had discovered that labyrinth during his escape, and had painstakingly recorded as many details of it as he could remember. Assuming nothing had changed since then, we should to be able to make our way through the lower levels without being seen. And even if the recent expansions had altered things, once we reached the servants' passageway we'd be able to move around without the Shadows seeing us and, hopefully, find another way to get to Tommy. The stealth fetter would help us deal with any servants who crossed our paths.

That was the theory, anyway. Granted, it was a scary theory, with all sorts of things that might go wrong, but the alternative was heading back down through Mystic Caverns to the crystal gate and working our way up through all the Shadows' security from there. None of us were crazy enough to think that was a good idea.

Sebastian had found his way out through the servants' labyrinth; we would find our way in by the same path.

We headed toward the building where the abbies lived. Both of the servants' outbuildings offered direct access to the manor house, but since abbies tended to avoid direct eye contact with their *homo sapiens* masters, we figured they might not look at us as closely as other servants would, making it easier for Sebastian's fetter to protect us. The fact that we were planning to exploit the submissive habits of an enslaved race was something I tried hard not to think about.

The abbie dormitory had fewer windows than the other outbuildings, and it looked deserted. We went around to the back of the building and found what appeared to be a kitchen entrance. Quietly, we slipped inside. We could hear movement coming from somewhere else in the building, but the source didn't seem to be close by, so we kept going, picking our way carefully through shadowy rooms. The few lamps that were present offered just enough light for us to make out a rough-hewn table and chairs, a simple iron stove, and boxy cabinets made of unfinished wood. All of it was simple and functional, with not a cent wasted on design. Given how wealthy and powerful the Shadows were, it was an eloquent statement about how little they valued these people.

As we neared the common room the sounds of movement grew louder. We pressed ourselves back against the wall, praying that whoever was ahead of us would move off in another direction. Any direction. I could hear some kind of communication going on, but it never resolved into actual speech. More like the sounds that animals would make, expressive but inarticulate. Were the abbies capable of true human speech? We hadn't thought to ask.

Then the voices faded, and we could hear bare feet padding away from us. Several pairs of them, from the sound of it. We needed to move quickly now, before they came back.

I stepped into the common room, intending to cross it as expediently as I could, to get to the door at the far side. According to our map, that would lead to the service tunnel. But when I saw what was in the room, I stopped cold.

"Jesse?" Rita's voice was no louder than a breath. "What is it?"

"It's all right," I breathed back. "Come on in."

I heard them enter the room behind me. Rita gasped.

There was more light here, enough to see that the walls and the ceiling were covered with drawings. Not formal compositions, set within neatly defined borders, but wild scrawlings that flowed into one another without visible boundary. Some of them were of recognizable subjects while others were totally abstract. Fractal patterns morphed into a Van Gogh sunrise, which morphed into a waterfall, which morphed into a herd of galloping horses. Then back to abstract patterns again. Dozens of different artists had left their mark here, with no thought for unity of design, each one just scribbling whatever came into his head. The result was as chaotic as you'd expect. Looking down, I saw there was a row of handprints along the bottom of one wall, child-sized; evidently the youngest abbies had been encouraged to contribute to the project.

Staring at the work, I could not help but feel a sense of awe. And fear. Not because of what the display was, but because of what it implied.

These people were human.

Really human.

Yes, in a technical sense I'd already acknowledged their species. They were close enough to us in form that there was really no way to deny it. But they were also from a different world, and they seemed to lack many qualities that I expected from human beings. So thus far, I had managed to keep my emotional distance, framing my sympathy for them in terms applicable to any living creature. Because accepting that they were people just like myself meant I would have to ask myself some pretty uncomfortable questions: *If I'd been born among them, and was treated like they are, would I have become equally spiritless? Could a soul that was like my own be beaten into this kind of submission?*

But though I might not recognize the subject matter of all the drawings, I recognized the artistic spirit behind them. It was the same spirit that had inspired the magnificent cave-paintings of Lascaux and drove mankind to decorate his environment wherever he went. Man's hunger to express himself through art was a feature that defined our species.

These abbies were my spiritual kin.

A camera shutter went off behind my ear, startling me. I turned around and saw Devon putting his iPhone back in his pocket. "For later," he said quietly. I realized that the revelation I'd just had was something he'd been struggling with all along. It was the presence of these creatures that had spared his own people from the nightmare of slavery in this version of America, and he could not look at the abbies without feeling the burden of their shackled humanity upon his shoulders.

"You two done with the museum tour?" Rita snapped. Evidently she was immune to the solemn significance of the place.

Without further word we headed to where the map indicated a service tunnel should begin, at the base of a narrow staircase. There wasn't any kind of door at the entrance; if a Shadow wanted to enter the building underground, there was no way the abbies could keep him out.

The tunnel itself was sized for diminutive hominids; even Rita would have to duck down a bit if she didn't want to bang her head on the ceiling. We could see a few yards down its length, but after that the ambient light from the dormitory petered out and there was only blackness. Devon reached for his flashlight, but I put a hand on his arm to stop him. If we wanted to pass for menials we couldn't afford to risk being seen with such a device.

I took out the small fetter lamp that Sebastian had given me and studied it. There didn't seem to be any kind of on-off switch, and when I held it out at arm's length and said experimentally, "Let there be light" (for lack of a better idea), nothing happened. How had Isaac turned it on, back in the Warrens? I tried to remember. We knew that the fetters Sebastian had given us were activated by touch, but this item, clearly, required more than that. What if the strange mental sorcery that powered the light would only work for him? No, that couldn't be true; Sebastian understood how Weaver tech worked, and he wouldn't have given it to us if it was owner-specific.

Closing my fingers over it, I shut my eyes and tried to visualize it glowing with light. I figured that since it was powered by mental energy, maybe that's what was needed to turn it on. And sure enough, after a few moments of concentration I saw a cool blue light begin to glow between my fingers. It wasn't as bright as when Isaac had used it; maybe the charge was running low. But there was enough light to let us see where the walls of the tunnel were, and to keep us from tripping over anything.

We headed into the tunnel single file, hunched over to avoid the low ceiling. Since Rita had the stealth fetter, we let her lead the way. What no one said aloud—but I'm sure we all were thinking—was that if we had to hurt someone, she was the best person to have in front. We all had our kitchen knives at hand, their improvised plastic sheathes duct-taped discreetly beneath our clothing, but I didn't think Devon was any more prepared than I was to slice into human flesh. Rita though . . . she looked ready.

The tunnel seemed to go on forever, and by the time we reached the wooden door at its far end I had a cramp in my neck from bending over for so long. I held my breath as Devon reached out to test the handle. If it was locked we'd have to go all the way back to the abbie house and seek another way in. I couldn't risk using Sebastian's fetter on this lock when we might need it later to free Tommy.

The door wasn't locked, although, as it swung open, the hinges made a dreadful noise that reverberated down the length of the tunnel and probably throughout the citadel as well. All three of us froze in place, and I thrust Isaac's glow lamp deep into my pocket so that its light wouldn't be visible. We could hear people in the distance, and we waited with pounding hearts to see if they would come our way. The darkness surrounding us was as thick and oppressive as it had been back in the caverns, and I reached out to put my hand on the wall, to keep from drowning in it. Then we waited.

And waited.

There was a dry lump in my throat. I had to fight not to clear it.

Finally Devon whispered, "It's all right, I think. No one heard us."

I took the lamp out of my pocket again. Its pale blue light revealed a large chamber with wooden boxes stacked up along the walls. Two tiny pinpoints of light down near the floor drew my notice, then startled me by moving suddenly. A rat. It was gone before I could draw my next breath, its pink tail twitching as it disappeared between two crates. I had a sudden flashback to our flight from the sewers, and had to take a moment to steady myself before I could go on.

Trembling and silent, we made our way past the rat, and into the Shadowlords' lair. Heading toward the nearest place where the map indicated an access point to the service passages below, we passed by several storerooms. Since our cover story was that we were here to deliver supplies, we peeked inside to see what was there. We stood a better chance of fooling people if we weren't walking away from the place where our supplies were supposed to be going. A quick glance in each storeroom told us that there was no food stored here; that was probably kept closer to the kitchen. Good enough.

At one point we saw another rat watching us, its beady black eyes all but invisible until the light glanced off them. Probably that's why the food was stored elsewhere.

This place is in serious need of cats, I thought.

As we moved further into depths of the building, we began to hear voices ahead of us. Clearly, we were getting closer to the areas where servants lived and worked. We hitched our sacks up to our shoulders, traded in our stealth-in-the-darkness body language for something that communicated *Of course I belong here!* and hoped we could sell it.

Suddenly we turned a corner and were face to face with a local, an elderly man who was so preoccupied with business of his own that he was clearly not prepared for three teenagers nearly running into him. I saw Rita reach up to activate the silver fetter.

"Kitchen?" Rita asked brusquely, before the man could say anything. The air of authority in her voice was naturally compelling, and hopefully the fetter would compound it. The man blinked, hesitated, then pointed us down a side corridor. We hurried in that direction, and I breathed a heavy sigh of relief when we turned a corner and he could no longer see us.

One encounter, and my nerves were already raw. How many more people would we have to fool before we found a way into the servants' labyrinth? How long would the stealth ward last?

The map indicated three possible entrances into the labyrinth, but only one of them was drawn in black ink. That was the one Sebastian had seen with his own eyes, and we knew that it was our best bet. But as we turned a corner to head in that direction, we found another rat in our path. It stared at us for a moment with its glassy black eyes, calmly, as if taking our measure, then turned and scampered off, heading in the same direction we'd planned to go. Not moving quickly, like it was worried that one of us might come up behind it, but casually, like it had business it needed to take care of, and just happened to be going in our direction.

I stared after it, not wanting to give a name to the fear that had suddenly taken root in my soul.

"Anyone other than me worried about that?" Devon whispered.

I remembered the mountain hawk that had searched for us when we'd first arrived, and Kurt's suggestion that someone connected to the Shadows was controlling it. And I remembered all the kids back on Earth who had died after run-ins with animals. Seemingly harmless animals, that had done things animals normally didn't do. Would a stealth ward have worked on them?

"It's gone on ahead of us," I said quietly.

"So if it's more than a rat—" Devon began.

"—they know we're coming," Rita finished for him.

What now? I thought despairingly. Never had Tommy seemed so inaccessible.

But we still had two other paths left to try. They were chancy at best, but still preferable to one that was likely to have a welcoming committee waiting for us. And if the Shadows were sending their servants to meet us at this entrance, that meant there would be fewer of them at the others. Right?

We needed to get to the Shadows' private levels underground as quickly as possible, so we could lose ourselves in the service labyrinth there. Up here we were sitting ducks.

We turned around and started to retrace our steps, Rita whispering directions to us from her map as we walked. When we got to the place where we had to leave the main corridor, we looked around to see if any rats were in sight. There was no point in changing our course if rat spies would just report our new route to their masters. But the hall looked genuinely empty, and it was lit well enough that we felt reasonably sure nothing was hiding in the shadows.

We travelled as quickly as we could, anxious to reach our goal before the welcoming committee at the first entrance realized we'd changed plans. But as we neared the place where the stairs leading down were supposed to be, we slowed a bit, wanting to take a good look around before committing ourselves to descent. And it was a good thing that we did. No sooner had we ceased walking than a small dark shape darted out of an opening on one side of the corridor ahead of us, ran across our path, and disappeared into an opening on the far side. It didn't appear to have seen us, but the fact that it was here at all meant that the Shadows had animal agents watching this area as well. Which meant they were probably watching the third entrance, too.

Which meant there would be no way to get downstairs without being seen.

Have we come all this way for nothing? I thought despairingly. The futility of it all was nigh on overwhelming; I could feel tears of frustration brimming in my eyes.

Devon put a strong hand on my shoulder, steadying me. We couldn't talk aloud because the rat was still close by, but Devon's touch spoke volumes: *It's not over yet. Be strong.*

I nodded and let him draw me back the way we'd come, wiping tears from my face as I walked.

The search for the third entrance led us through a series of work-rooms filled with tools, sawhorses, and various pieces of furniture in the midst of repair. The floor had been swept clean at some point, but a thin layer of dust had settled onto the stone surface since then; had a rat passed this way recently, its tracks would be visible. But there was nothing. I felt a knot between my shoulders ease up ever so slightly. We would leave our own marks as we crossed the room—there was no way to avoid it—but hopefully, by the time anyone saw them, we'd be long gone from this world.

The staircase wasn't exactly where the map said it would be, but we did find it eventually: a tightly coiled spiral leading down into pitch blackness. Unlike our other two options this staircase didn't lead to a service passage, but into the main part of the Shadows' private level. Still, what choice did we have? Our map indicated there was a place close by, on the lower level, where we could enter one of the hidden passages, so we decided to descend here and try to find it.

Standing at the lip of the black iron staircase, I found myself gazing down into utter darkness; it was impossible to see what lay beyond it. But that was a good sign, I told myself. Even the Shadows probably needed some light to see by, so the fact that this place was completely dark suggested that no one was nearby.

We hoped.

Rita started down first, knife in hand. I fell in behind her, and Devon behind me. My heart was pounding so hard I could feel the blood in my palm throb against the iron railing. I had to hold the glow lamp high with my other hand, so that everyone could see where they were going, and that made it harder to maneuver down the narrow stairs. More than once I had to wrap my left arm around the center pole to keep my balance, skewing the light that Rita and Devon depended on. One time she almost fell, and when Devon reached past me to grab her he almost knocked me down as well. We were still pretty high above the floor, so falling would not have been good. But eventually we all regained our footing and continued our precarious descent.

The staircase took us through two full twists, then deposited us in the middle of a large chamber. There were pieces of furniture all around us, in no particular arrangement. Perhaps things were being prepared for delivery to the workrooms upstairs. If so, we should get out of here quickly, before someone came for these items.

I turned toward the door which our map had indicated would lead to a service passage—

—and I was hit from the side by something so massive and heavy that it knocked the breath out of me, sending me sprawling into a row of wooden chairs. I heart Rita cry out "Shit!" as wood split beneath me, jagged splinters scoring my flesh. I struggled to right myself. But whoever or whatever had knocked me down didn't mean for me to have a chance to do that. Rough hands grabbed my arms and jerked me to my feet, nearly dislocating my shoulder. My fetter lamp went flying across the room, giving me a brief glimpse of the armed men who now surrounded us, including the two hulking freaks who now held onto me. I tried desperately to squirm out of their grip, but to no avail. I cursed myself for not having had my knife out when we were attacked. What was Rita doing?

I looked around and saw her a few feet away, also pinned in place by two goons. There was blood on her face, but maybe not her blood; it looked like she'd managed to slash one of her attackers across the cheek. Good for her. Next to her Devon was still struggling, and I saw one of his captors punch him in the stomach with so much force that he gasped in pain, then doubled over and vomited.

We'd been caught. It was over. The rats had herded us right into this trap, and we had fallen for it.

Tears came to my eyes, but I fought them back. I wouldn't let these bastards see me cry.

A chill blue light suddenly filled the room, stronger and sharper than the light from Isaac's lamp. Now I could see that there were many men in the room, maybe nine in all. The one who was holding the light was dressed in the same kind of long grey robes the Shadow at the Gate had worn, though this man didn't look nearly as unnatural. Someone else was standing behind him, his face hidden in the shadows.

"Search them," the man in the robes ordered.

The goon on my left grabbed both my arms and jerked them behind me, forcing my body taut as the other one ran his hands over me. All over me. I shuddered as his hands moved roughly over my body, feeling for weapons. My arms, my torso, my legs . . . his hands lingered on my breasts, and I could see a smile flicker across his face as he plucked the precious fetter from my shirt and threw it over his shoulder. I tried not to let him see how terrified I was, but he wasn't fooled. He ran his hands up the insides of my thighs, watching my face as he felt between my legs. Horrified, I realized that if he wanted to rape me in front of all these people there was nothing I could do to stop him. A sudden wave of sickness came over me, so powerful that I thought I would follow Devon's lead and vomit.

Then the man let go of me and stepped back, taking up his station once more at my side. You could see from his face how much he was enjoying my terror. Damn him. Damn him.

In his moment of lechery, however, he'd been less than thorough. He'd found all the weapons and tools I'd had on me, but he hadn't bothered to remove the papers in my pocket; I still had Sebastian's map. And he'd been so focused on mauling my breasts that he'd missed the small round pendant tucked into the center of my bra.

I still had the codex.

All of the other things that Devon, Rita and I had been carrying were now piled on the floor in front of the Shadow, including Sebastian's stealth ward. The burlap bags had been emptied, and all our alien treasures had been spilled out, with Devon's iPhone on top of the pile. One of the men retrieved the fetter lamp and the stealth ward and put them on the pile next to the phone—at which point the person standing behind the Shadow stepped forward to pick up the lamp, and as he did so I saw who it was: Isaac.

I lunged forward with such unexpected force that the goon on my left side lost his grip. "You son of bitch!" I yelled, struggling to get close enough to claw his face with my nails.

But the guy who'd lost his grip punched me in my stomach, so very hard it drove all the air from my body. I tried to draw a breath but my lungs wouldn't obey me. I would have doubled over if the goons who were holding me allowed it, but they didn't, so my stomach muscles clenched in a spasm of frustration, which made the pain even worse. I swallowed back on a rising tide of bile. Its bitterness seared my throat.

Through all of this, Isaac didn't move.

He looked just like the Shadow beside him. The same colorless skin, the same empty eyes. I hadn't known the signs well enough to recognize them. Had Sebastian suspected what he really was? Is that why he'd insisted we leave Isaac behind? Had the kids in the Warrens guessed the truth?

Isaac was like a rat in their midst, playing them all for fools. Playing us for fools.

Now I understood why he'd been so calm in the Warrens. The raiders would never have killed him. They wouldn't have killed us if we were under his protection. It had all been a sham.

When he saw that I could finally breathe again, and was able to focus on his face, he said very quietly, "You didn't really expect it to be that easy, did you?"

"You bastard!" I spat. "You sold us out."

"No. I returned to my family." His expression was as serene as a corpse's. "Just as you advised me to do. Because you were right, Jessica: the bonds of blood are stronger and more meaningful than any fleeting passion. I returned to my Guild because of you."

"That's not what I said!" Tears were coming to my eyes now, and I couldn't stop them. "Just let my brother go," I begged. "He's no threat to anyone. Do whatever you want with me, but please, just let him go home."

Isaac said nothing. He might have been stone for all he responded to me. The Shadow beside him gestured to one of the goons. "Tell His Lordship we have the intruders in hand," he ordered. "The guards can stand down."

"I'll tell him," Isaac said quickly.

The Shadow looked at him, one eyebrow slightly raised.

"I'm the one who told him people were coming. It's my duty to let him know the matter has been resolved."

The Shadow considered that, then nodded. "Very well, Apprentice. You do that. Meanwhile," he looked at our captors and ordered, "put them in holding until Lord Virilian can decide what he wants to do with them."

I tried to watch Isaac as he left the room. I ached for him to turn toward me one last time, to show me . . . what? That there was some tiny spark of regret in his soul? That he was sorry he'd had to betray us? That it pained him to be the one who crushed my final hopes?

But the goon who was holding me yanked me so roughly toward the door that I stumbled and nearly fell. By the time I had my feet under me again, and could look back, Isaac was gone.

29

SHADOWCREST

DOWN, DOWN, DOWN WE WENT, deep into the bowels of the earth, past the seven circles of Hell and beyond, into a realm of utter hopelessness. They tied our hands behind us along the way, and while I was lucid enough to remember the *Mythbusters* trick of pressing my wrists together sideways so that I would have some slack later on, it seemed a futile effort. There was no way we were going to come out of this mess alive.

The underground complex had been expanded since Sebastian's escape, and we passed through whole levels that weren't on his map. The upper ones looked fairly prosaic: Add a few windows and they could have been part of any Victorian manor. But the further down we descended, the less normal things looked. Below the residential area was a maze of shadowy hallways that were half Gothic in style, half . . . something else. Below that was a level finished entirely in black marble—floor and walls and ceilings and doors—all of it. The faces of the humans who stood guard there gleamed like polished skulls in the fetterlight as they waved us through. I thought I saw ghosts in the lower levels as well, or things that looked a lot like ghosts: wisps of smoke that were formless when you looked at them directly, but resolved into quasi-human shapes in the corner of your eye when you focused on something else.

For the final part of our journey through Hell we were squeezed into a cage-like elevator, whose rope-and-pulley mechanism was visible through the bars. God alone knew what was powering the thing. Given what we'd learned about this world, I figured there was probably a room full of abbies on treadmills, laboring endlessly in the darkness so that their masters wouldn't have to climb the stairs.

As soon as the elevator door was shut, the iron cage dropped out from under us, and for a moment it seemed as if the earth had swallowed us whole.

And then, at last, it was over. The cage stopped moving and our captors shoved us out of it, and I knew in my gut that the terrible journey had reached its end point.

We were in a cavern . . . or something that had once been a cavern, now adapted for the Shadowlords' use. Some of the natural features were still visible—undulating walls of glistening grey limestone, a few thick pillars that rose from floor to ceiling like ancient Greek columns—but most of the place had been slathered over with concrete, its gritty flow following the natural contours of the walls and floors. The result was disturbingly organic, as if some vast cave-creature had swallowed us whole, and we were now trekking through its innards.

They shoved us forward, and we stumbled to a place where alcoves with vertical iron bars across the openings lined both sides of the chamber. A sudden wave of panic overwhelmed me. They were going to lock us in, and leave us down here. In the caverns. In the dark.

I struggled vainly against my captors as they opened the door to one of the cells, throwing my body about in a desperate attempt to break free. Raw animal panic had taken over. Behind me, I heard someone else involved in an equally desperate scuffle, and then the sickening thud of flesh striking flesh.

But we were all as helpless as fish in a net, and eventually the three of us were thrown inside a single cell and the door was slammed shut behind us. The loud metallic clang resonated through the cavernous space, drowning out the softer click of the lock as it closed.

They left then, without further word. I lay on the concrete floor where I had fallen, trembling as I waited for the moment they would turn out the lights and leave us to the mercy of the cavern's suffocating darkness. I didn't think I could handle it. But endless seconds passed without that happening, and when I realized that the lights were going to stay on, some of my sanity returned.

I struggled to a sitting position and looked around. Our cell was one of half a dozen fashioned out of natural alcoves that flanked a long, narrow chamber. If you stood in the middle of the chamber you might be able to see into all the cells, but in our current position the undulating walls of the cavern obscured much from view. The only lighting came from a handful of glow lamps embedded in the ceiling and, because of their positioning, some parts of the alcoves were lost in shadow. I peered into each in turn, struggling to see if anyone was inside them. If this was the place where prisoners were kept, logic said my brother must be here. But nothing moved in the darkness. No one called my name.

"C'mon, girl, let's get these ropes off."

Someone took hold of my shoulder and tried to pull me back from the bars. I shook him off.

Across from us was a long, narrow cell whose depths were mostly in shadow. I squinted to shut out the glare of the nearest light, willing my eyes to adjust to the darkness. It seemed to me there was a deeper shadow near the back that didn't quite match the rest of the rock, but it was still. Too still. A live person would have been moving by now, wouldn't he? We'd made enough commotion on our way in to wake the dead.

"Tommy?" I called out tentatively. There was no response.

So I yelled the name. Why not? What did we have to lose anymore, by being heard? My voice resonated back from all the empty spaces surrounding us. I could hear an edge of hysteria in the echo.

The shadow stirred. My breath caught in my throat.

I heard Rita and Devon come to the bars, but I didn't turn to look at them; my eyes were fixed wholly on the figure moving toward us. It paused in the darkness, and I saw blue light glint from its eyes as it blinked. Then suddenly it lurched toward us, with the kind of inarticulate cry a wounded animal might make.

Please God, let it be Tommy. Please.

My brother hit the bars of his cell with the force of a bird flying into a plate glass window. His skin was pale and his eyes were grey pits of exhaustion—he looked like death warmed over—but he was alive. Alive! I wanted to reach out to him, but the ropes on my wrists kept me from even trying, so I pressed my face between the bars of my own cell, wanting to get as close to him as I possibly could.

"Jesse!" he rasped. His voice was hoarse, as if he'd been sick. "I knew you would come for me! I knew it, I knew it, I knew it!"

"Hey, kid," I whispered back. Ever since the night I'd watched the video on his computer I'd dreamed of what I would say at this moment, but now that it was finally here I was almost too overwhelmed to speak. "I couldn't leave you here alone, could I? Who would help me figure out my video games?"

"It's you they want." His voice cracked as he spoke. "You know that, right? Something about your dreams."

"Yeah," I whispered. Shutting my eyes for a moment against the sudden tide of guilt. All that Tommy had been through in this terrible place had been because of me. "I figured that out."

"I didn't tell them anything. I figured that as long as they stayed focused on me they wouldn't go after you, so I kept feeding them stories. To give you time to rescue me . . ." The corner of his mouth twitched slightly. "Of course, when I pictured that, I imagined you would be on the other side of the bars."

Despite myself I smiled. "Damn! I knew there was something we got wrong."

"How long has it been?"

I sighed. "A week, I think. I've lost track of time at this point."

"A week? Jeez." He shook his head. "We are gonna be *soooo* grounded when we get home."

I couldn't help but laugh, and then I cried, and then I laughed and cried some more. Eventually I slid down to the ground with tears pouring from my eyes, and when Devon and Rita finally got the ropes off my wrists I lowered my face into my hands and just let it all flow—all the sorrow, all the fear, and all the joy that I felt in discovering that, although my baby brother had been a prisoner of monsters for a week, he was still every bit as much of a snarky smartass as before. It was a good thing that there were bars between us at that moment, because if there hadn't been I would have grabbed him and hugged him so hard that all his anti-contact neuroses would have been squeezed out of him like toothpaste from a tube.

"Hey." Devon prodded me. The urgency in his voice brought me back to myself. "Someone's coming."

I wiped my face with my sleeve and hurriedly got to my feet. I felt more strength in that moment than I had for days. Never mind the fact that we had no fetters and no plan. Whatever came at us now, Tommy and I would face it together.

Footsteps were approaching. One person, it sounded like. I drew in a deep breath, trying to steady my nerves. Then he entered the chamber, and I stiffened.

Isaac.

Rita spat out a curse as soon as she realized who it was; I'm not even sure it was in English. Out of the corner of my eye I saw her looking around for something to throw at him. Of course there was nothing. We were helpless.

I just glared at him. I wondered if he really grasped how much I hated him at that moment.

Calmly he looked toward Tommy's cell, like one would look at a caged animal in a zoo. "So this is the infamous little brother? The one you risked your life to save?"

"Don't touch him," I snarled.

He put up his hand to reassure me; it was the kind of gesture one would use to calm an angry dog. Then something seemed to draw his notice. He looked around the chamber, startled. It was as if he expected something to be hovering in the air, that wasn't there. "There are no shades . . . ?"

"You mean the ghost things?" Tommy asked. "I sent them away."

The look of surprise on Isaac's face gave me perverse satisfaction.

"What do you want with us?" I demanded. "Haven't you done enough damage? What's left to do now, gloat? The fact that I can't get out of this cage to wring your neck doesn't mean I'm going to jump through hoops to amuse you."

He turned toward us. Well, he turned toward me, really. I got the sense Rita and Devon were peripheral to him.

"This place isn't the same as it was when the Green Man was prisoner here," he said quietly. "There are things stored here now that are of great value to the Shadows . . . and anything that we value, the shades of the dead guard for us. You would never have seen such sentinels, nor heard them coming. You would have walked through halls that seemed utterly empty, confident in your secrecy, while in fact your every move was watched and reported upon. And if you had dared to enter those places which are off limits to the living—they're never marked as such, because those who live here know all about them—you'd have been killed on the spot. Not captured. Not questioned. Just killed. Maybe then your dead spirits would have been bound in service to the Guild." He glanced at Tommy. "Maybe you'd even have been forced to stand guard over your brother, so that no one else could save him."

"Great," I growled. "So everything was hopeless from the start. Things could be much worse than they are now. Got that. Thanks so much for the update." I glared. "Anything more?"

He looked back at me. There was a turmoil in the back of his eyes that I could not put a name to. "You couldn't have gotten down here on your own," he said. The volume of his voice had dropped; no one outside this chamber would be able to hear what he was saying now. "The Shadows had to bring you down here themselves. There was no other way."

Devon drew in a sharp breath. "Are you saying . . . that you arranged all this . . . to *help* us?"

"Bullshit!" Rita spat. "You played us. You won. It's over. Go back to your friggin' undead playmates and leave us the hell alone."

But I was looking in his eyes. I saw what was there.

"Show me," I whispered.

He took out a key from his pocket.

The room fell utterly silent. In the distance I could hear a single drop of water fall from the ceiling to the floor. Softer than a pin falling.

"You came back to Shadowcrest to help us," I murmured.

"No, I came back because I belong here," he corrected me. "This is my world, and everything that has meaning to me begins and ends here. Sooner or later I would have tired of wandering and returned to my people. You were the one who made me realize that. Of course, it might have been years before that happened, but then I realized that if I came back today," his eyes held mine, "I could help keep you alive."

I had nothing to say. Even if I'd had the right words, I don't think I could have gotten them out past the lump in my throat.

He stepped forward and unlocked the door. Rita edged out of the cell with her back to the wall, eying him as if he were a wild animal who might pounce on her at any moment. Devon was a bit cooler, and he nodded to Isaac as he walked out, feigning a confidence I was sure he did not feel. I walked right up to Isaac, close enough that I could feel the heat of his body radiate against my own.

"They'll figure out that you freed us," I said. "You could lose everything."

"No I won't." He reached into his pocket, pulled out a couple of small items, and stuck one into the lock. The other he dropped on the floor just beneath it. A faint smile touched his lips. "What they'll discover is that one of the guards who patted you down did a lousy job."

Sticking out of the door was one of the tools that Rita had used to try to pick the lock in the sewers. The one on the floor was a broken fragment.

"You'll find an exit in that direction," he pointed. "Keep going, and it'll lead you down to the portal in short order. Bear in mind, the Gate is probably in use right now. How you handle that is up to you.

But the security along the way should not be a problem. This place is designed to keep intruders out, not to lock Shadows in."

I hesitated. We had the codex, so there was a chance we could get home safely. But Isaac didn't know that. Was he only pretending to free us from prison, while he sent us to our death between the worlds?

Devon voiced my thoughts. "If we go through the Gate without a Shadow to guide us, won't we die?"

"Or wind up in the wrong world?" Rita challenged him.

Isaac shook his head. "Every person is naturally attuned to his own world, and unlike Sebastian, you four haven't done anything to screw up your attunement. Odds are good that if you make it across safely, you'll come out in the right sphere."

"*IF* we make it across," Devon said sharply.

Isaac shrugged. "I didn't say there was no risk. If you want to stay here instead, no one's stopping you."

He walked over to Tommy's door and unlocked it. The minute the door was open my brother sprinted toward me, and to my astonishment he threw himself into my arms and hugged me like the world was about to end. So I hugged him back just as hard, marveling at the therapeutic power of alien abduction. When I finally drew back I saw there were tears in his eyes. Good ones. "Don't you *ever* go off to an alien world without me again," I told him sternly.

I stood up and looked at Isaac. The gratitude I felt toward him was more than I could express in words.

"Here," he said softly. "You'll need this."

He held out his fetter lamp. I took it. Then he took a small silver disk from his pocket and offered it to me.

The stealth fetter.

I felt my breath catch in my throat. "Aren't they going to notice if this is missing?"

"They would if it was yours. But this lamp is mine." A faint smile twitched his lips. "Now that I'm not hiding from my own people, I won't need it anymore."

On an impulse, I reached up and kissed him on the cheek. As my lips touched his face I could hear his sharp intake of breath, and I felt a tremor run through his body. I held the kiss for a long second, savoring the intimacy of the connection, then drew back. "I'll never forget you," I whispered.

"But I will forget you," he warned. Pain echoed in his voice. "It's the curse of my Guild. So if you ever do come back here . . . don't count on me for anything. Don't even tell me you're back in this world. I may not be the same person who cared enough to free you."

"Uh . . . guys?" Tommy coughed. "Maybe we should start moving? Not that I don't love this place."

With a sad smile I moved away from Isaac.

"Good luck," he murmured. "Be careful."

"You, too," I told him.

As we turned to head in the direction he'd indicated I patted my little brother on the head. Tommy muttered something about not being a puppy dog and batted my hand away.

He was gonna be all right.

‖‖‖‖‖‖‖‖

The last leg of our journey was a short one, for which I was grateful. Between my injured ankle and the various parts of me that had been punched, scraped, stabbed, and mauled, I was nearing the end of my physical reserves. Tommy didn't look so good either. A week's close confinement had taken its toll on him, and by the time we reached the place where the tunnel we were following joined the main conduit, I could see that he was straining to keep up.

"Almost home," I murmured to him. "Hang in there, kid."

We passed some wards, but whatever power was fettered to them was intended to keep people from entering the citadel complex, not leaving it, so they didn't affect us. Finally we came to a steel door, bolted on our side. It opened easily. Beyond that was a wide, well-lit tunnel, with glossy tiled walls and a gracefully arched ceiling. It reminded me of an old subway tunnel I'd once seen in New York. And of the ornamentation surrounding the Gate.

We were almost home.

We could hear voices ahead of us now—or rather, the hollow echo of voices, channeled to us by the polished walls and ceiling of the tunnel. It was impossible to tell how far away the sources were. Silently we crept toward them, not even daring to whisper to one another, for fear that the tunnel's acoustics would amplify our voices. No longer were we the confident kids who had smuggled ourselves into this complex days ago, recklessly defiant and ready to bluff their way through any encounter. Rita and I were visibly bruised and bleeding now, and Tommy looked like one of Fagin's kids. Devon's dark skin masked the worst of his bruises, but one of his eyes was swelling up, and it was clear from he way he walked that his right leg had been hurt. One time he lost his footing and nearly went down. Rita grabbed him in time to keep him from falling, but he wound up hitting the wall pretty hard, and the noise of it echoed down the tunnel ahead of us. For a moment we all froze, waiting for the inevitable sound of someone coming to investigate. But as with the creak of hinges in the abbie tunnel, the noise seemed to go unnoticed.

Only that last noise didn't go unnoticed, I reminded myself. *The rats were watching us all the time.* But there was no movement visible ahead of us, and though I turned back quickly a few times, to try to catch any pursuing rodents unawares, there appeared to be nothing behind us either. Given that the tiled corridor was straight and smooth, and a line of glow lamps in the ceiling provided fairly consistent lighting, even a rat would have trouble finding a place to hide. But that still left the spirits of the dead to worry about. I prayed that whatever Tommy had done to drive them away from our prison cells would apply here as well.

As we walked, I wondered what Isaac would have done differently, had the Shadows' pet ghosts been watching our reunion. Did he have the power to control them, like the Shadowlords did?

Soon we could see the stronger light of the main chamber brightening the tunnel ahead of us. I felt a nervous flutter of anticipation in my stomach. Would the arch look any different to us now that we understood its true significance? I reached into my shirt and pulled out the codex. The tiny gold lines were brighter than I remembered, and they seemed to shift position as I looked at them. Like the trembling of a compass needle.

Tommy's eyes grew wide when he saw it in my hand. Then he grinned. "Very *Men in Black*," he whispered.

"Shhh," I whispered back, and I mimed a smack to his head.

Other than the echo of our footsteps, the world appeared to have grown silent. Whatever discussion had been taking place in the chamber ahead of us was apparently concluded.

I remembered how the grey man in Terra Colonna had left the main chamber as soon as his job there was done, leaving the portal unattended. Since no one would be foolish enough to activate the Gate without a backup team of Shadows and Greys to get him through safely, there was no need to guard the thing when it wasn't in use. Which meant that if no one was using the Gate right now, the chamber might be empty.

As we neared the end of the tunnel we stopped walking, and for a few seconds we all stood very still, listening intently for any hint of movement. But there was no sound. None at all. Fortune seemed to be on our side, for once.

About damn time.

As we entered the chamber, Tommy's eyes grew wide. I suddenly realized how little he probably knew about this world. All the time that we'd spent running around like headless chickens, struggling to learn about Guilds and Gates, he'd spent sitting in a dark prison cell, alone.

I took his hand in mine and squeezed it. "Keep hold of my hand," I whispered to him. "No matter what happens to us, no matter how scared you get, *don't let go of me.*"

He nodded solemnly and gripped my hand, so tightly that it hurt.

There were three gurneys with sheet-covered bodies on them lined up neatly next to the Gate. Someone had left a clipboard and a pen lying on the stomach of the nearest one, and I had to resist the urge to go over and read the list of names on it. This time I would know what all the titles meant. This time I would understand exactly how each person on that list was helping the Shadows rape my homeworld.

Easy, girl. Stay focused.

Rita and Devon went over to check out the gurneys, just to make sure no one was hiding behind them. We didn't want to experience another ambush like the one upstairs. Of course, down here there were also a thousand and one dark crevices for people to hide in— we'd used a few of them ourselves, back on our own world—but those were around the periphery of the chamber, not near us. If anyone jumped out at us we'd have time to respond.

Rita took Tommy's free hand in hers; I could feel him tense up at the contact, but he didn't pull away from her. Good boy. Devon took up Rita's other hand. God alone knew what we were about to face, in that void that lay between the worlds, but at least we would face it together.

Trembling, I held up the codex and looked at it. The golden threads were glowing more brightly now, and when I focused my attention on them they began to move. Pattern after pattern took shape within the crystal sphere and then dispersed, each one leaving an impression in my mind like the afterglow of a sparkler. Mandala-like geometrics gave way to fractal spirals, which gave way in turn to clusters of filaments that rippled like wheat fields in the wind. As each pattern formed, it filled my mind, drawing my soul into the same alignment—and as each one vanished it left me briefly disoriented. They were the same kind of pattern that I had sensed back home, when the Shadowlord activated the Gate, but back then there had only been one design. This time there were hundreds, and while I sensed that I was supposed to recognize which one mattered to us, I didn't have a clue how to do so.

Then, for a moment—just a moment—the threads resolved into a familiar pattern. Maybe it was a design I had used in a painting once. Maybe it was a path I had walked in one of my dreams. I thought back to the thin lines of fire that had followed me in my last dream, recording my path as I walked from world to world—

And suddenly I understood what it was that I held in my hand.

A map.

As if in response to my thoughts, the chaotic swirling within the codex settled down. A single pattern was visible now, throbbing with golden light. The same pattern pulsed within my mind. It filled the air around me, and I embraced it in my soul, studying all its twists and turns. This was the path that would lead us home. Were we supposed to follow it like a road map? Or was it some kind of metaphysical programming for the Gate, which would do the work of getting us from point A to point B? I cursed myself for not having asked Sebastian more questions while he was still with us. *Activate this when you step through the Gate, and it will see that you reach Terra Colonna safely,* he had told me. Now it was time to test his words.

I looked at my companions. Something in my expression seemed to steady them; even Tommy stopped trembling. Devon took a last look behind us to make sure nothing was in the chamber that we needed to worry about, then nodded to me. I squeezed Tommy's hand—

—and they came out of nowhere, because that was their Gift: to come out of nowhere. We should have remembered that Gift. We should have realized that Greys could be in the chamber without our seeing them. We should have guessed that all the noise we'd made back in the tunnel would put them on alert, so that they would draw their Gift about them like sorcerous cloaks and wait for us to arrive. But we hadn't. We hadn't thought about them at all. That, too, was part of their power.

Grey hands slid out of nowhere, grasping hold of us. Grey fingers squeezed a pressure point in my arm with painful intensity, forcing me to release my brother. Grey arms grasped Tommy and pulled him away from me, while other hands grabbed Rita and Devon. It all happened too fast; by the time I reached out for Tommy, he was gone. I heard him scream my name. I managed to pull away from the Grey who had grabbed me, and I twisted around, but my little brother was no longer beside me, and I screamed. Not in fear, this time, but in fury.

The golden lines were gone now. The arch was gone. The only

thing left in my universe was rage—hot rage—an all-consuming desire to hurt the people who had tormented Tommy and threatened
my friends. Molten fury suffused my flesh, energizing my spirit and
banishing any pain that might have slowed me down. It was exhilarat-
ing and terrifying all at once, and I embraced it without reserve, ready
to confront these Greys who had *dared* to attack us, who had *dared* to
lay hands on my family and friends. Never mind that the worst physical confrontation I'd ever voluntarily indulged in was a game of
dodgeball in gym class. Never mind that I had no weapon of any kind,
and wouldn't know how to use one if I did.

A mother wolf doesn't have to be told how to protect her cubs,
does she?

I saw that my brother was struggling to bite the Grey who had
grabbed him, and doing so with enough ferocity that the Grey was
distracted by it. Good. I rushed forward with my arm extended, fingers locked together into a solid spear point of fingernail and bone,
aiming for his right eye. At the last second he saw me coming and
jerked his head to one side. As soon as his attention shifted my brother
took advantage of it, sinking his teeth into the man's arm, deep
enough to draw blood. The Grey cursed and jerked his arm away from
Tommy's mouth, giving my brother a chance to break free. I reached
down to grab his hand to pull him to safety—

But then someone grabbed my hair from behind, yanking me
back so hard it nearly snapped my neck. With a curse I tried to twist
around to face my assailant, but there was a gurney in the way. Pain
exploded in my hip as I slammed into it, but I was high on adrenaline
by that point and no longer gave a damn about pain. I grabbed the
gurney and rammed it into the Grey who was gripping my hair; he
lost his hold on me and went flying across the room, blocking the path
of two others who had been coming toward me.

Suddenly the whole room was full of Greys. I couldn't see where
Rita and Devon were, but I could hear them fighting. The Grey
Tommy had bitten grabbed hold of him again, this time with an arm
locked tightly around his neck, and despite my brother's valiant effort

to back-kick him in the groin, it looked like Tommy was about to be dragged away from me. Again.

Desperately I looked about for something that I could use as a weapon. Anything! I thought of the clipboard and pen I'd seen before, but those had been knocked out of place when I hit the gurney. The clipboard had skidded across the floor and was well out of reach, and though the pen was still on the gurney, it had rolled to the far end. Not worth the effort. I needed something that could make a definitive difference in this engagement, that would not only hurt one person, but could swing the tide of the entire battle—

And then, in a flash, I knew what I needed to do.

I threw myself across the gurney, grasping for the pen. The hard metal edge of the table hit my abdomen with a force that drove all the air from my body, and the gurney rolled out from under me and nearly sent me crashing to the floor, but my fingers successfully closed about the pen, and that was the only thing that mattered.

Staggering to my feet, I looked around for Tommy. There were two Greys holding onto him now, trying to pin down his limbs as he struggled with the ferocity of a maddened wildcat. I ran toward them. A Grey grabbed me by the arm, trying to pull me back, but I jerked loose from him and just kept on going. No one was going to stop me from getting to Tommy. *No one.* As I ran I took aim at the Grey who had the firmest grip on my brother. I don't think he saw me coming. Or maybe he did, and he just didn't think I could do any meaningful damage to him. After all, I was just some poor girl from Terra Colonna, trying to punch him on the side of his head, while he had a teenage wildcat to contain.

I stabbed him with the pen as hard as I could, putting the weight of my whole upper body behind the blow. It hit the side of his neck with a sickening force and slid into his flesh like a fork into a Christmas ham. A gush of hot scarlet blood told me that I'd hit my intended target—his carotid artery—and I yanked the pen out hard, jerking it toward me as I did so, to open the wound up as much as possible.

Blood spurted from the hole in his neck with such force it didn't seem real. But it was real. It was horrifying, too, and for a moment I couldn't take my eyes away from the gruesome sight. The wounded Grey reached up to his neck in panic, clamping a hand over the opening as he fought to keep his lifeblood from spurting out of his neck. One less hand holding Tommy. My brother sensed the opening and kicked out with all his might. He hit the wounded Grey on the inside of his knee, collapsing his leg, and the man released Tommy as he fell to the floor. Blood was splattering everywhere.

Now the Greys next to Tommy had to make a choice: either attend to their comrade and try to keep him alive, or risk his bleeding out on the floor while they tried to control my brother. For a moment the whole world seemed frozen. Then the Grey holding on to Tommy let go, kneeling down by his comrade's side. Another grabbed a sheet from the nearest gurney and started tearing off a piece of it. A third one pulled a small black crystal out of his pocket and did . . . well, whatever grey people did with small black crystals while their friends were bleeding to death on the floor. Then someone yelled, "Man down!" which was exactly what I'd been hoping for. For one precious instant all the Greys looked to see what the emergency was—and in that moment I grabbed Tommy and started running with him toward the Gate.

"Run!" I screamed, just in case Rita and Devon hadn't figured out what was happening. But they'd taken advantage of the moment as well, and they reached the Gate just as Tommy and I did.

Rita gripped my arm. Devon grabbed hold of Tommy. I grabbed the codex and pulled down on it as hard as I could; links went flying as the chain around my neck snapped.

We'd planned to destroy the arch after we got home, but I knew now that we didn't dare wait that long. The Greys knew how to work the Gate better than we did, and if they followed us into it they might get to the other side before we did. We had to destroy the Gate right here, right now. Close the door behind us forever, so no one could ever follow. Which, according to Sebastian. meant destroying the codex while we were still on this side of the bridge.

I focused my mind on the last pattern the codex had shown me, trying desperately to commit the arcane map to memory. Years of artistic training had honed my ability to remember images, but how well could I memorize under these circumstances? Well enough for us to find our way home without the codex in hand?

If not, we would just have to take our chances.

As we stepped through the Gate I swung the codex on its chain as hard as I could, cracking it like a whip against the stone foundation of the arch. By the time it struck we were gone from the Shadows' world, and darkness enveloped us.

We were nowhere. We were everywhere. All the things that normally made the universe a stable, comprehensible place had disappeared, leaving . . . nothing. A chaos of nonexistence surrounded us, destructive energies churning and cresting about us, crushing and rending to pieces everything they touched. I struggled not to drown in the terrible tide, sensing that if I did so I would face a fate far worse than death.

Was this chaos our creation? Had our destruction of the Gate set loose energies that were now destabilizing this entire realm, not just closing a single breach? I couldn't afford to dwell on such questions. I was the only one who could get us home now, and I didn't dare lose my focus.

In my mind I struggled to trace the pattern the codex had shown me, clinging to it like a lifeline. Supposedly, it was the path we had to follow to get home, but how was I supposed to apply it? Concepts like *distance* and *direction* had no meaning here. There were no doors in sight. So how was I supposed to make this work?

Black energies crested high overhead as I thought back to the thin line of fire in my dream. I remembered how it had marked the pattern of my steps on the ground as I wandered from door to door . . . from world to world. . . .

Suddenly I understood what the pattern really was. How many times had I sketched out designs just like it on napkins and tabletops, reducing patterns of human fate to geometric designs? Only this time it wasn't the destiny of a single person that I was looking at. This pattern represented the destiny of an entire world, each twist and turn revealing a time and place where another world drew close: a portal. These were the doors of my dreams, only now the distance between them was not measured in inches or miles, but in gradations of probability.

No normal mind could grasp such a thing. Or perhaps I should say, no *sane* mind could grasp it. But I had been wandering the plain of alternate realities in my dreams for years, and its geometric language was etched into my brain. Consciously, I might not be able to tell you what every twist and turn of this map represented, but deep beneath the layer of conscious thought, in that secret place where dreams take shelter, I *knew*.

Was this the Gift that the Shadows thought I had, that they so feared? Or only a precursor to something more frightening?

Shutting my eyes, I focused on the pattern before me. I imagined myself in the center of my dream plain, with doors beckoning to me at every turn. It was hard to hold the vision steady in my mind when the universe surrounding me was being swallowed by chaos, but I struggled to keep my focus. I pictured the pattern of the codex laid out on the ground before me, a thin line of fire that revealed what direction we must travel in, and how far we must go, in order to find the one door that would lead us safely home.

And suddenly the vision was gone, and the darkness vomited us onto a rocky surface. I lost my footing and barely managed to get my hands out in front of me before I hit the rock floor, hard. My palms landed on glass-like shards of shattered crystal. Overhead I heard a series of sharp cracks, and I looked up just in time to see a cluster of stalactites hurtling down toward me. I rolled to one side just in time, shielding my face with my lacerated hands as the cluster smashed into a thousand knife-edged fragments, that flew through the air like shrapnel.

Devon grabbed me by the shirt and started dragging me away from the arch. The whole floor was covered in sharp crystal fragments, that tore at my clothing and my flesh as I was dragged across them, but I wasn't about to complain. As he helped me struggle to my feet, I realized the ground itself was shaking. There was a loud rumbling sound, as if an eighteen-wheeler was driving straight at us.

"Shit!" Devon cried. "We need to get out of here!"

I looked around for Tommy, grabbed his hand, and then looked for Rita, but she wasn't there.

Wasn't anywhere.

"Where's Rita?" I demanded.

No one answered me.

I looked around wildly, panic surging in my heart. She was nowhere to be seen.

I started to run back toward the arch, but Devon grabbed my arm. The ground beneath my feet was shaking more violently now. It was hard to stand.

"She's trapped in there!" I screamed. "We have to help her!"

"Jesse!" There was agony in his Devon's voice, but he held onto me firmly. "There's nothing we can do! We have to get out of here."

But . . . but . . .

"We have to go!" he repeated, jerking me toward the exit.

Another massive formation broke loose from the ceiling and crashed to the ground not far from us; I put up my hand to shield my face as calcite shrapnel flew threw the air. The ground was shaking more violently with each passing second, and I could hear the cavern groaning and fracturing all around us. The sound of fault lines splitting open was as loud as the crack of lightning overhead. If we stayed here any longer we would surely be crushed to death.

Over the din Tommy screamed, "Jesse!"

We ran.

We got as far as the metal walkway before the ceiling of the great chamber began to collapse. The tunnel lights went out, but I pulled out Isaac's fetter as I ran and held it high. Its light was much dimmer than before; was it running out of energy? The thought of being trapped down here in the darkness while the cavern collapsed around us was too horrible to think about.

But the tunnel was more stable than the great chamber had been, and though the grate swayed beneath our feet like a rope bridge in a storm, the steel was flexible enough to remain intact. We ran as fast as we could, scrambling desperately over heaps of fallen rock whenever they blocked our path. At one point the rumbling of the earth around us quieted for a few seconds, and I felt a wave of relief. Then it started up again, twice as loudly as before.

Finally there were stairs in front of us—a long, narrow flight of them, carved into the native stone of the cavern. We climbed them as quickly as we could, falling to our hands and knees when the earth started shaking so badly that we couldn't stand upright any more, half-crawling and half-running to safety.

Just as we reached the top step, the shaking finally stopped. The rumbling faded, then was gone.

The earth was unnaturally still.

Breathless and bruised, we staggered through the half-demolished archway at the head of the stairs. The room beyond that looked like it had once been a tourist shop. Now it was just a big empty space whose ceiling had collapsed. The floor was covered in glass from shattered windows, and empty shelving units had fallen across the main aisle. We picked our way carefully through the mess, heading toward the main door. My legs were shaking so badly I could hardly walk, and all the injuries I'd been ignoring now hurt with a vengeance. But that was a good sign. My body knew that it was safe now. It was allowed to feel pain.

The door to the outside world was solidly stuck in its frame. We had to climb out through a window. More glass cuts. I didn't care.

I grabbed Tommy and kissed him, and then I grabbed Devon and kissed him, and then I dropped to my knees and bent down and kissed the ground like you see people do in movies. It never looks real, but it is real, it's so real, because when your lips touch the earth, and the taste of your world is on your lips, that's when you know—really *know*, to the depths of your soul—that your nightmare is over at last.

We were home.

30

MANASSAS
VIRGINIA

THE HOUSES IN OUR NEIGHBORHOOD weren't all visible from the road. Some were tucked so far back into the forest that you practically had to go up to the front door to see them. A stranger driving down our street would probably not notice if any houses were missing. But to my eyes there was a gaping void at our address, impossible to overlook.

Devon's dad drove us into the driveway—which now was little more than a smooth black strip leading to a field of rain-soaked rubble—and parked.

He was the first person we'd contacted, once we finally got a driver on Route 340 to stop and lend us his cell phone. Which took longer than you'd expect. Maybe the sight of three teenagers standing half-dazed next to the highway, their clothing tattered and their faces speckled with blood, had scared people off. Kitty Genovese Syndrome: *I-don't-want-to-get-involved.* Or maybe they just thought we were a bunch of smart-ass kids pulling a practical joke on passing motorists. We did look like refugees from a *Night of the Living Dead* cast party, so you couldn't really blame them.

When we'd finally gotten Devon's dad on the phone he didn't ask us a lot of questions, just verified that we were in a safe place and made immediate arrangements to come get us. After that Tommy and I called Mom, but she didn't answer. I tried not to get too alarmed over that. Our house phone had been a land line, and there was probably nothing left of it now but a blob of melted plastic. Maybe in the chaos after the fire Mom hadn't been able to transfer the number to a new phone yet.

I hoped that was the reason she wasn't answering.

Doctor Tilford had wanted to tell the police we were back, but Tommy and I begged him to hold off a bit. I didn't want Mom to hear that kind of news from strangers. Reluctantly Devon's dad agreed, on condition we let him tend to our wounds while his receptionist called around to find out where Mom was. That sounded reasonable, so we went to his office to let him slather us with antiseptic, while she started searching.

It turned out that Mom was still sick—really sick—and a relative I barely knew had come to Manassas to help care for her. Since being released from the hospital she had spent most of her time wandering around the ruins of our house. Not doing anything in particular, just wandering. She told people that when we came back that's where we would go to find her, so that was where she needed to be. For as long as it took.

And now here we were at last. Standing in the place where someone from another world had once tried to kill me. It seemed a lifetime ago.

At first all I saw was rubble. Not because there was nothing else to see, but because the rubble was so compelling that I couldn't bring myself to look away from it. Here was my life, and Tommy's life, reduced to blackened timbers and rain-soaked ash. All my art. My computer. My diary. The dining room where we'd celebrated birthdays together, the kitchen where we'd gossiped over pizza, even the office where my birth certificate, with its tiny footprints, had been filed. Gone. Not until this moment had the magnitude of the loss really hit me.

Then Tommy screamed "Mom!" and threw his car door open.

Squinting against the sunlight, I could just make out the forms of two women standing at the far end of the yard, half-hidden by the shadow of a great oak tree. And yes, one of them was Mom. But how thin she looked, how frail! The other women was a robust Oktoberfest type, and when my mother swayed at the sight of Tommy and me, overcome by emotion, the other woman put a hand around her shoulder, steadying her.

Suddenly the tears I had fought so hard not to shed at Dr. Tilford's office began to fill my eyes. And this time I let them come, because there are times in a person's life when it's okay to cry, and this was one of them.

Tommy sprinted across the field of blackened timbers, his arms waving wildly as he ran toward Mom. Suddenly I realized what was about to happen . . . or not happen. My breath caught in my throat as I got out of the car, my heart pounding more loudly than it had when we'd fled through the Warrens.

Tommy ran into Mom with such force that the impact nearly knocked her off her feet. And then he hugged her. After a moment's surprise she hugged him back, her arms wrapped so tightly about him that all the Shadows in the universe couldn't have broken them apart. And then she was weeping, and he was weeping, and they were hugging each other so hard that my heart ached. So many years of fear and frustration and unexpressed affection were in that hug, it was overwhelming just to watch it.

For a moment I just stood there, letting Tommy be the star of the moment. He'd earned it.

Then Devon prodded me gently in the back. Out of the corner of my eye I could see that he was smiling. "So now can we talk to the police?"

Wiping my eyes with my sleeve, I nodded. Then I began to pick my way across the field of rubble—a bit more carefully than Tommy had—to where my mother and my brother were hugging and weeping, to join in the reunion.

EPILOGUE

CRYSTAL GATES EVERYWHERE. *Razor-blade glass spines block-ing my way in every direction. I have to smash through bunches of them to peer through each archway. Gate after gate after gate. Never finding the world I want. The world I need to see.*

Calcite spines spattered red with blood mark the places I have already explored. A trail of crimson drops behind me sketches out fractal patterns on the ground. Connect the dots and it will lead you to other worlds . . . but not the right one. Never the right one.

"Rita!" I yell at the top of my lungs.

As if mere volume will change anything.

The ground beneath my feet isn't stable anymore or even solid. It's a sea of unchained energy, in which I somehow manage the fantasy of walking. Now that I understand what the black plain of my dreams represents, the walls of illusion that once protected me from its true nature are disintegrating. Each moment that I'm here I must struggle to impose my own mental order upon the place, or risk being swept away.

Rita!

I run to gate after gate after gate, smashing my way through crystal barriers, seeking a world where my friend still lives. But are these dream-worlds real? Am I seeing events that really occurred somewhere, or are these only potential realities, twisted echoes of the real thing? The simple universe of my childhood, in which events progressed in clean linear order, has been shattered. How many worlds are really out there? Do my dreams allow me to peer into places that really exist, or am I just imagining them?

All I know is that if I can find a single universe in which Rita managed to survive the explosion, then I will know that her continued existence in my reality is possible. But I cannot find any sign of her.

Scenes from the Shadows' stronghold unfold before my eyes like the pages of some dark novel. I watch as an arrogant Shadowlord is blamed for our destruction of the Gate, and I hear him swear vengeance upon us as he is cast down from power. I watch as Greys assess the ruins of their Gate, and discuss how to bring all their stranded tourists home. I watch as Isaac attends the trial of the guard who was blamed for our escape, and I mourn the lack of remorse in his eyes.

But I never find Rita anywhere.

What if the chaos between the worlds has swallowed her whole, so that she can no longer exist in any reality? If so, that's my fault. I brought her to that other world. I led her into the Gate under Shadowcrest, and failed to bring her safely to the other side.

Guilt floods my heart. Mourning suffocates my spirit.

Forgive me, Rita.

‖‖‖‖‖‖‖‖

The tourist shop at Mystic Caverns looked as if it had been abandoned for decades. The last intact sections of roof had succumbed to heavy rains following the earthquake, and part of the front wall had collapsed during an aftershock. Scraps of yellow police tape fluttered in the wind like battered carnival pennants, vying for attention with the bright orange condemnation notice nailed to the door. Hey! Don't go in here! Things may collapse on you! We won't be held responsible!

The authorities had wandered around the place for a week before finally accepting that there was no safe way to explore what remained of the caverns. The mystery of who had abducted three Manassas teens, and why they had done so, would remain unsolved.

I shivered as I looked at the battered building, and wrapped my arms around myself. Devon put an arm around me and squeezed gently.

"T'sokay," he said softly.

But despite the comfort of his touch, it wasn't okay. It would never be okay.

The police had questioned the three of us together, and apart, and in every combination and permutation imaginable. But they had learned nothing. Our memories of captivity were far too hazy and disjointed to reveal anything meaningful. We all remembered that Devon had showed up after the fire to see if everyone was all right, that he had found Tommy and me wandering around in a daze, stunned by our close brush with death, and that he had promised to give us a lift to the hospital. But then there was some kind of carjacking along the way. The details were hazy. Everything after that was just a blur.

We couldn't tell them the truth, of course. Not unless we wanted to spend the rest of our lives in a room where the furniture had padded corners.

Eventually the police deduced that we'd been drugged, probably with something like Rohypnol, the infamous date-rape drug. And since Rohypnol interfered with short term memory creation, there was no further point in questioning us. No big surprise there. We'd watched enough cop shows to know how to fake the right symptoms.

The Rophynol thing was Tommy's idea. Gotta love my little brother.

As soon as he got back online, Tommy launched a fictitious campaign to locate the person who'd been feeding him dream stories for his game designs. He appealed to his friends on Facebook, saying that surely they must have seen her postings somewhere, and he really had to warn her about something, could they please help him find her? He even arranged for a few of his gaming buddies to seed the social networks with comments by other people that confirmed the existence of his made-up dream muse. *Yeah, I remember her telling you about those dreams, they were friggin' weird. Haven't seen her recently, though.*

Of course that trail led nowhere. But we knew that the Greys had originally discovered Tommy because of his online activity, so it stood to reason that they might be watching there. If he could convince them that he wasn't really the source of the dreams that they were so worked up about, they would have no reason to come after him a second time.

And that was true enough, wasn't it?

A week passed before we had a chance to get away from everyone and return to Mystic Caverns. Between Mom's medical needs, the police having a million questions to ask, and the press trolling our home turf like hungry jackals looking for spicy neighborhood interviews, it was really hard to get away.

Truth be told, Mystic Caverns was the last place I wanted to go, but we had unfinished business there.

Standing beside Devon and Tommy, gazing at the ruined tourist attraction, I found it hard to absorb what we'd been through. Hard to accept that any of it had been real.

In silence we walked past the main building, crossed the open field, and then entered the woods beyond. It was a bit of a hike to the spot where we'd hidden our stuff, but we'd known when we did it that people would be searching the grounds pretty thoroughly once we returned home, and there were a few things we didn't want them to find.

They were still where we'd left them, wrapped in plastic that we'd salvaged from the snack bar in the tourist shop, buried at the base of an oak tree. Isaac's glow lamp. Sebastian's letter. The silver stealth ward. All intact. I felt a knot of tension in my shoulders ease when I saw the two fetters lying there. No, we weren't crazy, and this was the proof of it.

The only proof.

Breaking the seal on the letter, I discovered it was one large piece of paper, folded over many times. I spread it out on the ground before us, and Tommy pinned down the corners with rocks. It was a map.

At first glance it looked like North America. But it wasn't the North America I had studied in high school. This one had had no United States of America in it. Instead there was something called The United Colonies of New Britannia, that stretched from Florida up into Canada. Even the states had different borders than in our world, and some of them had different names altogether. And there were a lot fewer Indian names, I noticed. No Roanoke, no Chesapeake, no Shenandoah Valley.

New Britannia extended west as far as the Mississippi. Beyond that were some provinces with French names, and west of those, a large unmarked area called *the Badlands*. It extended well beyond the region where the actual badlands were located, so the name must have referred to something other than geological makeup.

California was an independent country. Okay, so maybe things weren't so different there after all.

I spent so long studying the unfamiliar political entities that I almost missed a tiny note scrawled at the bottom of the paper. The writing was smooth and elegant, in the same cursive form that you see in 18th century documents. I smoothed out the paper so I could read the words clearly.

Follow the dreamers.
S. H.

My hand on the paper trembled. Not because of what Sebastian had written. The fact that he had give us the map was a statement in itself; there was only one reason we might ever need such a thing. *You will return here*, he was saying to us.

I wanted to deny that prediction. I wanted to clench my fists and cry out to the skies that no, I would not ever go back to that terrible place, *ever!*

But I didn't. Because he was right.

He was right because Rita might still be alive somewhere, and we'd never know peace of mind until we found out what had happened to her. He was right because we'd just destroyed a Gate belonging to a powerful Guildmaster, and if my dreams reflected even a fraction of what had really happened to him as a result of that, Devon and I were the top two names on his shit list. He was right because Isaac's Shadow buddies now had Devon's cell phone, which meant they could now access a host of his personal information, as well as the names and numbers of his friends. No one we cared about was safe.

Somewhere on that other world was the woman who had given birth to me and then abandoned me. And she was the only one who could teach me about the Gift that was in my blood.

A Gift so terrible that all those who possessed it were destroyed.

A Gift that drove its users mad.

I stared at the map in silence for a long, long while. I didn't have to look at Devon to know that he'd come to the same conclusion I had. Or that he didn't like it any more than I did.

"Come on," I whispered, gathering up the map. "Let's go home."